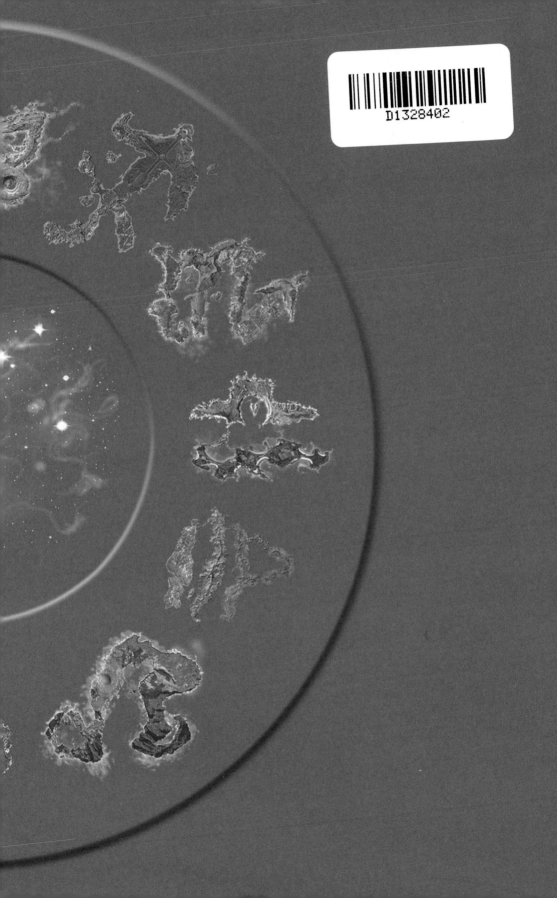

magic stones

First published 2007 by MiYu Magic Stones B.V.

ISBN 978-90-810858-2-3

Copyright © Tais Teng 2007

Typeset by Petsch BV, www.petsch.nl
Printed in Canada by Friesens, www.friesens.com
Published in North America by Winscott Corporation, www.winscott.com

www.miyumagicstones.com   **magic happens!**

THE EMERALD BOY

by Tais Teng

Stories from the
magic islands of MiYu

*This book is dedicated to all the people who know there's
a magic island behind every horizon.*

THE TWELVE MAGIC ISLANDS OF MIYU, THE PLANET SHIPS AND THE MASKED GOD OF QUICKSILVER

The twelve islands of MiYu girdle their water world like a belt of shining jewels. Each magic island has the shape of a zodiacal sign: Aquarius rises in a double zigzag of stone from the waves; Sagittarius is a slashed arrow, overgrown with ancient oaks.

Most people are born in the right month for their island. If you are born on the 24th of May, you're certainly born on Gemini. If you're born on the first of July, Cancer is your island. Only on Leo it sometimes goes wrong. Opal for instance was born on Leo but Sagittarius was really her star island. Hard luck, because only on your star isle can you use all your talents, all your magic powers. All wrong-born people yearn to visit their true country, even if only once in their lifetime.

The islands were created quite a long time ago, **98,636** years ago to be exact, on the third of April. Gliph Abar, the masked god of quicksilver, wove them from starlight and the cool night breeze.

Just like the other gods, Gliph Abar drifted through the warm ocean with never a care. He played catch-me-if-you-can with thirty feet long white sharks and nibbled on the most delicious jellyfishes. But one night he looked down and realized for the first time that his legs ended in ridiculous stubby clubs. He had feet, not a beautiful finned tail like the other gods.

I look like a fool, he thought, feet are for walking but in the whole world there's no place to stand.

He looked up.

The stars shone steadily. The stars were clearly solid, they didn't move up and down with every wave. Yes, the starry sky was the only thing strong enough to hold his weight.

That's just what I need down here, he decided. He snapped his fingers, caught the night breeze and the reflections of the stars promptly froze into rocks and sand. The drifting seaweed became forests and fields of heather. The tiny red crabs that scuttled across the seaweed turned into humans and animals.

It remains a fragile spell: at any moment the islands may sink back into the waves. To keep Gliph Abar's spell active the islanders light fires in the pattern of their island's constellation. From a mountaintop or the back of a flying whale you see the other islands, lying on the dark sea, glowing with manmade stars.

If one of these fires ever dies down, that part of the islands promptly sinks. To destroy an enemy island you only need to douse its fires.

Nobody ever tried. All the other islands would promptly invade and feed the guilty in extremely small pieces to the temple lobsters.

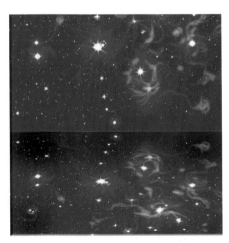 

There is one more, quite secret island:
The Isle of the Moon is deliciously cool, filled with singing silver streams, all of the hazelnuts you can eat, happy birds. Their single city is build from marble and the beaches are silvery sand.
There's one drawback and it is a rather large one. The Moon Isle changes with the phases of the real moon. You start out with quite a large disk and in the next weeks the island shrinks to a half moon, a sickle and then gone. With the new moon you find yourself bobbing in the middle of the sea, hundreds of miles from the next island.

The planet ships circle the islands. They are tremendous galleons and each moves at its own pace. The Mercury ship takes only 88 days to complete his journey, the Jupiter ship almost eleven years.
These ships are huge, big enough for complete orchards and forests, for green hills dotted with sheep. The silken sails stretch for miles, clouds form below the ceiling of the cargo holds.
The crew never visits dry land.
If they ever fish you out of the sea, they'll never let you go.
Don't ever mention your own isle. Insist that you are from one of the other ships. The sailors believe that the islands are no more than mirages, lies to lead their ship astray and wreck them on hidden reefs. Or, if the islands exist, they must surely be inhabited by devils.

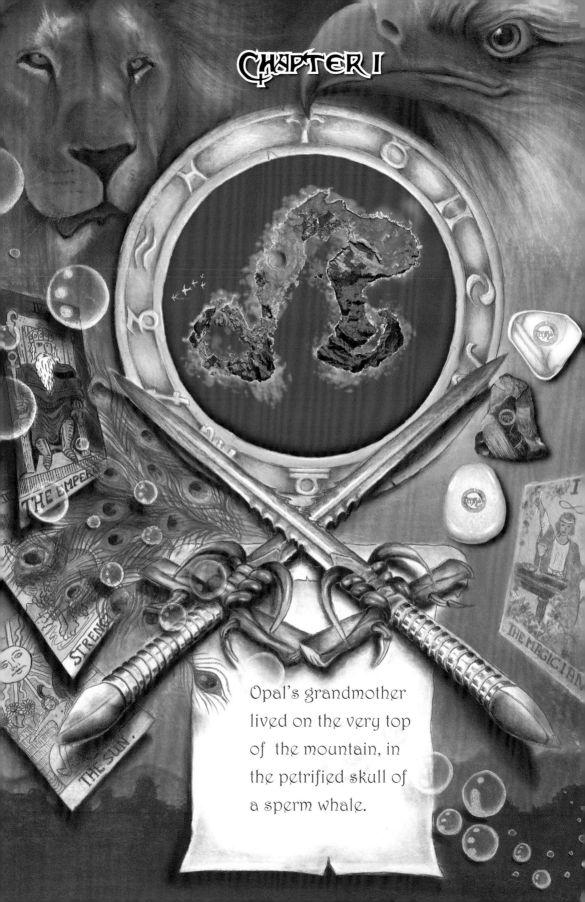

CHAPTER I

Opal's grandmother lived on the very top of the mountain, in the petrified skull of a sperm whale.

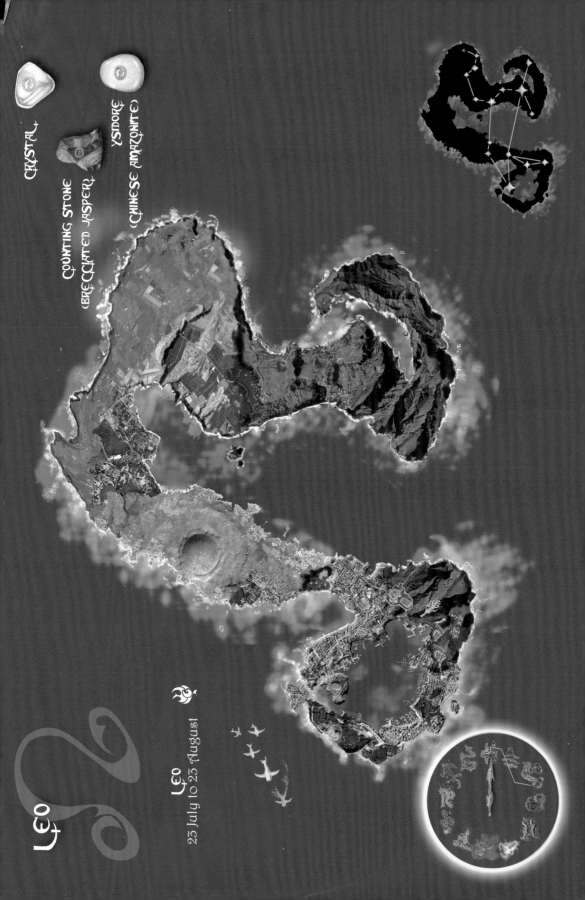

LEO

CRYSTAL

COUNTING STONE
(BRECCIATED JASPER)

YSIDORE
(CHINESE AMAZONITE)

LEO
25 July to 25 August

LEO

1.

'Opal! What's keeping you, girl? There're frost-flowers growing on your roasted locusts!'

Opal looked up. Her grandmother lived on the very top of the mountain, in the petrified skull of a sperm whale. Grandmother Rithka leaned dangerously far out over the sharp teeth of the jaw, and waved enthusiastically. Opal brushed a sweaty lock of hair out of her eyes.

A thousand steps and at least three hundred to go. She sighed. Even a mountain goat would get blisters on his hooves from such a ridiculously high staircase. Why didn't Grandmother Rithka live somewhere down on the quay? In a lovely little cottage, with a flower box filled with forget-me-nots?

'Almost there, Grandmother.'

'Hup! Hup! There're penguins paddling in your hot chocolate!'

Grandmother Rithka herself ran up and down the stairs daily, almost as if she had springs in her heels. And she often carried two heavy shopping bags.

Magic of course, Opal thought. No woman of eighty-four could be more fit than her own granddaughter.

The stairs took a final turn and Opal stood in front of the gigantic skull.

As she cautiously crossed the field of carnivorous plants, the cactuses hungrily lurched in her direction and rattled their spines.

'Down!' Grandmother Rithka ordered. 'Opal isn't food. She belongs here.'

Long ago Rithka was a wise-wife. Or maybe a witch is a better description and a witch you are forever. Only the most stupid of burglars ever tried breaking in. Grandmother's house should have warned them – nice old ladies seldom lived in giant skulls.

Opal squeezed through a gap between the teeth and stepped out onto the jaw.

Grandmother Rithka held out her hand and demanded, 'Show me your report.' Opal didn't ask how she knew the reason for her visit.

Grandmother Rithka sniffed the parchment, took a nibble and munched it thoughtfully. 'It is genuine.'

'Of course it's genuine!'

'I remember two years ago,' Grandmother said, 'The F that had been changed into an A.'

'Mother didn't notice,' Opal said.

'Your mother's not a witch. Not a single spark of magic in her fingertips. From you I expect better. Magic never skips more than a single generation.' Grandmother scanned the report. 'Conjuring fishes, a B; Dragon-lore, a C; D in gem-smelling; Ritual and sacrifice, an A.' Opal held her breath.

'An F-minus for magic! How ever did that happen, Opal?'

'I... Well? You see, maybe I just don't have any talent for magic?' Opal cringed and hoped the Earth would swallow her up. Rithka was her favorite grandmother and she couldn't stand disappointing her.

'And they still accepted you for the temple school?' Grandmother Rithka asked.

'I'm very good with ritual and sacrifice. My bowl of sacrificial rice is always empty the next morning. To the last grain.'

Grandmother snorted. 'The temples are crawling with rats. Burning incense and gossiping with gods isn't magic. For magic you need complicated spells and hard gemstones.'

'I did quite well in gem sniffing.'

Grandmother grinned. 'So you believe you've earned a reward?'

'Mother gave me two pieces of rose quartz and a blue agate,' Opal said.

'I see. And I shouldn't be stingy?' Grandmother Rithka gestured towards the huge earthenware bowl in the back of the skull. 'Try your luck.'

Opal hesitated. Two years ago, when she had changed her marks, the bowl had suddenly filled with thousands of wriggling centipedes and extremely slimy snails.

That was then, she decided, I didn't do anything wrong this time.

Fortunately all the stones remained hard and smooth.

She opened her hand.

'Good grab,' Grandmother said. 'A tiger-eye, an emerald and two moonstones.'

Opal clearly felt the magic in the stones: a soundless buzz she could only hear in her bones. Grandmother once told her 'bones are hard and white – just like gems. When you cast a spell, listen to your bones and never to your brain.'

'And Opal,' Grandmother continued, 'Tell me what it means that you got these particular stones.'

Opal automatically reached for Gliph Abar's Book Of All Answers.

It was small enough to fit into her pocket.

'No, don't ask a god,' Grandmother said. 'That's for stupid idol-huggers.

Think like a witch. Listen to the stones themselves.'

'Okay, fine. Two moonstones – they're identical and therefore quite powerful. Moonstones foretell a meeting. So I am going to meet two people and they have something to do with a tiger-eye and an emerald. How am I doing so far?'

'Sounds logical,' Grandmother said.

'Emerald glows green and warm. So, the first person will become a good friend. Tiger-Eye stands for wild and dangerous. I have to be on my guard when I meet him.'

'Really?' Grandmother said. 'I'm afraid your F-minus in magic was exactly right.'

'What did I get wrong?'

'If I keep telling you, you'll never become a witch.'

I don't even want to become a witch! Opal didn't say it out loud.

An F-minus in magic was bad enough.

Alone in the washroom, Opal rolled her new stones on the tiles. 'Tell me my future,' she whispered.

The stones lay in a triangle, the tiger-eye in the center. With her thumbs she measured the distance between the stones and next added up all the numbers until there was only one left. Nine.

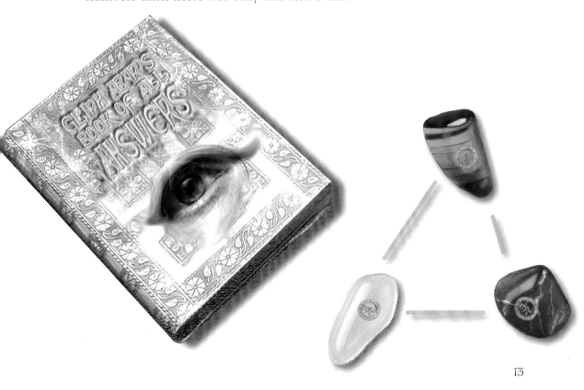

THROWING THE MAGIC STONES AND GLIPH ABAR'S BOOK OF ALL ANSWERS

If you throw your MiYu-stones, you can find the answer to any question in the most famous book:

GLIPH ABAR'S BOOK OF ALL ANSWERS

GABOAA is without the slightest doubt the shortest grimoire in history. It contains only nine answers, but they give the solution for any problem.

This is the way it works: First of all you ask your question. Don't whisper: Gliph Abar has to hear it and you're not the only one seeking his attention. You ask for instance: 'I'm in love with the boyfriend of my very best friend and I don't want to hurt her. What should I do?' Then you roll three stones. Use your thumbs to measure the distance between the stones. This time you find 3, 8 and 12. You add all numbers until you have only a single number left. 12 is 1 and 2 and that makes 3. Now add the other numbers: 3 + 3 + 8 = 14. Now add the remaining number: 1 + 4 = 5. Looking at answer number 5 you find:

THERE IS A BIRD FOR EVERY PROBLEM

slick, eh? Now you know exactly what to do.

THIS IS THE COMPLETE AND
UNABRIDGED LIST OF ALL THE
ANSWERS:

1
TURN LEFT AT THE THIRD SKELETON

2
IF YOU WANT TO EAT LAVA, YOU'D BETTER BLOW

3
ASK YOUR SECOND COUSIN

4
EARPLUGS AND TWO OUNCES OF
CANDY WOULD DO IT

5
THERE IS A BIRD FOR EVERY PROBLEM

6
AT LEAST MAKE SURE YOU
WON'T GET CAUGHT

7
YOU CAN'T EAT ROTTING
SPROUTS EVERY DAY.
SOMETIMES THERE IS ONLY
STEAK AND ICE CREAM

8
DUMP HIM (OR HER) RIGHT AWAY!

9
EVEN THE LONGEST JOURNEY STARTS
WITH FINDING YOUR TOOTHBRUSH

She opened Gliph Abar's Book Of All Answers to page nine.

EVEN THE LONGEST JOURNEY STARTS WITH FINDING YOUR TOOTHBRUSH

What the heck was the god talking about? Grandmother Rithka was right. This kind of magic was for idol-huggers.

The sun was almost touching the horizon when Grandmother Rithka asked, 'When do you have to go home?'
'Nobody is waiting for me.' Opal sounded a little bitter. 'Only the servants will notice. I'm sure Father is still scribbling in his books and polishing his coins. Mother's off somewhere, visiting and giggling with her friends.' She looked at her grandmother. 'I like your cooking a lot more. At home we always have those stupid suckling pigs, with marzipan apples in their mouths. And butterfly tongues. I hate them! My father doesn't care how food tastes as long as it's expensive.'
'Dried flounder and a hunk of brown bread is all I have,' Grandmother Rithka warned. 'And no lemonade. Only ice-cold water from the mountain brook.'
'Couldn't be better.'
From the whale's jaw, Opal had a perfect view of the city. The seaport of Idinde reached at least two miles into the ocean, like a strand of lustrous

green seaweed. The houses clung like barnacles to the cliffs while below glittered a hundred glass piers.

A mournful hooting drifted down and Opal looked up. A squadron of flying whales plunged from high in the sky. They hit the bay, trailing plumes of spray. In the red sunlight they seemed on fire.

Opal felt a stab of longing. The whales looked so carefree! The whole world was theirs' and the islands were no more than dots in an endless blue sea.

Virgo, the next island, lay like a gray smudge across the horizon. The first night-fires were burning already – blue and green stars. These fires had been burning for thousands of years. Opal knew that if they ever go out, the island would instantly sink beneath the waves.

Grandmother Rithka spat out a particularly big fish bone. 'Why the dark and brooding look?'

'It's the whales. I never go anywhere! Father wants me to marry some old fart who is at least as wealthy and boring as himself. The rest of my life I'll stay at home and complain about the servants.'

'He's trying to marry you off, again?'

Opal giggled. 'Last week's was such a boob! He collected seashells. Only shells with pale blue mother-of-pearl, he said. And he gave me such a goofy smile and whispered 'As beautiful as your eyes.'

'Your eyes are indeed a kind of pale blue,' Grandmother Rithka said.

'I think he meant it as a compliment.'

'My eyes are ugly! They're the color of dishwater.'

'You disliked him, so everything he said was wrong.'

'But Grandmother, he was thirty at least! Why would I marry such an old fart?'

Grandmother Rithka grinned. 'Yes, thirty is decrepit indeed. Was he a wealthy man?'

'Richer than us. I bet he sleeps on a mattress stuffed with butterfly wings and drinks only mermaid tears.'

'Yes, a palace on a mountain top and an army of servants makes a man quite a bore. A sailor with a hook, a wooden leg and a dragon tattoo would be a lot more fun.'

'I don't want to marry at all! I want to go away!' Opal jumped up. 'I want to leave this stupid island! I don't want to be rich and bored anymore.' She clenched her fists. 'This I swear, by the curling beard of great Gliph Abar himself!'

Opal's voice took on an eerie ring. Her words echoed through the skull, becoming louder, deeper. 'Gliph Abar... Gliphhh Abarrr...' To Opal, it seemed as if the sound spread in immense circles, over the whole ocean, touching the islands one by one.

Opal stood frozen by fear. She knew you should never pray to Gliph Abar. The masked god was the most powerful of all. He fashioned the islands of MiYu from trembling starlight. And He never, ever, listened to your prayers.

The tones changed.

'Away, away,' the echoes chanted. 'Never wealthy or bored again.

You'll see all the isles. Drink from every spring.'

The moment the echoes died away Grandmother Rithka clacked her tongue. 'That was a wish and I'm afraid someone heard it.'

'But Gliph Abar doesn't even have a temple! He never answers prayers.'

'Except when he's in the mood. Then he delights in answering prayers and fulfilling wishes – especially stupid ones.'

'Away from here', Opal repeated. 'Never wealthy or bored again.'

What's stupid about that? It's exactly what I want. And he promised I'd visit all the islands.'

'Gliph Abar loves practical jokes,' Grandmother Rithka informed Opal, 'But his victims seldom see the humor.'

2.

Opal almost drifted down the long staircase. She felt so happy and light that it seemed she barely touched the steps with the tips of her toes. Above, the sky shone the deepest satin blue, filled with enormous sizzling stars. 'Never rich and bored again,' she sang. 'Away, aye, away from here…'

Everything fitted like the last piece of a puzzle. Tomorrow she'd go to the temple-school. Hundreds of brand-new friends and Gliph Abar had promised her a wild and exciting life on top of that.

A servant intercepted her in front of the gate. 'The Lord, your father, is quite displeased. He's been waiting for half an hour. There is a guest.'

'But I ate already with my grandmother.'

'The Lord, your father, strongly urges you to change into something more becoming. Not an old rag covered with breadcrumbs and grease spots. Not to mention dirty sandals.'

Opal sighed. 'Tell him I'm coming.'

Opal was trying on a gown adorned with dancing peacocks when her younger sister slipped into her room. 'Father is fuming,' Pebble said. Pebble's real name was Tourmaline but she hated gems. 'He looks positively purple and he's foaming at the mouth.'

'Who's the guest?' asked Opal. 'Gustraph said something about a visitor.'

'It's another suitor for you. You remember shell-man from last week? He's asked papa for your hand and papa said; 'Of course you can marry her. You have my blessing.'

'No!'

'Don't panic. You aren't married yet. You have to agree first. If you don't say 'Yes, I do,' there can be no marriage.'

'As if he'll listen to his daughter of fourteen! If I say no, father will send me to a nunnery – somewhere high in the mountains – to make me think again. Then I can herd squealing marmots all day long and braid flower wreaths from gentians.'

Pebble rubbed her chin. 'You might be right. This is the nineteenth suitor in a row you've turned down. Father is starting to loose his cool.'

'If I marry, it won't be this one! Dinja is my witness!'

'You don't need the help of a goddess. Just make sure he doesn't want you,' Pebble suggested. 'First of all, get out of that gown. That's much too ladylike.' She rummaged through Opal's wardrobe. 'Yes, try this one.'

'That apron? But…'

'It looks expensive with all those paste gems and glitter, not like an apron at all,' Pebble said, 'Only when you look quite closely…'

'Or if you read the text,' said Opal pointing out the curly letters, beautifully embroidered with gold thread and blood coral beads:

'And She Also Can't Cook'

It had been a funny gown, the kind girls wore for the spring carnival.

'Do you still have those earrings?' asked Pebble.

'The ones with the monkeys sticking out their tongues? Great idea.'

'You know what to do?' Pebble whispered at the door of the dining room.

'I point and every time I look at you…'

'Yes, yes.'

The five meter high gate opened and two lackeys goose stepped forward, raising their silver trumpets.

'The highborn dame Opal tsal Everetto dun Maginoisse!' declared the chamberlain. 'And her sister, the highborn dame Tourmaline tsal Everetto dun Maginoisse!'

It was the same suitor, Opal saw. He was perhaps a little bit less ancient than she'd originally thought – more like twenty than thirty but he remained a terrible bore.

'This is my eldest daughter,' her father said. 'But of course you've already met Opal.'

The man nodded. 'And that was a real treat. Such a charming young woman.'

Now it is my turn, Opal thought. Dinja, make me strong, she prayed to her favorite goddess. 'I ate already,' she said in a clear voice. She pushed away her chair and stood up. 'If I may be excused?'

Her father flushed red. The veins in his neck stood out. 'Stay on your chair! You can eat again! We've all come here for you.'

Only then did Opal notice the other guests – lords and ladies wearing their most precious finery. Foaming ruffles and hats as complicated as cuckoo clocks. No doubt these were the relatives of shell-man. 'Lord Git tsal Usbenk dun Eggenbach wants to ask you something,' Opal's father boomed.

'What?'

Shell-man stood up and raised his wineglass. 'Dame Opal, I would like to…'

Pebble nudged Opal and pointed. Both of them exploded with laughter. Shell-man looked instinctively at his fly. Pebble giggled hysterically, almost falling off her chair.

Shell-man put down his glass. 'Young ladies! May I ask what's so funny?'

It's very easy to get the giggles. After the first snort you just kept on laughing. It also helped if you're nervous already.

Opal knew she'd won. It's impossible to ask a woman to marry you after you've called her a 'young lady' in that tone of voice.

Pebble pointed again. 'You, your…' She couldn't finish her sentence. 'Did you see…'

'Yes, oh yes!' Opal hiccupped.

Their father erupted like a walrus from the polar sea. 'Opal! Pebble! Go to your rooms right now! I'll speak with you later.'

In the corridor Pebble gave Opal a high five.

'I'm sure that creep doesn't want you anymore,' she said. 'Papa will stop the whole son-in-law thing.' Pebble frowned. 'I only hope he doesn't start with me instead.'

'You're only eleven. And anyway, I'll help you.'

'We'll marry mountain trolls or pirate captains,' Pebble said. 'Not wimps like shell-man. And that's if we marry at all.'

3.

The Rammstein butterfly wakened Opal with the squeal of his wings.
His wings were fashioned from stained glass and if you didn't oil them regularly they shrieked like the door of a ghost house.
She stretched like a cat. Yes, this was the better kind of morning for sure.
I go to the temple-school and I don't even have to marry. And, best of all, Gliph Abar promised me I'll visit every single island!

The dining room was empty except for Pebble and half a dozen servants.
Luckily, their parents were still asleep. Opal didn't want a thundering row to start the day.
'Did Papa come to your room last night, for that serious talk?'
Pebble asked.
'No. I think he's finally given up.'
Pebble moved closer. 'Are there any interesting boys at your school?
All the ones in my class are such babies.'
'Come and meet me when the temple school gets out,' suggested Opal.
'Then you can see for yourself.'
'That's okay? I mean, I'm your little sister.'
'Not so little and a lot more clever than I.'
 In fact, Opal didn't mind that there would be someone waiting for her after the first day.

The temple school lay on the western tip of the harbor, among the olive trees. Opal strolled past a row of tiny shrines, each with its own idol.
She stopped in front of a statue of Dinja-with-the-Bow and laid a grape on her altar.
'Thanks for saving me from that bore,' she whispered.
Dinja had also refused to marry the husband chosen by her father.
So her father had her imprisoned in a high tower, with only one jug of water and a single bunch of wrinkled grapes. Dinja's father had been even more strict than Opal's.
Dinja though, shot an arrow with a thread of spider silk into the moon and let herself down to the ground. A lot later, after some adventures that took a bard eight hours to sing, she married Gliph Abar and became a goddess.
You can be sure she didn't invite her father to the wedding.

The shrine of Gliph Abar was empty, as usual. On the altar lay several stone masks and a letter, made of marble. 'We'll contact you,' said the engraved message. Everybody knew what that meant. Praying to Gliph Abar was useless. He never listened.

But me he heard, Opal thought, my prayer he answered.

Halfway down the path Opal heard children's voices.

They sounded alarmingly subdued – nobody yelled or laughed. Opal slowed down. Each step was shorter than the previous one until finally, she was dragging her feet. This was wrong! Don't be so timid! If the other children saw you as a timid mouse on the first day, you'd never get a second chance. Opal took a deep breath and squared her shoulders.

All the new students were waiting in a half circle in front of the closed temple-gate. Opal knew the seniors started an hour later.

The gates were fashioned from fist-thick plate steel, streaked with rust and studded with corroded rivets. It certainly didn't look like a school door, more like the gate of a prison.

There was a motto chiseled above the entrance

HOW MUCH BETTER TO BE A DILIGENT ANT THAN A STUPID BUTTERFLY!

What rot, Opal thought. Who wants to study to be a busy ant?

'You don't?' a voice said next to her.

Ay, Opal thought, I said it aloud.

'Me neither,' the boy continued. 'Let the little ants sweat.' He waved his arms. 'Meanwhile we butterflies, we'll flit from flower to flower and suck all the honey!'

Opal smiled. The boy was so right. 'My name is Opal. What's yours?'

'In fact it's Shining Emerald but all my friends call me Smald. I'm the only son of the high priest.'

When she looked him in the face she understood why his parents had named him Shining Emerald. His eyes had that rich, gem glow; that sea deep green.

'Where did they put you?'

'The class of the Snorting Boar,' Smald replied.

HOW MUCH BETTER TO BE A DILIGENT
ANT THAN A STUPID BUTTERFLY!

'Me too!'

'Good.' He pulled a pendant on a silver chain from his shirt and displayed it on his palm. 'Ever seen an amulet like this?'

The pendant was a rather strange shape: a silver triangle with a golden circle and a small gold cube in the center. Or was the cube gold?

Something about the shine was subtly wrong – too oily for gold.

Opal recoiled. 'That isn't gold! It's py...'

'Oh no,' Smald said. 'The purest of gold. Believe me.'

It was a beautiful golden pendent, Opal saw now, just gold.

'I'm your best friend,' Smald said and Opal nodded vehemently.

Of course Smald was her best friend. He had always been and always would be. Smald turned to another girl. 'Hello. My name is Smald and I am your best friend.' He showed her his amulet too.

'That's great,' the girl said. 'I mean, about you being my best friend. I don't know anyone here yet. I, uh, they call me Onyx. Jade-Onyx.'

Jade-Onyx was quite beautiful. Her long, blond hair looked almost silver in the sunlight. Normally Opal would have hated her at first sight.

She was much too beautiful and girls with double gem-names were no good. If you didn't have a real name, like for instance 'tsal Everetto dun Maginoisse', a double first name didn't help. Even with three gem-names you remained a commoner.

But this time Opal smiled at Jade-Onyx and offered her hand.

Any friend of Smald's was her friend too, of course.

In the classroom Opal patted the seat next to her. 'Sit by me, Smald?'

A pity he didn't hear her. He walked to the front row and sat next to Jade-Onyx.

Too bad, but Smald was right. Jade-Onyx was prettier and for Smald, only the best would do.

'Is this seat taken?'

The moment she saw the new boy, she almost snarled 'No!' but that wouldn't work. The classroom was filled to capacity and this was clearly the only stool left.

Why does it always have to happen to me? Opal thought. Dinja help me, what a bumpkin! Just see his clodhopper sandals. Wooden soles and the leather is cracked. And that idiot sweater of his. Who ever wears a sweater of itchy sea-grass to school?

She sniffed carefully but smelled only pine needles, a whiff of wood smoke.

He doesn't stink. That, at least, is something. She studied him from the corner of her eye. Such a beanpole. A regular scarecrow.

'My name is Tiger-Eye,' he offered.

'Opal,' she muttered. Tiger-Eye was such a boastful name. Brave Tiger-Eye, eh? In one of Grandmother Rithka's tales, the hero's name was Tiger-Eye the Dragon killer. Well, this oaf was certainly not a dragon hunter.

'Opal is a beautiful name,' Tiger-Eye continued.

Oh no, he's trying to sweet-talk me. Opal kept looking straight ahead.

It wasn't an improvement. Now she had a clear view of Jade-Onyx whispering in Smald's ear.

Such a horrible cheap girl with her platinum blond curls. Smald deserved better. Someone with more class – like me, for instance. Now, if Smald had asked for my hand...

Opal imagined the happy, surprised look on her father's face; Mother clapping her hands for joy; Pebble embracing her older sister.

Pebble embraced me and...

Somehow the picture didn't gel. Pebble and Smald, that didn't fit at all.

Would Pebble dislike him? Was that the problem? No, of course she was jealous of me. Well, a pity for poor Pebble. If she wants Smald, he's already...

Don't think about Pebble! When I marry Smald I want to wear the same silver boots as the princess in The Three Sisters and the Shark god and a veil of...

'A right good morning, class!'

The voice of the teacher burst Opal's daydream like a soap bubble.

He closed the door and waddled to the lectern. Placing his arms – like two rosy hams – on top of the blotting paper he beamed at his students.

'They call me brother Gravel and I am a priest of Ordwin the river god. Now Ordwin is endlessly patient. He grinds even the hardest rock into sparkling silver sand. Alas, I'm not that patient yet. That is why the abbot placed me in front of a room filled with louts and giggle-girls that are only a little bit cleverer than chattering monkeys.' He lifted his stout walking stick. 'Whenever I catch anyone nodding off or giggling, I'll correct him with a firm whack of my trusty stick. The third time means a visit to the headmaster.' His grin now almost stretched to his ears. 'And the headmaster doesn't believe in sticks. He uses a cudgel studded with crooked nails.'

'He's bluffing,' Tiger-Eye whispered in Opal's ear. 'My nephew was in Gravel's class last year and the master didn't hit anyone.'

Smald jumped up and pointed to Tiger-Eye. 'He whispered, master.

Hit him!'

'Hit him?' The grin disappeared from brother Gravel's face and he clutched his stick a bit awkwardly. 'Well, I didn't exactly mean hitting.'

Smald raised his amulet and pushed it almost in the face of the master.

'You are the most strict master in the whole school. You always beat whispering pupils. He whispered. Give him a wallop.'

'The most strict,' the master repeated. 'Always a wallop and he whispered.' The master stopped in front of Tiger-Eye. 'Put your hand on the table. You've earned a wallop. Because of, of...'

'Because he whispered,' Smald offered.

'This is completely crazy,' Tiger-Eye said. He placed his hand on the table, palm up. The master's stick gave him a hesitant tap.

'You always hit a pupil harder,' Smald said. 'A lot harder'

The stick slammed down and Tiger-Eye gasped. Another slap, a third.

'Well, that's it,' the master said and turned away.

'My uncle hits me harder,' Tiger-Eye said to his back, but the master didn't seem to hear him.

That's a bit sad, Opal thought, getting punished on your first school day. But Tiger-Eye was stupid to whisper. Children who whisper deserve a good walloping. Smald said so.

The rest of the lesson Tiger-Eye kept his peace, thanks be to the gods. He didn't even look in Opal's direction.

Drawing on the blackboard, the master explained how to decipher the language of the swallows. While swooping, they swiftly wrote words in the sky.

He hooked a big picture down from the ceiling. A man with an oversized crown stood on one leg beneath a sky filled with swallows. He tried to pull off his left boot.

'Most of what the swallows write is pure rubbish,' the master declared. 'Drivel about eggs or that strange lopsided nest of the lady one roofing tile over. But there's an ancient legend that tells how the bricklayer's King of Virgo read in the sky that an assassin was hiding in his wardrobe. So the king tiptoed to his wardrobe and glued the door shut with spider silk.

Next he called his guards: 'This wardrobe is lousy with woodworm. Carry it to the sea and throw it into the deepest whirlpool.'

The wardrobe wailed and protested but the king only smiled. 'The woodworms are loud today.'

The bell started to toll and the teacher raised his voice. 'Good, you have a

half hour recess. So munch to your heart's content on your pancakes and drink your tepid buttermilk.'

Outside all the boys and girls surrounded Smald like a swarm of wasps on a honey cake. That stupid Jade-Onyx clung to his arm like a leech. Smald must have found that rather annoying but was too good-natured to protest.

Opal ended up on the edge of the group. She would have preferred standing next to Smald but a tsal Everetto dun Maginoisse didn't force her way in like a drunken farmhand at the dog races.

'Let me through!' shouted Tiger-Eye, using his elbows and fists to clear a path. He stopped in front of Smald and glared down on the much smaller boy. 'Why?' he asked. 'Why did you tattle on me? You don't even know me! Today's the first time you ever saw me.'

Smald laughed. 'I'm going to do something quite funny. I'm going to tell you the truth. Because, you know, a minute later you'll have forgotten it all. Look! Everybody loves me. Even if they consider me, in their heart of hearts, a pain in the neck. Their hate has to go somewhere so I chose you. I need a whipping boy, someone at the bottom of the pecking order and you are it.'

'Magic! Your amulet. You're using black magic!'

'You are so right and now I want you to forget. Forget all I've said.' He looked Tiger-Eye in the face. 'Is there something you wanted to ask me?'

Tiger-Eye shook his head. 'I don't know...' He sighed, 'No, nothing.'

'Look,' Smald said, 'I think it's a pity nobody likes you. But what can I do?'

Tiger-Eye nodded and stalked away.

4.

Opal angrily followed him. She only caught up with him halfway to the Alley of Gods, in front of the altar of the herring god.

'Why are you bothering Smald all the time?' she accused. 'Why are you trying to start a row?'

'Starting a row? Me?'

'He's your friend. He's everyone's friend.'

'So he says.'

What a killjoy Tiger-Eye was! Smald was trying his best to befriend him even though nobody liked Tiger-Eye.

'Are you going home?' Opal asked.

'You'd like that, eh? All of you.'

'I'm only asking,' Opal said. 'If not home, where?'

'To the tree. The Tree of Names. My nephew told me about the magic tree. If you carve your name in the bark then not even the headmaster can expel you.'

'Is it a kind of wishing tree?'

'Something like that, yeah.'

I could use a wish, Opal thought, and a bit of magic is always useful.

Not that I want a lot of magic. Just enough to catch Smald's attention.

He doesn't even have to sit down next to me. Just noticing me is enough.

'I'll walk along with you.'

'I can't stop you. But you don't need the Tree. They'd never expel the daughter of a wealthy merchant.'

'Maybe I have something else to wish.'

The tree was a giant, meters thick and as high as a watchtower.

Maybe he was as ancient as our very island, Opal thought. The very first tree Gliph Abar made out of seaweed.

Hundreds, no thousands of names had been carved in the bark.

They looked like scars – green and brown scars made from a smoother wood. The most ancient letters were so stretched, that they were impossible to read.

'Come to carve your names, children?'

A man sat among the coiling roots. Opal had completely overlooked him.

Not so strange – his cape was exactly the same color as the bark.

The man rose.

'I'm the Keeper of the Tree. I make sure that only names and wishes are carved in the bark. No filthy words or curses. It's for your own good. The Tree is slow to anger, but once he gets going... Ay, his roots can find evildoers everywhere. If necessary they'll pierce the hardest granite.'

'And then they'll strangle him?' Opal guessed.

'No, nothing that simple. Or merciful.'

The man's face had a thousand wrinkles, but somehow he didn't look old at all. It was as if his skin was too big for his face, hanging down in folds and wrinkles. Besides, the Keeper's actions were too supple for an old man.

The Keeper laid his hand on the bark. 'Please carve away. I'll just watch over your shoulders.'

Opal opened her penknife and drew a big 'O'. Would just 'OPAL' be enough? No, my complete family name. To be on the safe side.

'That's a whole lot of names,' the Keeper remarked while she, biting the tip of her tongue, carved the 'M' of Maginoisse. She almost cut her thumb. She'd completely forgotten about the Keeper.

'Do you have to creep up on me?'

'That is my duty. Please go on.'

Easier said than done. It was quite annoying having someone watch you. No matter, she had nothing to conceal.

Now for Smald's name. His true name: Shining Emerald.

She hesitated as she finished the name. An 'I-love-you heart' would be mushy. Also, it was dangerous to be too greedy when making a wish. In the end she drew an eye between their names. That should be enough. If the spell worked Smald wouldn't be able to keep his eyes off her.

The Keeper peered closer and rubbed the bark. 'Are you certain this is the right name?'

Beneath his fingertips the bark gave way like wet clay. The letters warped and slithered away.

'What are you doing?' Opal cried. 'Stop it! You're spoiling everything, you senile old fool!'

He stepped back. 'That's more like it.'

With a sinking feeling Opal stared at the bark. Smald's name was gone. 'Tiger-Eye' proclaimed the letters. The wood scars looked positively ancient, green with alga, as if they'd been there forever.

'Did you say something?' Tiger-Eye stepped from the other side of the tree, his clasp knife opened in his hand.

'That wretched Keeper!' Sputtering with indignation she pointed to the names.

'What Keeper?'

'You saw him yourself. The old man sitting among the roots.' She looked around but the Keeper had disappeared.

'It's just us two,' Tiger-Eye said. 'Nobody else. But what are you bleating about? What's spoiled?'

'Nothing,' Opal said, hastily covering their names with her hand. She felt horribly embarrassed. What if Tiger-Eye noticed his name below her own? She jerked her head towards school . 'Let's go. Recess is almost over.'

Next to the altar of Gliph Abar Opal noticed a limp mask hanging in the briars. It was probably left as an offering.

She unhooked the mask from the thorns.

It was unpleasantly slimy and too dense for velvet or cotton. It felt exactly like the flesh of a raw oyster.

Opal spread open the mask. It was a nasty thing, with empty eyeholes and a crooked nose.

She froze. It was the tree keeper's face.

Opal had an A for Ritual and Sacrifice so she instantly knew who had worn this mask.

Who else but Gliph Abar, the god of a thousand faces? He had disguised himself as the Keeper of the Tree.

O no! I cussed a god. Called him a senile old fool.

'Move it!' Tiger-Eye cried. 'The whole schoolyard is empty! Everybody is inside already!'

Opal dropped the mask and sprinted after him. Trouble with gods was bad enough. Late on her first school day was worse.

They flung themselves across the threshold with the final toll of the bell and flopped into their seats, gasping like fish on dry land.

5.

'So, that brings us to the end of your first day,' brother Gravel said.
'Don't forget your homework. All the capitals of the islands and the first nine words of the swallow language.'
Smald was the first to rise. The other pupils waited until he stepped into the hall. Opal nodded. Of course one waited. It wouldn't do to crowd Smald.
Out in the schoolyard, the pupils formed an orderly line, waiting for Smald to notice them and speak a few words. About twenty meters away Opal saw Pebble sitting on the corner of an empty fountain. She waved to her sister and went to join the line. Pebble could wait. Talking to Smald was the important thing right now.

Opal was last.
'Eh, Smald?' she said. 'Maybe you'd like to see my house? I mean, we have our own swimming pool in the garden and our cook, he makes divine ice cream.' She had never used a word like 'divine' before.
'No, sorry,' he said while placing his hand on Jade-Onyx's shoulder.
'Today I think I'll go with her. She has a twin sister who is even more beautiful. That's right, isn't it?'
Jade-Onyx nodded emphatically. 'Much more.'
Smald gave Opal a radiant smile. Yesterday she'd have considered it a smirk, a gloating monkey-grin. 'Are you jealous of her?' Smald pressed.
'It doesn't matter if you hate each other, as long as you both love me.'
'Ok,' Opal said. 'Maybe another time?'
She turned away. It was clear that Smald had more important business.

'Opal! I'm here!' Pebble raised her hand but kept right on talking.
Dinja save me! Her sister was talking to Tiger-Eye. Talking up a storm. Waving her hands, throwing back her hair. Nice job, sucking up to the dullest boy in the whole class. Pebble really knew how to pick them.
'Tiger-Eye tells me he's in your class,' Pebble said. 'It's crazy hot and he doesn't have a swimming pool at home. So he's coming with us.'
'Humph,' was Opal's only reaction. On the way home she trailed a dozen meters behind her sister and Tiger-Eye. What if Smald saw her walking with Tiger-Eye? What would he think?

Opal couldn't even sit in the garden. Pebble and Tiger-Eye were splashing

and spattering in the swimming pool. Through her open window she heard them clearly. Great gods, such fun those babies were having.

With pursed lips she thumbed through her schoolbooks and learned all the swallow words for the next two weeks.

Tiger-Eye left at seven, half an hour before dinner. At least Pebble hadn't invited him to stay for a bite. The moment the gate was closed she tore into her sister.

'What in name of all the gods do you want with him?'

'What do you think?' Pebble said. 'He is funny, he is gallant and not bad looking at all. But Tiger-Eye doesn't even notice me. I mean he only wants to talk about you. I told him you're a stuck-up, sugar-doll princess.

An even worse brat than Lady-Not-Good-Enough who dined on silver flowers and slept on seventeen mattresses. I told him you stick your nose so high in the air that you stumble across your own feet. He didn't believe me.'

Gliph Abar and Dinja

Gliph Abar still roams the islands. He's the god of quicksilver and as changeable as water. Gliph can take any shape he wishes.

Every drunken beggar who hammers on your door can be the god in disguise. Even the hated neighbor who confiscated your brand-new ball. So keep smiling and don't hit him with your baseball bat. If he's Gliph in disguise you'll have a big problem.

The god loves practical jokes.

If a complete street of marathon runners slips on a hundred-and-seven banana skins and end up in a three-meter high heap of albatross guano, you can be sure the toddler sniggering behind the fire hydrant is the god.

Gliph Abar has a rather childish sense of humor. He's a bit like a boy who pokes an anthill heap to see the little fellows panic. Or like your nasty little brother who puts centipedes in your new suede cowboy boots. Only Gliph would use a flaming torch and cobras, not centipedes.

Praying to Gliph Abar is useless. He never listens.

But if he likes you, you can have lots of fun. With Gliph there's never a dull moment.

Prayer rugs or temple statues always show Gliph Abar when he's just taking off his mask. Below that mask a second mask appears that's exactly the same. At his feet lies a heap of other masks.

Dinja started out as a perfectly normal princess and – like Opal – she refused to marry the boring oaf chosen by her father. She would rather run through the wood, hunting wolves with her bow. Her father however was a bit sterner than Opal's. He promptly locked her up in a high tower, with only one pitcher of water to drink and a single bunch of wrinkled grapes to eat.

Dinja had hidden her bow and arrow beneath her bridal gown. The moment the moon rose, she shot an arrow in the disk. She had glued a strand of spider silk to the arrow and she now used it to lower herself to the ground.

Soon Dinja was known as the best bow-woman of all islands. She could hit the eye of a scorpion at ninety paces and ran faster than a cheetah.

Every week at least a dozen princes or emperors asked for her hand, but she laughed in their faces. On a beautiful September day she chased after a fox. He dove into a bramble bush and Dinja hissed with frustration. A fox could sit for hours without moving. But wait, she heard a rustling.

A stag jumped from the brushes in a shower of leaves and Dinja immediately took chase. A stag was even better than a fox. She could already picture his antlers hanging above the fireplace in her humble cabin.

The stag jumped across a bottomless ravine, forded a river with icy water that came straight from the glaciers, sprinted through a field with man-high poison ivy. Dinja ran barelegged but she wasn't one to complain.

The stag danced from tussock to tussock, crossing a swamp filled with quicksand and vanished into a gloomy oak wood.

Dinja stood gasping at the edge of the wood. She had lost the trail of her quarry. It was the very first time that had happened.

From the forest a grunt sounded. Or more like a rumbling so deep you could feel it in the pit of your stomach. A huge wild boar studied her from the gloom. His eyes glowed like red coals. His tusks were ivory scimitars.

Well, Dinja thought, there is nothing wrong with a wild boar and she drew her dagger. An arrow doesn't work against a two-meter high wild boar. The monster boar turned around and fled into the woods.

Dinja pursued him for three hours, four. She wheezed, the sweat streamed down her back and filled her boots until they sloshed and still the boar ran on.

It is probably a magic beast and perhaps even invulnerable, Dinja thought. All the better, otherwise it wouldn't be fun.

In the end it was the wild boar that stopped. No matter how magical, he was completely winded. It was night and the moon stood high in the sky. If you looked you could still see Dinja's arrow and a trailing thread of spider silk.

'I give up,' the boar said. 'You caught me, fair and square,' and he changed into a well-muscled fellow with a wild beard.

'You could have fooled me,' Dinja said. 'So you are no animal but a man.'

'A god actually,' Gliph Abar said, 'and you caught me. What are you going to do with me?'

'I can't cut off your head to hang it above my fireplace,' Dinja said. 'People would talk.' She took him by both ears and pulled him closer to kiss his lips.

You can be sure that Dinja didn't invite her father to her wedding.

6.

Today I'll see Smald again! That was Opal's first thought when she opened her eyes the next morning. Everything felt exactly right. A ray of butter-yellow sunlight slanted down through a gap in the curtains, twinkling with specks of dust. Her butterfly flapped enthusiastically around the room and for once his wings didn't even squeak.

This is going to be a super day, Opal thought. I know it, I feel it.

If I run to school right now, without eating or washing, I'll be the first.

No other children. When Smald arrives I'll be waiting for him. Then he'll understand how much I love him.

Pebble stumbled into the kitchen, yawning and tugging a comb through her hair as Opal threw three peaches and a hunk of bread into her schoolbag. Forget butter or fillings. No time.

'What's the hurry?' Pebble asked.

'I don't want to miss a single second of the lessons. And, ah, I want to look through my homework once more.'

'Look through your homework? You? That would be the first time.' Pebble shook her head. 'I'm lucky I don't have to go to the temple-school yet. Just one day and you're already out of your mind.'

'See you this afternoon. I really have to run.'

Opal arrived at the schoolyard, out of breath and at least an hour early. Her heart was hammering and sweat streamed down her back.

Smald wasn't there yet. But Jade-Onyx was and the rest of the class.

Jade Onyx sniffed. 'You're the last. Perhaps you dislike Smald?' She opened her bag and showed off three closely written pages. 'I did all his homework. And you?'

'Hullo, boyz and girlz!' Smald strolled across the schoolyard. 'I polished my pendant this morning until it shone.' He waved his amulet. 'Have a good look. Doesn't it sparkle like there's no tomorrow?'

Immediately, there was such a jostling crowd around Smald that Opal didn't get to see the perfectly polished pendant at all.

Opal shuffled into the classroom, the last pupil, and sat as far towards the back as possible. No, not the last pupil – one seat remained free.

With the eighth chime of the bronze bell Tiger-Eye dashed into the classroom. Guess where he sat?

Today they had brother Marl teaching Advanced Fishing. The man was as skeleton-thin as a praying mantis. All the hair from his bald head had migrated to his flowing side-whiskers.

'Fishes, yes,' he started off. 'Well, of course one can sit by the seaside with a fishing rod, and stare at a motionless float for simply hours and hours. Most likely you'll go to bed with an empty stomach.'

Brother Marl turned his back to the class and Opal watched as Smald stood up. He raised his arm, taking aim.

'How much better it is to spread a net and play a happy mackerel-hop on your magic…'

Something burst onto his bald head.

'What?' His grabbed at his head; at the same moment a horrible stench spread through the class. It had been an albatross' egg and quite a rotten one, at that. The contents dripped in green slimy threads from his fingers.

'Who did this?'

'He did, master!' Smald pointed at Tiger-Eye. 'He threw the eggs. All three.'

'Is that true?' the master asked the rest of the class.

'I saw it myself!' cried Jade-Onyx. 'Tiger-Eye! It was him!'

Three eggs? Opal saw only one. And Tiger-Eye couldn't have done it. No way. He was sitting right next to me…

She closed her eyes but the picture in her memory remained the same. Smald had thrown the egg. But why did the rest of the class point at Tiger-Eye? We both sat on the last row, behind them, and the others didn't have eyes in the back of their heads.

'Tiger-Eye stays after school,' the master decided. 'The rest of the week. Weeding the school garden.'

'The rest of the month,' Smald corrected him. 'Pulling nettles. With his bare hands.'

'The rest of the month is a better idea indeed,' the master said.

'It starts with an egg…' He blinked his eyes in the glare of Smald's amulet and nodded. 'Unruly pupils need stern masters.'

Tiger-Eye didn't even breathe out loud for the rest of the lesson and Opal quite understood. She was furious, so angry she could scream.

What craziness was this? Why did the master believe Smald's story while the whole class had seen him, throwing that rotten egg? Tiger-Eye was just a big bumbling lout with a ridiculous sweater and stupid sandals, but that was no reason to accuse him falsely.

At recess I'll confront Smald, she decided. This has to stop! She couldn't

understand what she'd ever seen in that adder Smald.

'That girl is waving at me,' Smald said to the circle of kids surrounding him. 'Let her through please.'

He faced Opal. 'Something you want to tell us? For instance, that you threw the eggs and not your boyfriend?'

Several girls giggled.

'There were not three eggs. Just one and you threw it. I saw it myself!'

'You're wrong. Just plain wrong.' Smald said, raising his amulet.

'Tiger-Eye threw the egg. I mean all three eggs. Believe me.' He rubbed the point of his nose. 'And stop resisting. You adore me. What's your name? Opal? Love me like all the others.'

'But of course,' Opal cooed. What was Smald talking about?

Everybody loved him.

After school Opal took the mule wagon to the other side of the city. She hoped Grandmother Rithka would at least pretend to listen to her account of the first school days. Yesterday she had seen her parents only in passing.

'I'm so happy for you,' her mother had said, followed by 'Don't forget to do your homework.' And then she had turned to the maid to scold her for putting white roses in a pale yellow vase.

Her father had tugged on his fur-lined cape and said, 'Tomorrow I'd love to listen to your stories but now I have to run. There's an emergency meeting of the silkworm keepers of Scorpio.'

Opal looked up from the foot of the Grandmother Rithka's cliff.

The stairs still looked ridiculously high. Her ankles cramped spontaneously.

Only fools complain, Rithka always said. Use your brain and if that doesn't work, magic.

Why not both? Opal thought. Luckily the moon was hanging high in the sky. Magic was so easy! Moonstones belonged to the moon, to the sky. They wanted to go up, to join her, just like Opal.

She licked her two moonstones, waking their magic.

'Seek your big sister!' she ordered, pointing to the sky. Then she tied them around her ankles with a cord.

It worked like a dream. With each step they lifted Opal higher into the air. It was like having springs in your heels.

'You got to the top much faster this time,' Rithka smiled.

'Gran! We're learning the language of the swallows and I already know a

hundred words!' Opal burst out. 'And I've met an extremely interesting boy.'
'So. That is good to...' Her grandmother froze. She took a step in Opal's direction and grabbed her chin. 'Look at me, granddaughter.
Look me right in the eye.'
It only lasted a few seconds. Rithka let her hand drop and clacked her tongue. 'Somebody put his dirty fingers in your head and stirred your memory. You stink of fool's gold.'
'Pyrite? But pyrite magic only works when you see the stone itself? Clearly. Doesn't it?'

Pyrite was one of the most powerful stones. Islanders called the beautiful yellow stone fool's gold because it often looked the same as real gold.
The moment anybody hung a talisman of pyrite around his neck, he lied so beautifully that everyone believed his every word.
When a stranger walked into a village wearing pyrite, the first who met him immediately tried bashing his head in before he could say something like: 'You are all my slaves. Do everything I say.'
'I don't know anybody with such an amulet,' Opal insisted. 'I'm sure I would have noticed. And it only works when you see it.'
'He probably ordered you to forget his amulet. It doesn't matter.
I have the perfect defense.' She walked to the grab-vase and produced two earrings. Each one had a pendant, shaped like a black tear. A silver gleam shimmered with every motion across the surface.

'Hematite absorbs all magic,' Grandmother Rithka declared.
'As long as you wear these stones, a liar doesn't stand a chance.
No matter what he says, you won't believe a word.'

No guardian at the gate? This was a fine mess. Now every beggar could slink inside and fill his filthy pockets with singing toads.
Opal pushed against the gate. The wood didn't budge.
Locked? I didn't even know you could lock the gate!
'Hey, open up!' she called and kicked against the door. 'Let me in, you sluggards! It's me! Opal tsal Everetto dun Maginoisse!'
It was only after five minutes that she heard the bolt shoot back. By then Opal had shouted herself hoarse.
'It's Saint Umphard's Day,' Pebble said from the doorway. 'Did you forget?
All the servants sit with their slippers in front of the fireplace, trying to drink our wine cellar dry in a single day. You and mama have to cook today.
I've already swabbed the kitchen floor and walked the hunting dogs.'
'Saint Umphard. How stupid of me.'

'Hey,' said Pebble, stretching out her hand. 'You're wearing new earrings.'
'Grandmother gave them to me. They aren't for show but for protection against black magic. According to her, my head's filled with pyrite lies.'
'Smald!' said Pebble. 'He's wearing an amulet! I bet you it's a magic one.'
'I don't know. It was ordinary gold, not false.' Opal waved in the direction of the gilded columns at the entrance to their villa. 'Our whole house gleams with gold. I'm quite sure that... Wait a moment. Wait a moment. That amulet. It was like a jigsaw, all kinds of different pieces. A circle, a triangle, a square.'
'Pyrite crystals are square,' Pebble said. 'The circle and the triangle were real gold of course. So nobody would notice the square.' She licked her lips – a bit like a mountain lioness who'd just noticed a tasty little baby deer. 'When we tell the royal guard they'll dump Smald in the deepest dungeon and throw the key in an erupting volcano. Everybody hates pyrite liars!'
'If only it was that easy!' Opal said. 'Picture it. Smald waves his amulet and the guards promptly do everything he orders. Then it'll be us who end up in prison. Also, he's the son of the high priest. They are mortally afraid that Smald's father will call on a dozen gods and turn them all into cockroaches. No, I'll think of something.' She touched an earring. 'Knowing that all his words are lies is half the work.'
The rest of Saint Umphard's Day was great fun. The gardener complained that the soup tasted like brine and was quite undrinkable. Because Opal had made the soup, he was probably right. The maid insisted that Opal's mother polish her shoes at least three times before she declared herself satisfied.
That night the whole family slept on the potato sacks in the barn while the servants snored beneath silken sheets. Opal fell asleep with a smile on her face. If only it was Saint Umphard every day...

Arre Umphard

Arre Umphard was the god of the poorest servants, of the galley boys and the washwomen with hands that were red from the suds. His totem animals were the scurrying rats and cockroaches. To pray to Arre Umphard you had to pour a gush of sour milk onto a moldy crust of bread while you whispered your wish.

Afterwards a cockroach or magpie would bring you his answer in a dream. On Umphard's day the servants were in charge for one day and one night. They put on the satin coat of their master. They drove the coach through the formal gardens, straight across the flower beds and so they were happy for at least one day in the year. The god often sleeps in front of the fire, curled up like a kitten. Other times you see him hanging by his toes among the smoked hams. Only slaves, orphans on bare feet or servants who have just spent their last dime can see him.

7.

Next morning Opal had trouble not laughing in Smald's face. How seriously that little guy waved his amulet! And all the other pupils followed him like bleating sheep.

This was the day reserved for sport and games, the girls against the boys. Smald and Jade-Onyx were the captains, of course. So it was logical that Opal and Tiger-Eye spent the whole day sitting on the reserve bench.

'He doesn't like you, either?' Tiger-Eye asked. 'Smald and his silver-haired maiden?'

'I saw through him. Smald is nothing but a dirty little sneak, even if his father is the high priest.' She unhooked an earring. 'Do you have piece of cord so you can hang this around your neck?'

'A present? What's the occasion?'

'Not a present, more like...Yes, call it a shield. It is hematite.'

'Hematite drinks all magic.' Tiger-Eye was as quick on the uptake as Pebble. 'Smald's amulet! I thought they were just sucking up to him because he was rich, or because of his father.'

'Hah! Smald's father isn't even titled. Not a single noble ancestor. Put it on and he can't touch us.'

They sat silently for a moment.

'My grandmother,' Opal began, 'She once told me a fairytale. There was a hero in it named Tiger-Eye. Tiger-Eye the dragon killer.'

Tiger-Eye laughed. 'Killing them is the last thing I would want to do – me or my family.'

It's horrible when you're the black sheep, when the whole class snubs you. But if you're two victims together it is kind of fun. It was just fine with Opal: She and Tiger-Eye lazed on the reserve bench, in the warm sun, while the rest of the class ran until they were blue in the face and their feet nearly dropped off.

'Walk home with me after school?' Tiger-Eye asked, trying to sound nonchalant. 'I already visited your house.'

He is shy! Opal thought, followed by: at least he asked.

'Why not?' she replied. 'I have nothing better to do.' It didn't do to appear too eager when a boy asked you over. It only made them arrogant.

Directly behind the school Tiger-Eye turned right and crossed the Northern Bridge. Opal had seldom walked in this direction. On the other side of the bridge she remembered why.

The houses were at least six, seven stories high and so narrow they made her think of upright coffins. Washing hung on lines of braided sea grass. The shirts and shorts looked gray from the peat smoke. But Tiger-Eye inhaled the smoke with a smile on his face. 'Ah, there is nothing like the smell of honest pig crap and nettles! The stink of all those bloody flowers, that horrible jasmine in your garden, it made me want to puke.'

Was he pulling her leg? Everybody liked flowers. Didn't he? 'Flowers aren't too bad once you're used to them.' She tried to breathe only through her mouth.

'This is where I live,' Tiger-Eye mumbled, avoiding her eyes.

'With my Aunt and Uncle Slate.'

'Crazy!' Opal squealed and clapped her hands. Tiger-Eye's house might look like a hovel but the whole garden was filled with statues. Human-size statues carved from sparkling gemstone.

'By Dinja's bow! This is the most beautiful place I have ever seen.'

Opal stepped into the garden and studied the closest statue. The man's mouth gaped wide, in a soundless scream. He lifted his hands as if to repel some hideous devil. Opal didn't have the slightest idea what he feared. The sculptor hadn't seen fit to include the attacker.

She trailed her fingers across the chin. She could actually feel the bristles on his cheeks. Wow, that stone mole even sprouted a crystal hair.

These statues were classier than her family's – no banal kings with swords and crowns or posturing gods. Tiger-Eye's front garden was crowded with guys on bare feet, who were clad in rags. They weren't wearing many-pronged crowns or heraldic helmets, only a cap at most. How original.

'This is the best garnet stone I've ever seen,' she said. 'Such a deep blood red and the statue is one single piece. Your people must be even wealthier than my family.'

'If we could sell Great-Uncle Gneiss, sure,' Tiger-Eye said, 'but you don't sell family. That my great-uncle ended up as garnet is his bad luck. Only emerald is more expensive.'

'Great-Uncle Gneiss? What do you mean?' Opal wasn't following Tiger-Eye's story.

'You chucked Uncle Gneiss beneath his chin. If he was still alive, he would have given you a wallop.' Opal snatched her hand away.

'Luckily he's been petrified for thirty years.' He waved at the statues. 'All family. That's what happens when a dragon gets you.'

'A dragon? You're a...'
'Sure. Egg-snatchers. We
gather the gems wild
dragons lay.
You weren't far off with
your 'dragon-killer.'
Only it's the dragons
that kill us.' Some
things one didn't
mention: for instance that all
those beautiful polished gemstones
were in fact dragon-spawn.
The MiYu-dragons didn't dine on gallant knights
and screaming maids like some old tales told.
They much preferred a nice block of soapstone or
a bank of crunchy pebbles. They blew their white hot
flame across a rock and slurped up the bubbling lava.
The hardest pieces crystallized into dragon eggs.
Dragons spawned them like frogs, thousands at the time.
Only one in a million ever hatched. A fertilized egg glowed
in the dark, but sadly, it was a glow no dragon could see.
The dragons were very protective of their eggs. They knew the
location of every single one.
Egg-snatchers collected the dragon eggs and you could use
them for all kind of spells. To make your herbs grow, to raise
a storm when the fisherman, who dumped you for your best
friend, set sail…
Poaching gems was an extremely dangerous job, Opal knew.
Only the poorest of the poor would ever attempt it.
'Dragons are quite ill-tempered,' Tiger-Eye told her. 'When they meet
a lout lugging a big sack filled with gems, they take a deep breath and
bathe him in flame. The poor guy promptly changes into a stone statue.
The mightier the dragon, the more precious the stone.

It is possible to save the victim. Possible, but not easy. You cover him with his own weight in gemstones. The jewels promptly lose all their color and magic. They change into worthless quartz.

When you change into garnet, you're just out of luck. Your family and friends need at least twenty years to gather so many precious gems.

And if you scolded your wife and hit your kids, well, you'll end up as an oversized garden gnome. With every spring a bird nest in your mouth. Like Great-Uncle Gneiss here.'

The statues suddenly lost their luster in Opal's eyes. They were only sad and horrible. It was like having the mummies of your family in front of your house.

'Doesn't anybody ever steal them?' Opal asked. 'I mean they remain gemstone, even if they are really people. You are all so poor here.'

'Not that poor,' Tiger-Eye said. 'When you steal someone's statue, his ghost creeps inside your dreams. You'll never sleep until you put back the statue. And if you broke up his statue, to turn it into gems…'

'Yes? What happens then?'

'I haven't the slightest idea. Nobody was ever greedy enough to try.'

In the late afternoon Tiger-Eye's aunt offered them a slice of black bread with crumbs of stockfish. The blue fuzz growing on the bread made it extra tasty, Tiger-Eye said.

Opal surreptitiously dropped the bread into her schoolbag when Tiger-Eye looked the other way. She brushed the crumbs from her lips. 'That was delicious.'

'Do you want another slice? My aunt…'

'Oh, no, thank you.' She ostentatiously rubbed her belly. 'I'm stuffed.'

I have to distract him before he offers me another horrible thing to eat. 'You said you lived with your aunt. Did you have trouble with your parents?'

'Not at all. They live here too and I see them every day. Come, I'll introduce you.'

He halted in front of two statues. The statues looked quite dramatic: there was a panic-stricken man, who was obviously trying to flee.

With one hand he was wildly swinging about with a huge cudgel while dragging a woman with the other. She was still hanging on to a half-filled dragon-egg sack.

'They bumped into a dragon and didn't run fast enough,' Tiger-Eye said. He put his hand on his mothers curls. 'They turned into ruby, an extremely rare gemstone.' He bit on his lower lip. 'Each raid I search like crazy.

I've never found more than a few grains of ruby.'

'Oh no,' Opal breathed. Me and my big mouth. Tiger-Eye's parents were skin and bones but they still would weigh close to a hundred and twenty kilos. With a hundred and twenty kilos of ruby you could buy a complete country house, with a garden filled with strolling peacocks and marble fountains. Or a brand-new cargo ship. Even if they had died it would have been less awful. Now Tiger-Eye had to pass them everyday, knowing he would never be able to save them.

Tiger-Eye looked at the horizon and clacked his tongue. 'Half an hour to sunset. I'll walk you to the bridge It isn't clever to cross my neighborhood after dark.' He shuffled his feet. 'I asked my aunt if you could have dinner with us. Sorry, there just isn't enough food. Also, I guess you don't like kelp-soup with ground barnacles. That is fare for poor people.'

'What crap! I love ordinary food. I really liked your black bread.'

Tiger-Eye grinned. 'Sure and that's why you slid it into your school-bag. So you could nibble it at home.' He raised his hands. 'No, you don't have to protest. I can barely stomach it. We just didn't have anything else.'

Opal ears burned. So that was the reason Tiger-Eye wouldn't stay for dinner the last time. He was just polite. When poor people like Tiger-Eye's aunt invited a guest, their children go to bed with empty stomachs.

8.

A week flapped past like a startled pheasant, then a fortnight, and Opal discovered she could just ignore Smald. Not that Smald had given up easily. He waved his amulet, almost pushed it into Opal's face and hissed in anger. Twice he tried to sick other pupils on Opal and Tiger-Eye.

He quickly stopped that. Whenever he used a pyrite lie against Opal the earrings sucked all magic away and he couldn't use his amulet for at least half an hour.

It ended in a kind of armed peace. Smald pretended Opal and Tiger-Eye didn't exist and Opal returned the favor. It was all right with her: she had Tiger-Eye to keep her company. Also, she didn't really need the rest of the class. In the meantime she had met quite a lot of pupils from the other classes and as long as she didn't sit in her own group she was quite popular.

'Let's go visit the Tree of Names,' Tiger-Eye said during recess. 'I need a place where nobody can eavesdrop.'

The tree looked bigger than ever and her leaves overhung them like a dark green thundercloud. It was strangely silent: not a single bird sang, no chipmunk chattered.

Opal looked carefully around before she sat among the roots. No trace of the so called Keeper. It didn't prove much. Gliph Abar could very well have changed himself into an aphid.

'Spill,' Opal said.

'I have discovered where Dardamesh lives!'

'Fantastic. But who is Dardamesh?'

'Mighty Dardamesh, the Mother of All Dragons! Don't you rich folk know anything? No egg-snatcher ever found her hoard. Imagine: a whole cave filled with gleaming jewels. The eggs of centuries. At one stroke I'll be as rich as your whole family.' His voice dropped to a hoarse whisper.

'Wealthy enough to make my parents live again.'

'That would be wonderful. But why tell me? I mean, it's the discovery of the ages and I'm not even a egg-snatcher. Not even family.'

'You're the only one I can trust. And Pebble of course. The rest of my family... We have been poor for too long. It's doesn't make you very nice. Also, with egg-snatching you always need two. One to lure the dragon away. The other to raid the cave.'

'Count me in.'

'Well, I… There is a slight problem.'

'I'm listening.'

'We'll have to hire a boat and a whole lot of other things. Big spades, sacks of thistledown. A gong of first-grade green jade. I don't own a single wooden dime. Can you lend me some? I'll pay you back. Triple. Tenfold.'

Opal rummaged in her bag and handed him her sea serpent-leather purse. 'Here, take what you need. No, take the whole purse. We'll see if there is anything left afterwards.'

'See? That is what I meant. If I lent my uncle any money, he would run to the tavern and squander it all on booze. And the next day he would deny he owed me any money at all.'

'Inside our tea house hangs a gong of green jade. Nobody ever sounds it. When do we leave?'

'Tomorrow we walk to the North Harbor and we hire a boat. Right after school.'

'What in the name of all Three Sisters are you doing?' Pebble asked that afternoon. Opal put her bag down and brushed the petals from her bare arms.

'I'm gathering stuff. You know, thistledown and dandelion fluff. This whole bag, it has to be filled to the brim.'

'Something for school?'

'Not really. Not for school.'

Pebble folded her arms. 'You have a secret. Please tell. A secret is no fun without sharing.'

'Swear you won't tell father or mother. For them just about anything is too dangerous or undignified.'

Pebble snorted. 'Did I ever snitch on you? So it is insanely risky and completely foolish?'

'Tiger-Eye discovered treasure. A cave with the dragon-eggs of a thousand years.' She opened the bag. 'This thistledown is to keep the stolen jewels from clinking. When a dragon hears the slightest tinkle of a jewel, she comes rushing. Whoosh! A whacking great flame and you are a garden gnome for the rest of your life.'

'That sounds dangerous indeed,' Pebble said with a certain envy.

'That's why I agreed to come. And to help Tiger-Eye of course.'

'Sure, so he'll be wealthy enough to marry you.' Pebble jumped back to avoid Opal's kick.

'Don't be stupid! We're just friends.'

9.

'Wake up!' Pebble threw the shutters wide open and pulled Opal's eiderdown from her bed. 'Come on!'
Opal blinked against the sudden flood of sunlight. 'Who, where?'
'A fox killed all three roosters. The floor of the chicken run was covered with feathers. Even our cook overslept. There's only cold porridge in the kitchen.'
'Oh no!' Opal grabbed her coral red dress from the chair. 'I have to run. It will be a disaster if they make me stay after school.'
'Don't forget your bags with thistledown!'

She ran down the quay. This wasn't the first time she'd missed the first hour. Opal wasn't an early riser. Half way down the Avenue of Gods she discovered she wasn't wearing her hematite earring. She must have left it in the jewel case on her night stand.
It didn't matter. Tiger-Eye was still wearing his ring on a cord around his neck. Smald can't order us around. He probably didn't even know it's the earrings that gave them immunity.

The hours seemed to creep by. Even a snail on crutches moved a lot faster. When the last bell chimed Opal jumped from her chair.
Today we make Tiger-Eye rich. Rich enough to save his parents.
I only hope they won't think me a spoiled brat. Poor people always hate the rich.
Tiger-Eye and Opal were the first to leave the classroom. All the other children waited until lord Smald deigned to rise.
'You ready to raid a dragon?' Tiger-Eye asked.
Opal grinned. 'Just you wait, Darda-what's-her-name. We won't leave a single pebble in your cave.'
'Bought a wheelbarrow. I left it under the razor berry bush behind the bridge. I didn't want to make my uncle suspicious by taking our own.'
'A wheelbarrow? You're thinking big.'
She instantly regretted her remark. It had nothing to do with greed.
Tiger-Eye had to transport at least a hundred and twenty kilos of jewels to save his parents. Even more if those jewels were less precious than rubies. Without a wheelbarrow it would be impossible.

They proceeded slowly, what with a wheelbarrow loaded with oversized spades and bulging sacks. They were only half way along the coastal road when Smald stepped in front of the wheelbarrow.

'Where are you going with such big spades and all those sacks, Tiger-Eye? Going to muck out the royal stable and smear the dung in your hair?'

He looked at Opal and his eyes widened. 'No earring! This must be my lucky day.'

So he knew, Opal thought.

Tiger-Eye grabbed a spade. He raised it above his head like a battle ax.

'I still have mine! If you lift one little finger against her...'

Smald danced back, out of the reach of Tiger-Eye's weapon. 'Opal!' he cried. 'When I clap my hands, you jump from the cliff. Because you love me so much you'll do everything I ask.'

That would be fun, Opal thought. I've never jumped from a cliff before. If Smald asks it must be quite safe. I'll probably drift down like a feather. She walked to the edge of the road. The North Harbor lay at her feet, at least sixty meters down. The waves broke against the foot of the cliff. The spume looked like fine lace.

'Shall I clap my hands?' Smald asked.

'Yes, yes!' Opal cried. 'I want to fly!' She flapped her arms and giggled.

Tiger-Eye lowered his spade.

'Right,' Smald said. 'Now take off your earring. Throw it into the sea.'

Tiger-Eye obeyed.

'Good boy,' Smald said. 'Tell me everything. Where are you two going? Why do you need that wheelbarrow and so many bags?'

Tiger-Eye's mouth tightened and deep in his throat a rattle began. He tried to bite his tongue to stop the words. Nothing worked: The pyrite magic was too strong.

'I discovered a cave,' he whispered, his voice hoarse with anguish.

'Filled with jewels. I saw them glisten from above. The walls of the ravine were too steep to descend. You can only enter from the seaside.'

'The mother of all Dragons lives in that cave,' Opal helpfully added, 'and nobody has ever stolen a single jewel.'

'Well, well,' Smald said. 'A man can never get too rich. You know what? I'll go with you. You two can carry my bags of jewels.' He jumped on the wheelbarrow, sat down on the bags and languidly waved his hand. 'Proceed.'

Tiger-Eye pushed the wheelbarrow all the way to the left wharf of the harbor and stopped, gasping, in the middle of the basalt dam. The sweat

dripped from the point of his nose.

Smald stepped down from the wheelbarrow and stretched his legs.

'So far so good. Now you are going to hire a boat, right?'

A man waved from a neighboring jetty. 'Boats! You're looking for a dinghy, a fine sloop? I have the best there are and nowhere cheaper.'

The man sported the wild beard of a buccaneer and his hair stood out in all directions.

'Go for it,' Smald ordered.

Half a dozen boats had been moored along a jetty. Their sails were embroidered with parrots and squids. Copper lanterns gleamed.

'You won't find a better boat on all the twelve islands,' the man declared. 'Unbelievably cheap, too.'

'You're trying to cheat those children?' A woman jumped down from the pier. Six meters: The planks shook when she landed.

'Hey!' the man said. 'I didn't even mention a price, Di.'

'Pay the man whatever he asks,' Smald ordered. 'Don't haggle, Tiger-Eye. It isn't my money anyway.'

'Six agates for the whole day,' the man promptly said.

Tiger-Eye handed him a large moonstone. 'That's all I have left.'

'Exactly right,' said the man and pocketed the stone.

The woman shook her head. 'How about some change? A few shiny black pebbles for instance?'

'Obsidian, my lady? That beautiful black volcano glass?'

She stamped her foot. 'You know very well what I mean!'

'I only just started and don't forget it was her own wish. Two small stones then.' He nodded. 'Just strong enough to free their thoughts. Not enough to escape. Yes, that makes the game a lot more interesting.'

He rummaged in his money belt and handed Tiger-Eye a handful of pebbles. 'Your change, young man.'

Smald slumped against the mast and closed his eyes to continue his nap. 'Row me, Tiger-Eye,' he yawned. 'Row me rich.'

Opal pushed the boat away from the jetty as the woman raised her hand.

'You cried when I ate my last grape,' she told Opal. 'I'll never forget that.'

Opal didn't have the slightest idea what she was talking about and waved back a bit hesitantly. She knew the woman from somewhere. Was she an acquaintance of her parents or a second cousin from another island?

No, nothing that vague. Opal had seen her before. Not once, but often. At least she'd seen her portrait. The name was on the tip of her tongue.

She knew that face. Only the clothes were wrong and she should be carrying something in her hand. Something curved like a coat hanger? Tiger-Eye nudged her and she lost her train of thought.

'Smald is dozing,' he whispered. 'Open your hand.'

The moment Opal touched the stone a cool breeze seemed to blow through her head. All pyrite lies lost their grip, evaporating instantly.

Smald almost made me jump from the cliff! He wants to steal all our jewels. He made Tiger-Eye push him the whole way.

Somehow the last insult was the worst. She clenched her fists.

Nobody spits on my friends!

She watched Smald from the corner of her eye. That son-of-a-featherless-seagull still slept. His mouth hung open and he snored, loud enough to put a manatee to shame.

'Why can't we push him overboard?' she whispered. 'Feed him to the tiger sharks? I saw one following us a minute ago.'

'No, sorry. The boatman gave me two small pebbles. Just enough to allow me to think. But we still have to do anything Smald orders.'

'We'll get him,' Opal said. 'At least my thoughts are my own again.'

She folded her hands and bowed to the west.

'Help me take revenge, Dinja,' she prayed.

The goddess-with-the-bow knew everything about revenge and terrible retribution. Even her own priestesses only whispered about what Dinja did to her own father after she escaped from her prison tower.

A silver fish jumped from the waves and flapped his wings.

Opal smiled. Flying fishes were the hunting dogs of Dinja, every child knew that. The goddess had heard her prayer.

10.

Two hours later, a score of islets dotted the sea. No, they weren't islands, Opal saw, but trees growing in the middle of the ocean.

'How does that work, Tiger-Eye? I thought trees couldn't stand salt?'

'Mangroves love it. Six thousand years ago the Count of Ismadell planted a whole forest-reef in front of his coast. Mangroves stop even a tidal wave. The castle of the Count had been washed away by a tsunami the year before, see?'

They passed below the thick gray branches of a giant tree. A row of pale birds looked down. One lifted his bill and blew a yellow flame.

'Dragonets,' Tiger-Eye said. 'We are getting close.'

They dragged the boat up to the high tide line. Now even the most powerful wave couldn't float her away.

The sand was strangely smooth Opal saw, with only a few gull footprints and a single hyena spoor. 'I don't think many people visit this stretch of coast. Maybe we're the first?'

'In ninety-eight thousand years? Not a chance. It is really quite close to the city.' He scanned the sea cliffs and pointed. 'Bull's eye! That fissure must be the entrance on the sea side.'

It took Opal at least ten seconds to find the crack in the granite.

It was only a little darker than the rest of the rock. She would never have found the entrance on her own.

'You go first,' Smald said. 'I am the son of the high priest and worth a hundred times more than an egg-snatcher or the daughter of a mere merchant.

'You're just a coward,' Tiger-Eye said.

'Better afraid than slate.' Smald giggled and repeated his own joke.

'Better afraid than slate!'

Opal bent down and pointed to a smooth purple pebble. 'Amethyst!'

'Probably washed down from the cave,' Tiger-Eye explained. 'By the rain.'

Opal kept looking at the ground. Find a big enough piece of hematite and she would be free.

'Uh oh,' Tiger-Eye warned, raising his hand to stop them.

'We're clearly not the first visitors.'

A peddler crouched in the entrance of the cave. His boots were rose quartz while his backpack had solidified into the kind of off-gray soap stone.

'Her flame almost missed him,' Tiger-Eye said.

'What do you mean?'

He tapped on the stone man. 'This is all rather worthless stuff. In the center of her flame he would have changed into a much more precious stone.'

He sighed. 'Turning into stone is bad enough. To change into something so base…' He froze. 'Ay.'

The cave was filled with statues. It looked like a warehouse of garden ornaments: egg-snatchers; two shipwrecked sailors with the water dripping from their beards in diamond pearls; a fisherman with a malachite fishing rod. Dozens, maybe hundreds of statues.

'I, eh, I wonder if it was such a smart idea to steal Dardamesh's eggs.'

'We have no choice,' Opal said. 'Smald won't let us turn back.' She fished the jade gong from beneath the bags.

Though their ears were so small as to be almost invisible dragons had incredibly sharp hearing. The rattle of a pebble told them the taste of that stone from half a mile away. Most dragons considered jade the ultimate gourmet stone. The chime of Opal's gong would certainly lure Dardamesh from her cave.

'Tell me once more what you are going to do,' Tiger-Eye said.

'I know. No need to repeat.'

He kept looking at her.

'All right, you win. I hide behind a rock, a big boulder, and strike my gong. When she leaves her cave, I stop. When she returns, I strike it again.'

'Remember dragons only see moving prey. The moment you freeze you become invisible. But only if you keep as still as a statue. Twitch your little finger, lick your lips and she will see you again. And the second time her flame won't miss.'

Opal soon found the perfect hiding place. Some three hundred meters away a whole gallery of basalt columns had come tumbling down.

They lay in a heap at the foot of the cliff, forming a beautiful maze.

Opal entered a narrow corridor and climbed at least seven meters before she saw daylight again. The columns leaned together and their tops looked like the battlements of a tower.

From her lookout Opal had quite a good view of the cave entrance.

Smart dragon who finds me here.

Opal hit her gong. A clear note sung out across the beach. Somehow the gong sounded tasty indeed. Just like the bell of the man with the honey

cake pushcart. Opal could imagine Dardamesh running from her cave, saliva dripping from her maw. The best thing was that the sound bounced from cliff to cliff. For the dragon the sound would come from all directions at once.

Dardamesh coiled from her cave, supple as an eel. Each scale burned like a golden flame. She was so beautiful Opal choked up and felt tears burn in the corners of her eyes.

It was a deadly kind of beauty – the splendor of a roaring tsunami or a lightning strike.

Dardamesh lifted her mighty head and scanned the beach.

Opal hit her gong again and ducked.

When she dared to look again, Dardamesh was circling high above the sea.

Good, Opal thought, she didn't have the slightest idea where the sound had come from. I have to lure her closer. I can't allow her to see Tiger-Eye when he leaves her cave.

She hit the gong three more times and Dardamesh turned, looping back to the coast. The dragon alighted in front of Opal's watchtower.

Oops. This time Dardamesh didn't doubt the direction at all.

Opal didn't dare to move. Or even breathe.

From the top of the sky an angry screech drifted down.

It was a horrible sound, raw as the scream of a hungry seagull.

But if a seagull, then a two-thousand-pound seagull…

Two dragons wheeled. Males, Opal saw. They sported colorful crests and were as tattered as tomcats. Their wings were torn and ripped, their scales blackened by a hundred firefights.

Just what we needed, Opal thought, more dragons. She groaned.

Dardamesh lifted her muzzle to the sky and roared again, each dragon word was a thundering flame. Opal didn't need an A in dragon lore to translate. 'The jade belongs to me! Every single crumb! Back off!'

Seven seconds later the three dragons rolled across the sands, roaring and spitting fire.

Maybe more dragons was exactly what we need, after all, Opal thought.

She slipped from her tower and ran from boulder to boulder.

Tiger-Eye and Smald emerged for the third time from the cave, dragging their now extremely heavy bags. The bottom of the sloop sparkled, already ankle deep with shining dragon-eggs.

'We have to stop,' Tiger-Eye gasped. His bag was bulging and looked heavier than Smald's. 'A single agate more and the sloop will sink.'

'Don't be a ninny,' Smald sneered. 'The dragons won't stop fighting for the next three hours.' He looked at Tiger-Eye. 'In the cave, it looked as if you were searching for something. Something special. Even emeralds weren't good enough. What kind of gem were you hoping to find?'

'Rubies. Why?'

'I saw a whole heap of rubies. In the back of the cave.' He grabbed his amulet. 'Believe me.'

'Rubies. My mother turned into ruby.'

Opal saw Tiger-Eye's dreamy gaze. 'Smald's lying!' It was no use. Tiger-Eye desperately wanted to believe. The small piece of hematite didn't help at all.

Tiger-Eye grabbed a new bag and took a second one. 'We'll go back to the cave, one more time.'

Smald ran in front of them all the way to the cave. 'I'll show you where the rubies lie. Blood red rubies. A heap as high as your head!'

'You won't find a single ruby in the cave,' Opal hissed. 'Not even a grain. He is only saying that because he is such a greedy monster. He wants more jewels.'

'He must have seen them,' argued Tiger-Eye. 'Otherwise, why would he mention rubies?'

'Idiot! Because you told him you we looking for rubies.' She caught her breath. It was suddenly much too silent. In fact, alarmingly silent.

No roaring dragons, no hissing flames or crashing basalt pillars.

'Dinja save us,' Opal whispered. 'They have stopped fighting'

Wing-beats thudded and a giant shadow blocked the entrance of the cave. Golden eyes as big as wagon wheels glared down on them.

'And what do we have here?' Dardamesh rumbled. 'Three little human packrats trying to drag my beautiful eggs to their own nests?'

Dragons spoke all languages, even those of humans.

Tiger-Eye grabbed Opal's wrist. 'Don't move.'

Opal froze. She felt Dardamesh's gaze pass over her body without slowing down.

'I was wrong. There is only one little rat after all.'

Smald stepped back until his shoulders bumped against the wall.

'It wasn't me. They dragged me along. They kidnapped me!' He pointed to Opal and Tiger-Eye. 'They stole your most precious treasures, mighty dragon lady. Not me! I swear!'

'Who do you mean, little rat-boy? You are the only one here.'

'I am not. Not here! No.' Smald grabbed his amulet and held it high. 'I am invisible,' he intoned with a quavering voice. 'Believe me!'

'Pyrite? You stupid mortal. I gobble sulfur and iron and crap pyrite. Your magic won't work on dragons, and besides, we are the best liars of all.' She opened her maw and poison-green flames washed over Smald.

When the roaring fire stopped, an emerald statue filled the cave with a beautiful green glow. The boy still held his amulet high, trying to ward off the doom that had already overtaken him.

11.

Dardamesh stamped through the cave, grumbling, the smoke still hissing from her nostrils. She next flew to the sloop and emptied the bags in her cave. Thistledown drifted down and a piece of fluff landed on Opal's nose. It started to itch unbearably.

That was the beginning of the longest three hours of Opal's life.

Dardamesh crouched in front of the heap of pebbles and started to sort them according to color, all the while whistling through her teeth in the most annoying manner. Sand fleas climbed into Opal's shoes and bit her savagely between the toes.

When Dardamesh finally opened her wings and flew away. Opal was so stiff she might as well have been a stone statue. She itched all over.

Tiger-Eye pulled her stumbling from the cave.

'Shouldn't we take some jewels?' Opal protested. 'We came all the way and…'

'You saw how fanatically she counted her stones. Even a handful of grit she would miss immediately.'

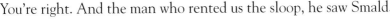

'I think you're right.' For safety's sake she even dumped the small piece of amethyst she'd found on the beach.

They were rowing among the mangrove trees when Dardamesh' enormous shadow swept across their boat.

'You're forgetting something.'

Smald's statue crashed into the sloop.

'I don't want that ugly thing cluttering up my clean cave.'

She hovered above them with slow wing beats.

'If you had taken a single egg,' Dardamesh continued, 'Or even a flake of amethyst you'd be stone too.' Her grin showed an incredible array of dagger-like teeth. 'I rather like you little ratkins that know how to keep grubby-fingers in their own pockets. I don't meet that kind of vermin very often.' She lifted into the sky so fast she seemed to fall upwards.

'Just what we need,' Tiger-Eye complained. 'What should we do with his statue? Drop it into the sea?'

'I'm afraid we have to take it with us. I only just thought of it, but if Smald has disappeared they'll comb the whole island. His father is too important.'

'You're right. And the man who rented us the sloop, he saw Smald.

Three departed and only two would return.'
'We have to tell everything. Well, not everything. Not about the cave. Just that a dragon petrified Smald. That can happen to anyone. Also, his father is filthy rich. All those sacrifices people make to the gods. A high priest can surely find a miserly sixty kilos of emeralds to save his son.'
Tiger-Eye pulled the amulet off over Smald's head. 'That cursed thing.'
The pendant splashed in the water and zigzagged downward. One last glint and the deep blue swallowed it.

The moment they moored a man came running down the pier.
'What are you doing with my boat? You dirty pilferers! What are you doing with my poor sloop?'
'A man rented us this boat!' Opal protested. 'We paid.'
'You didn't pay me!'
'He had a woman with him,' Tiger-Eye said. 'She had red hair.'
The man snorted. 'That really helps. Red-haired women, there are a thousand walking around. No, I think you were just trying to steal my boat.'
'That makes no sense at all.' Opal said. 'Why would we row back to the very same pier?'
'Some thieves have no sense.' He raised his voice. 'Guards! There're two thieves! Pirates!'
Two guards rushed forward, grappling hooks in their hands. A third jumped into a kayak to block any escape by the sea.
The biggest guard tugged his moustache, coughed. 'So, a stolen boat, eh.' He looked down. 'And what do we have here? A statue? It's solid emerald as far as I can tell and I'm an expert. For didn't I give my first wife a ring with a truly huge emerald on the day we married? Priceless! And half a year later she ran away with a squid-tamer. No, I'm sure you didn't come by that honestly.'
And that was only the start of their troubles.

12.

Opal inspected the cell.

'I thought this kind of dungeon only existed in fairy tales. Look at it: a tiny window with three bars, a crock of brackish water with a dead bluebottle fly.' She inspected the crust of bread. 'It is so dry a shark would crack his teeth on it. I mean, there are even spider webs.'

Tiger-Eye took the bread from her hand. 'What do you mean, stale? It hasn't even grown mold yet.' He took an eager bite.

Opal lifted her arms. The chains clanked. 'And handcuffs! Are they crazy?'

'Perhaps it's time to ask the advice of your holy book?' Tiger-Eye fished three pebbles from his moneybag and rolled them. 'I hope you brought it along?'

'Number seven,' he said after adding up the numbers.

YOU CAN'T EAT ROTTEN SPROUTS EVERY DAY, SOMETIMES THERE IS ONLY STEAK AND ICE CREAM

she read from Gliph Abar's Book of All Answers,

'You see?' Tiger-Eye said and took another grateful bite from his crust.

There were footsteps, the chink of mail and the door swung open.

'The judge has agreed to see you now,' the jailer said. 'You're in luck. He set everything aside and moved your trial up to this afternoon. He's never seen such a shocking case.'

'Shocking?' Opal said. 'That we hired our sloop from the wrong man? How could we know he was a fraud?'

'Nobody cares about that boat. It gets you another week detention, at most. No, it is the statue…'

'We didn't steal it! I already told the guards. A dragon turned him to stone!'

'Don't tell me. Tell the judge. I only work here.'

Outside two soldiers brandishing halberds joined them.

'I thought the courthouse was to the right?' Tiger-Eye said.

'You're so right,' the jailer said, 'But we're going to the Temple of All Gods Save Gliph Abar. Petrifying a minor, well, that counts as black magic. So it is a case for the priesthood.' He eyed Opal. 'Don't you have a grandmother who dabbles in magic?'

'Grandmother Rithka never turned anybody to stone. Dardamesh did it!'
'If our judge isn't a regular judge,' Tiger-Eye asked, 'what then?'
'You get the high priest himself. It's a great honor.'
'That is so wrong! How can he give us a fair judgment? Smald's his son!'
'The high priest always handles these black magic cases.'

The Temple of All Gods was fashioned from the skeletons of leviathans and sperm whales. A thousand lacquered bones and vertebras fit together like a jigsaw puzzle and gleamed in the sun. The two front teeth of a sea serpent formed the ivory gates.
Opal had visited the Temple only once before, to put her first milk tooth on the altar of the Tooth Fairy. The temple was kind of old-fashioned, mostly visited by senior citizens and pious sheep herders.
They followed along the gloomy hallway and the jailer opened a door made from gray driftwood. Barnacles spelled the names of several minor sea gods.
'Here are the murderous wretches!' the jailor cried, pushing them inside. 'Give them their just desserts, judge! Yes, hang them high and give their eye balls to the gulls!'

During a regular trial the spectators sat on the tribune, with the judge and the criminals on the little stage. In the temple they did it differently.
The whole tribune was filled with idols. Some were at least six meters high while a few would fit in the palm of your hand.
The high priest presided on the third row and wore a wig of dried lizard tails. The soldiers dragged Opal and Tiger-Eye to the table with Smald's statue.
The jailor prodded Opal. 'Stand up straight! Look the judge in the eyes. Only speak when he asks a question.'
'So here they are,' the high priest said. 'The villains who turned Shining Emerald into a pitiful statue.'
The high priest was extremely thin, skin and bones, with an imposing hooknose. He reminded Opal of a plucked crow.
He's afraid, she realized. Scared stiff. Beads of sweat gleamed on his brow and his voice sounded unsteady, strangely hoarse. Not because of us: look how he trembles every time he gazes at the statue but he can't keep his eyes away. He stares at the statue like a mouse at a cobra.
Holy gods, the amulet hung once again around Smald's neck! Opal knew exactly how such things went. It was impossible to get rid of cursed jewels.

Even if you dropped them in the deepest trench, threw them in an erupting volcano, they always returned to their reluctant owner. Clearly this was such an amulet.

'You!' The finger of the high priest pointed in Tiger-Eye's direction.

'You come from a family of egg-snatchers. You should have known better than to lure a child into dangerous dragon territory.'

'Smald forced us with his amulet. He owned a pyrite stone.

And he's no child. Smald is just as old as we are'

The high priest gazed at the emerald statue, blinked and scratched behind his ear. Opal had seldom seen such a bad actor.

'Amulet? I don't see an amulet. Not anywhere. Do you, dear jailer? Guards?'

The men shook their heads.

'No, eh, no amulet at all, Lord!' a soldier called and clicked his heels.

They were lying, Opal thought, or are they really unable to see the amulet?

'We threw the amulet in the sea. So nobody else could misuse it.

Only it returned. It's hanging around his neck, Dinja is my witness!' She looked up at the high priest but he turned his head. Now Opal knew for sure he could see the amulet. That he knew all about its pyrite power. 'He was your own son! You must know he wore a magic amulet!'

'Sorry, I never noticed an amulet. No, I don't think I can follow your strange story.' He turned his back to them and raised his hands to the idols.

'O gods, who are so much wiser than I, listen!' He spread his arms. 'Give us your holy and wise counsel, because I, your humble priest, am completely at a loss.'

They heard a strange scuffling followed by a rather nervous cough.

Then a hollow voice thundered through the hall. It was a true god voice, extremely loud and filled with eerie echoes.

'Banish them from our beautiful island at the first light of day, for, eh… what? Oh, for their crime is too heinous to be forgiven.

And let them take that cursed statue with them. They may only return when they have gathered enough emeralds to make Smald live again.'

The high priest breathed a shuddering sigh of relief.

'The gods have spoken! Take them away! Remove that horrible statue, too! I don't want to see them ever again.'

Back in the dungeon Tiger-Eye took the crust of bread from the bowl.

'You're sure you don't want any? It isn't smart to start a long journey on an empty stomach. And the book told you to eat what you have, not what you want.'

'If I take a single bite I'll throw up. Look, mice have nibbled on this corner!'

'So what? That's a good sign. Mice can smell poison.'

Opal turned her face to the wall. Her head felt strangely dull. As if all her thoughts were swimming through molasses. It was so unfair! Not their fault at all. Those two thoughts kept grinding in her head, like the ponderous turning of millstones.

A square of light with three dark stripes slowly climbed the wall.

After a few hours it turned red: the sun was setting.

A key ring tinkled and Opal jumped up.

'You have a visitor,' said the jailer.

'My mother?' They are coming to free me! My parents are rich.

They can bribe the jailer, smuggle us outside. Papa is a merchant. I bet he knows all about bribery.

'Your mother?' The jailer laughed. 'No, she looks a bit too young to be your mother.'

'Hey, Opal, Tiger-Eye.' Pebble edged past the jailer and closed the door in his face. 'Papa is next. They're still frisking him. I think the guards are afraid he'll try to help you escape. You're such tough criminals…'

She plumped down on the single chair. 'Tell me what happened.'

'I don't understand at all,' Opal said a bit later. 'The whole trial. I mean, the high priest is filthy rich, isn't he? He can find enough emeralds to save his son without the slightest effort.'

'It's not all that complicated,' Pebble said. 'I gather that he hates his son. How long do you think Smald owned the amulet? Perhaps since he was a toddler? Or even worse, it was the birth gift from a very bad godmother. They had to obey his slightest wish. Smald enslaved his own parents. This way the high priest can be sure Smald remains a statue. You'll never gather enough gems to make him come alive.'

'There was a god! An idol spoke!'

'Just a hollow statue with a priest inside – they do that all the time.'

'That is cheating! Sacrilege!'

'I don't think the gods care. They are much too lazy to punish every rotten priest.' Pebble rose and kissed them both on the cheek.

'I'll warn Grandmother Rithka. She is certainly as cunning as the high priest and I'm sure she'll think of a solution.'

'What did we ever do to deserve this?' her father wailed. 'I hardly dare to look the neighbors in the eye. Your poor mother swooned when the guard brought the news. Such a shame! She's still at home, lying on the couch.'
Opal couldn't believe her ears. He was complaining about her?
Keep calm. Don't call him names. We need his help.
'It's a misunderstanding.'
'A misunderstanding? My eldest daughter sits in jail.' He glowered at Tiger-Eye. 'In the company of a pickpocket and poacher.'
'I don't have to leave the island. Not really. If Smald comes alive…'
Her father was shaking his head.
'No?'
'If I gave you even the tiniest emerald and the high priest heard about it…
I am a merchant, you understand. Before a ship sets sail the high priest has to bless it, ask favor of the sea gods. If he declines, not a single sailor will dare to board. In half a year we would be as poor as temple mice.'
'So you love your gold more than your daughter,' Opal said. 'Good to know.'
'It isn't that at all. You have to understand. People depend on…'
'Go away! If you don't want to help, just go jump into the harbor!'
She squeezed her eyes shut and pushed her fingers in her ears. 'Go away!' she screamed.

Tiger-Eye pulled her hands away. 'You can stop. He has fled the cell.'
He massaged her neck. 'And I thought my family was bad…'
'Gold doesn't make you nice,' Opal said.
'Sorry for acting like a spoiled brat.'
Behind the little window the last red leached from the sky and stars began to glow.
'You know,' Tiger-Eye mused, 'You could see this as a fabulous adventure. We're heroes seeking a fantastic treasure.
And all the time we'll be free from school!'
'An impossibly huge treasure!
I'd rather be at school, writing a thousand lines each day.'
Tiger-Eye didn't give up so easily.
'We'll travel to the most wonderful islands.'
'Yes, in a leaking bathtub, on a sea filled with hungry sharks. You think they'll give us anything even slightly seaworthy? The high priest hopes we'll go down

before we reach the sea wall. Along with Smald's statue.'

'I only tried cheering you up.'

'Sorry, it didn't work.'

In the end Opal must have fallen asleep because the squeaking of badly lubricated hinges woke her. A whiff of steam reached her face and she smelled white hot metal. Her iron butterfly had alighted on the windowsill. He threw in a tightly rolled piece of paper and flapped away.

'What kind of animal was that?' Tiger-Eye asked.

'He brought a message from my grandmother. She gave me that butterfly when I turned six.' Opal unfolded the paper and a compass promptly rolled across the floor.

'Pebble warned me,' Opal read. 'I peered into my crystal ball and saw both of you crossing the sea on a flying whale. Such is the future and there's nothing I can do to change it.

This compass has an emerald needle. As long as my spell holds it'll point to the biggest emerald but one. See you soon on the quay.'

'Why the biggest but one?' Tiger-Eye asked. 'Oh, I understand. Otherwise the needle would always turn to Smald's statue.'

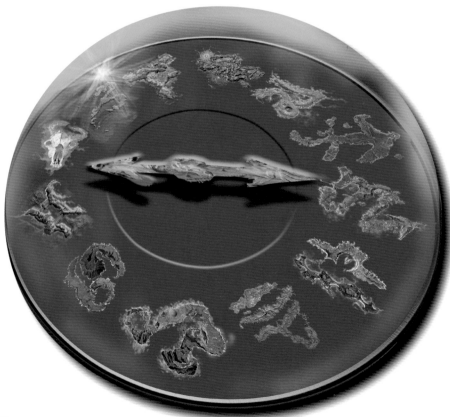

13.

The jailer took them to the quay. It was a dismal morning, with sudden freezing gusts, heavy with spray.

'Hear the albatrosses hoot and scream,' Tiger-Eye muttered.

'They are quarreling about who gets the first peck at our eyes when we sink.'

'Tut, tut,' said the high priest, 'Nobody wants you to sink. Look at this beautiful boat, complete with provisions for a week. With a bit of rowing you'll reach the next island easily. Your statue has already been loaded.'

Opal saw at once that Tiger-Eye had been right: their sloop was a drifting hulk that wouldn't keep afloat for very long. No sane sailor would even try to cross a goldfish pond with this sloop.

'Um, yes, so I wish you a very good journey. I'll leave you alone for a moment. So you can, well, say goodbye to your family.' He gave a limp wave with his hand and hastened back to the guards.

Nobody from Tiger-Eye's family had turned up. No aunt or uncle, not a single cousin. Not that Opal's parents did much to console her.

Opal's mother cried and sniffled. She patted Opal on her head and wasn't able to utter a word. Her father stood strangely stiff, as if he had swallowed a rake. 'It is, yes, a pity. When all is said and done, you are my eldest daughter. I had hoped...' His lower lip started to tremble. 'If only I could do something!' He swallowed and squeezed her shoulder. 'Raseiman protect you,' he whispered. Raseiman was the god of the merchants and just as greedy and untrustworthy as most of his worshippers. Opal's father looked at Grandmother Rithka. 'You wanted to speak with Opal?'

'Certainly and it is all grandmother-granddaughter stuff. Not for male ears. So make yourself scarce.' She turned to Opal. 'Let's not beat around the bush and call a skunk a skunk, eh? Did you steal anything from the dragon? Nothing? Good, so you won't find an angry dragon in your wake.' She took a Rammstein butterfly from her bag. 'Take this one. It's the most recent model forged by the dwarf smiths. He can flap thousands of miles before his sunstone expires and his steam wings stop. If you ever have a real serious problem, tie a message to his feet and throw it into the sky. He'll always find me.'

'So I'll have to send the butterfly the moment we step into the boat,' Opal said. 'This leaking bathtub won't reach the next island for sure.'

'Don't complain before the water fills your nose and the hammerheads start nibbling your toes. Your clever sister made a wonderful plan.'

'I stole a platinum travel pass from papa's office!' Pebble whispered. 'Here it is.' She slipped the metal card up Opal's sleeve. 'It's a travel-everywhere-pass. One of papa's buyers can step on any ship he wants and the captain steers the ship wherever he points. The best part is that the bill comes only at the end of each year. Papa won't miss the card for months.'

'How did you get the card exactly?' Grandmother Rithka inquired.

'It lay on Papa's desk. Gleaming out in the open. Almost as if he whispered 'Steal me! Steal me!'

'Your father's office?' Grandmother Rithka asked. 'Doesn't he close the door?'

'Usually. In fact, all the time and it's double-locked. A servant called me and said that papa wanted to see me. But when I arrived he was nowhere to be found. Why do you ask?'

'Isn't that a bit too… Well, let's say how often does he leave an extremely valuable travel pass lying around on his desk?'

'You think he left it on purpose?'

'What else? Your father did what he could. Which wasn't all that easy with the spies of the high priest looking over his shoulder all the time.'

'So he tried to help!' Opal felt instantly better. And my mother, she cried and cried and why should she if she didn't love me?

'Agate is my best friend,' Pebble said and Opal almost snapped: 'Happy for you.'

'She is also the daughter of a whale rider. I made a deal with him.

He'll fly you to the nearest island with emeralds.'

Maybe I won't have to drown today after all, Opal thought.

Suddenly everything seemed to slip and shuffle around in her head and to connect in new and interesting ways.

Tiger-Eye was right last night. This is a fantastic adventure! I'll visit all the islands of MiYu. Gliph Abar had promised.

'I would love to follow you,' Grandmother said. 'But have you ever seen me sail? Or even take a dip?'

'Never. Why?' What was Grandmother talking about?

'A witch is part of her island. The moment I no longer touch the ground I lose all my powers.' She showed the sole of her left foot. The sole was covered with a thick yellow-brown callus and was none too clean.

'A handful of dust and some dry bones can't help anybody, least of all my granddaughter.'

'A handful of dust?'

'That's what I would become the moment I left my island. A handful of dust and some dry bones. To be honest I'm not exactly your grandmother, more like your great-great-grandmother. I'm almost three hundred years old. Without magic all those years come rushing back at once.' She looked into the boat. 'How are you going to lug along that monster? Smald must weigh at least sixty kilos.'

'That could become a problem,' Tiger-Eye said. 'Especially if we're fleeing with stolen emeralds.'

'I'll think of something. Yes, Ysidore of course. Opal? If you meet someone in a dream be sure to be on your best behavior. Smile and curtsy. Especially if he likes playing with colored balls.'

'You there!' The high priest bumped his golden staff on the cobblestones and strode in their direction. 'Enough talk! This isn't a tea party. We are here to banish two criminals!'

Grandmother Rithka looked him right into the eyes. 'I'll speak to you later – in your nightmares.'

The high priest crossed his fingers to avert the evil eye.

'Tonight, young man,' Grandmother Rithka repeated. 'Hah, this will be a busy night for the dream imps.'

14.

The final mountaintop of Leo dipped below the horizon.
'Not a moment too soon,' Opal said. She laid aside the half coconut she had used to bail. She waved to the whale that had been circling them for the last half hour. 'They can't see us anymore, father of Agate. It is safe!'
The whale folded his wings and dove down like a hawk. He bounced from wave to wave, trailing a wide wake of foam. The whale stopped half a meter from the wildly rocking boat.
'Show-off,' Tiger-Eye muttered.
'Catch!' Agate's father lowered a rope ladder. 'Leave the statue in the boat. I'll hoist it up later.'

The cabins had been glued to the highest hump of the whale, huge bubbles of hardened glass. That way the passengers stayed dry even when the whale dove.
In the wheelhouse Agate's father poured them two big mugs of steaming chocolate. To complete it he added a handful of sliced hot peppers.
'Drink up. Your lips look gray from the cold.'
'Tha thankks, fafather of Agate.' Opal's teeth rattled against the rim of the mug. She was so cold her bones must have turned into bars of ice.
'Just call me captain Smoky Quartz. Father of Agate sounds kind of strange. Then I would have to call you 'friend of my daughter' all the time.'
After the second mug the captain folded his arms. 'And where exactly do you want to go, if I may ask? My daughter remained a bit vague about your destination.'
'This way.' Opal put the compass on the table. The needle turned three times and stopped. Opal noticed there were symbols for the islands carved on the rim.
'Libra,' the captain said. 'The island of the scales. Not the most relaxed people of MiYu but at least it is close. The second island from here.'
'What is wrong with them?' Opal asked.
'They are so, so accurate, nitpicking. Always measuring things and flipping through the pages of their law books. There are even regulations for the blowing of your nose. If you break a single rule they deport you.'
He nodded. 'Undesirable visitors are offered leaden boots and taken to the end of the wharf. Then they empty a cage full of shark-mice. So you get the choice: become mouse food or take a stroll on the sea bottom.'
'Nice people,' Tiger-Eye said.

'Well, you're perfectly safe as long as you keep their laws.'
'I doubt that stealing their emeralds is legal.'
'You've got me there.'

In their cabin Opal rolled their stones.
'Good book, give us your wise council! How can we steal an emerald without ending up in the jaw of a shark-mouse or on the bottom of the ocean?'
She threw the stones and made the calculation.
'Answer number six.' She opened Gliph Abar's Book Of All Answers.
It was curious that it was impossible to remember the whole list of answers no matter how often you used the book.

AT LEAST MAKE SURE YOU WON'T GET CAUGHT

Tiger-Eye chuckled. 'Now how does the book think of such a clever thing? At least make sure you won't get caught.'
Opal closed the book. 'As far as answers go, it is quite clear.'

The whale flew on all night. There was a steady rhythm. He gave three stately wing beats and then glided for sixty meters.
Opal sat upright in her hammock and gazed out across the sea.
They cruised so high that she could see all the island fires at once.
Virgo already slipped away below the whale. Three islands lay in the dark sea. Massive bridges connected the northern tips.
'Go to sleep,' Tiger-Eye said from the other hammock. 'Tomorrow we arrive in Libra. At cock's crow the captain said. If you stand swaying on your legs you won't be able to steal a broken brick.'
'You're right. I'm tired to the bones.' She closed her eyes.

Opal walked on an ink black ocean. It wasn't exactly water, because the ocean was filled with stars. With each wave they bobbed and swirled like fireflies.
I'm dreaming, Opal thought, for I'm lying in my hammock and stars never burn below the waves. Also, only witches and wizards can walk on water.
'Opal, wait for me!'
A walrus paddled in her direction. He gave a wriggle and heaved himself out of the starry water.

'Can you do this trick?' he asked. The walrus bounced a splendid blue ball in the air, caught it on his nose and kept it spinning. 'It took me a couple of million years before I learned. In the beginning it kept falling down.' He offered a flipper and Opal shook his foreleg. 'My name is Ysidore, the Walrus Who Balances The Whole World On The Tip Of His Nose.'

'Opal. But you must know already because you called me.' She gazed up at the swiftly spinning ball. 'Hey, I see our islands!'

Ysidore's ball was her world, blue as lapis lazuli, with clouds as fine as lace. Islands lay around the equator like a splendid belt.

'Your grandmother sent me. She's a dear friend of mine.

Each dream she gives me a mackerel from her apron. She told me you have to lug along a rather heavy statue. Now I'm already juggling a whole world.' He bumped the world ball with the tip of his nose and MiYu shot into the air, spinning wildly.

'Look out!' Opal cried.

'So what's a teeny weenie statue to me? Throw it here.'

Opal realized that she was carrying the statue across her left shoulder.

'It is heavy, but we need the statue for later, when we change Smald back into a little pest.'

'I won't take the statue itself. Only it's weight.' He plucked the statue from Opal's shoulder and bounced it high into the air. Together they arced across the sky, Smald and MiYu, sparkling green and shining blue.

Opal's eyes sprang open. She groped around in the darkness.

Yes, there was an ice-cold and stone-hard arm. She pulled and suddenly the statue lifted in the air. It weighed less than thistledown.

She put the statue back.

'Thank you, Ysidore,' she whispered. 'And thank you, Grandmother Rithka.'

YSIDORE

YSIDORE is the mighty walrus which balances the whole world of MiYu on the tip of his nose. In his magic dewdrop you can see any place and time. You can call him by licking an ocean-blue gemstone. The Ysidore stone would be the best but any blue stone will do.

Sometimes you have to wait a few dreams before he visits you. You're not the only one who wants to look into his magic dewdrop.

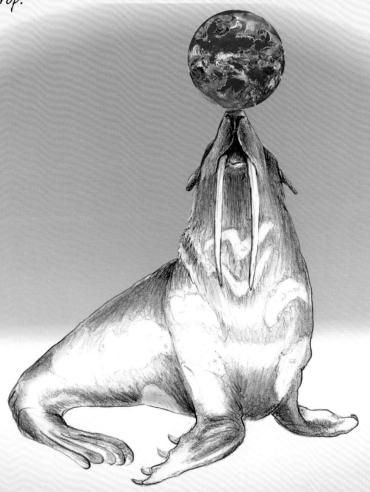

CHAPTER 2

Gliph Abar put his finger to his lips and Opal nodded.

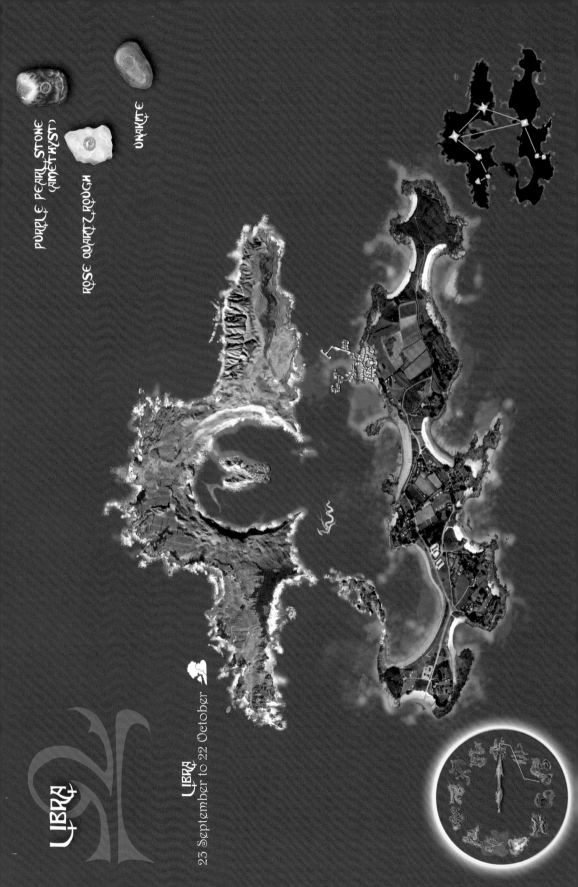

PURPLE PEARL STONE
(AMETHYST)

ROSE QUARTZ ROUGH

UNAKITE

LIBRA

LIBRA
23 September to 22 October

LIBRA

1.

It was early in the morning and the flying whale circled high above the port of Libra. Opal leaned over the low railing. Libra encompassed two islands: the lower was a fresh and open, with parks, white villas and inviting beaches made of sable sands. The upper island showed jagged mountaintops and steep cliffs. Gigantic waves rolled in and broke on the reefs in fountains of spray.

'Breakfast!' Captain Smoky Quartz hollered as he broke half a dozen eggs above a sizzling skillet. 'Never land without a decent breakfast.

It is impossible to stand those hair-splitters on an empty stomach.'

He rowed them to the jetty on a raft of pumice. 'I'd rather not go ashore. I hope you don't mind.' He shuddered. 'I can't stand all those forms you have to fill out in triplicate.'

'This way!' A high-ranking official announced from behind a lectern, his fountain pen ready. A stack of forms in all colors of the rainbow waited at his feet. A heavy rock made sure they wouldn't blow away.

'According to rule 23 A of the Revised Foreign Visitors Law of Libra and all surrounding reefs and islets I provisionally welcome you to Isola Verda, the Verdant and Shining Green Island. At least, after you've filled out the pertinent forms.' He offered them each a fountain pen. 'My name is Most Diligent Muskrat. Let's start with the emerald statue your friend is so unsuccessfully trying to hide behind his back. The levy on imported gems comes to a quarter of the value. Half a million, I'd estimate'

We are really off to a good start, Opal thought. 'That isn't emerald at all. It's a wooden statue. My friend painted it. Quite realistic, eh?

You really thought it was gemstone.'

'A wooden statue? Teach your grandmother to suck eggs!' He lifted the statue and almost fell over when it rose without the slightest effort.

'Right, a balsa wood statue then.' He leafed through the law book that dangled with a silver chain from his belt. 'It is a pity, but not a word about balsa wood statues. Happily I have some other forms here for you to complete.'

'This is the sixty-ninth form already!' Opal complained three hours later. 'And they want to know such stupid things such as the maiden name of my neighbor's wife. How many pets we have and what are the birthdays of my goldfish?'

Most Diligent Muskrat nodded. 'Yes, visitors have a lot less forms to fill out than native Librans. Here, have some more.'

There were a lot more forms to complete. Opal's fingers were covered in ink and stiff from all the writing.

'That's it,' Most Diligent Muskrat said and snatched the last form away. 'Now, that wasn't so hard, was it?' He lifted the whole batch of papers and threw them into the sky. A gust took them and scattered them across the sea.

'What are you doing?' Opal cried.

'Completing the forms is the important part. You think anybody wants to read that rubbish?' He buttoned his striped waistcoat. 'Follow me. Only the scales remain.'

At the end of the pier loomed an copper balance. It was truly colossal: you could park a horse on one of the scales. Next to the balance stood two pairs of leaden boots and a cage of hopeful shark-mice. They squeaked hungrily and gritted their teeth in a most alarming fashion.

'I'm quite ready, sir Muskrat,' a rather thin person piped up. Rubbing his hands he sat down on the scales.

'Now you people step on the other scale,' Muskrat ordered. 'We don't want our beautiful island to founder because a lot of fat foreigners are stamping around. Mister Dormouse here forms the counterweight. Each gram overweight costs you a rose quartz; each kilo a tree agate.' He smirked. 'I hope you're carrying enough gems. Otherwise I'll have to deport you.'

We're in trouble, Opal thought. Big trouble. Her purse was almost empty from the start. It was the end of the month and her allowance was almost gone. After the sloop and the shovels they might have two agates left at most.

She emptied the purse into her hand – one agate, the size of her nail and some lesser stones.

'Dormouse must be the thinnest man on the isle!' Tiger-Eye protested.

'Yes, convenient isn't it? He eats like a bird and there isn't a single ounce of fat on his bones. That way we always earn something from our visitors.'

'It's completely fair though,' he continued. 'For every ounce that Dormouse's overweight we pay you a rose quartz. Without any argument.'

Only a god can save us, Opal thought. Time to prove she earned her A for Ritual and Sacrifice. She was in luck: A blue pebble shone among the

small change.

Opal tossed up the pebble, letting it bounce on her brow. Only Ysidore's own priests succeeded in spinning a pebble on the tip of their nose but that was after years of practice. She hoped Ysidore would hear her anyway.

'Ysidore, help us,' she prayed soundlessly. 'Make us light as a feather. We don't want to take a stroll on the sea bottom.'

'We are waiting,' Muskrat said.

'Keep cool. We are coming.' Together with Tiger-Eye she stepped on the left scale. The balance rocked, creaked and suddenly tilted to Dormouse's side, banging the ground with a loud bump.

'This is impossible!' Muskrat cried. 'This has never happened before!'

He put weights down on their scale. First a gram, then a kilo and on up to ten kilos.

'This is, this is…' Muskrat threw up his hands, at a loss for words. An assistant had to drag in a second box of weights.

Eighty kilos, a hundred and fifty, two hundred. Only at two hundred and six did Dormouse start to rise.

'The last time you only weighed thirty-three kilos!' Muskrat wailed.

'I remember, now that you mention it. Still, I ate only half a biscuit this morning.'

Opal stepped from the scales and held her hand out. 'Correct me if I'm wrong but I think you own us two hundred and six tree agates.'

Tiger-Eye lifted the bag with jewels. 'We'll eat steak and ice cream the rest of the voyage! Sleep on eiderdown pillows.'

'If you don't mind I'll walk along with you,' mister Dormouse said. He eyed Most Diligent Muskrat. 'My boss is ready to explode.'

On the quay Opal collided with an extremely skinny man.

'Sorry, sorry! A thousand apologies! I was in such a hurry.' Water dripped from his hair and he had a bathing towel wrapped around his hips. 'Say, did you just come from the pier? I hope I'm not too late? Mister Muskrat called me for

a weighing but I was just taking a bath and someone stole my clothes.'
'He found someone else,' Dormouse said.
'Good for him. Then I'll hurry back and continue my bath.'
Opal stared at Dormouse. 'If that was the real Dormouse you must be…'
Gliph Abar put his finger to his lips and Opal nodded. When you disguised
yourself you don't like someone pointing at you and crying your name.
'I hope you don't mind if I help you now and then? It would be no fun if
you drowned at the very first island.' He winked, pinched Opal's cheek
and strode away.
'What did he want?' Tiger-Eye asked. 'Was he a buyer of your father's?
Another merchant?'
'Not exactly a merchant. He likes dressing up and, I'm afraid, he's actually
a kind of god.'
'No need to continue. I can guess who you mean.'

At the chapel of the Weeping Lady Tiger-Eye nudged Opal. 'Don't look
back but Most Diligent Muskrat has been following us for two streets.
He is writing in his notebook all the time.'
'Let him scribble.' She halted in front of a tavern. 'What do you think?
The Happy Kraken?'
'Hello there!' A beggar, squatting on a satin pillow, waved at them.
He was wearing a hat with a silver buckle and a peacock feather. 'Some
alms, good sir and lady? I'd be quite satisfied with tiniest silver ring or the
smallest ruby.'
'Move it, man,' Tiger-Eye said. 'You are wearing a cape with gold brocade
and you have three chins. No, four. Don't tell me you're poor or hungry.'
'Of course I'm not poor! A begging permit costs a thousand agates.
How can poor people ever pay such a sum?'
'I wouldn't give you a scratched pebble.'
'Miser! A curse on all greedy foreigners!'

The traveling pair hired a room in the tavern and ordered a sizeable dinner.
The terrace looked out on the second isle. Even in the warm sunlight it
seemed rather grim. Streamers of mist shrouded mountains like shark's
teeth. The cliffs rose directly from the sea. Only in the center they opened
up in a wide bay.
'There isn't a single spot of green anywhere,' Opal said. 'The other side
doesn't look exactly cozy.'
The innkeeper put a serving tray down with bowls of fish soup and a dish

of lobster claws in aspic. 'We call it the Dismal Isle and it is a name well-deserved. There are bad folks living there, lady. They dive for pearls and on their feast days it isn't a tasty plum pie they cut. No, it has to be human meat and fresh, too. You see that small island, in the middle of their bay? That black spot is the gate of their cursed temple. It is there that they sacrifice poor castaways to Hasdamin the One-eyed Sea Serpent.

In that temple they kneel to a colossal sea serpent idol. Each scale is made of the finest gold and his claws are diamonds.'

Opal laid the compass on the table and tapped it. The needle turned and pointed right to the entrance of the temple.

'Hasdamin the One-eyed Sea Serpent,' she said. 'Might that single remaining eye be an emerald?'

'Doesn't everybody know that? It's an emerald as big as a stonemason's fist.'

'Because of all the cannibals there is probably no regular ferry to their island, right?' Tiger-Eye asked. 'Would you know anyone willing to transport us to the other side?'

'My memory, it doesn't work too well right now. Maybe an agate would help.'

Tiger-Eye put a jade ring on the table. It was easily worth a dozen agates. The hand of the innkeeper snatched the ring away, as fast as a striking moray eel.

'The pearl masters cross once a year to the Dismal Isle – with a whole troop of soldiers to protect them. They exchange bags of meal and dried peppers for pearls as big as grapes. In their group there's not an ordinary fisherman to be found. Only wealthy people need apply.'

'I bet ordinary fishermen don't like that,' Tiger-Eye said.

'You are so right. Now you won't hear me say that Grubby Chipmunk smuggles pearls. He owns a beauty of a fishing boat. The windows of his cabin are leaded glass and his sails are made from silk. No man has seen him catch as much as a shrimp and he started with little more than a leaking rowboat. That doesn't prove a thing, of course. On moonless nights I sometimes see him leave the harbor. Where he is going?

Not the Dismal Isle certainly. Civilians are forbidden to go there.'

He gestured to the sky. 'Tonight there is no moon. Anyway, his ship is called the 'See If I Care.''

The good ship 'See If I Care' was moored all the way to the east, far from the other ships, and had its own jetty. The boards of the jetty were lacquered mahogany and decorated with silver nails.

'Grubby Chipmunk?' Opal called. 'We would like to hire your ship.'

'That's me, Grubby Chipmunk.' The man lifted his beer glass. The rim was adorned with gold leaf chipmunks. 'Drink a glass with me.

One shouldn't haggle with a dry throat.'

'Can you ferry us to the other side?' She rattled her moneybag. 'Tonight?'

'I don't need a handful of measly agates. No, I prefer a pair of willing hands. You help me with the loading of the pearls. You row when the wind fails. That will be my fee.'

'You're going to ferry us for nothing?' Tiger-Eye asked. 'And we're supposed to believe that?' He took Grubby Chipmunk by his beard and tugged.

'You won't trick me twice!'

Grubby Chipmunk roared and flung Tiger-Eye away. With a loud splash Tiger-Eye landed in the sea.

Grubby Chipmunk extended his hand and lifted him to the deck.

'Now, what was that about?'

'I, I thought your beard was false,' a dripping wet Tiger-Eye muttered.

'It is so full and curls so beautifully - it almost can't be real,' Opal cooed.

'Truly?' Grubby Chipmunk combed his beard with his fingers, clearly pleased. 'Good. We leave after midnight. When all prowling inspectors and pearl masters are lying on one ear.'

2.

By half past midnight they had already sailed halfway across the sound.

It was extremely dark without a moon, Opal discovered. In their wake the night fires made a few furtive gleams on the sloshing seascape. The fires were quite miserly, just big enough to keep the island above the waves.

'It is hogwash that they eat human flesh on the other side,' Grubby Chipmunk said. 'A fable we smugglers spread. Keeps the competition away.'

'Then why do the pearl masters carry half an army to the other side?' Tiger-Eye asked.

'I didn't say they are nice people. Some bodyguards with a bit of sharpened steel always helps you get a decent price for your dried peppers.'

'Then where are your soldiers?'

'They trust me. I'm almost family. My grandmother was a woman from the Dismal Isle.'

'So we load your pearls and sail away,' Opal said. 'As soon as we are sure everyone is asleep, you put us ashore in front of the temple.'

'When they are sleeping or dead drunk. The other pearl masters pay with meal and peppers. I pay in liquor.' He raised his telescope. 'I see a smuggler's lamp flickering. They are waiting for us.'

The ship scraped along the dark quay and Grubby Chipmunk threw a loop around the mooring post. Next he put ashore a basket of bottles.

'That's all,' Opal asked. 'Just six bottles?'

'Shhh. Don't talk so loud. They are rather shy, you know.'

Shadows stirred and moved closer. A few seconds later they solidified into Islanders.

'Cousin,' they whispered, 'dear, dear cousin. What did you bring this time?'

'They don't look like cannibals,' Tiger-Eye said. 'No bones through their noses, not even tattoos.'

'Well, they are. You'd better believe me.' Grubby Chipmunk took a step forward. 'Here I have two children. As fresh as fresh can be.
How many pearls do you offer?'

'Hey!' Opal cried. 'Is this some kind of sick joke?'

The Dismal islanders closed in. When she saw their grins she knew it wasn't a joke at all, not even a sick joke. Their teeth had been filed to needle sharp points.

'Who bids fifteen pearls for the girl? Do I hear sixteen?' Grubby Chipmunk roughly took Opal by the arm. 'Look what nice chubby arms she has.'

'I'm not chubby!' Opal screamed and yanked her arm away.

Immediately half a dozen hands gripped her and squeezed her arms, her legs, her cheeks.

'If you eat me,' Tiger-Eye threatened, 'I'll return as a ghost. You'll find me lying in your bed every night, cold as ice and stinking. I'll turn all your food into wriggling cockroaches. Yes and all your liquor into ditchwater. Muddy ditchwater!'

'Can he do that?' the chief asked. He was an ogre, a big lumbering monster. He scowled down at the struggling Tiger-Eye. 'It would be a waste of good liquor.'

'He is bluffing,' Grubby Chipmunk said. 'Boasting. He is just an ordinary boy.'

Opal pulled her butterfly from her bag and threw him into the air.

'Get help! Warn my grandmother!'

The steel butterfly instantly leaped into the sky, leaving a contrail of super-heated steam.

'Nice try,' Grubby Chipmunk laughed. 'A pity your island is a full day's flying from here.' He turned to the Islanders. 'Did I hear twenty pearls?'

In the end Opal went for twenty-five pearls, Tiger-Eye didn't do half as well.

'Is twelve really your final offer?' Grubby Chipmunk asked.

'Yes,' the chief rumbled, 'and we consider that quite generous. That boy is lean – just skin and bones. Not good eating at all.'

'All right, all right. They're yours.'

'You have 'till tomorrow,' the chief said when he closed the padlocks of their chains. 'We behead you the moment the first sun ray glitters in Hasdamin's single eye. Sleep well. This is a nice quiet cell.'

He closed the door of the dungeon.

'I'm afraid we were a bit too trusting,' Tiger-Eye said. 'The innkeeper was part of the plot of course. I bet he gets half of the pearls for every traveler he sends down to Grubby Chipmunk.' He inspected the cell. 'The stupid thing is that we came so close. They dragged us right under their idol.'

He pointed to the ceiling. 'See? Golden scales.'

Opal's head reeled. A hundred schemes and emotions bounced through her brain like mad ping-pong balls. She was too hyper to be afraid.

What was that sound? She sat bold upright. Footsteps? A shuffling outside the door?

'Hush,' she said.

The latch jumped back on its own accord and the door swung open.

The chief stood on the threshold.

'In a dungeon once again? I expected more from you, Opal.'

'Gliph Abar? You disguised yourself as their chief!' She offered him her chained wrist. 'Can you free us?'

'That would be cheating. Not the way to play the game of life at all.'

He lifted his hand. 'Now take care and it's been good to have known you, even if only for such a short time.' He turned and stepped into the wall. His flesh mask and the trousers of the chief fell to the floor. Gods can walk through solid granite walls, but that doesn't work for their disguises.

'Nice friend,' Tiger-Eye said. 'I thought he was your guardian angel.'

'Gods do exactly as they like. Gliph Abar mostly wants to have fun. I think that for him we aren't quite real. More like living tin soldiers.'

'Can't you ask your walrus for help?'

'I had only one blue pebble and I've used that' She stretched out her left leg to reach the trousers of the chief but her toes fell short by just a few centimeters. 'Can you reach them?'

'I can try,' Tiger-Eye grunted and then said, 'I've got them, but what a stink. If he washes it's once a year at most.' He looked up. 'Now what?'

'Go through his pockets. I heard a clink when the trousers hit the floor.'

'A key chain?' He patted the trousers. 'Here it is!'

The fifth key opened their shackles.

'Do you think Gliph Abar left them on purpose?'

'Gliph likes smart people. If we hadn't found the keys, he'd have shrugged and looked for some more amusing mortals.'

Opal opened the door as quietly as she could: no squealing hinges now!

Tiger-Eye had been right: Their dungeon lay at the very foot of the idol. Hasdamin the One-eyed Sea Serpent coiled all the way to the far ceiling.

'Such a monster,' Tiger-Eye said. Opal heard a certain reverence in his voice. Sea serpents were a kind of dragon and egg-snatchers had always looked up to the dragons. 'Do you think he's that huge in reality?'

'Maybe he doesn't even exist. He wasn't in My First Picture Book of Gods and Demons.' She gripped a scale and heaved herself up. 'This is as easy as the wall bars at school. Come on, we have to chisel out his eye. The Islanders will come to sacrifice us at the first morning light.'

Opal leaned against the curved horn on Hasdamin's snout while Tiger-Eye tried to get his clasp knife below the emerald eye.

'This gold is a lot tougher than I expected. Right, we do it this way then.' He hit his knife with a rock. 'Ah, there it comes.'

The emerald came loose with a strange, slurping plop. A blue liquid welled up. It smelled like brine and rusting iron.

'What is this? It looks almost like bloo…'

'My eye?' The serpent body shuddered. 'My eye!' The voice thundered like a breaking flood wave. 'I'm blind!'

Opal sprinted down the coils. She jumped from scale to scale and reached the floor rolling.

From the temple gate came the sounds of confusion, wild cries and the chime of a gong. A trio of temple guards with scimitars ran inside.

Tiger-Eye clapped the mask on his face. He had to tug on the ears to keep it from slipping.

'The mighty Hasdamin awoke too early and he has a foul temper!' he cried. 'Get reinforcements.' His voice didn't sound much like the chief.

'Yes, yes, we will get more guards! Warn everybody.' The guards fled and Opal guessed they wouldn't be back for at least a week.

'I saw canoes lying on the beach,' she said. 'At the left side of the quay.'

'Never had to row a boat so sluggish,' Tiger-Eye complained. 'This stupid…' He looked down. 'Oh no, the whole sloop is filled with pearls!'

'Keep rowing!' Opal ordered. 'Impossible to turn back now.'

'Strangle you!' Hasdamin's voice rolled over the waters. 'Break all your bones, eye-thieves!' He uncoiled from the temple gate and plunged into the sea. His bow wave almost toppled their boat.

'Row!' Opal hissed. 'Row!'

The boat didn't have a sail and the return journey went a lot slower.

The first sun flecks already danced on the water when the pier appeared from the morning mist. Opal's palms were covered with blisters. She steered for the end of the pier and stumbled up the steps.

'At least we have the emerald.'

'Our first emerald,' Tiger-Eye corrected her. 'Three kilos at most and Smald weighs at least sixty.'

'It is a start. You guard the boat while I go to the tavern and get Smald. Is that all right with you?'

'See you soon. Bring a piece of bread if the baker is awake.'

'Good news for empty bellies,' Opal said. 'I have fresh gingerbread and a jug of hot cocoa milk.' She lowered Smald's statue in the boat.

'What happens next? You're the egg-snatcher.'

'Hold the stone against his arm. The magic automatically flows from the gem.'

He rubbed the stone over Smald's left arm.

The eye of the sea serpent instantly lost its luster, turned an ordinary bottle green and kept on bleaching. When Tiger-Eye pulled the stone back.

The emerald had turned into a piece of colorless rock crystal. Smald's arm no longer sparkled and had turned back into his normal dirty pink.

'It's a pity. Look at that stone! A few seconds ago it was a priceless gem and now it's completely worthless.'

Smald's arm moved hesitantly. Pink fingers spread open and then made a fist. A second later he gave them the finger.

'He's alive again,' Opal said. 'At least partly. And he's still as nasty as ever. I mean, we're risking our lives and he gives us the finger!'

'Dear visitors, do you have a moment?'

Opal let Smald's statue slip from her fingers. It smashed with a rattling thud into the heap of pearls.

Most Diligent Muskrat stood with folded arms on the pier, a soldier on each side.

'Not only am I a Greeter of Visitors but I'm also an official pearl master.' He opened his notebook. 'Let me see. Didn't make the mandatory three bows in front of the altar of the Weeping Lady: a fine of ninety agates and five strokes of the cane. Refused an accredited beggar his alms: fifteen agates. The boy put his muddy shoes on a terrace chair: Sixteen agates and five strokes of the cane. And I didn't even mention the smuggling of pearls.' He looked into the canoe. 'Several score and high quality, too. While the smuggling of even the meanest, malformed pearl carries a penalty of a stroll across the sea bottom.' He returned the book to his pocket. 'As you have earned the capital punishment a hundred times over I wave the strokes of the cane.' He nodded to the soldiers. 'Arrest them. I'll arrange their lead boots and a cage with shark-mice.'

3.

'Do you think that he…' Tiger-Eye jerked his head in the direction of their captor. 'That he is you-know-who?'

'Not a chance. Not every person who makes trouble is a god in disguise.'

'Too bad.'

Most Diligent Muskrat personally wheeled the cage with shark-mice to the end of the pier. He left the carrying of the heavy lead boots to two underlings.

'Put on your boots,' he ordered, looking out over the sea. 'Blue sky and a bracing breeze. A nice day for a walk on the bottom.' He placed a hand on the bolt of the cage. 'You know how it works? I open the cage and you get the choice: jump or face the shark-mice. Shark-mice hate water. I guarantee they won't follow you.'

'I would like to pray,' Opal announced. 'Anybody who gets the capital punishment is allowed to pray. At least on civilized islands.'

'You have five minutes. Tell your favorite god your soul will be arriving, as soon as you have finished drowning.' The soldiers giggled.

Opal lifted her arms. There was only one god who would most certainly listen to her. But how did you call that particular god? She moved her whole body, trying to writhe like a snake.

'Hear me, mighty Hasdamin!' Always start a prayer with an respectful invocation and if you have their attention… 'You miserable blind earthworm! I stole your only eye and here I stand! Get me if you can!'

'Strange prayers those foreigners have,' one of the soldiers remarked.

'No wonder most of them end up on the bottom of the sea.'

Opal's prayer was answered sooner than she'd dared hope.

The sea opened in a whirlpool and she looked straight into Hasdamin's maw. Diamond teeth stood in three glittering rows. He burped and the stench of rotting haddock and spoiled seal fat rolled across the pier.

'My eye!' the serpent god screamed. 'Give me back my eye!'

His head shot forward and he devoured Most Diligent Muskrat and the cage with shark-mice in a single bite. A sweep of his black serpent tongue and the soldiers and the servants were gone. A half circle was bitten out of the pier.

And now? How do I go on? Opal kneeled, tugged at the fastenings of her boots.

'My eye…' Hasdamin's head swept back and forth in front of the pier.

So close, so very close. She didn't dare to breathe. She saw his mighty nostrils dilating, inhaling the smells of the new morning.

'Ah, gingerbread and cocoa milk. Ah. Mouse-blood. Yess, I smell you, eye-snatcher!'

'That's right' Tiger-Eye shouted. 'Come and get me, you blind worm!'

He had taken off his coat and held it like a matador from Taurus Island. 'Come on, you stupid lamprey!'

Hasdamin bellowed and stormed forward. Tiger-Eye sprang away. In passing he threw his coat over the horn.

'I smell you, I smell you!' the sea serpent screamed. 'You're so close.' His jaws snapped shut on thin air and he kept biting. 'You won't escape! I smell you!'

The sea serpent zigzagged away towards the horizon.

'Clever,' a voice said. 'Even if it only works for a short time. Until the coat falls from the horn.'

The 'See If I Care' bumped against the pier. Grubby Chipmunk stood behind the wheel.

'Jump aboard,' he offered. 'Going a few islands away doesn't look like a bad idea. It is bad smuggling with a roaring sea serpent as your neighbor.'

'Jump aboard and you'll sail immediately after Hasdamin,' Opal said.

'To sell us for a bathtub full of pearls. We know you.'

'Your walrus wouldn't like that.'

'Ysidore! You met him?'

'Yes, on my return journey a walrus hailed me. He bounced a most unusual ball around and was accompanied by a couple of sperm whales.

The compliments of Opal's grandmother he said. And I had the choice: saving you two or a whack with a whale tail. But when I returned the whole temple was in ruins and you were gone.'

Opal showed her platinum travel card. 'I'll charter your boat for the rest of the journey.'

Grubby Chipmunk touched the rim of his cap. 'Entirely at your service, ma'am!'

Opal walked to the box that Muskrat had used to dump the pearls.

'We have some luggage here.'

It was late that afternoon when Opal's butterfly landed on the rail and opened his steam whistle.

SCORPIO

SCORPIO
23 October to 21 November

GARNET

STORM STONE
(CHIASTOLITE)

PHANTOM AGATE

SCORPIO AND THE SUNKEN CITY

1.

It was late that afternoon when Opal's butterfly landed on the rail and opened his steam whistle. She hastily pulled the rolled message from his hind leg. The ear piercing whistle stopped.

'Dear Granddaughter,' she read. 'Ysidore told me you haven't been eaten after all. Not that I ever doubted your cleverness. Pebble also asks…' She put the message down.

'Why did you stop reading?' Tiger-Eye asked. 'What did Pebble want?'

'Nothing. It's just stupid.'

He snatched the message from her hand. 'Pebble asks have you kissed yet? Good question.' He threw the message away and put his arms around Opal.

Pebble was quite right Opal decided and returned the kiss enthusiastically.

Grubby Chipmunk wasn't bad company if you could forget that he would sell his best friend for half a pearl and a glass of beer. Scratch the pearl. He knew more tall tales than Uncle Jaspis, more dirty jokes than Cousin Turitella. Food wasn't a problem. The hold bulged with food and drink for months and that didn't mean hardtack and tepid water.

'How long to Scorpio?' Opal asked when she slid her third guinea fowl from the spit. The needle of the compass had rotated to Scorpio the moment Hasdamin's eye turned into quartz.

'A week's sailing,' Grubby Chipmunk replied.

'A fortnight ago you said the same,' Tiger-Eye protested.

'Well, the winds blow when they want. They don't listen to me. But if you want to row?'

'Stop quarreling for a moment,' Opal said. 'I see a sail on the horizon.'

Grubby Chipmunk jumped up and snatched his telescope from the table. He gazed for a full minute before he lowered his instrument. 'I have some good news and I have some bad news. The good news is that we must be pretty close to Scorpio. That kind of ship always hugs the coast. The bad news is that only Asarenian pirates embroider a cockroach on their sails.'

The sail was little more than a dot. Opal had also seen the vague outline of a mountain range on the other horizon. The tops were almost the same color as the sky, a blue only a little bit darker and she wouldn't have been completely sure.

'The raider is still miles away. Maybe we can outrun him? Reach a safe harbor?'

'No chance. There is only a slight breeze and they have more sails than we. More rowers too. It is a galley ship and their slaves are quite strong rowers. After a chase the pirates always feed the slowest slave to the sharks. No slave wants to be the slowest.' He snapped his fingers. 'Scorpio? Scorpio? The Imperial Coast guard! How went the distress signal again?'

He took the Handbook for the Able Sailor from the shelf. 'Distress dance of the three kites.' He looked up. 'Tiger-Eye! Yesterday you were flying a kite on the bridge. Can you make two more kites?'

'You launch three kites and the Coast guard comes running to save you?'

'Only if we give the right signal. With exactly the right kites.'

'Great glowing dragon turds!' Tiger-Eye wailed and tugged on the kite string. 'Fly, you sluggard!' His most recent kite made a somersault and plunged right into the waves. 'That's four already.'

He fished the sodden kite from the sea. 'Chipmunk, a kite shaped like a pike just doesn't fly!'

'You wailed exactly the same about the first two. 'A cockroach kite will never fly. His legs keep hooking the cord.' And 'your moon moth flies like an albatross.'

'Could you hurry up a bit?' Opal asked. 'I can see their shields with my naked eye.'

'You only have to worry when you see them twirling their grappling hooks,' Grubby Chipmunk said. 'Come, Tiger-Eye. The final kite.'

Tiger-Eye crossed several bamboo sticks and stretched the gray silk. Grubby Chipmunk started to paint scales on as fast as he could.

'There he goes!' Tiger-Eye said, letting out the rope. The kite wheeled and then started to rise in earnest.

'Thirty meters,' Opal declared. 'Eh, Chipmunk. Now the pirates are twirling their grappling-hooks. I hope you like rowing?'

The final kite joined the others.

'At last,' Grubby Chipmunk said. 'Let the cockroach pursue the humble night moth.'

Tiger-Eye tugged on the lines and let the kites swerve.

'Good. Now the pike. Let him chase away the cockroach.'

'Like this?'

'Perfect.' Grubby Chipmunk breathed a sigh of relief. 'The signal is completed. We are saved.'

In front of the ship the sea started to boil. From the blue depths a shadow darted up. Spume flew and water cascaded down from the deck.

It could have been a steel barracuda, but a barracuda as long as a warehouse, adorned with fearsome hooks and golden lanterns. On the bow glaring animal eyes had been painted, with bristling brows and a maw filled with sharp teeth.

'The pirate ship is turning!' Opal yelled. 'The're fleeing!'

Hatches opened. Soldiers in cuirasses of red lacquered leather emerged. They pointed their crossbows and jeered at the pirates. Their officer raised his saber. 'Fire!'

A swarm of crossbow quarrels hissed into the sky and swooped down.

They were a heartbeat too late. At most, half a dozen thudded into the hull. The rest fell short and sank.

An officer hauled himself on the deck of the 'See If I Care'.

He inspected the ship and it's three travelers.

'My name is Intrepid Peony, colonel of the Imperial Guard. I read the message your kites wrote in the sky – the pike that chases the cockroach away from the moon moth. The pike is the Scorpion Emperor of the Sunken City, of course, because pike live for a thousand years, just like the emperor. The moon moth is his humble subject.' He placed his hand on the hilt of his sword. 'The Imperial Guard only saves humble subjects of the Emperor. I hope you really are humble subjects of the Emperor. If I came running to save some foreign riffraff I'd as soon give you back to the pirates.'

'Bow!' Grubby Chipmunk hissed as he bowed so deeply his cap fell on the deck. 'Hail colonel! We most certainly are humble subjects of the Emperor.'

'That's what I like to hear. Well then, each ship that enters the harbor has to pay half her load to the Emperor. At least, when it concerns brand-new subjects.'

'What has to be has to be,' Grubby Chipmunk sighed.

'Throw us your strongest cable,' Intrepid Peony ordered. 'We'll tow you to the Sunken City before those cockroaches return with a dozen ships.'

The imperial submarine steamed to the distant harbor. It didn't exactly fly, but it came close. Chipmunk's ship careened from wave top to wave top.

Only within sight of the city walls did the submarine slow down.

Opal saw stairs descending straight into the sea. Below the hull, the spires of towers slipped past. In the blue green water an orchard grew, with brightly colored fishes nestling in the bare branches.

'Do you know the legend about our city?' Intrepid Peony asked.

'How Thousand Golden Domes became the Sunken City?'

'Tell me,' Opal said. 'Please.' She loved stories – especially legends about strange and exotic islands.

THE LEGEND OF SUNG-ARAD AND SONG-DAI AND THE LEMON OF IMMORTALITY

Sung-Arad and Song-Dai were twin brothers, sons of the emperor of Scorpio. They were heroes of course. They saved princesses, fished for sea monsters and wrestled with giant apes. Their most famous feat was stealing the Lemon of Immortality. The moment the Guardian went to take a pee (which he did only once a year, for he was a most conscientious guardian) they threw the

guard crocodile a drugged Maestrener ham and slipped into the Garden of the Gods.

Here Sung-Arad plucked the Lemon of Immortality. Song-Dai squeezed the precious fruit and filled two glasses of the finest crystal.

'To our health!' he toasted. 'May we live forever and a day.'

A heartbeat later the Guard returned with a whole army of howling demons and night-gaunts. He chained the brothers and dragged them to the throne of Gliph Abar.

'They drugged my crocodile and crept into my garden!' he accused them. 'Next, these jerks squeezed the Lemon until not a single drop was left and drank all the juice!'

'Interesting,' Gliph Abar said. 'So they are immortal and only gods can be immortal.' He looked them in the eye. 'All right guys, you're gods now. So build a temple and decide what gods you're going to be.' He waved them away. 'Next case.'

When they returned to their city they discovered that the old emperor had just died. The trial only seemed to have lasted a few minutes but on MiYu a full fifty years had passed.

'I'll miss father,' Sung-Arad said. 'Which of us is going to be the next emperor? We're exactly the same age.'

'Lets hold a shark-mouse race,' Song-Dai proposed. 'The winner gets the throne and the crown. The other takes a fleet with gold and sails away to find his own island.'

Shark-mouse races were quite popular on Scorpio then. They still are.

'Agreed!' Sung-Arad said and they slapped hands on the deal.

Song-Dai placed two shark-mice on the track. 'I'll count to three.'
On 'Three!' the mice darted away. They snapped and tore at each other's
ears and tails, and the blood splashed all around.

At the fourth circuit Sung-Arad's mouse started to slow down. He dragged
his feet and at last he couldn't even lift them and sat down on the gravel,
hissing with frustration.
'I win!' Song-Dai shouted. 'Long live the Emperor of Scorpio! Hurray for
me!'
The game hadn't been completely honest. Song-Dai had coated the feet of
his brother's mouse with a slow-drying jelly-fish glue. When Sung-Arad
discovered the treachery he waited till midnight and crept to the fire-pillar
in the center of the city. There he peed on the night fire till the last ember
sputtered out.
The city promptly sank down in the ocean. Before the townsmen could light
the fire again, half the city had disappeared beneath the waves. Sung-Arad
was long gone by then.
The brand-new emperor called all the court-magicians together and they
sent a roaring hurricane in pursuit of the fleet. Sung-Arads fleet went down
at Gemini, sinking with man and shark-mouse.
Sung-Arad was immortal and couldn't drown. His soldiers turned into
walruses and sea leopards. His Ladies-in-waiting became mermaids with
waving green hair.
Ever since, Sung-Arad dwells in the deep City of Coral and the brothers
deeply hate each other.

2.

Intrepid Peony indicated a dome, which drifted on the waters like a gorgeous decorated Easter egg. 'There's the imperial palace.
Tomorrow is a feast day. On the Day of the Daggers every subject can talk to the emperor. Even brand-new subjects like you.'
'Why do they call it Day of the Daggers?' Opal inquired. 'Strange name for a holiday.'
'Oh, it's just a name. Do you see the golden pillar behind the palace? That's where the Sea Lion King peed on our fire. At the start the pillar was just iron, but he was a god now and even his pee is magical.'

Imperial tax inspectors jumped aboard the moment the ship moored.
They shoveled pearls in pails, hauled away half the wine bottles and all of the smoked ham.
All in all it went quite quickly. Just three-quarters of an hour later Grubby Chipmunk put his footprint on a sheet of paper and they were free to go ashore.

Intrepid Peony got up from a public bench. 'If you want I can point you to an inexpensive tavern. Spending the night on a moored ship isn't allowed.'

He wants to keep an eye on us, Opal thought. He trusts us as far as he can throw a one ton rock.

'We'd rather walk around a bit on our own.'

'There's a floating market just around the corner.'

'Great idea,' Grubby Chipmunk said. 'I have to replenish my stock of smoked hams.

Somehow we suddenly haven't any left.' He opened his order book.

'Opal, could you sign? Luxury cruise to Scorpio for two persons and a statue.'

The market consisted of hundreds of rolling vendors boats. You could cross from boat to boat on unpleasant narrow planks. Each time a customer lost his balance and splashed into the oily water all the merchants hooted.

A merchant pushed a chain of rattling coins under their noses. 'An amulet for every problem, lords and lady – be it pirates, no luck at gambling, a jealous wife!'

'What kind of whistles are those?' Tiger-Eye asked. 'The ones shaped like birds?'

'That is a really excellent set, sir. They're birdcalls for every bird in the world, from hummingbird to bald eagle!'

Tiger-Eye pointed to a whistle in the shape of a gull. 'Show me how it works.'

'You ask and we blow.' He put the whistle to his lips. An extremely raucous gull screech sounded across the market. Ten, then twenty gulls turned in the direction of the booth and began diving down. In the blink of an eye the booth was covered with screaming gulls.

'Send them away!' Tiger-Eye swung his arm like a windmill until the feathers flew. The number of gulls only increased. 'I'll take the whistles! I'll take them all'

'Good decision, sir. All right, now I'll blow the black-headed-gull-devourer's whistle. They are mortally afraid of that animal.'

The next whistle produced a weird strangled hooting. The booth emptied in a heartbeat.

'You can bring us to the tavern now,' Opal said. 'One with a good hot bath. I want to wash the gull crap out of my hair.'

Tiger-Eye halted in front of the tavern. 'Intrepid Peony, do you see that ship there?'

Opal saw a ship entering the harbor. It looked unpleasantly familiar.

'Something wrong with that ship?' Intrepid Peony asked.

'You could say so! It has a cockroach on its sails. Dinja's bow, it is the very same ship that pursued us!'

'What is the problem? The pirates are also humble subjects of the emperor. They pay him a third of all booty and attack only foreign ships.'

'A fine state of affairs,' Tiger-Eye muttered.

Opal completely agreed. The stupid emperor of Scorpio was no better than a pirate captain. Worse than a pirate captain: a real captain wouldn't take such an indecently large part of the booty.

That evening Opal sat on the balcony of their room, her compass on her lap. She gazed out over the harbor.

'Three guesses where my compass is pointing now.'

'That drifting Easter egg?' Tiger-Eye said. 'The imperial palace?'

'Tomorrow you can go there,' Grubby Chipmunk said. He took a bite from the yellow-green foam on his kelp beer and emptied his mug.

'Ask the emperor if you can borrow his emerald for a moment.' He laughed so loudly the beer sprayed from his nostrils.

Opal slept like a rose that night. She was too tired to dream.

The barking of a seal woke her the next morning. A choir of seagulls answered him. Beyond the window the light was gray and cold. The sun still tarried somewhere below the horizon. She rubbed the sleep from her eyes and frowned. Something had changed in the room, had been shifted…

Smald! The statue was leaning against the wardrobe when she went to bed. Now it was gone.

Wait a moment, the doors of the balcony. Had they been open last night? Smald's statue had crawled all the way to the balcony. His living arm hung across the rail and his hand opened and closed spastically.

He tried to escape, Opal thought. He hauled his weight all the way across the room. Why did he drag himself to the balcony? Why not the door of the room?

'Opal?' Thirty meters away a woman balanced on the gilded knob of a flagpole. She lifted her bow: An arrow thudded in the wood of the rail.

A gossamer thread stretched from the flagpole to the balcony. The woman danced across the thread and jumped down next to Opal.

'Dinja?' Opal asked.

'I wanted to warn you before,' The goddess said, 'but your sleep was too deep to dream about me.'

'Sorry.'

'Smald has been scattering leaflets all over the city that say 'Help! I've been kidnapped!' A night fisher found two of them and raised the alarm. The guards are already on their way to your tavern.'

'I'll wake the others now.'

'Then you'll have to waken yourself first.'

Suddenly Opal was back in her bed. A seal barked, a choir of gulls replied. She opened her eyes as wide as possible and rolled out of her bed. I hope I woke up for real this time.

'Wake up!' She snatched Tiger-Eye's pillow away. 'Smald's betrayed us!'

A thunderous thud shook the door.

'Open up! In the name of the emperor!'

The second blow broke the bolts.

Intrepid Peony stood in the doorway with his sword in his hand.

Behind him two soldiers put their battering ram on the floor.

'You disappoint me,' the colonel said. 'One day you're humble subjects but you're criminals the next.'

'I'm starting to find this irritating,' Tiger-Eye said. 'We have to go to jail, I guess?'

'Ah!' Intrepid Peony said. 'You have been there before?'

'A dungeon is just a waste of time,' another officer said. On his helmet at least six plumes bobbed. 'We've already called for Judge Thistle Ball. He'll come to the courtroom as soon as he has shaved and fed his vulture.'

Grubby Chipmunk raised his hands in protest. 'I have nothing to do with them. I hardly know them. I am just a humble smuggler.'

'Is that so?' Intrepid Peony asked.

'It is true,' Opal said.

'Throw him in the dungeon. Smuggling carries a sentence of ninety-nine years.'

3.

Judge Thistle Ball wore a robe with such wide sleeves that the lower tassels swept across the floor. On his left shoulder crouched a vulture.

A silver scorpion formed the knob of his walking stick. He doesn't look like a lenient judge, Opal thought. Sentenced to life for a broken window would be the least.

'A grave crime indeed,' the judge declared after reading Smald's note. 'They've petrified a poor little boy and kidnapped him, too.' He looked up. 'Guilty as a pussycat with the feathers of the canary still in his whiskers. Intrepid Peony, tell them their choices.' The judge hobbled away, followed by his flapping vulture.

Intrepid Peony cleared his throat. 'Well yes. Look, you have two choices. Jump in the tub with wholy fire-jellyfish on the birthday of the sea god, that would be, yes, in three months time. Or you can choose to become emperor and empress for one day.'

'What do we do then, exactly?' Tiger-Eye queried.

'Our emperor rules Scorpio in infinite wisdom and his mercy is great. Not all of his subjects think so. That is why the emperor dismisses all his guards for one day. On the Day of the Daggers they can tell him all their grievances and complaints. Or, if they seriously disagree, they can creep into the palace with a poisoned dagger.'

'I get it,' Tiger-Eye said. 'And of course it isn't mister emperor himself sitting on the throne. Just some dupe like me.'

'You don't quite understand. Whoever wears the emperor's crown is the emperor of the Sunken City. You'll put on his emerald crown and your empress…'

'Did you say emerald crown?' Opal cried. 'Hold on. You've convinced us. We'll do it! Happily.'

'Are you crazy? We…'

'Shut your mouth!' she hissed at Tiger-Eye. 'We'll never get another chance like this. Or would you rather swim with the jellyfish?'

The next morning they floated in a barge to the imperial palace.

The hull was inlaid with hundreds of facetted gems. The sails were billowing gossamer, so thin you could look right through them.

Thousands of humble subjects hailed them from the quays and houseboats. Toddlers strewed rose petals on the water.

'Long live the emperor!' they cried. 'May he rule for a thousand years.

Long live the empress! May she always remain young and beautiful!'

They moored at the palace. Intrepid Peony preceded them through a window on the sixth floor. The windowsill lay a few centimeters above the high water line. A servant followed, carrying Smald in his arms.

They ascended a staircase with steps of smoked glass, walked through a copper gate and then stood in the throne room. The Keeper of the Crown stepped forward with the emerald crown and Intrepid Peony put it on Tiger-Eye's head.

'Bow!' Intrepid Peony roared. 'Bow deeply for the emperor and empress of Scorpio!'

The ministers and chamberlain promptly knelt. They bowed low until their foreheads touched the floor. Happily the throne room was covered with an ankle deep rug.

'That is enough,' Tiger-Eye said. 'Rise. Who organizes things here?'

A gentleman with a head as bald as an egg and a curling moustache that reached all the way to his shoulders raised his hand. 'I'm Learned Gentian, your councilor, o Emperor of Emperors. Whatever you order becomes law.'

'That is the way things should be. These are my orders; free Grubby Chipmunk. Load his ship with provisions and everything else he asks for. Tell him to wait for us. Yes, and shoot him if the tries to leave without us.'

'It will be done.'

'Now, everybody leave. The empress and I want to be alone.'

'Hail!' the ministers cried. They bowed and marched from the throne room. The councilor looked back from the doorway.

'In a minute the first subjects arrive. You can't send them away, you know.' Opal heard a certain glee in his voice.

'No problem, my dear man,' Tiger-Eye said. 'I quite like talking with my humble subjects.'

The moment the gate closed, Tiger-Eye took off the crown.

'It looks a lot bigger than the eye of the sea serpent. We are making progress. Which parts do we change this time?'

'Maybe his legs? I'm guessing the crown is big enough. If Ysidore's magic ever falters, we don't have to carry him. He can walk on his own.'

'Sounds logical.'

The color swiftly leaked away. It disappeared first from the knobs, then from the rest. A few shards of green stone remained. Probably the maker had used some other cheaper kind of gem instead of emerald, malachite or amazonite.

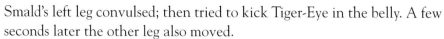

Smald's left leg convulsed; then tried to kick Tiger-Eye in the belly. A few seconds later the other leg also moved.

'It worked,' Tiger-Eye said and then gave a strangled yell. A man had his arm around Tiger-Eye's neck and held the point of a dagger against his jugular vein.

'Put the crown down, my emperor,' he said. 'Carefully. No sudden movements.'

A second assassin lowered himself on an almost invisible thread from the ceiling.

'What are you doing, Pale White Grave-Lily? That crown is clearly a fake. Every child can see that. Ordinary glass and not even green. No crown, no emperor.'

'I'm sorry,' Tiger-Eye said. 'It isn't my fault. They pointed me to this throne and set this thing on my head.'

'It is a scandal!' the first assassin said. He put his dagger back into its silken sash. 'I'll stop the other team. Nightshade, you go stand in front of the secret passage to warn everybody away we might have missed. We aren't paid to kill the wrong person.'

The other clacked his tongue. 'The other times there's been no problem killing the emperor. No worries about false emperors.'

Ruling was a piece of cake Tiger-Eye and Opal discovered. Tiger-Eye promised a weeping widow that he'd have a talk with her good-for-nothing son. He tasted a dozen home baked cakes and praised them enthusiastically. Nobody mentioned his crown.

The empress kissed wailing babies and received a lot of hand made drawings. Several times she had to autograph a plaster cast.

At a quarter past eight a man with a horn stepped into the throne room. He lifted his horn and blew five notes. The humble subjects instantly grabbed their belongings and left the hall.

Opal touched a woman on her shoulder. 'What is going on?'

'The Day of the Daggers is now officially ended.' She nodded at Tiger-Eye. 'He there, he isn't the emperor anymore. Just an ordinary nobody. No use talking to him.'

The secret door in the wall behind the throne opened and the councilor stepped cautiously into the hall.

'You're still alive?' he asked. 'How surprising.' His eyes darted while he inspected the throne. He stepped closer and felt behind the embroidered pillows. 'Where did you hide the real crown, if I may ask?'

'It is hard to believe, I know, but…' Tiger-Eye lifted the crown from his head. 'It suddenly lost all color.'

'What!' The councilor gasped for breath. His eyes protruded and he turned a deep crimson. 'Guards!' he roared. 'They have switched the crown! Guar…'

KABONK!

Opal set Smald down. 'He may be light as thistledown but his head is still as hard as stone. Is he still breathing? I didn't want…'

Tiger-Eye kneeled next to the councilor and felt his wrist. 'Just unconscious.'

'Let's make tracks then. The Day of the Daggers is done and they don't need an emperor anymore. I'd rather not have them asking about the crown.'

Escaping the palace proved easier than they had feared. Nobody recognized

them as last afternoon's emperor and empress. Not even Intrepid Peony who commanded the soldiers.

There were some good reasons. Tiger-Eye, for one, walked on his hands past the guards while he crowed like a rooster. Opal snatched a soup tureen in the form of a porcelain hen from a side table and put it on her head. She hopped past the soldiers while she clucked: 'Tock, tock. Lady Boiling-Hen, that's me and nobody can ever catch me!'

4.

Grubby Chipmunk sat singing a rather naughty sailors ditty in the light of a dozen flaming torches. His brand-new armchair had been upholstered in glossy sable. Next to his seat stood a box filled with wine bottles.

Half a dozen rolled along the deck with every movement of the ship.

'Pal and Tigger.' He raised his wineglass in a toast and sank back.

'Nayzz you zinking of me. A cell, bores you stiff after a day. No matter nineteen nine year.'

Tiger-Eye hauled in the gang-plank and cast off.

'Soh?' Grubby Chipmunk said. 'We's leaving?'

'Put your head in a pail of water, you lush,' Opal said. 'Otherwise somebody will come along to hack it off.'

'It's all trouble and noise.' Grubby Chipmunk muttered, sadly shaking his head. ''Twas too good to last anyway.'

Grubby Chipmunk proved right about the trouble and noise. They had only just hoisted the sail when a loud alarm sounded from the watchtowers.

'Crown-snatchers!' The amplified voice rolled like the thunder across the Sunken City. 'Dirty foreigners have stolen the crown of our beloved emperor! Catch them, faithful subjects, crush them! Smoke them out!'

'Do you think that's the voice of the real emperor?' Opal asked.

'That loudmouth?' Grubby Chipmunk snorted. 'They whisper that the emperor is a most vicious man. That he drinks baby's blood each morning to keep young. But roaring like a hysterical schoolmaster, no, that wouldn't be his style.'

Opal recognized the voice now. 'It's Learned Gentian, the councilor.'

'The emperor would have been better,' Tiger-Eye said. 'We only spoiled his crown. Opal knocked the councilor down with the statue.'

Grubby Chipmunk looked up and hissed in fright.

'What's that?'

'A tracking owl – they're worse than bloodhounds and he's hanging right above us.'

The owl circled and hooted twice.

'He's found us,' Grubby Chipmunk wailed. 'I never should have left my cozy cell. Ninety nine years isn't that long.'

'Soldiers,' Tiger-Eye pointed. 'They're lowering canoes at the piers. We're trapped!'

An insistent rapping came from just below the rail.

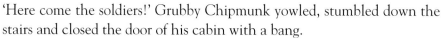
'Here come the soldiers!' Grubby Chipmunk yowled, stumbled down the stairs and closed the door of his cabin with a bang.

Opal looked down. A mermaid drifted alongside the hull

'You have no direction to jump,' she said. 'Except one.' She pointed. Between her fingers grew webs. 'Nobody thought of guarding the night fire of the city.' She chuckled. 'Did they already forget the treason of their emperor?' She reached beneath her in the water and handed Opal a glass pail. 'Perhaps this will help? With the compliments of the Sea lion emperor of Gemini.'

'A pail? Oh, I get it. I stand there with a pail of water and threaten to douse their precious fire if they won't let us go.'

'I wouldn't stop with a threat,' the mermaid said. 'When their city suddenly starts sinking again nobody will have time for a couple of crown-nappers.' She pushed off. 'Don't tarry! Give them no chance to intercept you.'

She dove with a majestic sweep of her tail.

The pillar with the night fire extended a gilded pier into the harbor.

Opal threw a loop over the mooring post and ran up the winding stairs.

She rested Smald on her shoulder like a club. Tiger-Eye followed her more slowly with the pail of water.

The fire was surprisingly small – just a brazier with glowing charcoal.

The stoker was slumbering on a marble bench. His thin mustache fluttered with each whistling exhalation. You could smell the liquor on his breath from the other side of the fire. At his feet stood an alarm clock in the shape of a mechanical frog. Dwarf made, Opal thought, just like her butterfly. The frog watched the flames intently and would croak the moment the fire started to smoke.

'Tie up the stoker,' Opal said to Grubby Chipmunk. 'You're the sailor so you should know everything about knots.'

'Hey you!' the frog called with a weird rattling voice. 'What are you guys doing with my master?'

'We're tying him up to keep him safe,' Opal answered. 'So he won't tumble down the stairs in his sleep.'

'Oh, that's all right then.'

A screech drifted down from the sky, followed by an angry 'Uhu!'

'Our owl is back,' Tiger-Eye said. He lifted the pail and bent his knees.

'Let him come. I have my pail at the ready.'

Barely five minutes later the warships closed in on the pillar. From their masts flew the shark-mouse banner of the emperor. Drums boomed, heavy as the heartbeat of a leviathan.

Two heralds jumped onto the pier and blew their trumpets. Three other servants proceeded to unroll a scarlet carpet.

'His majesty,' the heralds proclaimed. 'The Emperor of Scorpio!'

Just like when we entered the throne hall, Opal thought, only it's for real this time.

A man in a red cape followed them and put on his crown. He gave the crown a half turn, canted it and grimaced.

Opal walked to the edge of the platform.

'Only him. Only the emperor! The moment a single soldier steps ashore, we empty the pail on your fire.'

'We'll do it your way.' The emperor gave a jerk with his head and the heralds scuttled back to their sloop. 'Is it all right with you if I bring my councilor along? He sometimes gives rather sensible advice.'

'That weirdo?' Opal laughed. 'No problem. Only lay down your weapons. Especially the concealed ones. No, I have a better idea. Come in your underwear. Otherwise it's a no go.'

'With your feet bare,' Grubby Chipmunk amended. 'Emperors often put poisoned daggers or tame scorpions in their boots.'

In his drawers and barefoot, the emperor of Scorpio proved to be a rather skinny guy. It was easy to believe him a druggist or a taxidermist until you noticed his eyes. They were so cold, Opal had met tarantulas with a friendlier expression.

'You are wearing the crown of emerald,' Opal said. 'How?'

'Did you really believe I would let a false emperor put my crown on his head?'

'He's talking nonsense,' Tiger-Eye said. 'Emerald my foot. His new crown is made of green glass. I have to admit, it looks a lot like emerald. Only an egg-snatcher would see the difference.'

'A connoisseur,' the emperor said. 'You're right of course.' He licked his lips. 'A full pail and a night fire that doesn't burn all that well. Hmmm. As far as I know glass pails are only used in the city of my brother. But that doesn't matter. You'll want a safe-conduct away from here. If you don't throw your bucket of water and I leave your heads on your shoulders that can be done. Just return my crown.'

'That's a bit of a problem,' Tiger-Eye said.

Opal saw the councilor walk around the fire and sit down next to the stoker. Tiger-Eye now stood with his back to the councilor. Coincidence? The councilor rubbed his upper lip, pushed against his moustache and suddenly Opal understood what was wrong. Opal had quite recently knocked him down with a stone statue.

'The councilor is an imposter!' she cried. 'He doesn't have a lump on his head!'

Tiger-Eye instantly reacted and threw a splash of water on the fire.

The embers hissed and a white cloud billowed. The councilor put his fingers in his mouth and drew a supple rapier from his gullet.

'Stop right there!' Opal said. 'One more step and it's the whole pail. Then you can all walk among the fishes.'

'Well, we tried, didn't we?' the emperor said, nodding to the false councilor. 'Make yourself scarce, please.'

'Hi!' the assassin cried. He pinched his nose and jumped down from the platform.

'We still have a problem,' the emperor said. 'I can't allow you to leave with my crown. An emperor without a crown is…'

'Hogwash,' Tiger-Eye said. 'Nobody will ever guess that it's glass.'

'Except for a jeweler or a goldsmith. But I can imprison all goldsmiths and jewelers of course. Better yet, I'll feed them to the shark-mice.'

'You see?' Tiger-Eye said. 'No problem at all.' Suddenly he uttered a piercing scream and his right arm twitched. The contents of the pail splashed on the last embers.

'Kai ai!' Tiger-Eye screamed and danced around, wind-milling his arm.

A flying fish had fastened its teeth onto his wrist.

'Silverfin!' a clear voice sounded across the water. 'Down girl! Come to your mistress.'

The fish let go of Tiger-Eye's wrist and flapped away.

The last ember died and the city shuddered. Waves rolled in and overturned the war ships like cockleshells. From the ocean rose a groaning rumble. Towers swayed and slipped down into the dark water. Two miles farther on the imperial palace turned on it's axis and went bubbling down, all the way to the ninth floor.

The eyes of the stoker flew open and he immediately grasped the situation.

'My inside pocket!' He waved his bound wrists. 'I have a fire starter there. Behind the woodpile I've hidden a jar of rum, one-hundred proof. It burns like a phoenix in a fireworks factory.'

The emperor dove behind the woodpile and pulled the cork from the jar. The others sprinted down the stairs and jumped aboard. Tiger-Eye severed the mooring line with his folding knife, while Grubby Chipmunk pulled up the anchor chain, grunting with the effort.

The sea was filled with wreckage and floundering soldiers. Luckily they had more pressing problems than catching a couple of crown-thieves - such as keeping afloat in thirty kilo suits of armor.

'Hey you!' The mermaid surfaced next to the bow. 'Throw me the anchor. I'll tug you out to sea.'

A mud-gray shadow emerged from underneath the ship and took the anchor in his jaws. A hooked back fin rose from the waters.

A mighty jar shook the ship and she groaned in all her timbers and then leaped forward in the slipstream of the shark.

'Relax,' the mermaid said. 'The rest will go smoothly. As easy as drowning a sailor.'

Tiger-Eye glared at her and rubbed his bleeding wrist. 'That stupid mongrel. I bet she was yours.'

'You stood dawdling with your pail. I just gave you a little nudge.'

'Thanks for nothing,' Opal said. 'Stealing a crown was bad enough. Now all of Scorpio will pursue us.'

'But you have gained the everlasting gratitude of my master. The emperor of Gemini is in your debt.'

The thirty meter long white shark dragged them past the piers, into the open sea.

The mermaid looked back. 'It's a pity. The city has stopped sinking. The emperor must have started the fire once again' She smoothed her waving green tresses. 'Well, four floors lower isn't too bad. The next time they'll get a real ducking and there'll be no coming up either.' She looked at them. 'Where do I point your shark?'

'Our shark?' Tiger-Eye asked. 'What do you mean, our?'

'Do you want to drive the shark on your own?'

'I gather we're stuck with you,' Opal said. 'Perhaps you could tell us your name?'

'Lady Barracuda.' She gripped the anchor-chain. 'What direction?'

'I'll ask.' Opal took out her compass and tapped on the glass.

'Where should I be going now? Please tell us.' The needle turned three times all the way and finally stopped, quivering, in front of a constellation. If it had been a dog he would have cocked his head.

'Sagittarius,' Opal declared. 'The island of the bowman. Why did my compass hesitate?'

'We'll find out, I'm afraid,' Tiger-Eye said.

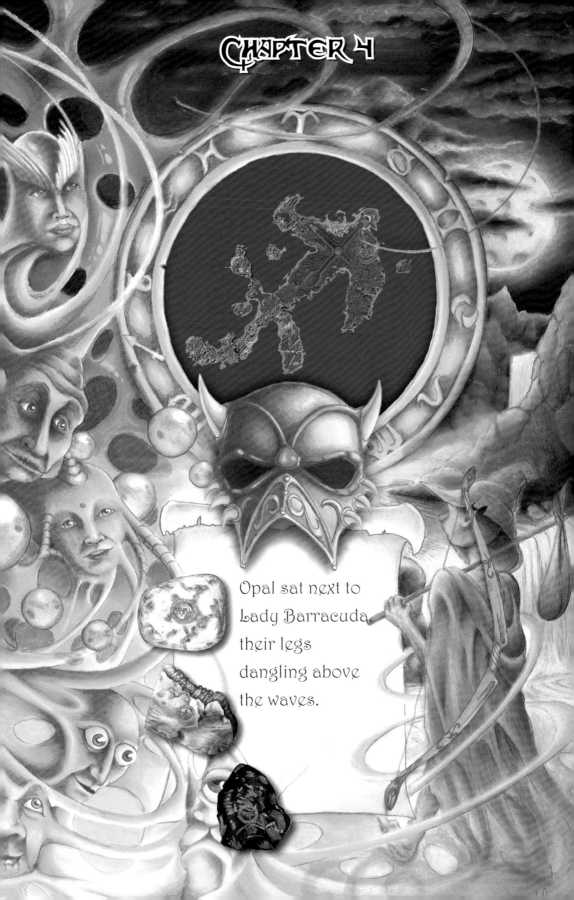

CHAPTER 4

Opal sat next to
Lady Barracuda
their legs
dangling above
the waves.

SAGITTARIUS

SAGITTARIUS
22 November to 21 December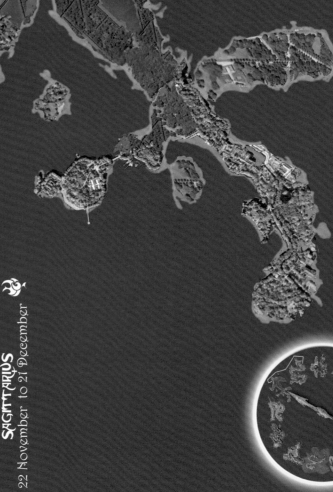

SNOWFLAKE OBSIDIAN

PETRIFIED WOOD

TREE AGATE

SAGITTARIUS

1.

Opal sat next to Lady Barracuda, their legs dangling above the waves.
'Can I ask you something?' Opal said. 'It is kind of personal.'
'Fire away. It is pretty hard to shock a mermaid.'
'It's about your legs. How do you do it? When you are swimming you have that big beautiful fishtail. The moment you touch the deck the tail splits into legs.'
'It's like werewolves. Only I don't need a full moon. Mermaids are a kind of were-fish.'
'I get it.'

The next morning Opal woke completely rested, with a mercifully empty head. It felt as if the night wind had blown away all nagging thoughts.
From the open port drifted a most enchanting smell – cinnamon apple-pie, straight from the oven as only her grandmother could bake it.
Their own cook put weird, expensive dried fruit in the batter and topped it with a mountain of whipped cream. Wrong, completely wrong.
Opal inhaled the smell with a smile before she realized how impossible it was: smelling Grandmother Rithka's apple-pie on the middle of the ocean.
Their ship might be the pinnacle of luxury, filled with all conveniences a smuggler's money could buy, but an oven she would have noticed.
Tiger-Eye leaned against a mast and carved a dragon from a piece of gray driftwood.
'Do you smell that, too?' Opal asked.
'That nasty stink you mean? Like something is burning in the oven?'
'Not burning at all!' Opal protested. 'That is just the way fresh apple-pie should smell. The bottom should have a nice thick crust.
Dark brown, so it crunches between your teeth.' Imagine bad-mouthing Grandmother's apple-pie!
'I haven't the slightest idea what you're talking about,' Tiger-Eye said.
'No matter what smell, it comes from the west. Sagittarius must be quite close, Grubby Chipmunk said so this morning. A flock of stippled silver-gulls flew over. According to him they always keep close to the shore.'
Opal noticed that the sea was covered with bobbing gulls. The moment they noticed the back fin of the shark they flew off screaming.
A yellow and green striped bird alighted on the railing and started to sing.

Opal automatically hummed along.
'Oggy Boggie Barabas
dances
bare feet
on newly broken glass.
Give me an E,
Give me an A,
Oggy takes all the girls away!'
Opal always smiled when she heard little children sing that song.
Her father had taught her that song on his knee and with 'away!' he dropped Opal right on the grass. That was before her father made so much money and became too important and busy to spend time with his family. Opal was quite sure he had never taught that song to Pebble.
'Give me an A,' Opal sang and suddenly she froze. The bird didn't only sing the melody, but also the words.
'He talks!' she called to Tiger-Eye. 'Do you hear? He talks!'
'He won't be the only bird that talks.'
'But it's my favorite song!' It could have been chance. Still, Opal felt herself welcomed. First the apple-pie, then her song… Almost as if the island was expecting her. Suddenly she realized that it must be literally true. Sagittarius was her star isle. She was born on the 26th of November and was a Sagittarian. Only if you reached your star isle could you become completely yourself, releasing all your powers and talents.
She spread her arms and yelled: 'Sagittarius, here I come!'

The isle of Sagittarius stretched in front of them, luxuriously green.
A golden shore glowed in the sunlight and Opal was quite sure there wasn't a mosquito to be found on the whole island. At least not one that would bite her.
My island, she thought, and she felt an enormous smile splitting her face.
Grubby Chipmunk tapped her on the shoulder and offered her his account book. 'If you could sign here please? Luxury cruise for two persons and a statue.'

The moment she stepped ashore a whole horde of excited animals burst from the shrubs. Turtles almost tripped across their own feet in their enthusiasm to reach her. Little monkeys waved flags they had made from palm leaves and bamboo.
'Opal! Opal!' the parrots screeched. 'Opal O, Opal ay, Opal hurray!'

MY FIRST BOOK OF GODS AND DEMONS

Aerdelick the Sower

Aerdelick the Sower had been the 308th son of Gliph Abar and Dinja. While his brothers went bear hunting or surfed on tidal waves, he carefully and lovingly collected seeds. Sagittarius was in fact his holy isle. All gardeners prayed to him. If you want him to answer your prayers you have to stand with your bare feet in a flowerpot filled with fresh earth. Whoever forgets to water his plants or kicks toadstools will surely get a visit from this god. Many a toadstool kicker has been found dead in his bed the next morning, his mouth filled with pine needles. When you plant a seed, first make a hole in the earth and then spit into it. Next intone this prayer: 'This is Aerdelick's water. Grow, in His name!'
On Taurus some people pee in every flower pot while calling: 'This is Aerdelick's golden water.'
Most serious gardeners consider that vulgar.

Opal stopped, raised her hand and the choir fell silent.

'I want to thank you. All of you. I'm also very, eh, delighted to reach my very own island at last. And thank you for this wonderful reception. You really know how to make a girl feel welcome.'

She must have said the right thing because the animals jumped up and down and cheered. The monkeys blew kisses.

'Ask them if they know about emeralds,' Tiger-Eye whispered in her ear.

'Not now!' Opal hissed. 'That would sound so greedy and ungrateful. The emeralds will take care of themselves. Let's just relax for the moment. I mean, for once nobody is lying in wait for us and there isn't a cannibal or monster to be found on the whole island.'

'How do you know?'

'It's my star isle! Of course I know!'

They strolled some miles along the coast. Among the trees they discovered fallen pillars, collapsed huts. An abandoned fishing village extended two piers into the sea. The harbor had silted up and the ships lay stranded on the sand. They weren't much more than hulks and their hulls were so weathered the wood looked silver-gray. From one of the sloops grew a tree.

'I don't like this,' Grubby Chipmunk sniffed. 'Everything is abandoned. No people anywhere, only animals.'

'What is wrong with animals?' Opal stroked a striped wildcat that had jumped on her shoulder. Fairies with colorful butterfly wings swarmed around her head. 'From the sea we saw a huge green dome. Maybe all the people live there?'

2.

It was the fifth day, or perhaps the sixth? Opal lazed in her hammock.
She drank grape juice out of a hollow calabash. Under the hammock
waited baskets filled with breadfruit, blood oranges and bundles of smoked
fish. Bees buzzed a drowsy summer song.

'Dame Opal?' A parrot landed on her left knee. 'Is everything right with
the world?'

Opal gave the thumbs up. 'Couldn't be better.'

Tiger-Eye argued that animals couldn't talk, just like on Leo.

He argued that even the parrots were just chattering. Maybe he was
right.

But Opal could understand them quite well. That's only logical; this was
her isle, those were her animals. Cancer was Tiger-Eye's star isle. On the
bare star islands of Cancer he would probably hear voices in the howling
wind, in the thunder of breaking waves.

'Something else?' the parrot inquired. 'Some fertilizer for your roots?'

'No thanks. I have all I need.' Fertilizer for your roots! Sometimes the
parrots were a bit hard to follow.

She dozed.

'Opal! Come on, Opal!'

That stupid Tiger-Eye shook her hammock and didn't want to stop.

All the rest of the crew stood around her hammock. 'Leave me in peace,
Tiger-Eye. I don't want to do anything.'

'You've already lazed around in your hammock for a whole week, stuffing
yourself until you're as fat as a potbelly pig.'

'A week is an exaggeration.'

Tiger-Eye put his hands on his hips. 'This is the eighth day since we
arrived.'

'That is right,' Grubby Chipmunk agreed. 'And you didn't once ask your
animals about the emeralds. You see that green dome overtopping the
trees? It could very well be made of emerald. Every time Tiger-Eye asks you
to come and see, you only say 'soon.''

'Why don't you go to the dome yourself if it's that important?'

'Your wretched island won't let us get through!' Lady Barracuda said.
'The moment we step into the forest the path is suddenly overgrown with
twining plants and brambles. Snakes hiss at us. Now snakes don't matter
to a mermaid, I have poison fangs myself. But the others would die when

they are bitten.'

'All right, all right, I'll come.' Opal snarled. 'I'll even walk in front to chase away the bad animals.'

Opal wondered what Tiger-Eye had been complaining about: the path was wide and clear. She didn't see a single bramble brush and all the serpents were darlings. They greeted her with darting little tongues and their eyes shone like drops of amber.

'You have been wearing those flowers in your hair for three days,' Tiger-Eye remarked. 'Why don't they wither?'

'The parrot gave them to me.' What would be next?

'They look bigger than yesterday and more brightly colored, too.

Take one from your hair. Please.' Opal took a flower by the stem and tugged. She got a painful jolt. 'I can't get them off. They're glued to my hair. Dried sap I guess.' 'Try tugging harder. Here! Let me tug.'

'That hurts. Stop it!'

She strode away, getting in front of them. 'If I want them to grow on my head, that is my own choice.'

'Opal, Opal,' the leaves rustled and she instantly felt calmer. This was her island. Nothing bad could happen to her here. 'Dear, dear Opal. Grow green

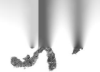

and flower. Grow green just like us. Us, us, us. We are waiting for you.'

The path opened upon a meadow filled with daisies and buttercups.

In front of her a lake shone with dark green water. It went on for miles to the north and the south.

She leaned over the granite rim. Just below the surface carp drifted past, silent as ghosts. Their scales looked as if they were made of ancient, weathered gold. One carp turned on his side and gazed at her.

His eyes were endlessly calm, wise as the mountains.

'There is the dome,' Tiger-Eye said. 'We…'

'Water!' Lady Barracuda rejoiced. 'Not a second too soon.' The mermaid sprinted across the field and dove into the lake. When she surfaced she held a wriggling carp in her mouth.

'Hey!' Opal protested. 'That's my fish!'

'Was your fish,' the mermaid corrected her and she bit the head off.

She opened her mouth shockingly wide and swallowed the whole fish without chewing.

Tiger-Eye took Opal's compass from his bag. 'What direction should we take for a nice big emerald?'

The needle promptly swung away from the dome. It pointed to a new island and seemed quite certain this time.

'Very funny.' Tiger-Eye said. 'So on the whole island there isn't a single emerald to be found? Why do we go here then?'

'I guess it was because of Opal's question,' Grubby Chipmunk said.

'I think she asked 'Where do I have to go now?' Not 'Where do we find the next emerald?'" He opened his arms and continued. 'Everybody has to go to her star isle at least once in her life. And the sooner the better.'

Opal saw the dome lying on the horizon, a beautiful green pearl no bigger than her fingernail. The soles of her feet started to itch. I have to go there, she thought. That is where I belong.

She started to run.

She felt as if she was flying. The flowering meadow fled away under her feet and she barely touched the grass. A swarm of parrots raced with her.

'Hup, Opal, hup!' they screeched. 'Opal is the champion!'

When she looked over her shoulder a quarter of an hour later the others had dwindled to dots. They ran, too but it didn't matter.

They hadn't a ghost of a chance at catching up with her.

She sprinted across a bridge that wasn't more than a slippery trunk and stopped when she reached the entrance of the dome.

This must be some kind of record, Opal thought. A three-mile run without sweating.

In the entrance a creature waited. He wore a cloak made of twigs and trailing Spanish moss.

I bet that's a god, Opal thought and at the same moment a picture surfaced. He had been described on page nineteen of her My First Book Of Gods And Demons.

'You're Aerdelick! Aerdelick the Sower.'

Aerdelick was the god in charge of all things that flowered or lifted green leaves to the sky. Sagittarius was in fact his holy isle.

At home the gardener bowed at least three times in his direction on Sagittarius before putting a spade into the ground.

'Aerdelick is my name and you must be Opal. All the animals were talking about you. Welcome on our island.' He indicated a huge ceramic flower box filled with delightful humid compost. 'Your pot is waiting for you. Take off your shoes and try it.'

'That's nice.' Opal's feet itched more than ever. Cool earth was exactly what she needed. She stepped across the rim and worked her toes deep into the earth.

Opal stretched and raised her arms high. Somehow that was the only right posture.

Aerdelick lovingly touched an ankle. 'I'll take good care of you. Water you every day. In my temple you'll dream green dreams and live for centuries and centuries.' Opal turned the palms of her hands towards the sun and closed her eyes.

She was already deep in a green dream filled with sunlight and babbling brooks when her friends finally caught up to her. Their voices drifted into her ears. She heard them but human words had already lost all meaning.

'Wood,' Tiger-Eye said. There was a catch in his voice.

'For crying out loud, her arms are covered with bark! All Opal's hair has turned green.'

Lady Barracuda climbed on the pot and put her ear against Opal's breast.

'She's still alive. I can hear her heartbeat. The change has only just begun.'

'Did it happen spontaneously?' Tiger-Eye said. 'Something in the air? Or is it a spell, someone's curse?'

'This here,' Grubby Chipmunk said and kicked against a pillar of serpentine. 'This is some kind of temple. I guess we'll find the culprit inside.'

'Does anyone carry a weapon?' Tiger-Eye asked and he opened his jackknife.

'Always.' Grubby Chipmunk pulled a concealed strangling cord from his belt.

'These are weapons.' Lady Barracuda opened her mouth wide and Tiger-Eye realized how sharp her teeth were. Not pointed, just honed like a woodworker's set of chisels. 'And these too.' Her nails lengthened into claws.

'It is a start,' Tiger-Eye said. 'Still, it seems prudent to ask Gliph Abar's council before we storm inside. He has helped us before.'

He rolled his stones, made a calculation and opened Gliph Abar's Book Of All Answers.

THERE IS A BIRD FOR EVERY PROBLEM

he read.

I hope we'll understand what he means by that before we turn into trees ourselves.

The dome was filled with a serene bottle-green glow. Brooks murmured everywhere, moisture dripped from fresh leaves. They walked along a wide avenue. At the end towered a throne made of petrified wood. The god looked down on them. His gaze was horrible, blind yet aware of the tiniest detail. Each socket was filled with a spiked chestnut.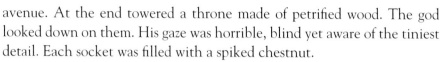

'My name is Aerdelick the Sower and somehow I don't think you've come to worship me.' His voice sounded like the rustling of leaves.

A whole forest of whispering leaves that stretched for hundreds, no, thousands of miles.

Tiger-Eye took a step forward. 'Give her back! Give me my Opal!'

His voice sounded hoarse and a bit tremulous. It almost got lost in the rustling.

'No. Why should I spoil her beautiful dreams about humid earth and sweet rising sap? Opal is mine. Just like all of the others.'

'What others? Oh.'

The tree lined avenue wasn't tree lined at all Tiger-Eye realized.

Scores of humans were planted in huge flowerpots. Their bodies had hardened into tree trunks. Leaves sprouted from their fingers.

'A tree grows best on her own island,' Aerdelick continued.

'Anywhere else she's only half as strong. Each of my trees was born under the sign of Sagittarius.' He indicated the dreaming wood. 'Each tree rustles my name. Every tree adores me and thanks me for the water, the filtered sunlight. They know that no grub will ever gnaw at their roots, that no caterpillar will hurt a single leave. Here, in my wide hall, they are safe from the woodpeckers of the world.'

'They are humans, not trees!'

'They're trees now. The moment Opal is firmly rooted, I'll re-pot her. She'll get a place of honor in my temple.'

'If I only had a axe,' Tiger-Eye muttered.

'You don't have an axe. Go away.'

Eyes appeared among the trees. Leopards with fur as green as moss and giant, pale scorpions joined them, their stingers ready to strike.

Tiger-Eye closed his knife. 'We'll leave.'

Once outside Tiger-Eye walked to the edge of the water and looked around. The meadow was strangely silent, just like the forest. Not a single bird sang. Even the trees seemed frozen. It was a deeply threatening silence. The whole island was against them, to the last blade of grass.

'You're giving up already?' Grubby Chipmunk asked.

'I'll never quit. Not if it concerns Opal. It was just that I suddenly understood what Gliph Abar meant. There is a bird for every problem.

Opal decided on her own that she wanted to become a tree. We have to teach her that being a tree isn't all that nice.' He took the case of birdcalls from his bag. 'Now I seem to remember seeing one for luring woodpeckers.'

'I don't think you'll find a single woodpecker on this island,' Grubby Chipmunk said. 'Aerdelick wouldn't allow it.'

'I'm hoping the sound is enough to wake her.' Tiger-Eye sat next to Opal and put his arm around her trunk. 'Listen, Opal.'

A loud rattle sounded from the whistle.

The trunk shook and just for a moment the bark on Opal's legs disappeared, her hair looked just a little less green.

'Once again?' Tiger-Eye asked. He turned the whistle and blew on the other side. A mocking woodpecker laugh echoed through the woods.

Opal screamed, at least as loud as the woodpecker laugh.

She tore her feet from the ground and jumped from the pot. 'Woodpeckers! Where, where?'

Tiger-Eye grabbed her hand. 'All over the place! Woodpeckers everywhere. But you'll be safe on the ship.' He threw the whistle to Grubby Chipmunk. 'Keep blowing!'

They ran through the woods while behind them sounded the hammering of bills, the laugh and chattering of at least a hundred woodpeckers.

When they pushed the ship into the sea the last trace of green had disappeared from Opal's hair.

Opal looked back. Sagittarius had shrunk to a green strip, already too distant to pick out individual trees.

'I had such a horrible dream,' she said. 'I had turned into a tree and that was kind of fun, but suddenly woodpeckers were climbing all over me. With such sharp bills...' She shuddered.

'It isn't easy to be a tree,' Tiger-Eye said. 'Think of all the beetles. The woodworms.'

'And woodpeckers.' Opal shivered.

'Yes, woodpeckers.' Tiger-Eye picked the last wilted flower from Opal's hair and threw it into the sea.

CHAPTER 5

Ysidore
disappeared
and Opal was
promptly wide
awake.

AQUARIUS

RHODONITE

COBWEB AGATE
(CRAZY LACE AGATE)

BLACK TOURMALINE

AQUARIUS
21 January to 19 February

AQUARIUS

1.

That night Ysidore swam into Opal's dream.

'You might find this kind of interesting,' the walrus said and lifted a flipper.
On the flipper quivered a drop of water that was as big as melon.

It slumped a bit, like a stranded jellyfish. 'I would have visited you before but you stayed on Aerdelick's island. Aerdelick is a rather jealous god. He allows no other god on his isle.'

Opal looked into the water. It was a kind of crystal ball, but made of water.

'It happened about a fortnight ago,' Ysidore said.

In the heart of the drop the emperor of Scorpio sat on his throne.

Intrepid Peony knelt on the carpet with his sword in front of him.

'I launched my fleet,' the emperor said. 'Steam-butterflies flap away and alert all my allies. To Virgo, Capricorn, Pisces and Libra. The moment that ship enters a harbor, ah, they'll find themselves in chains before they can drop anchor!' The emperor shifted his crown, turning it around.

'This wretched thing doesn't fit at all!'

'With your permission,' Intrepid Peony said, 'Nobody sees a difference, o mighty and most wise emperor. I don't, for sure.'

'I feel a difference and that's all that matters. Disguise yourself and search all the islands. I want my crown back! And don't be hasty. Only take their heads when you hold my crown in your own two hands.'

'Should I bring back their heads?'

'Certainly not! What would I need their heads for? Just bring me my crown.'

Ysidore disappeared and Opal was promptly wide awake.

She found Grubby Chipmunk on the forecastle where he gazed into a half full glass of wine.

'We are going to Capricorn, aren't we?'

'That is the general idea. According to your compass we should find quite a lot of emeralds there.'

'Ysidore entered my dream. Allies of the emperor are waiting for us on Capricorn. We have to choose another island.'

Grubby Chipmunk finished his glass and rose. 'I'll warn the others.'

'Gemini,' Lady Barracuda proposed. 'Let's go to Gemini.
In the City of Coral we'll be safe. My emperor will protect you.'
'Are you crazy?' Grubby Chipmunk said. 'Gemini, that is on the other side
of the world. Months of sailing. Where would we get food? Drink?'
He lifted his empty glass.
'Months, yes, but only if we're sailing. There are faster ways to travel.'
She folded her arms. 'I'm a mermaid. The water horses obey me.'
'Water horses?' Opal didn't know the word.
'Water horses is a fancy word for monstrously big waves,' Grubby Chipmunk
said. 'Thanks but no thanks.'
'I don't think we have much choice,' Lady Barracuda said. 'Look up.'
An owl flew over, a second followed, then a third. The first uttered a
mocking 'uhu!' and turned to the southeast. Lights showed all along the
horizon. Ship's lanterns twinkled; war drums throbbed. The fleet of the
emperor had found them.

2.

'There's no hurry,' Grubby Chipmunk said. 'They are still hours away.'

'Not all of them,' Lady Barracuda said. 'Turn around.'

'Ay. Yes, that is a kind of problem.'

Sails gleamed in the moonlight. Half of the ships showed the flag of the emperor; the shark-mouse. The other sails proudly bore the cockroach of the pirates.

'Water horses it is,' Grubby Chipmunk declared. 'Please.' He opened his arms and shrugged. 'Nothing wrong with drowning, eh? It has to happen sometime. Every sailor knows that!'

'Hold on to something solid,' the mermaid warned. 'It would be good if it could float, too, just in case something goes wrong.'

That didn't sound too encouraging, Opal thought. She collected three huge bottles in wicker-baskets and knotted them with a rope to her belt. She fastened a second rope to the mast.

'Everybody ready?' Lady Barracuda called. 'Here we go! She took a tsunamite stone, spat on it to activate it and raised her hands to the sky. 'Hear me, o horses of Sung-Arad! Let this ship be your chariot. Ride the waves and bring us fast as an arrow to the coasts of Gemini!'

A thud shook the hull. A second thud and the ship suddenly rose up two meters higher on the water. Two horses' heads overtopped the railing. They shook their manes and snorted spume and spindrift over the deck.

'Gallop!' Lady Barracuda suddenly held reins of golden seaweed.

When she flipped them, the horses neighed their answer.

The mainmast creaked and the ship shot away.

The 'See If I Care' rode the top of a thundering tidal wave.

A warship flashed past no more than a stones throw away. Opal saw the bowmen reach for their arrows.

'Down!' she screamed as a dozen arrows thudded into the mast.

A heartbeat later the flood wave overturned the warship.

The wind shrieked in their ears and they were still accelerating.

In front of the bow the ocean lay mirror-smooth in the moonlight. The water was so still Opal saw the reflections of the stars. The sea must have looked like this, she mused, long ago. The night Gliph Abar made the islands.

Behind Opal the sea was a horror of white-crested waves and whirlpools. Ships wheeled like leaves in a vortex, their masts broken and sails torn.

She heard the screams of sailors and the wailing of pirates.

'The emperor will have a fit!' Tiger-Eye yelled. 'But he only has himself to blame. We did return his crown.'

'Excuse me,' Grubby Chipmunk said, 'but is there a way to stop the horses?' For a salty sea dog he looked a bit too green around the nose.

'I hope so,' Lady Barracuda replied. 'This is the first time I've called them.' The main mare was colossal, a horse-wave of at least fifteen meters high. All the other horses followed her.

'What a mess,' Grubby Chipmunk complained while he tugged arrows from the mast. 'My poor ship looks like a pin-cushion.'

When Opal looked back a quarter of an hour later the fleet was lost in the distance.

'We are going rather fast.'

'Yes,' Lady Barracuda replied. 'Good going. We'll arrive by dawn's early light at the City of Coral.' She turned her head. 'Did you hear that? Someone is singing.'

The notes drifted across the water. They were fragile as cobwebs and they made Opal think of dewdrops in the morning or of swirling through the sky on a plane of silk strands. It was the most beautiful music she had ever heard.

'Can we go nearer?' she asked. 'It is so beautiful! I want to hear all their songs!'

'Well, my mares have the same idea. Look, they have already turned to the north.' Lady Barracuda slackened the reins. 'No need to lead them. They know the way better than me.'

The music filled Opal's head and pushed all her thoughts away.

The song titles popped up automatically: A whale in my web, All the bluebottles of September, Eight legs and not a single less, Enter my web and buzz, buzz, buzz!

'Aquarius must lie in that direction,' Grubby Chipmunk said. He thumbed through the Handbook For The Able Seaman. 'Look, there's Aquarius. Funny, they put a skull behind the name. I haven't the slightest idea why. According to the map there isn't a single reef to be found.'

'Read aloud,' Opal urged. 'Does it say anything about those beautiful songs?'

'Aquarius is also called the Isle of the Hunting Spiders. The spiders of Aquarius fling their nets far into the sea. They catch whales and sharks, fishing boats and sometime even whole war fleets. They lure their victims

with their irresistible songs and suck them dry. The beaches are covered with wrecked ships and gleaming white bones. At night the waves shine with a purple glow. That light is used to lure tone-deaf sea birds and fishes.' He closed the book. 'So now we know.'

'Beautiful song is right,' Opal said, 'and as for being sucked dry, they said nothing about girls or egg-snatchers from Leo. Also, people that sing so beautifully can't be all bad.'

'There is nothing wrong with being killed,' Tiger-Eye said.

'Singers have to eat, too, don't they?'

Opal had the vague impression that Tiger-Eye's reasoning was a bit flawed. It didn't matter. A new song drifted in on the night wind and she sang along at the top of her voice.

'Step into my arms,

my hairy arms.

Do you want to be

a nice little tidbit

for me?

My favorite midnight snack?'

At the horizon the mysterious purple glow strengthened. It flared as if the sea itself was burning.

'That must be the night light,' Grubby Chipmunk said, 'to lure the deaf fishes. We are sailing in the right direction.'

The sun rose and the first morning light glittered on the waves.

The water was so clear that you could look down for tens of meters.

'Land ho!' Lady Barracuda called from the crow's nest. 'I already see the first webs!'

So of course they all started to sing The Webs of Aquarius.

It was such a perfectly appropriate song.

'Webs in the wind,
webs across the roaring sea.
Aquarius, fair Aquarius
is where I wanna be!'

Grubby Chipmunk handed Opal his telescope. 'You can see the sperm whales thrashing around in the webs.'

Opal saw that he was right. And there were not only sperm whales but a

merchant ship too. Spider silk covered it from keel to mast and it dangled in a cocoon from a thick cable. The spiders themselves were almost as big as the merchant ship. Even the pups were the size of a haystack, not including their legs.

'The sun glitters so splendidly in the threads,' Lady Barracuda sighed. 'It looks like diamonds.'

The nearest cable was as thick as their mainmast. Waves broke against the anchoring point and sprayed like a fountain meters high.

'Move the ship deeper in,' Grubby Chipmunk said. 'With all this tossing about we won't stick properly to the web.'

'No problem.' Lady Barracuda gestured to the water horses.

The bow collided with a cable and stuck with a sucking plop. Three spiders rushed forward. The hairs on their back and forelegs glowed in all the colors of the rainbow and looked like living jewels.

'Come step on our web,' the first said, 'my dear, dear friends.'

'Into our arms,' the next whispered, 'our hairy arms.'

'Be our little tidbit,' the last said, 'our midnight snack.'

'Keep off!' Hasdamin the No-eyed Sea Serpent erupted from the sea next

to the ship. 'They're mine" he screamed. 'They stole my eye!
Go back! Back!'

His head darted forward and he severed a thick anchoring cable of spider silk. The whole web recoiled and shook. The spiders hooted in dismay and their song faltered for just a moment, but it was enough to break the spell.

Opal's heart missed a beat and she gasped for air. Spiders, monstrous spiders. So close she could count the hairs on their legs. Not to mention an angry sea serpent.

'Mine! Keep off!' Hasdamin hit the ship with his tail and the 'See If I Care' broke away from the web.

'Give those to me!' Opal snatched the reins from Lady Barracuda.

'To the open sea and don't let them eat us,' she commanded.

The water horses reared and sped away.

A mile off the coast Opal looked back. The web bounced.

The spiders jumped all around the sea serpent and tried to entangle him in their threads. Hasdamin wasn't a very good victim. His whole body was coated with a thick slime, just like an eel. There was no way that spider silk would stick to him.

'Hiya!' Opal cried and shook the reins. The tidal wave raised the ship higher above the sea and accelerated. The islands of Aquarius dwindled in the distance and slipped below the horizon.

CHAPTER 6

With nightfall the mighty
tidal wave had
shrunk to a mere
water hill that murmured
rather than roared.

CARNELIAN

TSUNAMITE
(BLUE HOWLITE)

PETRIFIED CORAL

GEMINI

GEMINI
22 May to 21 June

GEMINI AND REGINALD'S FIST

1.

With nightfall the mighty tidal wave had shrunk to a mere water hill that murmured rather than roared. Grubby Chipmunk searched the horizon.

'Still no trace of Hasdamin,' he reported. 'Not that I'm complaining.'

'Perhaps the spiders got him?' Opal said.

'Not a chance.'

'My horses have to rest tonight,' Lady Barracuda told them.

'They are so tired a sick jellyfish could outrun them.'

'Just what we need,' Grubby Chipmunk said, lowering his telescope. 'Another ship.'

'Of the emperor?'

'Most certainly! There's a shark-mouse on the banner.

The good news is that it's the flagship, all show and no speed. A mere lumbering beer barrel with only one mast left. The rest must have been broken by our bow wave.'

Opal took her turn at the telescope. 'Their sails are rags.

More holes than silk.'

'Good. We're still a lot faster. Even without water horses.'

Ysidore entered Opal's dream with his water ball the moment she closed her eyes. He had clearly been waiting.

'This is what is happening right now,' the walrus said, without letting the globe of MiYu wobble for a moment. 'I thought it might interest you.'

Opal peered into the water ball. Intrepid Peony stood on the forecastle, talking to the captain. The deck was a mess, festooned with ropes and torn sails, broken water barrels. The stairs to the hold were barricaded by heaps of stinking sea weed. Most of the masts had snapped, leaving only splintery stumps.

Her own ship was a dot on the horizon. While she watched, her own ship shrank almost to invisibility.

'Can we overtake them if we use all of our rowers?' Intrepid Peony asked the captain.

'Almost all of our oars are broken. The same is true for most of our rowers' arms.'

'We'll do it this way then.' He put a bird cage on the rail. Opal could see that the bars were made of silver. An expensive bird! No, wait. Silver.

Silver bars were the only way to cage magic animals. To keep ghost-birds or were-foxes.

Intrepid Peony opened the door of the cage.

'Find them,' he ordered. 'Get those miserable crown-nappers.

Dive into their dreams and tear their souls from their bodies!'

The owl turned his head all the way around, nodded and opened his wings.

They were striped like a tiger. A ghost-beast for sure.

Tear their souls out of their bodies...

I have to warn the rest! Opal thought. I must wake up.

'Ysidore?'

The god had vanished. Opal was dancing with ten other girls through a garden decorated with horrible pink paper chains. When she looked down she discovered she was wearing patent leather shoes and a green satin skirt with bows.

My sixth birthday, she thought. When I stumbled over a stuffed tiger and fell face first into my own birthday cake.

'I don't belong here!' she cried. 'I have to go back to my ship!'

'Come on, Opal,' her mother said. 'Blow out the candles. That's not so difficult, is it?'

'I don't want any candles! I want to go back!' Even her voice sounded wrong, a whine.

'Blow!' her mother ordered and her voice was the growl of a grizzly.

There is only one way to get out of this dream, Opal thought.

To stop this stupid nightmare in it's tracks. She took a deep breath and fell face first into the birthday cake. A loud giggle filled the whole room. Once again her ears grew hot.

It worked. The party was gone and she stood next to her bed.

Or it didn't work all that well. Opal saw her own head on the pillow, with the eyes closed.

I'm still not really awake but at least I'm back on the ship.

I have to find Tiger-Eye. Maybe I can enter his dreams and warn him.

The ship was at least six times bigger than before, filled with brand-new stairs and hallways. Almost all the doors were closed and from behind the doors came the most annoying giggling and snorts of laughter.

Still, it seemed to Opal that the surroundings were almost real – that she was sleepwalking through the ship.

This door then?

Tiger-Eye was snoring below an open porthole.

She hauled him upright, shaking him.

'Please wake up! You have to wake up!'

'Hu uh?'

An owl sat in the open porthole. His feathers were tiger-striped.

'Go away!' Opal screamed. 'Get out of here!'

The owl completely ignored her. He swooped down on Tiger-Eye and flew straight through his head. Opal saw the owl vanish through the porthole. In his claws he held a whole string of colorful memories.

I have to stop him. Silver. Silver is the only thing that works against a ghost-bird.

Next to a plate with a moldering blueberry muffin was a cake-fork.

Like all Grubby Chipmunk's cutlery it was made of pure sterling silver.

She threw the fork at the owl. The bird emitted a piercing cry and suddenly flew slower. He turned and fled to the south. That, at least, was something. The flagship was coming from the north.

'What, what! Where?' Tiger-Eye sat bold upright. He shuddered and his eyes sprang open. 'Where am I? Who are you? You're not my mother!'

His voice sounded horribly wrong. Just like in Opal's first dream he sounded much too young. The voice was one of a fearful toddler.

But this isn't a dream any longer, Opal thought. I'm wide awake and so is he.

'Who are you?' Tiger-Eye wailed. 'I want my mother.' His lower lip started to tremble. 'I want my moh… hother…'

They all squatted in front of Tiger-Eye. Grubby Chipmunk had found a honey-lollipop and Tiger-Eye had at least stopped crying. It was impossible to think with a toddler screaming in your ears Opal had discovered.

'The owl has stolen his soul.'

'Yes,' Grubby Chipmunk nodded. 'Your soul is made of memories and without them you're nothing and nobody. Do you think the owl fled back to the flagship?'

'I threw a fork and hurt his wing. He panicked and turned in the opposite direction.'

'An owl has to land somewhere on dry land,' Grubby Chipmunk said. 'He isn't waterproof like a gull. When he lands in the sea his feathers get soaked and he swiftly drowns. And if he's wounded he won't get far.'

He opened his Handbook on the maps.

'Here,' he finally pointed. 'This should be it. Reginald's Fist is the only island between us and Gemini. Not much more than a sea cliff.' He turned to Lady Barracuda. 'Are your water horses rested yet?'

'Rested enough for a brisk trot.'

'It is getting old,' Grubby Chipmunk said, 'but they put a skull with Reginald's fist, too. Three, no less. Most irritating and there isn't any further explanation.'

Long before they reached Reginald's Fist, they passed five buoys.

They must have been centuries old, because there were only flakes left of the once gaudy paint. Yellow and black, Opal noted, the stripes of a wasp. On MiYu that was the universal sign for danger. Yes, she was right, for the upper part of the buoy was decorated with a cast-iron skull and crossbones. On the next buoy the skull was three times as big.

'They want to make it perfectly clear,' Grubby Chipmunk said, 'that going on is kind of stupid.'

'Whatever it is that awaits us,' Lady Barracuda said, 'we don't have to be afraid. Not with me in the company.' She bared her sharp teeth, extended her claws. 'I'm the monster here.'

Lady Barracuda was a bit of a show-off sometimes, Opal thought.

'Wait a moment,' Grubby Chipmunk said. 'Here comes another buoy.'

He peered through the telescope. 'This time I can read the words.

They're made of gold and gold doesn't rust.' He frowned. 'Don't tickle?'

'They really wrote that?'

'Yes. Don't tickle.'

2.

From a distance, Reginald's Fist looked like a smudge in the sea haze.
The cliff sharpened to a stony knoll that rose on a pillar from the waves.
'Now I understand why they called it Reginald's Fist,' Grubby Chipmunk
said. 'Because it is a fist. Do you see that curved peak there? Doesn't it look
like a thumb? And those four ridges are exactly like fingers.
With a little imagination you can even make out the nails.'
'What a job, carving a complete cliff.' Opal said. 'Each finger bone is as
long as a boathouse. Hey, he's wearing a signet ring on one finger.'
'Reginald,' Lady Barracuda mused. 'Reginald. When I was no bigger than a
shrimp we had a song about Reginald. Something about the ogre Reginald
who... Something about stamping on everybody until they were as flat as
pancakes.'
'An ogre,' Opal said. 'Isn't that some kind of giant? A very bad tempered
giant? Strange that anybody would erect a statue for him. And then only
his fist. Although that would be the most important part of a hoodlum.'
'Sorry,' Lady Barracuda said. 'That's all I remember.'
Opal raised the telescope once more. An owl flapped through her field of
vision. His wings were tiger-striped and he flew rather stiff-winged.
'We've found the right island,' she said. 'I just saw the owl.'

Reginald's fist rose straight from the waves. No trace of a beach or a
sheltered bay.
'Not the easiest place to moor,' Grubby Chipmunk said. 'Look at those
waves! Five meters high and then smack, you're up against the rocks.'
'Men,' Lady Barracuda declared, 'men are such softies! Drop the anchor
and give me the mooring line. I'll knot it around his thumb. Then you can
use the rope to climb to the top.'
She jumped into the water. An incoming wave took her and threw her
halfway to the top. A normal woman would have had all her bones broken,
but mermaids are sturdy. Lady Barracuda hooked her claws into the wet
rock and scuttled upward before the next wave could wash her away.
Opal saw her throw a loop around the thumbnail. The rope tightened and
jumped from the waves. The owl swept down and circled Lady Barracuda,
screeching indignantly.
'I've found his nest!' she called a bit later.
'And Tiger-Eye's memories?'
'Better see for yourself.'

That didn't sound good, Opal thought. But first she had to get Tiger-Eye to the island. Opal hoped he didn't suffer from fear of heights.

It went extremely well.
'Yes, great!' Tiger-Eye crowed the moment he saw the rope and he hooked his leg around the line. 'I wanna climb!' He gripped the rope and scuttled up like a tree rat.
Now it's my turn, Opal thought. The rope swayed with every wave.
It tightened like a guitar string and then fell slack a moment later.
Halfway to the top Opal made the mistake of looking down.
She arrived with trembling legs and tightly closed eyes on the other side.
'My, oh my, you're looking a bit green,' Lady Barracuda gloated.
'I hope you don't have to puke.'
'Witch,' Opal muttered. 'I hope you swallow a fishhook.'
'Here's the nest!' Grubby Chipmunk called from the next finger.

The ghost-owl had made a nest between the knuckles of the index finger and the middle finger. A rather pathetic affair made of dry sea weed and fish bones.
'You said that Tiger-Eye's…' Opal started.
Lady Barracuda extended a foot. 'Here.'
All that was left from Tiger-Eye's soul was a wilted string. Here a memory gleamed of a slice of bread with three candles and a sardine. To little Tiger-Eye it must have looked like a fantastic birthday cake. A bit beyond lay a piece of Opal's face. No more than her mouth and nose, but you could still see that she smiled.
'We're too late. The owl has gobbled up all his memories.'
A tear crept down her cheek and she angrily wiped it away.
'Try that magic book of yours,' Lady Barracuda proposed.
'Your god gave you good advice before with the woodpecker whistle. Blubbering and beating your breast, well, you still can do that later.'
'All right.' She selected and threw three tiger-eyes.
It wouldn't hurt to make completely clear to Gliph Abar who she meant.
'Book, how can I get Tiger-Eye's soul back?'
She rolled the stones and calculated.

YOU CAN'T EAT ROTTEN SPROUTS EVERY DAY, SOMETIMES THERE IS ONLY STEAK AND ICE CREAM

the book told her, 'Only steak and ice cream?' She looked at the others.
'You can't always get what you want?' Grubby Chipmunk said.
'Sometimes you have to take potluck. Eat things like sea grass and jellyfish.'
'It is clearly about vile food,' Lady Barracuda said. 'Vile food is good for you?'
'Vile food is good for him,' Opal decided. 'For Tiger-Eye.
He should eat something quite foul to get his soul back.'
Grubby Chipmunk knelt down. 'Would an owl pellet do?'
'That's it! Gliph Abar's answer is clear as glass. Dragons eat rock and only the most beautiful part, the most important part, remains – the gems they lay. With owls it must work the same way. Only the most important memories are indigestible. They disgorge them as pellets.'
Opal put her fist in the air and yelled. 'We are saved!'

'No,' Tiger-Eye declared. He clenched his teeth. 'I won't eat that.
It is filthy.'
Opal had to agree with him. The pellet was a dirty green, full of mouse hair and pale rodent bones.
'A pellet is delicious! Look at me.' She opened her mouth wide and mimed taking a delighted bite
'You're not eating. Not really,' Tiger-Eye complained. 'Don't wanna eat!'
'That won't do,' Lady Barracuda sighed. She took Tiger-Eye by the throat and shook him until his teeth rattled. 'Now you eat that pellet!' she roared. 'Or I'll pulverize you!'
'Yes, yes!' Tiger-Eye screamed. He pushed the pellet into his mouth and swallowed.
'Wow,' Opal said. 'Is that the way to do it?' Her parents had never screamed at her.
'That is the only right way,' Lady Barracuda said.
'And I should know. Mermaids have up to three hundred babies with each litter and there's no time for 'I don't like fish, mamma."

Tiger-Eye looked around, still a bit dazed and spat out several small bones. Then he pointed and said 'Opal. Grubby Muskrat.'
'Almost right,' Grubby Chipmunk said. 'It is Grubby Chipmunk.'
'Lady Barracuda.'
We are getting there, Opal thought. At least he knows our names again.
'How did I get here?' Tiger-Eye scratched his chin. 'The last I remember, I

was lying in my bed with the blankets pulled up to my chin.'

'You've got everything back,' Opal said. 'Well, almost everything.
A ghost-owl tore your memory out of your head. We let you eat his pellet
and now you're back.'

'Ah. A ghost-owl ate my memory.'

'Nothing to it' Grubby Chipmunk said. 'It could've happened to anyone.'
He put his cap on. 'Maybe we should go on?'

Opal already had her hand on the mooring line when she saw a bright red
flash from the corner of her eye. The sun had emerged from the mist and
made the ring on the third finger glow. Opal had thought that the ring was
carved from sandstone and that the gem no more than a chunk of basalt.
In the sunlight the ring had an unmistakable gold glow and the signet
stone was blood-red, filled with reflections.

'Look at that!' she pointed. 'That gem must be the size of a wagon wheel!
A pity it is only a stupid ruby. If only it had been emerald!
We could have turned around right now and gone back to our island.'

'Ruby!' Tiger-Eye grasped Opal's arm. 'My parents were turned into ruby.
With that gem I can save them!' He ran to Grubby Chipmunk.

'Do you have a hammer on board? Something I can use as a stone chisel?'

'I've got both of them, dear boy. A sailor is always ready for any emergency.
Even for jewels that have to be chipped away as fast as possible, before the
villagers come running with pitchforks and cudgels.'

He went down to ship's hold and returned with a sledgehammer and a
stone chisel as long as his forearm.

'Have fun.'

Opal studied the stone ring finger. Tiger-Eye sat hammering on the gold
and somehow she didn't like that picture. Not at all. She had strong sense
of déjà vu, like it had happened before.

A final tap and the jewel came free. Tiger-Eye tensed his muscles and
heaved. The ruby didn't move a centimeter.

'Lend me a hand, Grubby Chipmunk, Lady Barracuda. I can't shift it.
I think I'm still a bit weak because of the owl.'

'Move over. For this job you need a mermaid.' Lady Barracuda gave the
stone a half turn and pried it up. 'Heave ho!' She lifted the jewel and
it hurled away like a skipping stone. The ruby had a flat underside – it
skipped three times across the water and landed lightly on the deck, where
it kept spinning for several seconds. It was probably more of Ysidore's

magic, making all heavy stones light as a feather.

Lady Barracuda folded her arm. 'See. That's the way we mermaids throw a skipping stone.'

Reginald's ring finger moved and curled.

'Oh no,' Opal groaned. 'Not again.'

Reginald's Fist hadn't been a carved cliff after all, just like Hasdamin hadn't been a golden idol. It was exactly what the name said: Reginald's fist.

3.

'Now I remember!' Lady Barracuda exclaimed. 'That song was about a horrible giant that had been turned into stone by a wizard. The wizard made a ring with a magic ruby…'

Opal knew enough fairy tales to finish the story. The moment the giant put the ring on his finger he changed into stone. Guess what happens when you take the magic ruby away?

'All the screaming ninnies of November!' Lady Barracuda cursed. 'Couldn't it go the easy way just for once?' She grabbed Opal and Tiger-Eye by the collar and jumped down. They splashed into the water a stone's throw from the boat. 'Cut the mooring rope,' she called. 'Haul up the anchor!'

Grubby Chipmunk landed with a thud on the deck and immediately cut the rope.

'How long do we have?'

'I haven't the slightest idea if giants are early risers or not.' Lady Barracuda put her fingers to her lips and whistled up her water horses.

The waves rolled in – six, seven and still no trace of a horned horse head.

'Can't say that I disagree with them,' Lady Barracuda said. She turned to Grubby Chipmunk. 'Raise the sails.'

The fist had turned into a spastically grabbing hand. It rose at least a hundred meters and then slipped down again. A mile away the sea started to boil and a mighty nose emerged. Mussels and seaweed covered it from the top to nostril. Two lips like gray whales followed.

Reginald sat up and looked sleepily around. He raised his hand and stared at his ring.

'My ruby! They have stolen my ruby!'

Lady Barracuda hung over the rail and drummed on the wooden hull. 'Listen to me! Come here, you dumb sharks!' Her shoulders slumped. 'Even my sharks act as if they suddenly can't hear me.'

Reginald searched the sea and Opal felt his gaze slipping across the ship. She felt an eerie pressure that lifted all the little hairs on the back of her neck.

'Dinja,' she prayed. 'Save us this last time. Make Reginald overlook our ship. For a giant our ship would be no more than a cockle-shell with a feather for a sail.'

Dinja didn't hear her. Or perhaps too many distressed maidens were praying to her right then.

'You…' Reginald's voice rolled from horizon to horizon, loud as a seaquake. No, even louder, because Opal saw the clouds swirl with every word.

'You are the stealers of my most precious jewel. I see my gem. Glinting and sparkling on your very deck.'

He bent down. It was quite a slow motion. They would have whole minutes before he would crush them between his fingertips.

If Dinja couldn't help, perhaps Gliph Abar would?

Opal shook the stones, threw.

'What is the answer' Tiger-Eye asked. He had the book already open on his lap.

'Number five.'

THERE IS A BIRD FOR EVERY PROBLEM

What does he mean? What bird? Even the gulls fled when Reginald stretched his arms.'

'There is only one bird left,' Opal said. 'And it's the bird that started all this.' She made a trumpet with her hands and shouted 'Owl!'

An angry screech answered her.

'Owl! Are you still hungry? No creature has a bigger soul than a giant. A head filled with memories, owl. Thousands of year's worth of memories.'

The owl let rip a hunting cry, full of pleasure and greed. He dove straight through Reginald's head, trailing a mile long streamer of memories as he flew away.

Reginald halted, raised a dripping hand and rubbed his brow. The owl kept on flying, draping half the sky with memories. They flapped in the breeze like satin mainsails, filled with scintillating colors.

'My ring… They stole my beautiful… My beautiful what?' He peered at his hand.

The owl dove again. This time the banner of memories looked more ancient, like streamers of trembling northern lights. Opal saw Reginald as a toddler, riding a blue whale. His little legs were no longer like century-old oaks.

'Who am I?' Reginald rapped with his knuckles on his temples.

'Where am I? What am I doing here?'

He suddenly sat down in the sea sending flood waves rolling away in monstrous ripples.

The owl flew a circuit through his brainpan and took Reginald's last memories.

'Baby tired,' Reginald sighed and he lay down on the sea bottom.

Only the tip of his nose still jutted above the waves. Every fourth minute a roaring fountain jetted into the sky

'And there we have the water horses and mister shark,' Lady Barracuda said. 'When nobody needs them anymore.'

Tiger-Eye sneezed three times and started coughing.

It sounded quite alarming. Each bark seemed to come from the bottom of his lungs.

'What's wrong?' Opal asked.

'Just a cold,' Tiger-Eye gasped and then his eyes turned up and his knees buckled.

Opal felt his brow. He was hot, a regular furnace, and his face was suddenly covered with purple spots.

'Tiger-Eye!'

His eyes were closed and each breath rasped. New bumps appeared, red this time. They burst and started to bleed.

'Did something bite him?' Grubby Chipmunk asked.

'Something poisonous?'

'How would I know?'

'We must set course immediately for Gemini,' Lady Barracuda said. 'Gemini has the best healers of all MiYu.'

The shark took the anchor in his mouth and the water horses put their shoulders under the hull. The ship tore across the ocean, eighty miles an hour, a hundred, two hundred, faster than any other vessel. Opal prayed it would be fast enough.

4.

Gemini rose in front of their bow: an enormous stone rectangle where only seals, albatrosses and cormorants lived. The only humans on the rocky island were a handful of hermits and egg collectors.

Everything that counted lay below the waves.

The ocean was quite shallow here. Opal saw coral gardens slip away beneath their hull, temples of white limestone with giant mussels for roofs, acres filled with waving sea anemones.

'Our capital is quite a lot bigger than the Sunken City,' Lady Barracuda boasted. 'You only see the upper quarters. The buildings go down for miles. So deep the fishes carry lanterns above their eyes and all the jellyfish shine.'

'How do we descend?' Grubby Chipmunk asked. 'Do you use submarines, like the emperor of Scorpio?'

'We have something much better than submarines. Water spiders.'

She threw a handful of gray grains into the water. 'Dried shrimp eyes. Spiders love them.'

Bubbles rose. Bubbles as big as a fist. Below each bubble dangled a hairy spider.

'With their bubbles they filter oxygen from the water. Put four, five spiders on your shoulder and they weave an air bubble around your head.'

Lady Barracuda fished several little sacks from her bag. 'But keep feeding them shrimp eyes.'

'And if we don't?' Grubby Chipmunk asked.

'They start eating your eyes.'

'Spiders.' Opal shuddered when the first spider ran up her leg and settled on her shoulder. 'They'll never be my favorite pets.'

'Hello,' the spider hoarsely whispered in her ear. 'Do you have something to gobble, like? I love eyes.'

Lady Barracuda slung the unconscious Tiger-Eye across her shoulders.

'Let's jump in. The sooner we get him to a hospital the better.'

With her head in an air bubble and her hair crawling with spiders Opal swam down into the City of Coral. It was market day. Merchants displayed their cages with colorful moray eels. Musicians blew a bubbly air on conches or drummed on poisonous puffer fish. A clown with a striped jellyfish as a hat danced past, juggling giant sea urchins.

Opal had always believed it would be silent under the sea.

She couldn't have been more wrong: Every third fish whistled or grunted and even the shrimps rattled like castanets.

'Over here,' Lady Barracuda said as she towed Tiger-Eye into a building. Above the entrance a gilded staff hung, with two coiling sea snakes.

It must be all right. On Leo the healers used the same sign.

Opal's stomach contracted when she saw Tiger-Eye. He looked so horribly limp and she didn't like the eager swarm of tiny fish that followed him.

They smell his sickness, Opal thought. That he'll soon be fish food. Suddenly she feared it was already too late. Was he still breathing? But no, he moved, his hand opened and closed.

A sneeze echoed through the hall, so loudly that all the fishes fled.

The walls of the sickroom were covered with spiders. Their bubble of air reached all the way to the ceiling though the water still sloshed around her ankles.

'This boy is the guest of the emperor!' Lady Barracuda declared.

'A most esteemed guest.'

Two healers rushed up and bent over Tiger-Eye. They prodded his arm, felt his wrist, smelt his breath. The eldest healer put a snail on Tiger-Eye's brow and started to count. On the count of thirteen, colored stripes and circles appeared on the snail's body.

'That isn't good,' the healer said.

'Yes, you can say that,' his colleague nodded. 'The only sickness I don't see is the whooping cough. I take that back: that zigzag there. Whooping cough for sure. Watch that pulsing asterisk there. Only one in a thousand…'

Opal gripped his wrist. 'What is wrong with him? Tell me! I have to know!'

'What is wrong with him? Just about everything, lady. The flu, a cold, measles and chickenpox, earaches and rubella.'

All childhood illnesses, Opal thought. You get them only once and if you survive you are home free. Your body knows what to do the next time, how to get healthy. It remembers what to do.

'He didn't get all his memories back,' she said. 'He forgot how to fight all those diseases.'

'That is a problem. There is no way we can save him from all these illnesses at once. We would have to give him so many medicines that we would poison him. I give him four days at most.' He gestured with his hands. 'Sorry. It is a pity.'

'Hogwash!' Lady Barracuda took him by his embroidered collar and lifted him. 'Save him! You are the healers.' She bared her teeth and it wasn't a nice smile. 'You have a simple choice: Heal him or die yourself.'

'Lady, mighty lady, I…'

'The emperor owes him a favor. The emperor always pays his debts.'

'Put my colleague back on the ground,' the other healer said.

'I have the solution.'

'Tell me.' She didn't put the healer down and Opal quite agreed.

What kind of worthless healers were they that they couldn't cure a common cold?

'There is only one place where you always are in the best of health,' the other healer told them in a rush. 'Your very own star isle.'

Lady Barracuda turned to Opal. 'When does Tiger-Eye have his birthday?'

'I haven't the slightest idea. I've only known him for such short time!'

Why did I never ask? What kind of worthless girlfriend doesn't even know the sign of her friend?

She looked at Tiger-Eye. 'He's unconscious, too far gone to tell. Or could you…'

The healer shook his head. 'Waking him would be fatal.'

'Names,' Grubby Chipmunk mused. 'On Leo everybody has the name of a stone, don't they? How do their parents choose? Has it anything to do with his birthday? Just a question.'

'You're a genius!' Opal cried. 'On our island they always call you after a stone that belongs to your sign. Opal belongs to Sagittarius. Tiger-Eye, yes, it's Cancer. The Lobster Isles!'

Lady Barracuda threw the healer on a stretcher. 'We go and this time I'll use the racing horses of the emperor. Cancer is pretty close, the first island to the east.'

They rode on the crest of a twenty-meter high tidal wave, a veritable mountain of spume and roaring water. Gulls flashed past and they seemed to fly backwards, falling behind the horses in a heartbeat.

'Don't you ever get the feeling that…' Opal asked, 'That you'd love to be bored? Even if only for a few hours? No assassins or ghost-owls, no petrified giants. Just sitting on the deck and gazing in the distance, thinking of nothing special?'

Grubby Chipmunk shook his head. 'No, I wouldn't like that.

Why do you think I am still a smuggler? While I walk on slippers of snow-tiger fur and drink my mint tea from golden cups? I really like a bit of excitement, arrows zapping around your ears and a howling wolf or two.'

'It would be lonely without enemies,' Lady Barracuda declared.

'Imagine that you were a wimp, an ever-smiling sissy-girl that nobody hated? Friends are nice and quite useful but mortal enemies are what you really need.'

'No doubt you're right.' Opal raised her hands. 'Forget it.

It was just me babbling.'

CHAPTER 7

The setting sun painted
the sea a deep arterial
red making it look as if
they were racing
across an ocean of
blood.

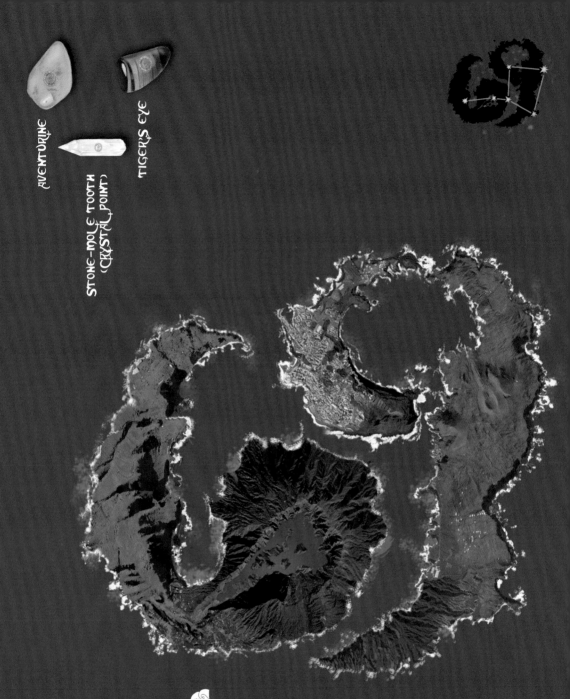

AVENTURINE

STONE-MOLE TOOTH
(CRYSTAL POINT)

TIGER'S EYE

CANCER

CANCER
22 June to 22 July

CANCER

1.

The setting sun painted the sea such a deep arterial red that it looked as if they were racing across an ocean of blood. The ruby on the deck was almost the same color.

A gust of sulfurous fume suddenly enveloped the ship, smelling of coals and hot steel. The water in front of them turned opaque, a milky white. From the haze a mountain chain materialized and Opal saw the glow of a night fire. It was a wavering column of fire, at least a hundred meters high. It drew an inky contrail across the sky.

'The smoking Isles of Cancer,' Lady Barracuda announced.

'This is where the dwarf smiths toil day and night, grubbing in the earth and hammering away. Do you smell their foundries? We'd better slow down a bit and send the horses back before they think we're an invading war fleet.' She tugged on the reins and the tidal wave sank down into the sea.

'What do you mean 'war fleet'?' Opal asked.

'Sometimes there are problems. Slight misunderstandings.

That often happens between neighboring islands.'

'Go on,' Grubby Chipmunk said.

'In fact, well, we have been at war with Cancer for the last seventy years. I quite forgot in all the hurry and the excitement.'

'Stop right... there!' The Rammstein butterfly alighted on the steering wheel and drove his claws deep into the wood. For a moment Opal hoped her grandmother had sent the butterfly, but no, this butterfly was more robust, a no-nonsense butterfly with wings of bulletproof glass and soldered joints. His head was a small, but quite functional, crossbow.

'Turn ... around,' the butterfly rasped. 'You... are not... welcome. No... body welcome... from Gemini.' With each syllable steam spurted from his body. 'Last... war... ning.'

Better not leave the talking to Lady Barracuda, Opal thought and she leaned over the hissing butterfly. 'We aren't enemies. We need your help.' She waved in the direction of Tiger-Eye who lay on a mattress, white as a sheet. 'He is from here. I mean, his sign is Cancer and he is dying.'

'Name?'

'Tiger-Eye.'

'Tiger… eye… is Cancer… stone. Honor… ary citi… zen. Wait… here.'
The butterfly scuttled up the mast, fast as a cockroach, and launched himself into the air.

A warship intercepted them half-hour later. The bow was decorated with a mechanical lobster. He lifted his claws and clicked them threateningly. Iron albatrosses circled the mast. They bore flame-throwers in their claws.

Not exactly a jolly festival boat, Opal thought.

A foghorn boomed as the ship came alongside and a dwarf jumped over. He wore the leather apron of a blacksmith and from his belt clacked an impressive collection of hammers, from a tiny nutcracker to a massive sledgehammer. On his head grew an impressive mohawk.

'They call me Ulrich Sledgehammer,' he said. 'Where is my star brother?'

'He is there,' Grubby Chipmunk pointed. 'On the mattress.'

'He doesn't look too well. Are you sure that he isn't dead?'

'Tiger-Eye is deathly ill. Only his star isle can heal him.'

'You were quite right to bring him here. The healthy smoke of our coal fires! The delightful sulfur fumes!' He nodded empathically. 'I understand.' He raised his thumb to the ship and Opal saw that his nails had been blackened by the fire and that his calluses were covered with burn holes. 'Call the ram-fishes back! It is all right.'

Two steel-gray forms surfaced next to the hull. Their function was quite clear to Opal. One of the bows ended in a drill as thick as her fist.

The drill slowly rotated, slowly but somehow hopefully.

The other bow sported a circular saw with diamond teeth.

A wooden ship didn't stand a chance against these kinds of weapons.

'I'll pilot you to the harbor of Schmutzberg,' Ulrich Sledgehammer said. 'There are several reefs with pointed poles, a number of sea mines and some shoals with ill-tempered walruses. These things can be a problem for foreigners when they arrive uninvited.'

The twin islands of Cancer hugged each other like two oversized tadpoles. The northern island was bare – mostly uninhabited. Surprisingly Schmutzberg didn't lie in a sheltered bay. They didn't even have a breakwater. The waves rolled in unhindered, straight from the ocean, and smashed against the shore. You had to anchor outside, in the deep water, and row to the quay.

'Better take that glass pail of yours along,' Ulrich said. 'We'll need it."

On the quay he loaded Tiger-Eye, mattress and all, onto a wheelbarrow and pushed him at a jog trot across the cobbles.

On each street corner gas lanterns hissed. Big, wavering flames were circled by dozens of grimy night moths.

Ulrich halted on a small square, next to a pump. Frame houses crowded the square, their roofs covered with blueberry bushes.

'Shouldn't he go to the hospital?' Opal asked.

'Of course not, healers are for wimps. A real lobster boy only needs a lungful of fresh air, a splash of water from his very own star isle.'

'I get it,' Opal said. 'It's a medicinal well.'

'You could say that.' Ulrich pumped the handle until the water gushed forth.

'Shall I lift up his head so he can take a sip?' Opal asked.

'No need.' Ulrich lifted the pail and threw the contents into Tiger-Eye's face. 'Wake up, sleepy-head!'

'Idiot!' Opal screamed. 'He's deathly ill!'

'Not any more.'

Tiger-Eye rose sputtering and sneezing. The water dripped from his hair.

'What kind of stupid prank is this?'

His face was unblemished. There wasn't a trace of the stinking sores. Not even the tiniest red spot.

Ulrich filled a small bottle. 'Take a sip every evening for a week and you're good for another hundred-and-fifty years.'

'Thanks, I guess, but where am I?' Tiger-Eye looked around, pushing wet hair out of his eyes. 'It feels very familiar here somehow. Like… like everything is exactly as it should be for the first time in my life.'

'This is your star isle,' Opal said. 'Cancer.'

'I smell smoke and coal. Hot iron. Almost a dragon smell. I've always been quite jealous of them, you know? Not their gems; their fire.

A white hot fire is the most beautiful thing in the universe and even in winter we never used more than a handful of coals.'

'We are the smiths of MiYu,' Ulrich said, 'And we don't need a dragon for our forge. Tell me, when exactly is your birthday?'

'The fifth of July. Why?'

'I knew it! I knew it! The same day as me!' The dwarf jumped in his arms, pounded Tiger-Eye's back. 'At last, my star brother! Did you know that nobody else was born on the fifth of July? On the whole island?'

'What happened with that house?' Tiger-Eye asked. 'It looks like Swiss cheese, all holes.'

'You're telling me!' Ulrich said. 'Our mayor lived there, you know. It was a brand-new city hall, not even fifty years old and the pride of Schmutzberg. Stained-glass windows, a gate of iron wood, marble pillars and now look at it…' He snorted. 'Vermin!'

Now Opal noticed the holes too. They sometimes went right through the cobblestone, like termite tunnels. So many bites had been taken from the bust of the mayor it looked like a gnawed apple core.

'Vermin,' Ulrich repeated. 'Pernicious vermin.' He raised his hammer. 'Here we are! This is your tavern. Outlanders usually stay here. It's the only house without a forge. I hope you have a good night's sleep. See you in the morning.'

'Wait a moment, brother,' Tiger-Eye said. 'Do you mine emerald here?'

'That green stuff? Worthless rubble.' He scratched his Mohawk. 'We sometimes pulverize it, to surface garden paths.'

'Could we buy some? Say sixty kilos?'

'As much as you want. Even if you need a thousand kilos. And buying? What rot! You're my star brother! I'll bring a whole wheelbarrow of the stuff in the morning.'

2.

The owner was quite tall for a dwarf. He reached almost to Opal's chin.

'Four guests and hungry too,' he complained. 'How do you plan on paying?'

'How about pearls?' Grubby Chipmunk said. 'I have a couple of the most beautiful pearls in my money bag.'

'Pearls it is. If you dissolve them in vinegar they give a delicious drink. Though not everybody thinks so.' He pushed four hammers across the counter. 'Your tools.' He nodded to the north. 'It is a rumble night, but you know that. Real mole weather.'

Opal lifted her hammer. 'Nice hammer. Quite, ah, hefty.' Don't ask any stupid questions. We are on the island of the dwarf smiths.

Of course no dwarf goes to bed without a hammer next to his pillow.

'Have a good hammering tonight,' the innkeeper said. 'The stuffed shark will be served in half an hour. For the connoisseurs I have a side dish of sea grapes.'

After dinner Opal went out into the city with Lady Barracuda.

The others claimed they were too tired. Even Tiger-Eye went straight to bed.

'I want to find some temples,' Opal said. 'At school I had an A for Ritual and Sacrifice. All journey long I haven't made a single sacrifice, only prayed for help when I was in trouble. That doesn't feel right.'

'We only pray to our emperor who is a god himself,' Lady Barracuda said, 'And he doesn't like us talking to other gods. Especially not to his brother. That keeps things simple.'

It wasn't easy finding the quarter of the gods. In Opal's city the gods had a whole district, and shrines everywhere.

She asked a dwarf.

'We don't pray to the gods,' the dwarf said. 'They come to us – asking for magic weapons and coats of invisible mail. But I think there are some temples in the slums where the lemming-herders live. Most of them are from off-island and they have some strange customs.'

Opal finally found the gods. Their quarter was no more than a single street, with the garbage dump in the back. Clearly the dwarfs didn't need the gods.

The shrine of Gliph Abar was closed, the only entrance bricked-in.

A small sign on the steps said: 'Back soon.'

Right! Opal knew when she wasn't wanted.

Three candles burned on the altar of Dinja. Opal laid a bunch of grapes on the offering bowl and fed the holy spider a few sugared bluebottles.

'Thank you, Dinja. You have been a good friend.' Opal didn't really see her as a goddess, more like an extra sister. When she was little Opal had talked to Dinja: talking nonstop and showing her all her toys, quite willing to share.

'Now for the smallest,' Opal decided.

Arre Umphard had always been an easily overlooked god.

As a deity of the servants and the rats, he kept to the darkest corners. He loved all animals, even cockroaches and earwigs.

His shrine was indeed in the darkest corner of the street, inside an old beer barrel. Opal knelt and was shocked at how gaunt the statue of the god looked. Arre Umphard had always been a god of the good life, smiling and fat. This statue had never had a single offering. It had shrunken, with a skull-face, and Opal could count his ribs. The plate in front of him was cracked and dusty.

'Poor little one,' Opal said and she emptied her pockets on his altar including the huge black pearl she'd kept apart for emergencies.

'I hope this helps a bit.'

She turned away. Gods liked their privacy and accepting an offering was the most private thing of all.

'What were you doing down there on your knees?' Lady Barracuda asked and peered into the beer barrel.

'Making a sacrifice to Arre Umphard.'

'Is he an invisible god?'

'What do you mean invisible? There is a statue there.'

'All I see are cobwebs and a dead centipede.'

Opal looked again. Lady Barracuda was right: no statue, not even the cracked plate. But also, no black pearl.

It was close to morning and Opal hadn't slept a wink. Now she understood what the innkeeper had meant with his merry: 'Have a good hammering!''

All the dwarves had a good hammering and none of them seemed inclined to lay their heads down. The whole city reverberated with the sound of pounding hammers. Sometimes, just for variety, a dwarf drummed on an empty beer barrel or tossed about a couple of manhole covers.

The sound changed. From the south came a low rumble and the flowerpots on the windowsill swayed. A volcanic eruption or an earthquake?

'Tiger-Eye!' she whispered. 'Did you hear?'

No answer. The poor boy was completely out of it, tired to the bone.

First his memory was stolen then all childhood illnesses descended at once. For dessert he was splashed in the face with ice-cold water. No wonder he slept like the dead.

'Is anybody else awake?'

'They don't hear you. You're only dreaming that you are speaking.'

Dinja sat on the windowsill. Her bow gleamed in the moonlight. The Rammstein butterfly with the crossbow head had alighted on her shoulder.

'You've come to warn us again?' Opal asked.

'Not about soldiers this time. Do you hear that rumbling?'

'Hard to miss. Volcanoes?'

'Worse than volcanoes. Maybe you noticed the dwarfs hammering all night long? It's not that they like to work at night. They'd rather sleep but moles hate the sound of hammers.'

The windowsill was empty. No trace of the goddess and it took Opal half a minute before she realized she was awake.

The flowerpots rattled again on their saucers. The pounding of the hammers became louder, panicky.

Moles hate the sound of hammers. Moles.

'Vermin,' Ulrich had called them, 'pernicious vermin,' and the city hall had been filled with holes. Not holes but tunnels. Mole tunnels.

The rumble had come a lot closer and suddenly the sound was answered by a scratching in the wall. It could have been rats but the walls had been fashioned from basalt. Stones a meter wide and certainly gnaw-proof.

'Skroink?'

Grit rained down from a hole in the wall and a pointed snout followed

by a grey head popped out. More scratching and the mole's clawed forepaws appeared. The nails sparkled with pure diamonds. The gnawing and scratching started up again, but this time from the granite floor and ceiling. Stone dust drifted down from the ceiling.

Opal jumped up, snatched the blankets away and tugged on the others' noses.

'Wake up! We have to get away! The tavern is coming down; they're eating all the walls!'

The walls of the tavern were already swaying when they ran outside. The roof went down in a roar. A roofing tile smashed near Opal's feet, showering her with sharp shards.

'Out of the way!' Dwarfs darted past Opal's legs. 'Out of the way! We are in a kind of hurry, dear lady!' The whole street was filled with running dwarfs, fleeing towards the harbor, as fast as their short legs would carry them.

On the top of the hill Opal looked back. An invisible flood wave rolled over the city. Houses toppled, sank abruptly in the ground. The only thing left was rubble and churning banks of pebbles. The sound of scratching

claws and gnawing teeth was everywhere.

'Don't stand there gawking like a cow!' Ulrich grabbed her hand and rushed her along. He used his other hand to steer a wheelbarrow filled to the brim with chunks of emerald. 'To the harbor! Stone moles tunnel straight through anything. Granite, flesh or bones, it doesn't matter to them. The only safe place is floating on the sea.'

Ulrich ran to a mooring pole, took the rope and hauled in a sloop.
The harbor was packed with boats, beer barrels, oil drums, washtubs and wooden wardrobes.
A cobblestone split at Opal's feet and a tiny grey head popped up.
With a triumphant 'Skroink!' the stone mole dove into the wheelbarrow and started to crunch emeralds. A second mole followed, a third.
A few seconds later the whole wheelbarrow crawled with vermin.
'I hate this,' Opal muttered. 'I hate this!'
'Look out!' Tiger-Eye yelled. 'Your bag!'
Just in time she slung her bag away. Shreds of leather flew while two moles fastened their rock crystal teeth onto her bag. A third mole sped after Opal's rolling compass.
'No, not my compass!'
'Get into the boat! Forget that stupid compass.' Tiger-Eye grabbed her and jumped into the water.

Opal hauled herself onto the deck of the 'See If I Care'. She was exhausted and close to tears. 'We had it all! A wheelbarrow filled with emeralds and Tiger-Eye was healthy again. Now we've even lost the compass…'
'You're alive,' Ulrich said. 'You even have all your fingers and toes.
Why cry about a couple of green pebbles? If it had been a nice clump of meteorite iron now…'
Sixty meters farther on, the quay slumped into a bank of rubble.
Not a trace was left of the city.
'This happens every fifty years,' Ulrich said. 'Wretched moles.
As soon as they get overcrowded they roll down from the hills, eat our city and drown in the sea.' He clacked his tongue. 'And the next three years nobody dares to set foot on dry land. Not all moles drown and those that are left are pretty hungry. So, I'm afraid you're stuck with me in the meantime.'

CHAPTER 8

Lady Barracuda
flipped the reins
and the water horses
surfaced with a
gurgling neigh.

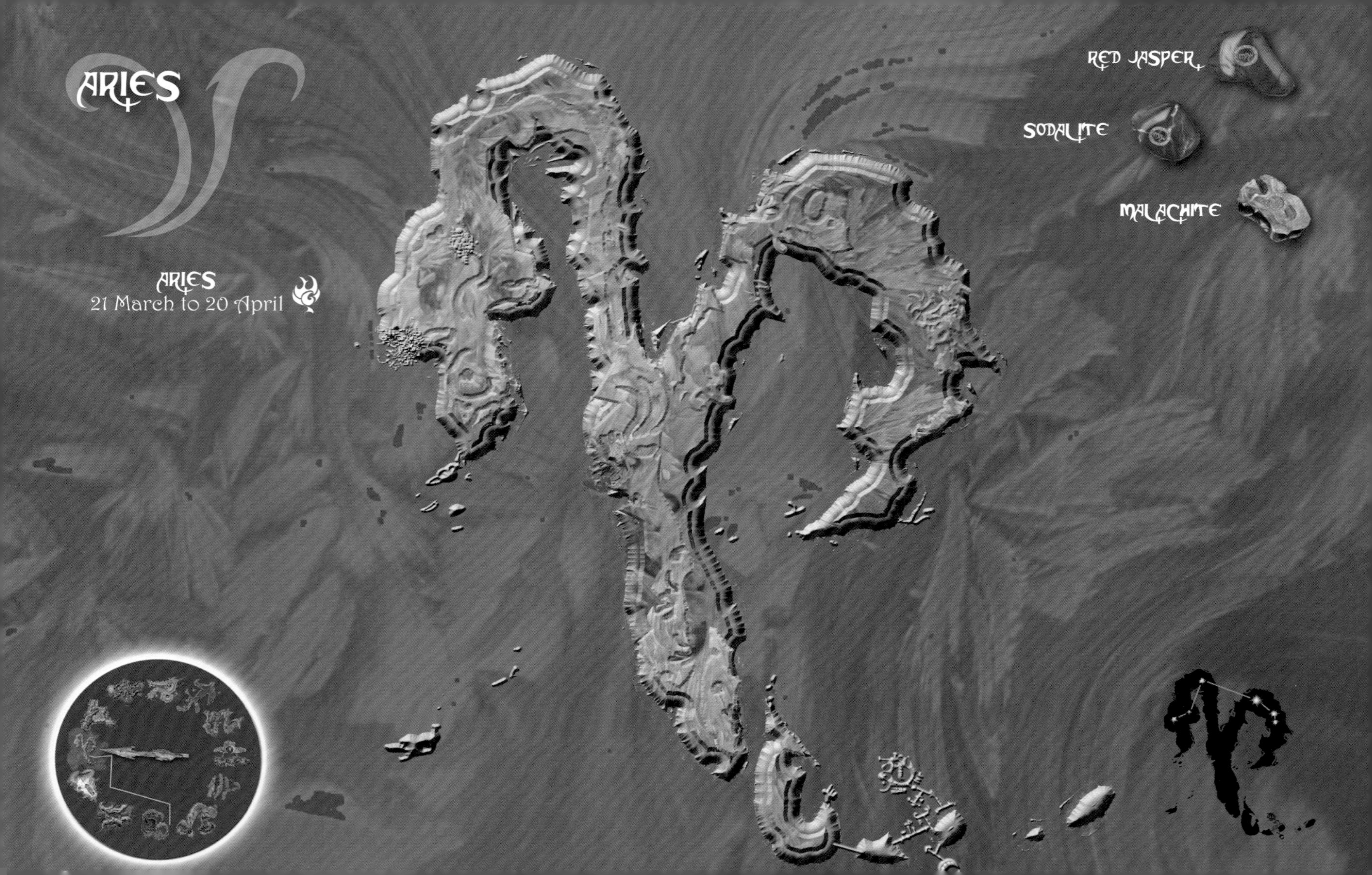

RED JASPER

SODALITE

MALACHITE

ARIES

ARIES
21 March to 20 April

ΑRIΕS

1.

Lady Barracuda flipped the reins and the water horses surfaced with a gurgling neigh. A second tug and the ship raced across the ocean on a curling tower of roaring spume.

It wasn't a moment too soon. The shore was grey with moles. The moles in front were pushed into the water and started to swim. The dwarfs hastily paddled into deeper water in their wobbling bath tubs. Until they drowned, the moles remained deadly dangerous.

'Where do we go now?' Lady Barracuda asked.

'An island with emerald,' Opal said. 'The last two stops it didn't go all that well and now we've even lost the compass.'

'No problem!' Grubby Chipmunk assured them. 'I still have the Handbook for the Able Sailor'. He leafed through the book, muttering 'emerald, emerald' all the time. 'Got it! Aries, the island of the ram. No, that's wrong. They're saying they have no emerald. Not a grain.'

'Could you read it aloud?' Tiger-Eye asked.

'Foreigners often call Aries the Isle of Emerald, but the name couldn't be more mistaken. From afar our poor island indeed appears to gleam like a green jewel. Alas, appearances are deceiving! Our island is made of dull green serpentine, or malachite of such deplorably low quality one wouldn't even want to carve it into toilet bowls. In our whole country there isn't a single grain of emerald to be found. Or any other jewel. So sorry, lords and ladies, treasure hunters and pirates, better look elsewhere.'

'This article about the islands,' Opal began. 'Was it written by people from that island?'

'Probably. Outsiders often get things wrong.'

'So they must be right about the emeralds. Well, we have still some islands left where nobody is angry with us.'

'It seems they have a bit of emerald on Taurus,' Grubby Chipmunk said after some more thumbing. 'Each morning a six meter tall emerald weathercock greets the rising sun on the palace of the deaf Khan of Taurus. His crowing sounds so loudly that the courtiers sleep with their fingers in their ears. And here: On Quakariquac villagers go heron fishing. As bait they use emerald frogs. Quakariquac lies on Pisces.' He closed the handbook. 'You're paying, Opal, so it's your decision: Taurus or Pisces?'

Something glittered in the corner of her eye. Opal turned and grandmother's butterfly alighted on a beer barrel. It held a rolled message in his front legs.

'Could you slow down a little, granddaughter?' Opal read. 'At this pace we'll never overtake you. Signed: Rithka and Pebble.' Opal shook her head. 'It must be a forgery. The moment Rithka leaves her island she turns into dust. She has to keep in contact with the earth or her magic fails. She would age instantly, all three hundred years in a heartbeat.'

'I'm sure it's Grandmother Rithka's butterfly though,' Tiger-Eye said. 'It had a scratch on the left wing and one of the rivets wasn't quite flush to the surface, but projected all of three millimeters.' People with Cancer as their sign tend to notice things like that.

'So Intrepid Peony caught her butterfly and switched the message. He's still following us. He would like it very much if we stopped.'

'You're right! Never trust a single soul. Not even your nice old grandmother.' The voice of Grandmother Rithka came from the stern.

'Grandmother, it is really you!'

Opal's grandmother had thrown a grappling hook and water-skied on the boiling water. Pebble sat on her shoulders and waved enthusiastically.

'Is that your grandmother?' Ulrich inquired. He held oversized hedge-clippers. 'Should I pull in the rope or clip it?'

'It is my grandmother. Dinja knows how she did it, but it is her.'

Grandmother slung a leg over the rail and toppled to the deck with such a thud that the mainmast swayed.

'Without my island I would die instantly,' she explained. 'So why not take a part of my island with me?'

'It was my idea!' Pebble called. 'Mine! We filled her wooden shoes with earth. That way grandmother is always standing on her native soil.'

'Ysidore told me you could use some help.' Grandmother reached inside her cloak. 'He lent me his water ball.'

The magic dewdrop was as big as a grapefruit and it rested quivering on the palm of her hand. She blew on the drop.

'Show us our enemies, wise spy-drop.'

In the center of the drop the ship of Intrepid Peony appeared.

The flagship no longer wallowed across the sea. The mainsail was still in tatters, no more than fluttering rags. Yet the ship raced across the sea. So fast it left an eight-meter high wave in its wake. Hasdamin the Sea Serpent had hooked both anchors in the corners of his mouth and towed the ship. White owls circled the mast.

Lady Barracuda leaned over the dewdrop. 'They are moving fast. But only half as fast as we are. It still is a sea snake racing against galloping horses. They haven't a ghost of a chance to overtake us.'

'Does Intrepid Peony know our position?' she asked Rithka.

'Probably not. His owls can't fly too far from the ship. All the more so now he's going so fast.'

'Taurus,' Opal said. 'Set course for Taurus. With the weathercock we can turn back Smald at one go.'

Grubby Chipmunk took the steering wheel and gave it a half turn.

'Taurus it is.'

Ulrich entered the cabin, nervously plucking at his hammers.

'I guess there is nothing to forge on this ship?'

'Starting a nice roaring fire on a ship' Grubby Chipmunk said, 'is always a bad idea. And I don't own an anvil anyway.'

'Do you have a piece of stone, then? As hard as possible. Sometimes, when we get snowed in during the winter, I carve diamonds or hammer a garden gnome from onyx.'

'We carry a piece of ruby as big as a wagon wheel in the hold,' Tiger-Eye said. 'It's yours as long as you leave us half.'

'Yes!' Ulrich rubbed his calloused hands and selected a file as long as his upper arm. 'How about I carve you a nice cuckoo clock?'

'I couldn't stand it at home anymore,' Pebble said. 'After you left mother sent all those weird suitors after me. I mean, that's stupid. I'm only eleven! It'll be years before I can wed.'

'Do they ever talk about me?' Opal asked.

'About you? Every day. Papa sent butterflies to all islands. He ordered all his captains to search for you.'

So he really cared after all, Opal thought. Such a search must cost him quite a lot of money. 'And the high priest?'

'He still hopes you'll fail. That you'll never return. You only have to whisper 'Smald' and he goes pale and starts to tremble.'

With Pebble at her side the ship suddenly felt completely different.

Tiger-Eye was the best boyfriend a girl could wish. Grubby Chipmunk hadn't betrayed anyone for several islands. Lady Barracuda had taught her spear fishing. But they weren't sisters – they didn't' giggle and gossip.

'And then Carneola put a piglet in Jaspis' bed,' Pebble hiccupped.

'With a huge bow around his neck! A blue one!'

Opal shrieked and got the giggles so badly she had to bite her pillow to stop.

'You can't do that to me!' Lady Barracuda screamed. 'We're in the middle of the ocean. Hundred of miles from any island!'

'I can. The emperor said so.'

A flying fish sat on the water barrel and bared all his needle teeth in a mocking grin. 'Our emperor owed Opal, four floors worth for the sinking of his brother's city.' The fish spread his fins. 'That debt's been paid in full by now. He needs his horses back.'

'A single day,' Lady Barracuda pleaded. 'Taurus is so close.

An hour then?'

'Tomorrow the sea fox hunt starts. Do you want our emperor to hobble across the waves on a draft horse?' He opened his wings. 'Go home!' he ordered the horses, prudently out of reach of Lady Barracuda's claws. 'The stable awaits you! Racks filled with fresh sea weed and squirming sea anemones!'

The tidal wave subsided and the horses galloped away behind the flying fish.

Opal saw the horses disappear with a sinking feeling in her stomach.

'A fine mess,' Pebble said.

'Well, we're in luck,' Grubby Chipmunk said and started to hoist the mainsail. 'There's a stiff breeze. Two weeks, three at most and we sail into the harbor of Taurus.'

'We don't have two weeks,' Grandmother said. 'I've been spying on Intrepid Peony for the last few days. The ghost-owl told him you're looking for emeralds and he can read, too. Every ship has a Handbook for the Able

Sailor. No, Taurus is just too obvious. He'll be waiting there for you.'

'Well, if you put it that way.' Grubby Chipmunk plucked at his side-whiskers. 'So Taurus is out, Pisces too.'

'Aries,' Opal said. 'According to the handbook there's not a grain of emerald to be found. Aries is the last isle he'll think of looking.'

'I can't believe my ears!' Ulrich reddened, he slapped his sledgehammer against his palm. 'Tiger-Eye don't tell me we're fleeing! We are brave lobsters! Afraid of none!'

'Well,' Tiger-Eye said. 'Intrepid Peony has a ship full of soldiers, an angry sea serpent and I don't know how many shark-mice. Do you know shark-mice? No? Shark-mice would eat stone moles for breakfast.'

'There is nothing wrong with hiding so you can lure an enemy into an ambush.' Ulrich waved with his sledgehammer. 'Go, go! Hoist that sail!'

2.

After the departure of the water horses the ship seemed impossibly slow. And it was so frustrating that as soon as the wind died the boat just stopped!

On the sixteenth day they had to go on short rations: dried seaweed and rancid shrimp crackers. The barrel with drinking water began to stink.

Even the Rammstein butterfly started to fail, his solar stone almost exhausted. A circuit of the mast was all he could manage.

On the twenty-fourth day Grubby Chipmunk lifted his head and inhaled the sea breeze. 'Guano! The gods be praised. The stink of caking gull droppings! We are close to land, Opal!' He opened his account book.

'If you could sign here? Luxury cruise to Aries for six persons and a statue.'

A few minutes later a broken twig drifted past. The leaves were still green.

'It lies just behind the horizon,' Grubby Chipmunk said. 'You see that cloud? Like a pancake with a hole in the middle? Such clouds only form around mountain tops.'

Grandmother Rithka stepped onto the deck. The dewdrop gleamed on her palm.

'Hasdamin has found our scent. They'll arrive inside of two hours.'

She offered her dewdrop. 'See for yourself.'

The flagship crossed the sea like a skimming stone jumping from wave top to wave top Hasdamin's fins whirled like a windmill. If you looked very closely you could see a minuscule Intrepid Peony standing on the bridge with one foot in front and his scimitar raised high.

'Do we reach the island before they get there?' Opal asked.

'Only just, if we're very lucky.'

Grubby Chipmunk said, unrolling a map. 'We can forget the harbor of Worthless Greenstone. I'll steer straight for the coast. The moment we run aground, you jump in and wade to the shore. The flagship draws about seven meters I estimate. They have to anchor at least half a mile from the coast

217

and lower a sloop. We can use that delay to hide.'
'Hiding won't work,' Opal said. 'Hasdamin doesn't have to anchor.
He followed our scent for hundreds of miles so what's a few miles more?'
Grubby Chipmunk shook his head. 'Hasdamin is blind and a sea serpent's
sense of smell only works at sea. We can dance a cancan in front of his
nose and he won't notice a thing.'

Their ship ran aground with a long groaning rattle. Opal could see to the
bottom: blood red coral shrimps with waving feelers swarmed around the
ship. The pebble shore was no more than thirty meters away. It shone with
a vulgar, eye-hurting green, so blinding Opal had to avert her head.
'Jump overboard!' Grubby Chipmunk roared and followed his own advice.
They waded through the tepid water to the shore, Opal carrying Smald on
her shoulder like a stockfish. Ulrich balanced the half empty water barrel
on his head.
A fearful lowing rolled across the waters – the hunting call of a sea serpent.
Opal looked back. The flagship was a gray silhouette on the horizon,
Hasdamin a wriggling line.

The moment the first pebbles crunched beneath Opal's boots Smald started
to thrash wildly. His legs kicked, he waved his single living arm.
'Stop it, you fool! If you fall you'll break in a thousand pieces!'
Emerald statues seldom listen, in that way they are even worse than
puppies. Smald gave such a tremendous heave that he spun through the
air and hit the pebbles with a crunch.
The pebbles promptly lost their luster. Meters around all green pebbles
turned into colorless rock crystal when the statue sucked all their magic
away.
Emerald, Opal thought. They lied about their isle to keep the treasure
hunters and pirates away. The whole of Aries was made of emerald.
Smald struggled to his feet. There wasn't an single spot of green to be
found on his whole body.
'You kidnapped me!' he
screamed, sounding like an
hysterical little boy. 'Then
you left me behind
with the dragon.
Opal used me like
a cudgel. In the

tavern you hung me upside down in the wardrobe!' He grabbed for his amulet. 'I hate you! Hate you all!' The pyrite dazzled in the sunlight and a yellow spark jumped right into Opal's head.

'Walk into the sea,' Smald ordered, 'and keep on walking. Yes, across the bottom of the sea until you drown.'

A walk on the bottom of the sea. Opal nodded. Smald always had such good ideas. Nice, cool water and breathing is for wimps. 'Come on, Pebble!' she called and sprinted for the flood line. 'The last one in is a sea grape!' Pebble ran right behind her. Such fun! Dancing on the bottom of the ocean with your sister.

'No, stop.' The voice sounded so self-assured that she instantly stopped in her tracks. The water already sloshed around her ankles and almost reached Ulrich's nose. 'Stay right there.'

The Rammstein butterfly stretched until he was almost two meters tall and dropped his wings of stained glass. They broke into tinkling shards. The creature had no face, only a mask of quicksilver that kept changing all the time. Gliph Abar extended his hand. 'Perhaps it would be better if you returned the amulet, Smald? Until you're a little older? Like eighty-four?'

Smald jumped back. 'It is mine!' he shrieked, gripping the amulet.

It was a stupid thing to do – the moment his fingers covered the stone, the pyrite spell was broken. Opal ran forward, kicked Smald on the shins and snatched the amulet away.

'Catch!' she called. Gliph Abar snapped the amulet from the air like a hungry gull and swallowed it.

Opal put her hands on her hips and glared up at the god. 'You gave the amulet to Smald? Are you completely crazy?'

Gliph Abar shuffled his feet. 'His father had to be taught a lesson.

The high priest stole the most precious jewels from our altars.

He ate all the cinnamon cookies you had baked for Dinja. They were much too salty and burnt besides, but

that was no excuse. So when Smald prayed to me after his father gave him a beating…'

'You gave that little pest the most dangerous amulet of MiYu and he became even worse than his father.'

'Yes, it was quite amusing. I laughed like crazy when he ordered his father to eat mud pies. Made from real mud, of course.' Gliph Abar raised his hand. 'Have a nice journey back.' He turned and strode away, faster and faster. Each step was at least five meters longer than the last.

'No, stay!' Opal sprinted after him. 'We still need your help! Intrepid…'

She stopped. The god had shrunk to a pinpoint and with his final step he vanished beyond the horizon.

'Stupid gods,' Opal said. 'They are nothing but trouble. Those meddlers! It was his entire fault! Without that amulet…'

Ulrich tugged at her elbow. 'Perhaps we should run, Opal? As fast as we can. The flagship…'

Hasdamin's hunting cry rolled across the emerald beach and echoed from the precious hills. Opal started to run.

The sea serpent followed their scent trail through the water and stopped at their ship. Hasdamin sniffed at the bowsprit, licked the mast, the dangling anchor.

'Nothing and nobody! Their ship is empty.' He smashed his tail against the ship and the 'See If I Care' tumbled through the air. Hasdamin's head darted forward and he bit the ship cleanly in two.

3.

It was evening and still unbearably hot. Without Ulrich's water barrel they would have died of thirst hours before. They hunched behind a two-meter tall emerald, on the top of a hill. Soldiers swarmed across the land like ants, prodding with their spear points into every hole, turning over every stone.

Ulrich was already on his third emerald, polishing and carving quite fanatically. He moved the point of his stone chisel and tapped with his number three hammer. The shards whistled around Opal's ears.

She didn't complain. Everybody had his own way to handle his fear. They didn't have to keep quiet anyway. The soldiers roared marching songs and beat on meter-high war drums.

'Why don't they use their owls?' Opal asked Grubby Chipmunk.

'With their eyes they would have found us in minutes.'

'Owls are blind in daylight. The moment the sun sets…'

'We don't have to wait for sunset,' Grandmother Rithka said.

'Intrepid Peony just carried a cage of shark-mice ashore. Shark-mice have no trouble following a lead on dry land and sunlight doesn't bother them.'

A horrible shrill squeaking rose the moment Intrepid Peony opened the cage. Gray blurs flashed across the pebbles. Shark-mice were swift.

'They have discovered our trail,' Grandmother Rithka said when the mice suddenly took a sharp left turn and ran to the hill. 'I hope they break their teeth on my bones.'

'Can't you use a spell?' Pebble asked.

'Like what?'

'Uh. Make them sneeze like crazy so they can't smell us?'

'Shark-mice are much too savage to put under a spell. Any incantation they will tear into pieces and devour it with hide and hair.'

The underside of the sun touched the horizon and from the mainmast streamed a curl of white smoke. No, not smoke. They were spots.

Winged spots. 'Don't bother with shark-mice. There you have the owls already.'

The mice halted in a circle around the stone. Above Opal's head wheeled a swarm of hooting owls.

Intrepid Peony climbed on Hasdamin's head and raised a speaking conch to his lips. 'Not a step farther,' his voice boomed, 'or the shark-mice bite your toes off! We're coming to you.'

Intrepid Peony slid down a tusk.

'The crown,' he growled. 'No more tricks, no clever excuses. The crown. Right now!'

'The crown?' Ulrich shook the grit from his last emerald and presented it to Intrepid Peony. 'Were you looking for this?'

Opal's held her breath. This crown was endlessly more beautiful than the first one – all sweeping curves and flashing facets. Ulrich had even carved a band of snarling shark-mice and phantom owls. It was exactly the right crown for a god-emperor.

'This isn't his crown,' Intrepid Peony said and Opal groaned with disappointment. 'Just like a glorious rose doesn't look like a wilted buttercup.' He took the crown with awestruck reverence, turned it, marveling at each new detail. 'My emperor won't have anything to complain about with this crown. Not a thing.'

'And, ummm,' Opal said. 'I mean, is it all right this way?'

'The emperor wanted his crown returned. He didn't ask for your heads. So you're free to go, though I wouldn't try to visit Scorpio for the next hundred years if I were you.' He stepped back and looked up at Hasdamin. 'They are all yours, oh mighty and wise sea serpent.'

The sea serpent uncoiled and rose to his complete length and stood swaying like a cobra.

'They stole my only eye,' he hissed. 'They tore it from it's socket and ran away giggling! Crushing and drowning them would be too merciful!'

'We just needed a sample,' Ulrich said and offered two polished emeralds. The lowering sunlight filled them with leaping flames.

'What is he talking about, Intrepid Peony?' Hasdamin asked. 'What do you see?'

'Two perfect sea serpent eyes with a heart of fire. Eyes even a dragon would hesitate to meet.'

'Eyes of fire?' Hasdamin whispered. 'Dragon eyes?'

'More savage than dragon eyes,' Ulrich promised. 'Lower your head and I'll screw them into your eye sockets.'

The sea serpent swam away, into the sunset.

'I am the best!' Hasdamin roared. 'The most savage and the most beautiful!' and everybody who looked into his flaming eyes would certainly agree.

The flagship of Intrepid Peony followed in his wake. The war drums thundered.

Tiger-Eye followed them with his gaze and his shoulders drooped.

'That's over but now what? Our ship is wrecked and we haven't a bite to eat. How we'll ever get home is a mystery.'

Opal took his hand and tugged him down next to her. 'Stop it.

I don't want to hear another word. Nobody is hunting us. No sea serpent, not a single ghost-owl, not even assassins. Ulrich told me we have water for at least four days. What more do you need?'

'You are quite right,' Tiger-Eye said and he put his arm around her shoulder.

On the other side of the bay the first lamps started to twinkle.

So, they have a city there, Opal thought. Maybe man-eating giants dwell there, with six arms and three heads. Or wise elves in crystal towers. Tomorrow we'll see. Now we can just sit and stare. She gave a sigh of contentment and leaned back against Tiger-Eye's shoulder.

4.

Pebble woke early in the morning, still tired. Above the sea the light was the color of ashes and everything seemed dreary and hopeless.

'It isn't fair,' Pebble muttered.

Grandmother Rithka opened her eyes. 'What exactly isn't fair?'

'Everything! Opal's so special. I mean, gods talk to her. She's got the most interesting boyfriend of MiYu and at first she didn't even want him! And me? I'm just her little sister. I get to tag along.'

'Adventures aren't much fun while you have them. Wait till you get really hungry and you have to eat raw sea anemones. Adventures are mostly uncomfortable, trust me.' Grandmother Rithka shook the Ysidore's huge water drop from her bag. 'I'll have a look at your future anyway. I bet there are lots of adventures in it.' She peered in the swirling depths.

'Oh my, oh my…' Rithka sounded almost like a normal grandmother, the kind that wears a flowered pinafore and says 'Oh my, oh my'. So Pebble knew Rithka was pulling her leg.

'What do you see?'

'You are so lucky! You're going to meet a mysterious stranger. He's tall and handsome, even though he has the clothes sense of blind pack horse. And there's also a dragon. With a sail no less.'

'Let me see!'

Grandmother Rithka dropped the quivering drop back in her bag.

'Sorry. The vision just ended.'

'There is no mysterious stranger. You made that up!'

'Wait and see.' Rithka yawned and closed her eyes. 'I'll try and catch some more sleep. It is still quite early.'

Pebble strode along the flood line, stamping on the biggest and most beautiful shells. Each crunch helped a bit, but she was still fuming.

Nobody takes me seriously.

She looked back. The others were no longer visible, hidden behind the hill.

'Gmeep?' Some kind of a rabbit hopped closer and sniffed her sandals.

He was quite a cuddly little fellow, with white and black stripes, long fluffy ears. His eyes were green, almost the same color as Pebbles own eyes.

'Hey, who are you then?' She kneeled, stretched her hand to scratch him behind his oversized ears.

'Look out! Zebra-hares bite!'

Pebble snatched her fingers back.

'They mostly eat dried sea weed. A finger would seem to be quite a juicy treat.' A boy sat on a big boulder, a driftwood staff in his hand.

Pebble hadn't noticed him because he wore clothes in exactly the color of the crusted rocks, a grubby green-brown. He showed his hands.

'That's why I'm always wearing these padded gloves.' He leaned forward and did a double take. 'You're not from here.'

Pebble was instantly on the defensive. If someone on Leo said 'You're not from here' it was seldom friendly. You knew he was looking for trouble. 'How do you know?'

'Your clothes. They are beautiful. The only permitted color here is vomit-green and nobody ever wears a necklace.' He touched a bead.

'What do you call this color? I only see it when the sun sets.'

Pebble pulled the necklace over her head. 'Orange. This stone is yellow, this one turquoise.'

'Everybody has to wear drab clothes and no gems at all,' he said.

'Our whole island is made of emerald. If the foreigners ever discover that, well, they would try to steal it all. Pirates and treasure hunters.'

'That doesn't make sense. You can't steal a whole island. And if so much emerald circulated it would become worthless. As cheap as diamonds or rock crystal.'

'Tell that to the Guardians! They never let anybody off the island. You have to be thirty-three at least before you're even allowed to go fishing.' He clenched his fists. 'And that is ancient, much too old to have fun.'

He is tall, Pebble thought, at least a head taller than me, and his clothes are even worse than Tiger-Eye's. Maybe Grandmother was right.

And it was easy to talk to him, not like the boys in her class. They were such babies.

'The Guardians don't like foreigners?' she asked. 'Not that I'm one.'

'Even castaways are never permitted to leave. The Guardians catch them and send them to the mines. They quarry slate and work from sunrise to midnight.' He nodded. How many people came with you?'

'Eh, five others. No, six.' Smald was somebody she would like to forget.

'And nobody is wearing green? They are all as colorful as you?'

'I'm afraid so.'

'We'll say you are traveling troupe. Circus people. In the South there is a floating city. Everybody is crazy there, they say. Some even wear blue caps. Can you do tricks?'

'Lots of them.'

He offered his hand. 'By the way, my name is Clever Mayfly.'

It could have been worse, Pebble thought. He could have been called Wriggly Earwig. 'I'm Pebble.' She waved to the ocean. 'Is there a city on the other side of the bay? We saw lamps last night.'

'Worthless Greenstone is one of the bigger towns. We can go there and steal a ship, right? Sail the seven seas. Maybe become pirates?'

Pebble hooked her in arm in his. 'I've heard of worse plans.'

They walked back to the hill, followed by at least fifty munching, meeping zebra-hares.

'Do you trust him?' Opal asked. 'That Mayfly fellow?'

'He is a hare-herder,' Tiger-Eye said. 'I talked to him. He has to gather all their dried droppings for the city gardens. He has to shear them every fortnight and knots gray carpets from their hairs. I can't think of a more boring job. He would do anything to escape this island.'

They were walking down an almost invisible path, a hare trail.

The beach was still mostly emerald. So much green, you almost forgot any other color existed. Opal yearned for a red pebble, a single yellow fish bone. Even the sky had a green tinge.

'I can juggle seven sledgehammers at the same time,' Ulrich boasted. 'And if one drops on my head, why, that is a big laugh. Anyway, I am a dwarf. That is all you need to be in a circus.'

'I have a crystal ball,' Grandmother Rithka said. Well, a ball at least. And telling the future is easy. Just talk about tall, mysterious strangers.'

'Yes,' Smald said, 'that is exactly where you all belong. In a circus. Though a zoo would be even better. If you think that I'll …'

'We can do a comic act' Lady Barracuda proposed. 'Smald and me. I whirl him around and finally throw him in a bathtub with trained electric eels. He'll whoop and dance around with his hair standing on end.'

'That would be very funny indeed,' Grubby Chipmunk said. 'Or maybe something with lobsters, too?'

Smald didn't make a peep for the rest of the walk and trailed a long way behind.

That night they saw the lights glow on the other side of the bay. It didn't appear as if they'd walked any nearer and Opal noticed for the first time that all the lights looked green.

The next morning their hare trail joined a dozen others and became a highway with big slabs of polished emerald. Several farmers joined them, sitting on big wheeled wagons pulled by giant storks.

'Almost there,' Mayfly said. He was quite excited, throwing his staff high in the air, and singing at the top of his voice.

'I'm going to steal me a ship,
ay, doddi do!
A big golden ship
With two wings
and a tail,
ay doddi day!
Sailing away

and never ever coming back.'

'Should you sing so loud?' Pebble asked. 'I mean about stealing a ship?'

'Do you see a Guardian anywhere? Anyway, nobody listens to a hare herder.'

They passed through an open gate of bleached driftwood and suddenly the city lay at their feet. It was huge, bigger than Opal's own city.

All the houses were drab: in the flowerpots grew only grey sea thistles, dusty poison ivy and prickly pears.

'Where are the ships?' Opal asked. Piers stretched into the sea but there wasn't a ship to be seen. 'Are they all out at sea, fishing?'

'You see that island there? That is where the ships live. You have to blow on a conch and they sail in and pick you up at the piers.'

'Wait,' Opal said. 'These ships are alive?'

'How could they swim otherwise? The Guardians take their eggs, put a spell on them, and when they hatch the first person they see becomes their owner' He looked at them. 'Don't the other islands use sea dragons for boats?'

'Eh, these sea dragons…' Grubby Chipmunk said. 'They never eat their passengers?'

'Only stowaways I guess. And of course any smuggler or pirate who tries to land. The spell is quite strong. No dragon has ever broken it.'

'I get it,' Lady Barracuda said. 'We steal an egg. When it hatches it is ours.'

It happened quite fast. The road was blocked by a wagon filled with man-sized baskets. A whistle shrilled and suddenly the lids flew off, rolled across the street and a dozen soldiers emerged, clutching cudgels and sticks with lassos. Opal whirled around. More soldiers.

A portly man stepped forward. 'My name is Yellow-jacket, inspector-guardian third class Yellow-jacket. Some people reported you singing a rather curious song about stealing a ship.'

Clever Mayfly blanched. His staff fell from his hand and clattered on the green-glass cobblestones. The hares huddled whimpering around his ankles, feeling his fear. 'It, we…'

Grandmother Rithka hobbled forward. It was the very first time Opal saw her hobbling or with a bowed back.

'Ah, my good boy,' she said, 'we were just rehearsing.'

'Rehearsing a crime?'

'No, no, my dear boy. It is an act. A comic act. We are performers from the south. You know, the floating city? Right.' She grabbed Smald by his collar

and effortlessly lifted him. 'He plays a foreigner who tries to steal a ship.'
'Completely filled with emeralds,' Opal added.
'That is why he is singing that song. Foreigners are so stupid!'
'I'm not…,' Smald protested but Rithka shook him till his teeth rattled and he wisely fell silent.
'But the dragon ship hits him with his tail and he falls in the water.'
'In with a school of electric eels!' Lady Barracuda added with a smile.
The guardian smiled back. 'That sounds quite amusing. Those foreigners, uh oh! When is the performance?'
'Tomorrow evening.' Rithka took his hand. 'I'm the famous Madame Rithka and I can read your future in the lines of your hand.'
She gave a whistle. 'Such a future. I see you. It is some festivity. With a medal?'
The guardian leaned forward. 'They are making me chief? Finally!'
'I also see a beautiful woman. She is kissing you.'
'My wife is quite fat and has the face of a bulldog.'
'So this isn't your wife,' Grandmother Rithka said. 'But she is still kissing you. Enthusiastically.'
'Does she have red hair? Curling red hair, like the most beautiful sunset you've ever seen?'
Rithka peered in her ball. 'Yep. Lots of curls.'
The man glowed. He didn't look like a dour guardian anymore but almost handsome. 'Dancing Moth is going to kiss me,' he whispered. 'Me.'
Grubby Chipmunk scribbled and tore a page from his account book.
'Take this. It is a free ticket for you and your date. Don't tell your wife.'
The guardian turned to the soldiers. 'Move the wagon. These people, they are famous artists' He doffed his cap. 'I'll take you to a good tavern.'
Lady Barracuda fell in step with him. 'The island of the sea dragons, I guess it is guarded?'
'Of course.'
'And the dragons only come when you call them.' She clacked her tongue.
'Ay. I'm thinking about the play. How does that beastly foreigner get to the isle? We want the play to be as realistic as possible.'
'Perhaps he steals a conch?'
'Good idea, he blows the conch and the dragon comes.'
'Yes, and eats him. That would be the funny part. The dragon comes when you sound the horn but he won't obey you. You need a secret word, a password, so that he knows you are his owner.'
'Do you have a boat?'

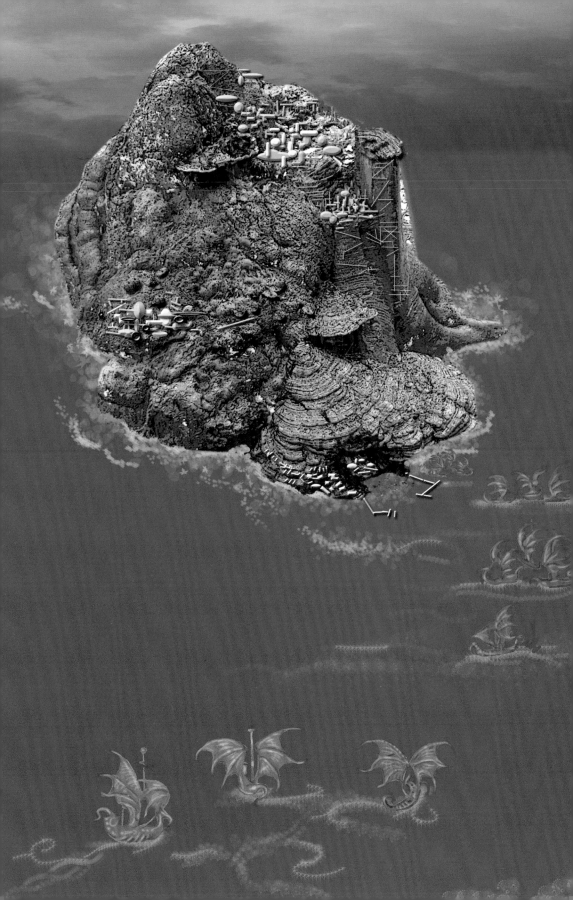

'A ship. All sailors call their boat a ship.'

'Could I borrow your horn? To make it look more real tomorrow? You'll get it back after the performance.'

'Of course!' He hooked a gilded conch from his belt. It was one of those intricate shells, with lots of hooked prongs and knobs. 'Blow three times. That is the way it works.'

Lady Barracuda shook her head when he dropped them off at the tavern and left with a jaunty wave. 'I don't get those drylanders. Why did he trust me?'

'You have curls,' Grandmother Rithka said. 'Even if they aren't red.'

They ate a very satisfactory meal of whitefish and shaved almonds.

The hares slept outside, hanging upside down from the branches of a tree.

'Sea dragons,' Opal asked Mayfly, 'do they spit fire?'

'I thought all dragons did? If their flame hits you, you'll turn into stone. But I think a dragon won't take the trouble to flame you if he's annoyed. He'll just bite your head off.' He reached inside his clothes and showed a piece of stone on a string. 'This is my secret stone, red jasper. It makes you immune to fire. Even magic fire.'

'Could you get some more?'

'It's expensive.'

'We still have a lot of pearls,' Pebble said. 'Ulrich brought them along to make soup.'

It was midnight and quite dark. There was no moon at all.

They crept to the end the pier. Tiger-Eye walked in front, rolling the big ruby. It meant the life of his parents and he never went anywhere without it.

'Everybody knows what to do?' Pebble said. Her sister had become a bit bossy Opal thought, ever since she hooked up with that Mayfly boy.

'Lady Barracuda blows the horn and we all have a piece of jasper.'

'I don't!' Smald protested.

'Well, almost all. So the dragon can't hurt us.'

'He can still bite our heads off,' Lady Barracuda said. 'Or flatten us with a flap of his wings.'

'That is why Grandmother Rithka has a spell ready. She knows…'

Three loud hoots interrupted her.

'I have just blown the conch,' Lady Barracuda declared and stuck the conch back in her curls.

A distant hoot answered her. A second hoot followed, this time quite a lot closer.

The ship slipped in, silent as a moon shadow. Two raised dragon wings acted as sails and many rows of webbed feet drove the ship.

A savage dragonhead on a supple snake neck formed the bow.

Two eyes like glowing lanterns turned to them, lighting the pier with an eerie phosphorescence.

'What do I see? Seven very edible foreigners.'

'Wrong. Six edible foreigners and a witch.' Grandmother Rithka's voice deepened and she suddenly sounded just like the guardian.

'I'm your master. Obey me.'

'You sound like my master, but I'm not quite sure. Just for this kind of situation, we have a failsafe, a password. There is one thing you have to tell me, one question to answer.'

'Don't bother with the question. The answer is 'red curls."

'Hah! You got it.' He slapped his wings together, hooting with laughter.

'So steal me! Rob that pompous beer barrel who called himself my master!'

'I'm happy you're taking it this way,' said Grandmother Rithka.

'Oh but biting your heads off would have been quite funny too.'

'Stop! Hold it right there!' Torches flared and the guardian came running along the pier, followed by a dozen soldiers.

'You fraud!' he cried. 'You can't predict the future at all! She slapped my face when I asked her to come to the circus!'

'We'd better leave,' Grandmother Rithka urged.

'We haven't loaded anything!' Ulrich protested. 'No food, no water!'

'Hold it, I said.' Opal counted nine soldiers kneeling on the pier.

They had crossbows and were only fifteen paces away. It would be impossible to miss.

'I can burn them, captain-lady,' the dragon offered. 'Turn them to stone.'

'Not fast enough,' Grandmother Rithka said. 'I hate this.
We came so close!'

Clever Mayfly walked closer to the soldiers. He raised his arms.

'You want me. Not them. I organized it all. They are just dupes. I hired them to steal a ship.'

'Not a step closer,' the guardian said. 'I'll shoot! I'll shoot!'

He sounded a bit hysterical.

Clever Mayfly snapped his fingers. 'A fox! Get him!'

The darkness suddenly was filled with swift darting movements.

The soldiers stumbled, started to scream. Torches fell hissing in the water. Every soldier was covered with zebra-hares who nipped at their heels and bit through the bowstrings and peed in their eyes.

'Now we leave,' Clever Mayfly smiled.

The sails caught the breeze, dozens of legs churned the water and the pier slipped away, swallowed by the dark.

'I spent years training them,' Clever Mayfly explained. 'What else was there to do? Also, foxes like a nice fluffy hare. But a score of nice fluffy hares that keeps kicking and biting is quite a different kettle of fish.'

He grinned. 'If any fox hears my hares he walks a big circle around them.'

'I see where you got your name,' said Grandmother Rithka.

'Talking about clever,' he said. 'How did you know that you had to use the voice of the guardian?'

'They lied to you. Newly born dragons are just like kittens. They are born blind and can't see for a week. So their owner is the first human they hear when they crawl from the egg, not the first they see. It must be the voice of their master that completes the spell.'

They passed Sea Dragon Isle in the first light of the morning.

Hundreds of dragon-ships dotted the sea and their veined sails shimmered with all colors of the rainbow. The island itself was a steep peak, abruptly rising from the water. Clever Mayfly pointed to a silver dome.

'That is where they hatch the eggs. The little ships are kept in a big swimming pool and eventually lowered to the ocean in a bucket.'

'Why on an island?' Opal asked. 'Why not just in the ocean?'

'They don't want any wild dragons escaping to the sea,' the dragon said from above. His head had twisted around. 'We are sea dragons, the moment we step on dry land we turn into stone.' He looked at Grandmother Rithka. 'Where do I go, captain-lady?'

'Go south to the next isle. We need food, we need water.'

'There is a water cask in my hold. No food though.' He nodded. 'Taurus is the next isle. Nine days sailing.'

CHAPTER 9

At the end of the fifth
day Opal saw the
sun go down.

TAURUS

ROSE QUARTZ

HAWK'S EYE

HELIOTROPE

TAURUS
21 April to 21 May

THE DESERT ISLE OF TAURUS

1.

The water cask lasted only four days, even with rationing. At the end they drank only a teaspoon every third hour.

At the end of the fifth day Opal saw the sun go down. It had been a searing hot day and her lips were cracked, her throat so horribly dry she could only croak. She saw double. It was two suns going down in a sea that seemed to burn.

'I hope you people don't die of thirst,' the dragon said. 'I wouldn't like that. The spell compels me to return to the harbor if my owner dies.'

'Everybody has his own troubles,' Opal said hoarsely. 'I wish I had yours.'

She lay down on the deck, her head on a coil of rope. She prayed for a cool breeze. A rainstorm was probably too much to ask: Aerdelick was the only rain god she knew and he most certainly wouldn't listen to her.

Not after she had refused a beautiful flowerpot in his temple.

She closed her eyes and Ysidore promptly surfaced in her dream, shaking the dream drops from his pelt.

'Are you people stupid or something?' he asked. 'Dying of thirst, when there's so much to drink?'

MiYu slowly turned on the tip of his nose, showing one splendid island after another.

'What do you mean?'

'Rithka still carries my magic dew drop in her bag. It contains ten liters at least!'

'But that is magic. It is to see the future.'

'If you don't drink it you won't have any future. And it is easy to get another drop.'

Opal's eyes flew open. 'Grandmother! Ysidore just came in my dream and…'

They were back to the teaspoons when the dragon finally reached Taurus. First they sailed through a narrow passage, guarded by grim watchtowers each topped by a shark-mouse. It opened into a natural bay, the left eye socket of the steer's skull that formed the island of Taurus.

The great city of Cock's Crow made a half circle, all around the bay.

'Ah,' Grubby Chipmunk said, 'There's the palace of the deaf Khan. You know, with the famous emerald weathercock that crows so loudly in the morning that his courtiers have to sleep with their fingers in their ears.' He sounded pleased that his Handbook had been right.

The palace was made from bottle-green glass and looked like a collection of soap bubbles. Rather big bubbles though, each with a diameter of at least fifty meters, and decorated with silver filigree Zodiac signs.
The magic cock perched on the uppermost bubble.
We are lucky we don't have to steal that cock, Opal thought. The Khan can keep his emeralds. We only need a few casks of water.
'Ship ahoy!' the harbormaster stood at the end of the pier. He caught their rope and fastened it to a bollard. 'Dragon ship, eh? First I've ever seen here. You must come from Aries.'
'Yes, we do,' she said. 'I'm Opal.' No, wrong! People from Aries are always named after insects! 'Opal beetle. That, eh, is a very little beetle with wings the color of opal. That is why I'm called Opal beetle.'
'You all look a bit dried out.' The harbormaster indicated a terrace with gaily-colored parasols. 'They sell water there. Quite cheaply too.
Only a pound of moonstone per glass.'
A pound of moonstone would buy a racing horse on Leo. Or several casks

of the very best, half a century old, wine.

'What is that in pearls or rubies? That is the only thing we have.'

'Nobody wants rubies here. Or pearls either.'

He looked at the floating dragon. 'Nice ship. Would be worth at least a couple of hundred liters. When did you steal it?'

'We didn't…'

'You don't have to be shy. We get all kinds here. Pirates, were-sharks, all looking for desert roses. The big strike.'

'What are desert roses?'

'The most precious stone of them all. They absorb all water for miles around and turn even the greenest forest into a desert. But if you plant it in a place where there is no water at all, they quickly grow into the most beautiful palaces. Every emperor or filthy rich crime lord dreams of owning a desert rose palace. They are a bit hard to find, though. They are exactly the same color as the sand.'

'Lets go to the terrace and drink a glass of water,' Grubby Chipmunk said. 'I bet I can make a deal with the waiter. I'm good at making deals.'

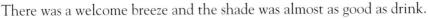
There was a welcome breeze and the shade was almost as good as drink.

A waiter walked to their table. 'Something to drink, lords and ladies? We have sparkling water with real ice cubes, chilled mango juice with a cherry and a little paper parasol.' He grinned. 'So the drink doesn't get hot. You get it?'

'We are travelers and we don't have any moonstones,' Grubby Chipmunk said. 'But we carry a lot of other interesting things.'

'I'm afraid we only accept moonstones.' His voice sounded distinctly cooler. 'Just wait a moment. The guest at table sixteen is calling me.'

He stalked away, took a new order and went inside.

The man from table sixteen rose and sat down at their table. 'I heard you're rather thirsty voyagers and don't have any moonstones right now?'

'Yes?' Opal asked hopefully.

The waiter returned and put down a tray with glasses and a three liter carafe of water.

'Drink all you want!' the man said. 'On me.' He sat down on a chair and leaned eagerly forward.

'I have a proposal. You know what desert roses are?'

'The harbor master told us.'

'I'm organizing an expedition to the interior. To gather desert roses. I'll give you all the water you can drink while you are prospecting. You get a barrel of water for every desert rose and every third rose you can keep yourself.'

'If I was you I'd jump at the chance,' the waiter said. 'You won't get any better deal.'

'We get three water barrels for every rose,' Grubby Chipmunk said.

'Two.'

'No, three. That's our last offer.'

'Done!' The man grinned such a wide smile that Opal knew they'd been taken, played for the foreign fools they were.

'Are you leading the expedition?' Opal asked.

'Do I look like I'm crazy? The searing sun, salt storms, sand spiders lurking behind trapdoors to catch prospectors! No, I own a well and that makes the whole deal possible. Water for roses and everybody is happy.'

He took a couple of contracts from his crocodile-leather briefcase and they all signed. They didn't have any choice.

'See you in the morning, at the east gate. That is where the great salt desert starts.' He sprinkled salt on the sheets to dry the ink. 'Such contracts are binding. If you break them it is the salt mines.'

Opal took her contract. Perhaps we were a bit hasty, she thought. Perhaps we should have read the contracts before signing them?

'Did you notice the waiter?' Opal asked when they walked down to the harbor.

'No shadow you mean?' Tiger-Eye said. 'Do you think he is some kind of spirit?'

'More like a god. A certain god.'

'You mean Gliph Abar is still meddling?'

An ancient sailor waved at them. He took the pipe from his mouth and blew a smoke ring. The smoke transformed into a silver ring and fell clanking onto the cobblestones and rolled into the gutter.

'My dear Opal,' he said, 'I promised you would visit all the islands of MiYu. Well, there are still a couple left.'

'I don't want to see them anymore! I only want to go home!'

'Wishes once made cannot be unwished.' He didn't have a shadow either. Of course he didn't have a shadow.

'See you on the next island!' The god was gone.

Grandmother Rithka bent and retrieved the silver smoke ring from the bone-dry gutter. 'He is getting sloppy. Never leave anything of your own when there is a witch around. This is almost as good as a fingernail or a hair.'

'You think you can put a spell on a god?' Opal asked.

'I can always try. Witches like to meddle, too. Wait a moment, he also left his pipe!' She smiled and it certainly wasn't the smile of nice old granny. Even a troll couldn't produce a better smirk.

The harbormaster waited beside their ship, fuming.

'Who said you could moor here? This is a holy pier! Reserved for the great Gliph Abar Himself!'

'Well,' Opal sighed. 'It is a bit hard to explain. Just point to where you want us to go.'

'He has a shadow,' Tiger-Eye remarked.

Opal nodded. 'And I bet he didn't when we arrived.'

'I have been reading up on Taurus and desert roses,' Grubby Chipmunk said. He tapped on the Handbook for the Able Sailor. 'Now there is a kind of stone that helps you locate roses. They call it a hawk's eye and it's striped with hundreds of lines that are changing all the time. It gives the

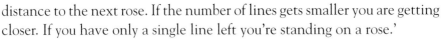

distance to the next rose. If the number of lines gets smaller you are getting closer. If you have only a single line left you're standing on a rose.'

'Sounds good,' Clever Mayfly said. 'Let's steal one.'

'They are magic stones,' Grubby Chipmunk said, 'And there are the usual problems with these types of stones. Only one in a thousand really works.'

Clever Mayfly thought a moment. 'So do we steal a thousand stones?'

'MiYu Magic Stones,' the sign on the shop said, 'You have the problems; we have the gems!'

A lady wearing a white lace headdress stood behind trays with gleaming jewels, open treasure boxes with sparkling necklaces, jade shark-mice and golden bracelets in the shape of sea serpents. The treasure boxes showed the dragon sign of Scorpio.

Opal looked at the floor: the woman threw a shadow. She relaxed.

Not a god or a goddess then.

'Can I help?'

'We are looking for a hawk's eye.'

'We just got a fresh supply from Last Well. Follow me.'

They went down a winding stair and it got almost cool. It couldn't be more than thirty degrees centigrade down there.

She opened a chest. 'Make your choice.' The chest was filled to the brim with stones, thousands of stones.

'Do they all work?'

'They are all authentic hawk's eyes. That is all we guarantee.

Magic is such a personal thing. What works for me perhaps doesn't work for you at all.' She nodded. 'Take your time. You'll find me upstairs.'

'It's too dark here to see any lines in the stones,' Opal complained.

'Does anybody have a bright idea? Grandmother?'

'The magic of a hawk's eye is subtle. If there are too many magic stones it gets lost in the background noise – like listening to the swish of a moth's wing while a hundred parrots are screaming at the top of their voices.'

'Srweek,' Stones rolled and Opal heard the patter of tiny feet.

The stones moved again and the pointed snout of a fat rat emerged.

'There are rats here!' Ulrich sounded a bit shrill and he clutched the handle of his sledgehammer. 'I hate rats! They are always nibbling at things. Just like stone moles!'

Opal stopped him saying, 'Rats are okay. They are sacred to Arre Umphard and they never, ever eat stone.'

'Skort,' the rat agreed and spat a hawk's eye on the floor. 'Arre skeurk! Umphard.'

He turned around and disappeared into the jewels.

'Did he speak?' Pebble asked. 'I thought he said…'

'Yes, Arre Umphard. The god sent him.' She took the gem. 'I think we buy this stone and only this stone. At any price. We must have something she wants – even if they have no use for rubies or pearls.'

'We'd like this stone,' Opal said. She opened her embroidered moneybag. 'Perhaps we can swap stones.'

'Only one? Well, you are in luck. You are the 73rd customer this week so you all get a free stone.'

2.

'COCK-A-DOODLE-DOO!'
Opal almost fell out of her hammock. She lay trembling beneath her covers. Such a horribly loud sound. No wonder the people slept with their fingers in their ears. That is what happens when you're ruled by a deaf king.
'COCK-A-DOODLE-DOO!'
Opal sighed. I might as well get up. I'm wide awake now.
'COCK-A-DOODLE-DOO!'
How many times would that wretched cock crow?
She heard the others stirring, yawning and cursing.

It was quite early in the morning but the day was already stifling hot. Beyond the East Gate shimmered the Great Salt Desert, hundreds of miles of crusted salt and black iron bushes covered with glass flowers.
They were the last to arrive. Half a dozen prospectors sat in the shadows, wearing wide brimmed hats and wrap-around shades made from volcanic glass.
Gesdit Yucca, the foreman, mounted his ostrich. 'Men!' he roared, 'Eh, women too! We go prospecting in the wild white lands, looking for our fortune and I bet, finding it too!' He raised a trumpet and blew.
'And off we go!' The ostrich took off at an easy lope. The foreman turned in the saddle. 'Just follow the footprints of my bird. See you in the evening, at the tavern of Last Well.'

There were stupid fools from all over MiYu, Opal discovered.
An extremely fat man from Scorpio with a tattoo of a moray on his bald head; Crazy Sunflower was probably a pirate. No, she shouldn't be prejudiced. Even perfectly nice people could have a tattoo of a moray. Crazy Sunflower probably patted little children on their heads and kept a canary at home.
The headmaster from Libra was a different case. From his belt hung several broken silver chains but not a single book of law or even the tiniest notebook. Learned Rabbit had probably narrowly escaped walking the sea bottom, Grubby Chipmunk told her. They only took your books away when you committed a truly awful crime.
There were twin sisters from Virgo, Rainbow and Snowflake.
They were as alike as peas from the same pod.

The last two were monks under a vow of silence. At least Opal thought so, because they never answered a question and never said a word, even to each other. There weren't any natives at all. People who lived on Taurus knew better than to go prospecting for desert roses.

'At least the trail is easy to follow,' Pebble said. The line of prints stretched to the horizon, grey where the feet of the ostrich had broken through the salt crust. 'Did you look at your stone?'

'I counted the lines at the last stop. Seventy-four. The same number when I counted them on the ship. I think it isn't dry enough yet for desert roses to grow.'

'Can I count them?'

'You can be our official counter' Opal said handing her the gem.

'Keep the stone.'

A minute later Pebble whooped. 'It is seventy-three, Opal. We are getting there!'

'There are still seventy-two lines to go,' Grubby Chipmunk warned.

'You were right,' Pebble said half an hour later. 'The number of lines is now up to eighty-seven.'

Everybody had his own method of looking for desert roses. Crazy Sunflower used a pair of trained scorpions that ran around, overturned stones and sniffed at pebbles.

The monks stopped every half hour and whispered the secret name of a desert rose and listened for an answer. The twins prodded the ground with iron staffs.

The sun crossed the sky like a burning snail and dropped down to a row of low hills. Nobody had found a single desert rose, not even a broken petal.

Finally they passed a wooden sign with that read:

LAST WELL

Population 19

and whichever fools walk all the way here

to look for desert roses.

There should have been vultures sitting on the sign, Opal thought, but it is too hot here for vultures.

'Good evening, brave travelers!' Gesdit Yucca stood in front of the only tavern in the village.

'The innkeeper has already prepared the evening meal. Fried desert rats, prickly pears and all the water we can drink.'

248

'Desert rats?' Smald wailed. 'Is there nothing else?'
'There are some leftovers from yesterday – meat buns made from pressed salt flies.'
'Never mind.'

'We are getting there,' Pebble said. 'Now I count sixty-four lines.'
'I see you have a stone,' Yucca said. 'Hawk's eyes seldom work. Only one in a thousand has the proper magic charge.'
'How do you look for roses then?'
'I never do. I'm the foreman. I just collect the roses you guys find.'
He stood up and looked around. 'There are things you probably don't know. If you ever see a desert rose don't run straight to it. Trapdoor spiders often use them to lure prospectors. They dig a deep hole and hide behind a trapdoor. So prod the ground carefully before you walk to your prize.'
'Are those spiders big enough to eat humans?' Clever Mayfly asked.
'Big enough to devour an ostrich and still be hungry.'

Opal was so tired, she slept the moment her head hit the pillow.
Nobody visited her dreams.

'All the crows of September!' Pebble's blistering curse woke Opal.

'It's gone!'

'What's gone?'

'Somebody stole our stone, Opal! I had hidden it in the toecap of my left boot.'

'You should have hidden it better,' Grubby Chipmunk grumbled.

'I mean, look at the people around us. They are scum. You must be pretty desperate if you go prospecting for desert roses. And the toecap or below your pillow is the first place a thief would look. I would.'

'I still have the spell I used to make the compass,' Grandmother Rithka said. 'I can modify it so it points to hawk's eyes.'

'Couldn't it…' Tiger-Eye started.

'No. Only nice jewels. A desert rose is pure black magic, as bad as pyrite.' Grandmother took a needle from her sewing set.

'I didn't know you could sew.' Opal said.

'The needles are just for a voodoo doll. Now hand me a cork and a glass of water.'

The rest of the group already sat at the big sandstone table in the dining room. Grandmother Rithka placed the glass with the drifting cork-and-needle in the middle and made a magic pass.

'Needle, needle,' she intoned. 'Show us true. Point to the hawk's eye in our midst.'

The pointer rotated and stopped. The needle clearly pointed to Learned Rabbit, the headmaster.

Pebble clenched her fists. 'You stole our gem!' She seemed ready to scratch his eyes out.

'I think you're making a mistake, young lady.' He reached in his pocket and produced five hawk's eyes. 'Your magic needle only points to hawk's eyes. These gems are mine, have been mine all the time.'

'I bet one is ours,' Pebble muttered.

The headmaster smiled. 'Prove it.' He put the jewels back.

The next day they went out into the hills. The headmaster found a desert rose. The following day he gathered two more roses and no one else had the slightest success.

'It seems I own the one stone in a thousand that works,' he smiled.

Pebble ground her teeth. If looks could have killed they would have been carving Learned Rabbit's headstone.

'I have an idea,' Clever Mayfly said. 'We wait until he has gathered a dozen desert roses and then we jump him. In the middle of the night.
Steal them all.'

'He doesn't have them anymore. He gives them to Yucca and the foreman puts them in the big safe of the tavern.' She kicked at one of his hares.
'Why are they always crowding us? They are making me stumble.
Look, they are almost climbing your legs.'

'They're afraid. I guess they can smell the trapdoor spiders.' He froze.
'Their traps! They bait their holes.' He spread his hands. 'I have an idea.'

'Oh, please. Not another one.'

'No, this would work. Spiders often put a desert rose on their trapdoor to lure humans. So they must collect them. Maybe they have hundreds of desert roses! Down there in their holes.'

'You want to go spider-hunting and steal their roses? You're crazy!'

'No, no, he's right,' Ulrich said. 'Spiders can't be any worse than stone-moles.' He slapped his sledgehammer in his open palm. 'And with a proper hammer, say a fifty-pounder, you can squash even stone-moles.'

The others joined them, attracted by Ulrich's whistle.

'What do spiders like?' he asked Grandmother Rithka. 'Except for humans
I mean? You're the witch. You know all about spiders and creepy-crawlies.'

'Flies. Even a man-eating spider would prefer flies if they weren't so small.'

Ulrich nodded. 'We'll build a better, bigger fly to lure a spider from his hole. When he jumps from out…'

'Yes?' Opal asked.

'I'll think of something.'

They had to work in secret. It was a trick that would probably only work once and a large crowd would make the spider suspicious.
Ulrich used an empty calabash for the body, wings made from lace, several pieces of barbed wire for the legs. Tiger-Eye looked through his collection of whistles and found one for the red-billed bee bird. The little bird fed on bees. He lured them from their hive by imitating a very excited bee that had just located a whole field of flowering clover.

When they left the next morning they turned to the west, looking for the

place where the hares had clung to Mayfly's legs.

'They are walking closer and closer to me,' Clever Mayfly said. 'Look, that one is trembling and her ears are hanging down.'

Ten steps farther on and the hares jumped whimpering onto his shoulders and tried to hide in his jacket.

Ulrich planted the fly in the sand, unrolled a long cord and tied it around a rock the size of an orca. 'Now we hide behind that dune.

I don't want him to see us.'

Tiger-Eye lifted his whistle and suddenly the whole desert was filled with a deep, drowsy drone. As if a giant bee, an enormous juicy bee, had landed in front of the trapdoor, buzzing with contentment.

The spider was fast - a mere blur as he landed on the fly and bit down.

It was a monster, at least the size of a wild pig and just as bristly.

'Got you,' Ulrich whispered when the spider hugged the fly with his powerful legs.

The spider gave an astonished hoot and tried to pull a leg away. It didn't work: Ulrich had coated the whole fly with extremely powerful glue.

The spider rolled through the sand, getting tangled in the rope, smearing glue all over his body.

The hares ran around the spider squeaking with glee. One produced a stream of pellets and started pelting the spider with them.

At the bottom of the hole they found a dozen desert roses. They were rich beyond all dreams of avarice – if they could smuggle them off the island.

Opal took the smallest rose to their foreman.

'Good for you' he said, 'Now, keep on looking. You have already earned three barrels of water! Who knows what tomorrow may bring?'

Opal shook her head. 'No, we are leaving this evening, walking back to the city when it is cooler. We only wanted to earn enough water to travel on.' She smiled at him. 'We are not greedy.'

After a dinner of desert rat soup and coarse brown bread that crunched between their teeth they packed their bags.

The two monks sat below the sign.

'We know that you found a lot of desert roses,' the first one said.

'We saw the spider,' the other continued.

'But don't worry.'

'We won't tell anyone.'

'Who doesn't already know.'

Opal stiffened. 'What do you mean, who doesn't already know?'

'The headmaster knows.'

'We saw him whispering with the pirate.'

'So the pirate probably knows, too.'

Opal looked down. Her own shadow stretched almost to the hills in the setting sun.

The two monks didn't throw a shadow at all.

'Thanks for telling me, I guess,' Opal turned to the others.

'We'd better hurry. Our secret is out.'

When she looked back the monks were gone, of course.

I didn't know he could disguise himself as two different people at the same time. That's a very special trick. But he always forgets his shadow.

3.

The warehouse with ship supplies was still closed when they arrived at six o'clock in the morning. They sat down on the steps and dozed.

When the door finally opened they got their three barrels of water, a hundred kilo bag of ship's biscuit and rolled them down to the harbor.

'You took your own sweet time,' the dragon said. 'It's three times now that people have tried to hijack me.' He nodded to the three limestone statues on the pier. 'Do you want to take them along? Not many people have a real pirate as a garden gnome.'

'No thanks,' Opal said. 'Just raise your anchor and leave.'

'We are rich,' Opal told the sea dragon when Taurus was no more than a thin white line on the horizon. 'We found a dozen desert roses.'

'You won't be wealthy for very long I am afraid.' He lifted a clawed flipper and pointed.

Sails dotted the horizon. When she looked through the telescope she saw the cockroach on the sails. Crazy Sunflower had been a pirate after all and he hadn't wasted any time following them.

'They waited until we had passed beyond the ten mile zone.
Taurus hasn't any authority here. They didn't want to share their spoils with the Taurans.'

Opal sighed. 'I didn't sleep all night and I am too tired to weep and scream. Any suggestions?'

'I'll sail as fast as I can. Still, they have a lot more sails than I plus ten oars for every one of my flippers.'

The sea dragon was very fast. It took the pirate fleet a whole three hours to overtake them.

The leading ship came alongside. Opal saw the headmaster and Crazy Sunflowers standing at the rail. The headmaster waved gaily.

'Would you like to know how I found you out? It was at the last dinner.
I was looking at my stone and when you passed suddenly almost all of the lines vanished. There was only a single line left, quite thick too.
I had never seen that before, even when I was almost standing on a rose.
There must be whole lot of roses, I decided, and pretty close too.'

He indicated the pirate. 'Crazy Sunflower and I, we have been working together for years. I scout around for victims and he takes them.'

'You want the roses?' Opal asked.

'Yes, all of them.'

'And then you'll let us go.'

'Of course, my dear girl.'

'He's lying,' Pebble whispered in her ear. 'He'll take our ship and kill us all.'

'I know.'

'It isn't that hard a choice,' the dragon ship said. 'Your life or the roses. The roses drink all the water, you told me. All the water for miles around. And ships need water to float.'

'I see.' Opal shook the desert roses onto the palm of her hand and threw them in front of the other ship.

'Go!' she called to the dragon ship. 'As fast as you can!'

Not even a dozen desert roses can drink the whole ocean dry, but they can try…

Suddenly an enormous whirlpool gaped in the ocean as the water was absorbed by the roses, sucked down like a super sponge. It was a monstrous maelstrom, at least a hundred meters wide and the pirate ship was caught, whirled around. Whirled around and tugged down, down to smash against the suddenly bone-dry bottom of the sea.

The dragon ship lowered his sails to the left and the right and suddenly they were wings again. He flapped them: Two, three mighty beats and the ship leapt into the sky. They drifted like a giant flying fish for half a mile before the dragon turned into a ship again and fell back into the sea.

'That was fun,' the dragon ship said. 'We should do that more often.'

Opal looked back. The ocean was choppy, filled with spume and waves. They sailed past the very edge of a monstrous whirlpool.

There wasn't a single sail to be seen.

'Do you think they drowned?' Pebble asked.

'They can't,' Grandmother Rithka said. 'But they might die of thirst. The pirates will be sitting on a piece of dry land, imprisoned by sixty-meter high walls of thundering water. The desert roses can keep drinking for years.'

CHAPTER 10

They held a
council of war
in the captain's cabin
in the stern, as far
from the dragon's
head as possible.

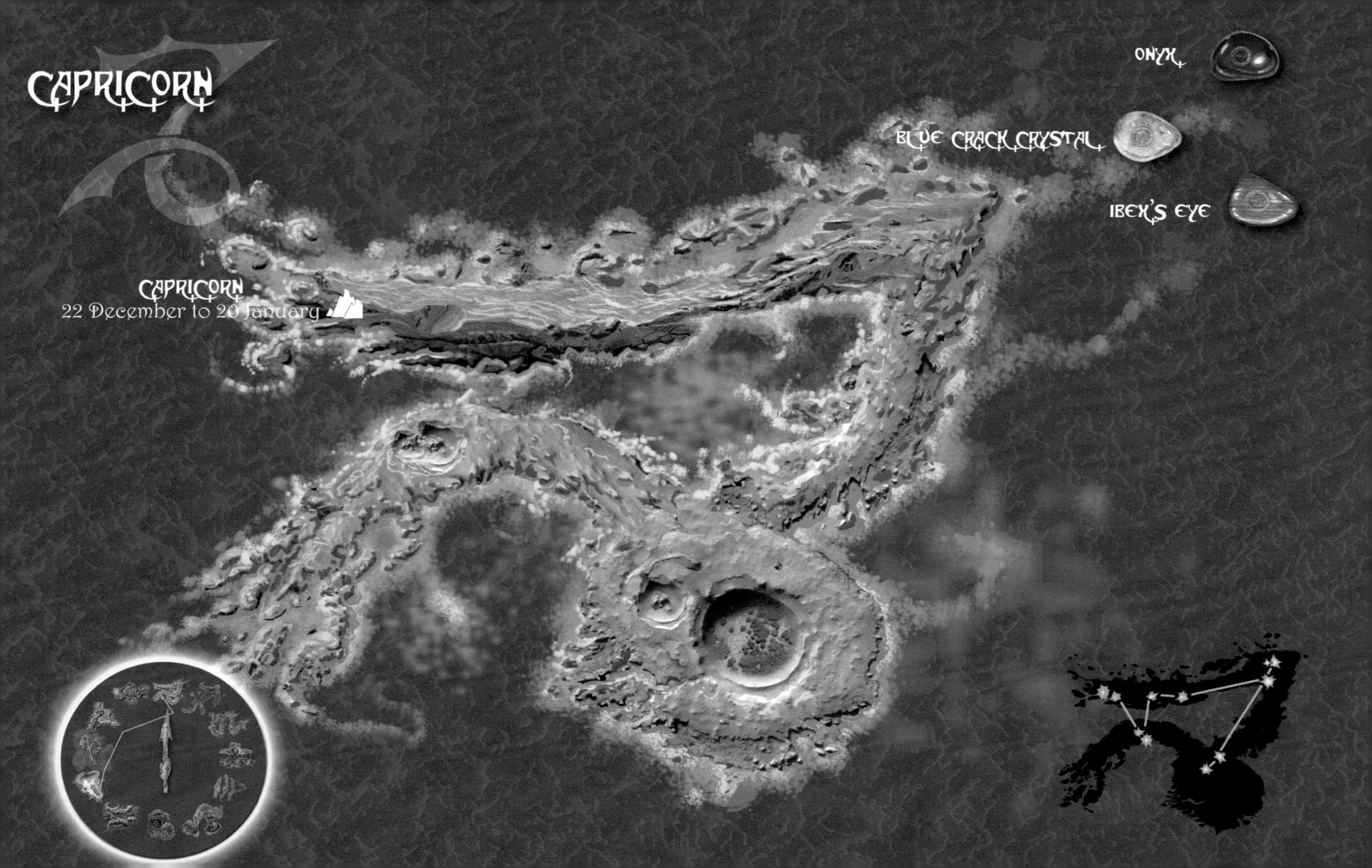

ONYX

BLUE CRACK CRYSTAL

IBEX'S EYE

CAPRICORN

CAPRICORN
22 December to 20 January

THE SECRET GARDEN OF CAPRICORN

1.

'Ah! Look at that full moon!' the dragon said. Two weeks had passed.
'I so love to see the light of the full moon as it paints the waves silver.'
'It looks very pretty,' Opal agreed.
Grandmother Rithka snorted. 'I didn't know dragons were so poetic.'
'I have a good reason to love the full moon.' His lantern-eyes glared down at her. 'Especially this full moon. Only it isn't exactly a full moon any longer. It was a full moon yesterday.'
'So?'
'Every full moon my owner has to change my password – it's part of the spell. It isn't 'red curls' anymore. Red curls is no longer valid.
Now I can do as I please!'
'You are bluffing.'
'Order me to turn right, captain-lady.'
Grandmother sighed. 'Turn to the right. I, your captain, command you to turn to the right.'
The sails shifted and the ship heeled sharply to the left.
'I could eat you,' the dragon said. 'Or turn on my back and drown you all.'
'But you won't,' Grandmother Rithka said. 'May I ask why?'
'I am still under a spell. It transformed me into a ship with cabins and a hold. My tail is a rudder and my beautiful wings became rigid masts and flapping sails. I can't even dive down to hunt sperm whales and giant squids.' His voice became a whisper, heavy with longing. 'You're a witch. If you break my spell and free me I'll carry you all straight to your home.'
Grandmother Rithka sat down on a water barrel and folded her legs.
'They put the spell on you when you were still an egg. Do you remember any of the words?'
'Every single word. A dragon never forgets.' He started to recite the spell. It was quite a long spell. He spoke for at least five minutes and some of the words sounded like gargling or the strangling scream of a loon.
Grandmother Rithka shook her head when he grunted the last syllable.
'Sorry. That's much too complicated for a humble witch. And I'm not very good at transforming. No, I need the help of a magician.'
'According to the Handbook the most powerful magician lives on

Capricorn,' Grubby Chipmunk said. 'In the Secret Garden.'

'How do they know he's the most powerful wizard?' the dragon asked suspiciously.

'Nobody's ever returned from the Secret Garden.'

'That's all right then.' His sails snapped and caught a new breeze.

'Capricorn here I come!' the dragon yelled and his tail wagged like a dog's.

They held a council of war in the captain's cabin in the stern, as far from the dragon's head as possible. Tiger-Eye kept tooting on the whistles at the same time while Ulrich sang a dwarfish drinking song at the top of his voice. It was impossible for the dragon to eavesdrop.

'What got into you?' Rithka fumed. 'The Secret Garden must be about the most dangerous place on the whole of Miyu. Nobody has ever escaped!'

'I had to say something,' Grubby Chipmunk protested. 'He was ready to dump us in the waves when you said you couldn't help him. He was that angry.'

'So you gained us some time.'

'Yes. We just row ashore at Capricorn and never go to that magic garden at all. He can't follow us on dry land. He would instantly turn into stone.'

They took a wide detour around Aries, never getting closer than a hundred miles. The dragon certainly didn't want to get caught now that he was almost free.

2.

Opal sat writing on the table in her cabin when Grandmother Rithka knocked and stepped inside without waiting for a reply.

Opal hastily covered the strip of parchment with her hand.

'Opal,' Rithka said, 'you are a bully.'

'What do you mean?' But her face grew hot and she was quite sure her grandmother could see her blush. 'I'm no bully. Smald's a bully.

He almost made me jump from a cliff!'

'Do you really think I wouldn't notice you and Pebble using magic? Especially black magic? Smald hasn't slept for three days.

The moment he closes his eyes he wakes up screaming.'

She took a blue stone with the drilled hole and rolled it between her fingers. 'A wishing stone. You write a message, roll it and push it into a hole. If you put it under your pillow you'll dream about whatever is written.' She lifted Opal's hand and took the dream paper.

'Spiders and centipedes. They creep all over you.'

'It isn't real,' Opal said. 'Just dreams. And nobody likes Smald.

He deserves it.'

'Who thought of it first? You or Pebble?'

'The dragon. He hates Smald too.'

'Don't you see what he's doing? He wants us to hate each other and trust no one. That's the only way he can control us.'

'I'm sorry,' Opal said. 'It was stupid. It was mean.'

'Smald is difficult to like, I know, but I don't want any granddaughter of mine acting like Smald. Not even a little bit.'

'I'm sorry,' Opal whispered. I acted just like Smald. A bully.

She felt filthy. Soiled.

'I'll go to your sister now.'

3.

'Capricorn,' Grandmother Rithka said. 'It means 'rock-goat' in the ancient language that only gods and witches remember.'

Capricorn was beautiful in the morning light. The majestic peaks seemed to float like clouds made of stone. With the telescope Opal could see rock-goats jumping across ravines, traversing steep cliffs along paths that were only about an inch wide.

Capricorn seemed quite welcoming. From the mountains blew a cool, bracing breeze and Opal smelled flowers and pine needles.

Two flying whales glided past and slid down to an unseen port. A good island to jump ship. We could even ask a whale to fly us home.

'So this is what we'll do,' the dragon rumbled. 'Opal and Clever Mayfly go ashore. Also Lady Barracuda, to kill any monsters you meet, and… yes, Grandmother Rithka to talk to the wizard. The rest stay here, on the ship. That way I am sure you'll return.'

'You heard us,' Opal said with a sinking feeling.

'We sea dragons, we are like sharks. We hear with our whole body. Tiny little ears all over.'

The dragon ship halted alongside a stone quay. At the end a marble staircase wended upwards to a distant pass. There was no sense of menace, only calm sunlight and the slap of waves. 'Jump ashore,' the dragon said. 'I'll wait for a month. If you aren't back by then I'll know you have betrayed me. I'll sail to the middle of the ocean and dump the others.'

'We understand' Lady Barracuda said. 'No need to elaborate.'

Ulrich handed her his hammer. 'You can use my sledgehammer. It cracks the hardest skulls.'

'Thank you.' She gave him a dazzling smile. 'I would like that.'

Lady Barracuda and Ulrich had a kind of understanding though Opal had never seen them kiss. Perhaps it was enough to know that you both liked wrestling bears and sea leopards? To sit together around Ulrich's whetstone, sharpening your blades and battle axes? Tiger-Eye slipped a stone into Opal's hand. 'A remembrance of me.'

'As if I'd ever forget you! You are my boyfriend.' She opened her hand. It was a wishing stone. Just like the one she and Pebble had used against Smald. 'What did you write?'

'If you know it stops working.'

They walked through a triumphal arch, decorated with flowers, a bow-and-arrow and several masks. In the center stood the following message:

WELCOME, O GODS,
TO MY HUMBLE GARDEN!!!

'Never trust anybody who uses the word 'humble',' Grandmother said.
'They seldom are. And he used three exclamation points.
That is even worse.'

It was a magic staircase. The moment they mounted the first step it started moving with a deep rumble.
'Moving stairs,' Grandmother snorted. 'How lazy can you get?
Use moving stairs to climb to your home and pretty soon your legs drop off.' She clearly disliked the magician already, before she had even met him.
They moved quite swiftly, about twice the pace of a racing horse running all out. The ship shrank to a golden sliver; the quay became a thin white thread. Soon the walls of the pass closed in and they lost sight of the harbor.
An hour passed and the pass widened, becoming a green valley.
The rumbling ended and the stair stopped moving.
'Looks good,' Lady Barracuda said. 'Reminds me of home.

Although it should be under a mile of water…'

'I told you we couldn't trust him,' Grandmother said. 'Look back at the pass. There isn't a pass anymore.'

Mighty cliffs rose, at least two miles high. There wasn't a sign of the mountain pass, not even a crack.

'I guess the wizard wants us to stay,' Opal said.

It was the most beautiful garden Opal had ever seen. It made her garden on Scorpio look like a garbage dump. Even Sagittarius hadn't looked half as green, nor sported such splendid flowers.

A path of shining gemstones wound past fountains made of porcelain. Wind gongs chimed.

'Friends!' A man walked down the path, followed by a little dog.

'Welcome, welcome. Thrice welcome in the Secret Garden of my master! You are gods?'

'Not exactly,' Grandmother said, 'Actually, we came to see the wizard. But we know several gods. Some are quite good friends of ours.'

'You can't see the wizard. So sorry, but he is sleeping right now.'

'When he wakes then?'

'You'll have to go to the palace. Ask for the chamberlain. He is in charge of the wizardly bedchambers.'

The little dog walked up to Opal and sniffed at her boots. Opal kneeled to scratch him behind his ears. 'Hey, little fellow.'

'Hey yourself,' the dog replied.
'You can talk!'
'I'm a magic dog. And I'm not a fellow. I'm a female dog.'
'Do you know the way to the palace? We have to see the wizard. It is rather urgent.'
'The new ones always want to see the wizard. And it's always urgent.
A dragon is burning their farms. The trolls came down from the mountains and ate their king. What is urgent about that? But I'll show you.'

It felt good to stroll through the park. It was so peaceful.
No monsters lurking anywhere, not even a platoon of soldiers trying to catch you. I could string my hammock between those two trees and just doze.
'Almost there,' the dog said. 'Just a moment.'
She went to the statue of a man with a goatee and a swirling mantle.
The dog lifted a leg and peed on his boots.
'I really like doing that. He always wanted his boots shined perfectly.
They had to be like mirrors.'
'Who is it?'
'The big wizard himself, of course.' She ran ahead. 'There's his palace.'
It rose from the greensward and Opal didn't like it. It was just too big, overdecorated. It looked like the wedding cake of a crime lord. Vulgar was the right word.
'He made it to impress the gods,' the dog said. 'It didn't.
Dinja couldn't stop laughing when she saw the palace.'
'Dinja visited the wizard?'
'A long time ago. And she didn't exactly visit. She was summoned, ordered to his garden. He is so powerful that he can command the very gods.'
He ordered Dinja around. She hadn't met him but she already hated this wizard. He is a bully too. Nothing but a bully.

The gates of the palace automatically opened at their approach.
More magic, Opal thought. It only annoyed her. And look at those gates: pure gold and decorated with about a thousand dragons and running nymphs.
'He is a kind of show-off,' the dog said. 'He started out a dirt-poor cobbler who did tricks at children's parties. Later he learned real magic.'
Trumpets sounded and a man appeared in a puff of smoke.

'I'm the chamberlain of the wizardly bedchambers.' He sounded rather self-important. Opal had met his kind before. Uppity servants.

'My name is dame Opal tsal Everetto dun Maginoisse,' she said in a ringing voice. 'I want to see your master. I must see him right now!'

'He is sleeping, taking his afternoon nap. But my master will probably wake soon. I'm sure he would be delighted to meet such a high-born lady.'

'We'll wait.' You had to be firm with servants. 'Bring us something to drink.'

'Very good, my lady.'

He returned a few minutes later with a tray floating in front of him.

More tricks, Opal thought. Or perhaps magic. It didn't matter.

'I have tea,' the chamberlain said. 'And these glasses are rainberry wine.'

'Thank you.' Opal didn't see him leave.

The chairs were quite soft, very comfortable. Opal took a cup of tea and nibbled one of the cakes. I'll just close my eyes for a moment, doze a bit. The chamberlain will warn us when the magician is ready to receive us.

When Opal awoke the room was filled with the wine-red light of the setting sun. She yawned and stretched. The others awoke at the same time.

'What are we doing here?' Clever Mayfly asked.

Opal looked around, noticed the tray. 'Drinking tea I guess.'

Lady Barracuda felt the pot. 'It's cold now.'

Grandmother Rithka nodded. 'And all the cakes are gone.

Let's go outside.'

A little dog waited for her outside. Opal didn't remember owning a dog, but that was all right. A lot of things were kind of vague.

'Did you see him?' the dog asked.

'See who?'

'It always happens like this,' the dog said. 'They never remember.'

She sounded a little sad.

Clever Mayfly fell in step with her. 'We were together I seem to remember. Are you my girlfriend?'

'I guess so.'

Opal showered in fountains and chased Clever Mayfly's zebra-hares with her little dog, though they never caught one. There was an old woman that seemed to know her and another one who was always messing around in the swimming pool. The trees were heavy with fruit and several fountains spurted wine and sparkling raspberry juice. Every night there was a barbecue.

She kissed several times with her boyfriend but it somehow didn't work. Kissing should be more fun, more exciting. She still liked Clever Mayfly but as a boyfriend he was a bust.

Life was good, life was like one endless summer afternoon.

Of course it had always been like that because she had always lived here.

Three more weeks passed though Opal didn't keep count of the days. Why should she?

On the twentieth day she found a little stone on the bottom of her bag. It was blue, more like a bead than a stone. A little strip of paper had been pushed through the hole.

A wishing stone, she thought. How did it get here? Who would give me a wishing stone? Clever Mayfly surely never would. Stuffing a live frog in her bag was more his style.

She remembered how it worked. You had to put the stone beneath your pillow and it would heal you, give you pleasant dreams.

You shouldn't unroll the message. If you did, it immediately stopped working. After the barbecue she put the stone beneath her pillow and closed her eyes.

Opal awoke with a keen sense of loss. She felt so badly she almost cried. She had dreamed about a boy with a cape made of sparkling gems.

No doubt a prince and he had been her boyfriend – her real boyfriend.

I have been cheated, she thought. I shouldn't be here. Not without him.

The dream had been quite clear and there had been others in it. A captain, a dwarf, a girl who felt so familiar, so safe, that she must have been her sister.

There was only one place she could find an answer. With trembling fingers she took the wishing stone and unrolled the strip of paper.

It was quite a short message. There wasn't all that much room on the small strip of paper.

Please dream of me, Opal.
I love you

Tiger-Eye.

Tiger-Eye! And her own name was Opal. A flood of memories filled her head. The woman in the swimming pool was Lady Barracuda.

The old woman was her own Grandmother Rithka and a witch, too.

We went to see the wizard... There was a man, the chamberlain.

He must have given us a potion to make us forget our very names.

Opal went to the swimming pool.

'You are Lady Barracuda,' she said. 'You are a mermaid and you wrestle giant squids for fun.'

Opal saw the light of memory return to Lady Barracuda's eyes.

They lost all their drowsy softness. Names are powerful.

'He dared!' Lady Barracuda hissed. 'Turning me into a tame goldfish!'

When she named her grandmother, Rithka only nodded. 'That was why I felt so listless. Witches aren't made for holidays.'

'What do we do with him?' Lady Barracuda asked. 'Tear him to pieces and feed him to Clever Mayfly's hares?'

'Maybe later. First we have to see the wizard.' She stiffened. 'Hecate help me! It is the twenty-first! The last day!'

The chamberlain must have seen them coming. This time the gates didn't open automatically. Opal heard a dozen bolts snapping home. It only slightly delayed them. Lady Barracuda still carried Ulrich's sledgehammer.

The chamberlain stood trembling in the middle of the hall, an opened conjuring book in his hand. Grandmother Rithka glared at him. 'I am a witch and you are no magician. Read a single word and I turn you into a frog.' He dropped the book. 'Didn't mean... None can disturb my master. He is sleeping.'

'Still?' Lady Barracuda said. 'Take us to him and I'll shake him awake.'

'You don't understand! He...'

'Take us to his sleeping room!'

The magician slept. He slept right on his throne and Opal could hear him snoring. The cobwebs were as heavy as draperies. He must have been sleeping for centuries.

'You are right,' Grandmother said. 'We don't understand. So explain.'

'It's a sad story,' the chamberlain said, and he began:

MiYu

THE SAD AND DISTRESSING STORY OF RED IBEX

Red Ibex, the king of Capricorn, was a powerful wizard – the most powerful wizard ever known in MiYu. He could lift a mountain just by snapping his fingers; he could turn muddy water into the very best wine; walk on clouds. These were his easier spells.

He conjured a garden in the heart of Capricorn and looked around. It was perfect: fruit trees, flowers as big as wagon wheels, birds of paradise.

'Surely my Secret Garden is even more beautiful than the Garden of Gods. I'll invite them for a party and ask them to bring me the Lemon of Immortality. I'm more powerful than the gods so I should be immortal too.'

The gods came. They had no choice: Red Ibex knew more magic than even Gliph Abar himself. If he hadn't bragged so much he would have become one of the gods. That is the way gods handle too mighty a wizard, they make him one of them.

'Hello, Di,' Red Ibex said, 'Look, I have a bow too.'

Dinja scowled. Only her very best friends could call the

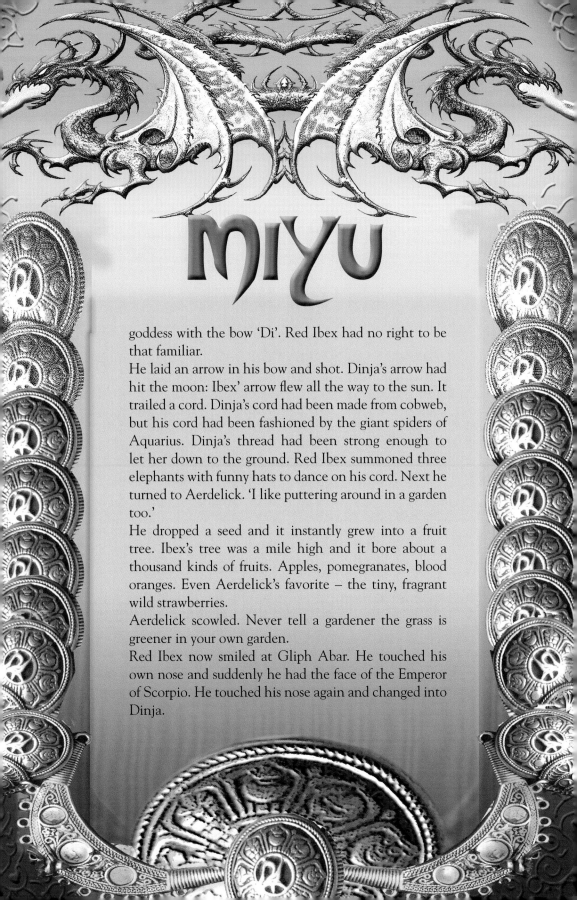

MIYU

goddess with the bow 'Di'. Red Ibex had no right to be that familiar.

He laid an arrow in his bow and shot. Dinja's arrow had hit the moon: Ibex' arrow flew all the way to the sun. It trailed a cord. Dinja's cord had been made from cobweb, but his cord had been fashioned by the giant spiders of Aquarius. Dinja's thread had been strong enough to let her down to the ground. Red Ibex summoned three elephants with funny hats to dance on his cord. Next he turned to Aerdelick. 'I like puttering around in a garden too.'

He dropped a seed and it instantly grew into a fruit tree. Ibex's tree was a mile high and it bore about a thousand kinds of fruits. Apples, pomegranates, blood oranges. Even Aerdelick's favorite – the tiny, fragrant wild strawberries.

Aerdelick scowled. Never tell a gardener the grass is greener in your own garden.

Red Ibex now smiled at Gliph Abar. He touched his own nose and suddenly he had the face of the Emperor of Scorpio. He touched his nose again and changed into Dinja.

MIYU

'I don't have to use a mask or any other disguises. What's more, I can even do shadows.'

Gliph Abar probably scowled. You couldn't tell because he was still wearing a mask. You can tell a hunting goddess she can't shoot for beans, a fertility god that his radishes taste like crap, but never ever tell a performer you can do better tricks.

Gliph Abar smiled. No it was the mask that smiled. 'You are the best. You deserve to be a god.' He took a crystal bottle from his cape. 'This is the juice of the Lemon of Immortality. We already squeezed it for you.'

Red Ibex uncorked the bottle and a heavenly smell filled the garden.

'This is the lemon for sure. You probably put some quick acting poison in it. It doesn't matter. There is no poison on all of MiYu that can hurt me.' And he drank the potion down to the last drop.

'It isn't a poison,' Gliph Abar said. 'Just a magic sleeping draught. You are immortal now. You'll also sleep forever.'

Red Ibex didn't hear him. His eyes had closed and he now sat slumped and snoring on his throne.

'I see," Grandmother Rithka said. 'There is no way to wake him?'

'He'll sleep forever. Not even Gliph Abar could shake him awake. But you can ask him questions. Red Ibex sometimes talks in his sleep.'

'I can try.' Grandmother Rithka looked up at the loudly snoring god. 'We have a sea dragon. He has us, is more like it. A spell turned him into a living ship. How can I reverse that spell? Make him a dragon again?'

Red Ibex muttered in his sleep. 'No, Myra dear. I want two clumps of sugar in my hibiscus tea. Not three. What spell? Recite it.'

'I wrote it down.' She took a piece of paper from her bag. Witches have good memories but not as good memories as dragons. 'I'll read it.'

'Did you get it?' she asked after she had recited the whole spell.

'Perfectly. Yes, Myra, these muffins are quite nice. Take one yourself. Those with blueberries are especially nice.' He smacked his lips. 'It's the spell of a rank novice. Worthless. It is so easy to reverse. Did you walk the dog?'

'Walk the dog?'

'Just recite it backwards, Myra, and the spell is broken.'

'Just recite it backwards?' Grandmother Rithka slapped her brow.

'It can't be that easy!'

'Red Ibex is the most powerful wizard of MiYu,' the chamberlain chided.

'The most powerful of all sleeping wizards,' he corrected.

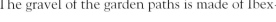

'One more question,' Grandmother said. 'How do we get out of your garden? All the roads are dead ends and the cliffs are too steep to climb.'

'You need the eye of an Ibex, of a real rock goat with her clever hooves to climb those cliffs. You have to jump from ledge to ledge and most are only half an inch wide.'

'That's nice to know. Sadly, I don't have the eyes of a deer. Or clever hooves either.'

'Eh, mighty lady witch?' The chamberlain said. 'I think he refers to a magic stone. It's called Ibex-eye and it makes your eyes so sharp you notice the slightest crack. It also gives you the balance of a rock goat.'

He took a string of amulets from his cuirass and pointed to a beautiful brown stone. 'This stone.'

'I'll pay you seven pearls for it,' Grandmother said.

'Done!' the chamberlain said, much too quickly.

'I guess they aren't that rare.' Grandmother commented as she counted out the pearls.

'The gravel of the garden paths is made of Ibex-eyes.'

'How does this particular stone work?'

'Rub the stone against your eyelids. Then touch it to your soles.'

'Myra,' Opal asked, 'That's Myra he was talking to in his dreams. Who's she?'

'Myra was his wife. He was always putting her down. There was nothing she could do right and he finally turned her into a dog.'

'I see.'

Opal's little dog sat waiting outside, as usual.

Opal sat next to her. 'You are Myra, aren't you? His wife.'

'It isn't something I'm particularly proud of.'

'We can try to change you back. My grandmother is a witch.'

'No thanks. I like being a dog. It is so much better than the wife of a brutish magician. I get to pee against all his trees. They are practically mine. And everybody saves their bones for me.'

'I understand.' And Opal did. There is nothing wrong with being a dog in a park with a thousand trees.

Opal rubbed her eyelids with the stone and then touched her feet.

When she opened her eyes she didn't understand why she had ever thought the cliff was unclimbable. There were so many ridges and ledges. Some were even a quarter inch wide! And there was a pipe along which you could practically run to the top of the cliff by zigzagging a little.

The stairs began at the top of the cliff. It started moving the moment Opal touched the first step.

The stairs went as fast as the first time. It seemed horribly slow to Opal.

The sun was hanging low in the sky and getting lower all the time.

Two hours and it would slip behind the horizon.

The pass made a bend and she saw the harbor. Dinja be praised, the ship was still moored…

'We're almost there. Don't leave!' Opal wheezed. 'We're coming!'

She heard a loud whoop. Pebble jumped over the rail and ran down the pier. She hugged Clever Mayfly and covered his face with kisses.

When she came up for breath, Clever Mayfly held her at arms length and studied her.

'You must be Pebble, I guess.'

'You guess?' Pebble sounded indignant. 'What do you mean, guess?'

'Long story,' Grandmother said. 'There are some things we have forgotten.'

'You have forgotten me?'

'Ahum,' the dragon said. 'Sorry to interrupt this tender scene, but you people sure like living dangerously. You have only one hour left.'

If he had worn a watch he would have tapped on it.

'It wasn't easy to get away from the Secret Garden,' Opal said.

'But you did get the counter-spell?'

'It's as easy as ABC,' Opal said. 'You, owwh!' Her grandmother had kicked her on the chins, hard.

'The magician didn't have the spell, sorry. But he did tell us where to find it. It's a spell of transformation, ship to dragon, eh? The frog-wizards of Pisces know all about transformation. They are doing it all the time. Frogspawn to tadpole; tadpole to frog. You see?'

'Frog-wizards? I've never heard of any frog-wizards.' He sounded suspicious.

As well he should be: Grandmother was making it up on the fly.

Grandmother folded her arms. 'Well, now you know. Come on, dragon. Hoist the sails! Pisces is waiting!'

The dragon pushed off from the pier without any further argument.

He had swallowed the bait after all, swallowed it hook, line and sinker.

'Hey,' Opal said, 'Where's Tiger-Eye?'

'I had to lock him in the closet. He tried to escape twice to look for you.'

Opal and Pebble were sitting on the bridge as far from the dragon's head as possible.

PISCES

PISCES
20 February to 20 March

PURPLE CROCODILE STONE
(AMETHYST ROUGH)

OCEAN JASPER

BRONZITE

THE MISTY, MYSTIC SWAMPS OF PISCES

1.

Opal and Pebble were sitting on the bridge as far from the dragon's head as possible. Not that it gave them any privacy: as they'd learned the hard way, the dragon had ears all over his body.

'Tell me,' Pebble said. 'Tell me true.'

It almost sounded like some kind of spell, Opal thought. She braced herself. This meant trouble. Her sister sounded too intense.

'Did you kiss him? You were gone for almost a month.'

'I didn't! He is your boyfriend and…'

'You are lying.'

Opal sighed. 'Well, we did, but only a few times. Because he thought I was his girlfriend. I didn't like it.'

Pebble nodded. 'Then it's all right. Kisses don't count if you don't like it. Then it is like kissing your least favorite aunt.'

'I really didn't like kissing him.'

'You don't have to plead. I believe you.'

That evening Grubby Chipmunk was reading aloud from his Handbook again.

'Pisces is the most beautiful of all islands! It has a thousand creeks and lagoons. Everywhere you hear the rustling of reeds and the languid 'croak' of the many-hued frogs. The inhabitants are easy-going.

They loll in their hammocks, drinking their 'flutwar,' a delightful local drink fermented from water lily bulbs. Even visiting pirates find a peaceful harbor here. They are often moved to return their ill-gotten gains to their victims. Nature-lovers can hire a flat-bottomed boat and pole down the waterways, looking for crocodiles and giant frogs. The island is saturated with magic. Flowers whistle and many animals can talk.

Pisceans can read the thoughts of all visitors, using the ocean jasper stone. They also sell crocodile leather purses. Be sure to buy one!'

'Hmmmm,' Opal said. 'I don't know. It sounds almost like an advertisement. Remember Aries? If this part is written by the Pisceans themselves, I don't think we can trust it.'

'The capital has the beautiful name of Quakariquac,' Grubby Chipmunk continued, ignoring Opal's outburst. 'The houses are raised on piles and you can fish from your very doorstep.' He closed the book. 'Sounds perfect!

We could use a holiday.'

'Your book didn't say anything about frog-wizards,' the dragon said from above their head.

'Frogs don't write. But the book mentioned giant frogs. No doubt some are wizards.'

2.

'Now, read the map most carefully,' the dragon said. 'There are sandbars and shallows everywhere around Pisces. I don't want to run aground.'

'I'm a captain!' Grubby Chipmunk sputtered. 'I have been sailing for years and I've never…'

'Right now the tide is out. If we run aground we're stuck.

We'll have to wait for high-tide and that doesn't come for about a month.'

'Turn to starboard,' Grubby Chipmunk directed. 'Now follow the channel until you get to the third branch.'

Pisces was a green line along the horizon. They had been zigzagging among the mud banks for hours and it didn't look any closer.

Grubby Chipmunk threw the map on the deck. 'This thing isn't worth the paper it's printed on! Pure fantasy! Why don't they mark the channels? Some buoys would be handy.'

'The saltwater crocodiles would only eat them,' a voice said.

A canoe bumped the bow of the ship, steered by a small boy. He was six years old at most but probably not even that.

'I'm Little Stickleback, your pilot. For only three pearls I'll guide you to Quakariquac.'

'How do you know we have pearls?' Grubby Chipmunk asked.

'I just read your thoughts.' He showed a gem. 'Ocean Jasper.

It's easy once you get the hang of it.'

'Aren't there any older pilots? You seem kind of young.'

'They are lying in their hammocks, too lazy to earn an honest pearl.

But you have to hurry. When the tide turns the crocodiles start patrolling, looking for stranded boats.' He opened his shirt and showed them a string of jagged purple stones. 'I'm not afraid of them. I have a lot of Purple Crocodile stones.'

'Are they magic?' Grandmother asked. 'That is one stone I have never heard of before.'

'Not really magic, but it saves your life and that is all the magic I need.

Look, saltwater crocodiles, will gulp you down without chewing.

They have a stomach filled with sharp stones that take care of the chewing.

Grind you into hamburger. Those stones get smooth very fast, though, and then they spit them out. Now if a crocodile spots you, you throw your purple crocodile stone as far as you can. The crocodile will swim after your stone. There are always lots of people and animals to eat but only a few sharp stones.'

'I get it. Better sell us some of those stones, too.'

'A pearl each. And for one pearl more I won't tell them your big secret.'

'What big secret? I don't have a big secret!'

'Well, then I can tell them, can't I?'

'You're a greedy little pipsqueak, you know.'

'Yes, captain, and proud of it.'

Grubby Chipmunk paid. Even the extra pearl.

'What secret?' Opal asked.

Grubby Chipmunk gritted his teeth and snapped, 'It's a secret!'

'Do you know about frogs?' the dragon asked.

'Lots of frogs here. Oh, you mean an enchanted one that can break your spell? I'll guide you there in the morning.'

They didn't meet a single saltwater crocodile. Opal thought that the boy had probably made them up to sell his stones.

In front of Quakariquac they passed their first buoy. It was studded with iron spikes. Like the Secret Gardens and Last Well it had a sign:

You're entering Quakariquac,
the harmonious city
where greed and anger are unknown.
Population: 0 – 30,000

'Why zero to thirty thousand people?' Opal asked. 'Couldn't anybody be bothered to count them?'

'We sometimes have to evacuate the city,' Little Stickleback said. 'When the frogs get bad or the blue swamp berries bloom. Don't worry. It only happens once or twice a year.'

They moved deeper into the city. It was a city of piers and wooden bridges, of stately houses perched on ironwood stilts. There were nets hanging everywhere, clotheslines with drying stockfish. Opal saw the skin of a giant frog stretched on a rack to dry. From toes to nose it measured at least five meters. The open mouth was filled with needle-sharp teeth.

This was the kind of frog that wouldn't be satisfied with eating

bluebottles.

Smart idea, Grandmother. Having us look for a frog wizard.

'I'll bring you to my uncle's tavern,' Little Stickleback said. 'He burns his food and the toilets are filthy but his mosquito nets are the best of the city.'

He turned to the left and crossed a lake with hundreds of quacking ducks.

'There it is,' Little Stickleback said. 'The house with the stork nest on the roof. Remember, don't eat his food and stay inside after sunset.

I'll see you in the morning.' He paddled away to stash his pearls.

The landlord nodded to them. He closed his eyes and touched the ocean jasper around his neck. 'Don't say a thing,' he said in a solemn voice.

'I see that you want four rooms and a good meal.'

'Don't go mystic on me,' Grandmother said. 'I'm a witch. And you can't read thoughts very well. We certainly don't want to eat here.'

'Oi, somebody warned you.'

Opal and Pebble went shopping. Their boyfriends stayed at the tavern, fishing from the porch and telling stupid jokes to each other. No problem. Boyfriends were useless for shopping anyway. They always started yawning when you'd only tried on a dozen shoes.

'Didn't Lady Barracuda want to come?' Opal asked. 'She is always wearing such expensive gowns.'

'She went with Ulrich, looking for swords and stuff. They both like sharp and pointy things.'

She darted aside. 'Look at those handbags, Opal! The label says they're real crocodile-leather.'

The owner waved them deeper into the shop. 'The crocodile-hunters personally cured and stitched them. But I have even nicer handbags here.'

The handbags were dyed a deep green and yellow, made from beautiful soft leather.

'They are a bit more expensive but quite exclusive. I'm the only shop in town that sells them. They bring in the hides after curing them with duckweed or the pollen of the swamp buttercup.'

'Who brings the hides in?' Pebble asked.

'Swim the hides in is more to the point. The crocodiles bring them after they've caught a hunter.'

'That seems only fair,' Pebble said. 'I want one.'

'Me too. The stone-moles ate my last one.'

'Hey, what about that shop? It sells fudge? I haven't eaten…'

'First the handbags.'

'Where is everybody?' Pebble asked two hours later.

The sidewalks had suddenly emptied. Shutters were rattling down, doors slamming.

'Closing time I guess,' Opal said. 'But why the hurry?'

The door of the last shoe shop opened a crack, the one where they had tried on no less than twenty-one high-heeled sandals.

'Why are you still standing there?' the shopping-girl asked. 'Go home! The sun is going down.'

'We are big girls,' Pebble said. 'We are allowed to stay up late.'

'Are you crazy?' the girl asked. 'The mosquitoes are coming!'

She bolted the door.

'What did she mean?' Pebble said. 'The mosquitoes are coming?'

'Listen,' Opal whispered.

From the swamp beyond the city rose a menacing buzz. It was a sound as deep and growling as an earthquake and it was getting louder. It was the sound of millions of hungry mosquitoes searching for blood.

'Crocodiles grow up to twenty meters here,' Opal said.

'Would mosquitoes…'

'Run!' Pebble cried.

The sky suddenly darkened. It wasn't clouds or even the sun setting.

The whole eastern sky was a solid black and the thunderous drone made the side walk shake.

A sparrow sized mosquito dove at the vein on Opal's neck. She swung her new handbag and two kilos of fudge hit it hard, sending it bouncing away. It landed in the water, at least twenty meters away.

'A home run!' Pebble cried.

'This way!' Tiger-Eye's voice could be heard above the buzz. He was covered from head to foot with a steel-mesh net – a walking mosquito net.

'Duck inside! They are too big to get in!'

A droning cloud of mosquitoes surrounded them. She saw hairy legs waving. Their black glittering eyes looked like blackberries. But Tiger-Eye was right: they were too big to squirm through the holes.

Opal started trembling only after the door of the tavern was safely bolted

behind them.
'I was wrong,' Pebble said. 'I'm not old enough to stay up late.'
The next morning the boy was waiting on the porch, eager to depart.
'Are you ready to go? It is quite a voyage – first up the coast, then around the North Cape to reach the Misty, Mystic Swamp. The frogs are somewhere in the middle.'
'Are you sure they know magic?' the dragon asked once again.
'Their chief-frog is as big as a horse. If that isn't magic I don't know what is.'

It was the perfect day for a trip, sunny, with a bracing sea breeze.
Opal leaned against the neck of the dragon and she felt that all was well with the world. She was seeing the islands, making the grand tour and crossing the entire world of MiYu. She was as free as a flying whale.
'Could you sell me one of your ocean jasper stones?' she asked.
'Reading thoughts would be fun.' Especially Grubby Chipmunk's secret.
'No sorry. An ocean jasper stone is very personal. We never sell them. Anyhow, it takes you many weeks to learn. Reading thoughts isn't easy.'
'A pity,' Opal said. She didn't believe a word. He just doesn't want us to read his thoughts. She didn't doubt for a moment that Little Stickleback was hatching a dozen schemes right now.

The North Cape was carved in the smiling face of a drowsy god.
A colony of gulls nestled on his brow and his head was streaked white with guano. It didn't seem to spoil his humor in the slightest.
'That is Avindra,' Little Stickleback said. 'God of ease and good living. He is taking a little nap, so all his followers walk on tiptoe and speak in whispers. His little nap has already lasted three thousand years.'
He lifted his hand. 'Listen. There it comes again.'
The snore rolled across the sea, a deep rumbling yet utterly peaceful sound. He blew a stream of protesting gulls from his nostrils.
I bet nobody from Leo has ever seen a god sneeze gulls, Opal thought.
I hope this journey never ends.

Behind Cape Misty, the Mystic Swamp began: a million reed islands, grey mud banks and channels with milky water. Water scorpions followed the boat, clicking their claws, hoping for a traveler stupid enough to go for a swim. They were pale as grubs and as long as Opal's arms. She had seen them before, in the creeks at home. Only on Leo they grew no bigger than

a finger bone.

'They taste like chicken,' Little Stickleback chuckled. 'I wonder what they say about our taste? Maybe we taste like chicken too!' He waved with his paddle. 'Over to the left now. We are almost there.' Opal could already hear them: a chorus of excited croaks.

The dragon pushed through the reeds and they entered a small lake.

A frog squatted on a raft made of overturned canoes.

'Hey,' the dragon complained. 'My feet are getting tangled in some kind of net.'

'We use the great net to catch pike,' the frog said. 'We seem to have caught something bigger this time.'

Opal didn't like his tone of voice. It was too much like the lazy drawl of a bully. Still, it never hurt to be polite and flattery often worked. Even with bullies.

'Are you perhaps a prince?' Opal asked. 'In fairy tales talking frogs are always enchanted princes.'

'No, I'm not a prince, though I have eaten them.' He smiled and he certainly didn't have the teeth of a prince. Fangs. Lots and lots of poisonous fangs.

'Remember,' Little Stickleback shrilled, 'I get their pearls and stuff!'

He turned his canoe and swiftly paddled away.

'We keep our promises,' The frog said. 'Come back tomorrow.'

He ogled them. 'I've always wondered what a dragon would taste like…'

The dragon snarled. 'Eating me? You and what army?'

The frog pointed.

'Oh,' the dragon said. 'That army.'

They were surrounded by hundreds of frogs. Even the smallest was the size of a mastiff and they were all grinning.

Ulrich hefted his brand-new axe. It looked extremely sharp and somehow thirsty. It wasn't the kind of axe one used to chop wood.

'Eating us won't come cheap. My axe is stainless steel so frog blood wouldn't rust it.'

Lady Barracuda stood next to him. 'I've never killed a frog before but it's never too late to learn.'

They are boasting, Opal thought, like the barbarian heroes in one of those ancient tales who run around killing everybody they meet. Bluffing, trying to make the frogs afraid. I don't think it'll work.

It didn't.

'Oh, you could kill some of us,' the frog replied. 'It doesn't matter. We are not afraid to die. If we die we are instantly reborn as frogspawn and we start over again.'

'Do you have a spell?' Opal asked her grandmother. 'Even a dirty trick? Turn them all into princes perhaps?'

'Let's throw the stones,' Tiger-Eye said. 'You haven't asked Gliph Abar's advice for weeks.'

There was a loud croaking and the frogs started to advance.

Opal threw the stones and counted. 'Number five!' she called.

THERE IS A BIRD FOR EVERY PROBLEM

Tiger-Eye read from the open book. 'I get it. My whistles.'

He thumbed through his birdcalls. 'Gull, woodpecker, hummingbird. Stork!'

Opal understood. Storks are a frog's worst nightmare. No frog is born a giant. They all started out as small baby frogs and the storks ate them.

Tiger-Eye put the birdcall to his lips and blew. The raw screech of a stork rolled across the water.

The frog sniggered. He had clambered on the stern and jumped around, easily avoiding Ulrich's blows. 'It's true that I was once afraid of storks.

But now I'm a big frog. A huge frog. I eat any stork that lands in my pool!'

'Blow again,' Grandmother said. 'Everything here just keeps on growing. They're all gigantic – the frogs, the mosquitoes. So why not storks?'

'Yes, keep on blowing, boy!' the frog laughed. 'Maybe we'll get storks for dessert' He landed in the middle of the deck, opening his maw.

'We came looking for storks but it seems we get frogs' legs today.'

The leader of the frogs froze when he heard the grating voice. It was a cold and somehow scaly voice. The golden eyes of the frog widened in alarm. Crocodiles emerged from the reeds, sliding down in the pool.

The frogs were huge but the crocs were even bigger.

'And him?' one of the crocodiles asked, pointing at the ship with a frog's leg still flapping from the corner of his mouth.

'Nah, that is a dragon,' their leader said. 'He's a reptile like us and we don't eat our own. And besides, I'm not hungry anymore.'

'Eh?' the dragon said. 'Do you know anything about the breaking of spells? Transformations like turning a ship back into a dragon?'

'No. Sorry. That's something the frogs would know. Their king would have known. He was a kind of magician.' He gestured with his stubby foreleg. 'Sorry, no king and no frogs left.'

They were at sea, ten miles beyond the North Cape of Pisces.

'This is the most worthless island I've ever visited,' the dragon complained. 'A complete waste of time!'

'There was a frog-magician,' Grandmother said. 'We didn't steer you wrong. Not our fault he got eaten.'

'Where do we go now?' the dragon said, sounding a bit forlorn.

'Leo perhaps?' Opal asked.

'No way! That's where your family lives. You'd signal your father somehow and a hundred flying whales would...' He shook his head.

'No, none of your own islands.'

'There is Virgo,' Grandmother Rithka said. 'None of us are from Virgo. None has ever visited it on this voyage. It should be safe for you.'

'Good, but that isn't enough. How can they help me?

Are they magicians, too?'

'No, something even better. They are serious. When you give them a problem they won't rest until they have solved it. Turning a ship back into the dragon is just the kind of problem they'd like.'

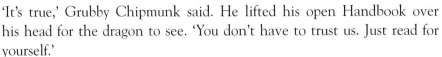

'It's true,' Grubby Chipmunk said. He lifted his open Handbook over his head for the dragon to see. 'You don't have to trust us. Just read for yourself.'

'I see,' the dragon said after a quick glance. 'Well, we go to Virgo then.'

He can't read, Opal thought. Grubby Chipmunk held the page upside down and nobody can read a whole page in three seconds.

'I want to show you something,' she said to Grandmother Rithka.

'It's in my cabin.'

She opened her friendship book and wrote: 'Walls have ears but no eyes and even if he had, the dragon can't read.' It was the first time she had written anything is her friendship book. 'Why Virgo?'

'Because of your wish – Gliph Abar made it quite clear: You have to visit all the islands before you can get home. It doesn't help to try for Leo before that. Virgo is the only island left. And it's the closest island to Leo.

There is also another good reason. Virgo is my star isle.'

'What do we do in the meantime?'

'Try to keep the dragon satisfied and act like we're looking for a counter-spell.'

CHAPTER 12

It was a long journey
to Virgo. Two
months, even on a
dragon-winged ship,
that used his webbed
feet for oars and
never slept.

VIRGO

SODALITE ROUGH

ELFSTONE (FLUORITE)

YELLOW CRACK CRYSTAL

VIRGO
24 August to 22 September

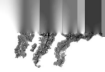

THE EAST-BRIDGE OF VIRGO

'Actually, Virgo is three islands,' Grubby Chipmunk said. 'Mighty bridges connect them and most people live on them. They are often miles wide, with houses, parks and fields.'

'Have you ever been there?'

'No, I got it from the handbook. Libra and Virgo don't exactly like each other. They are both very finicky, doing everything according to the rules. However the rules are quite different. Also, like doesn't like like, as they say. It is easier to hate your neighbor than a complete stranger.'

He nodded. 'So don't tell them I'm from Libra.'

'I didn't think you were so law-abiding,' Opal said. 'I mean, you're a smuggler, you trade with cannibals! You lie and steal.'

'No, I'm very much a Libran. My only rule is that I don't obey any rules and I keep that rule religiously. I never break it.'

It was a long journey to Virgo. Two months, even on a dragon-winged ship, that used his webbed feet for oars and never slept. By the time the ship bellowed 'Land ahead!' Opal had almost given up hope of ever reaching a shore again.

They came in from the northeast and the first thing Opal saw were the bridges. They straddled the horizon. Some of them were so huge the clouds passed below them. They looked very strange, more like mountains than something manmade.

Two ships instantly converged on them. They moved quite quickly though Opal couldn't find a trace of oars or sails. Perhaps they were mechanical, like the submarines of Scorpio?

One of the ships came up alongside their dragon. It towered over them, so big that the dragon looked like a toy boat.

A rope ladder unraveled and a customs officer rushed down, fast as a monkey.

'Welcome to the Republic of Virgo!' He was cleanly shaven, everything polished and shining from the silver buckles on boots to the badge on his cap. 'My name is Modest Thunder. Are you here for pleasure or business?'

'Business,' the dragon instantly said. 'Very important business.

We are looking for a magician to reverse my spell. I may look like a ship but I'm really a dragon.'

'A living ship! You came to the right islands. We know all about living ships.' He indicated his own towering ship. 'Our ships start out quite small, no bigger than whales. The first bridge we built on their back is no bigger than a cottage.'

Living ships? Opal gazed down into the water. It was a quite clear: you could see for at least twenty meters. An enormous fin moved languidly, stretching way beyond their keel. Their own dragon ship rocked in the turbulence.

Their whole ship is a fish. A monster fish. He could eat whales for breakfast.

The officer noticed her open-mouthed stare. 'Have no fear. Our ship-fishes only eat seaweed. If they swallow a fishing boat it's only by accident.'

The officer piloted them through the harbor. The ships were moored at least twenty meters from each other and Opal could easily understand why. Each deck was like the tip of an iceberg. The bulk of a ship-fish lay underwater.

They ended up in the shadow of the bridge, between two splendid yachts.

'Esteemed dragon,' the officer said. 'You can moor here.'

'How much are the harbor dues?' Grubby Chipmunk asked.

'No harbor dues, my dear captain. You are our guests.'

'Say, what about my spell?' the dragon asked.

'I'll have to consult some of our ship bree, uh, shipbuilders. They...'

'Shipbuilders?'

'Magicians I mean. Stay here. Relax. I'll be back in a few hours.'

He jumped to the pier and gave a jaunty wave.

'I don't like it,' Grubby Chipmunk said. 'I don't like it at all. No fee. Every time you moor you have to pay. He said he was a customs officer but he didn't ask if we had anything to declare. Not even once.'

The dragon agreed. 'I have been in a lot of harbors and this is the pier where you have to pay through your nose to moor. It is only for yachtsmen, for ships with gold trim, mahogany masts and silk sails. Not the place you would ever put a worker ship.'

'Shall we follow him?' Opal said. They were in this together.

The dragon was an enemy, but on a strange island, where you couldn't trust anyone, even an enemy was a kind of friend.

'You and Tiger-Eye. More would be conspicuous. The rest will try to get water and food in case we have to leave suddenly.'

'Right! We'll be seeing you!'

Opal ran down the pier with Tiger-Eye, hiding behind bales of puffin

feathers and crates with sea urchin needles. Modest Thunder took the left pier to the city-ferry. No problem, the ferry was so crowded there wasn't the slightest chance he would notice them.

'Look at the price list for our berth,' Tiger-Eye said. 'GOLDEN HARBOR. Mooring fee: 10 moonstones/hour.' He shook his head.

'You'd have to be a prince or a very successful smuggler to pay such a fee.'

'He wanted us a long way from the entrance. I bet he'll call the guards if we try to leave and tell them we haven't paid our dues.'

It was only a short trip. The ferry crossed to a stone quay and they disembarked.

'Keep him in sight!' Tiger-Eye called and Opal had to use her elbows and a few judicious steps on toes to stay with him. Tiger-Eye himself could look over most heads and he didn't have to hide. Modest Thunder had never seen him. It was a precaution. Always keep someone hidden when your ship is boarded.

An elevator dropped down from the high bridge and the officer went inside.

'We take the next one,' Opal said. 'It's too risky to stand in the same one. There are only five people in the cage.'

The upper side of the bridge was a whole new world. There were meadows with flocks of grazing geese; villas with glass cupolas; tall gray buildings that must be factories. Windmills whirred on every roof and the sky was filled with kites.

'I would like to meet someone nice for a change,' Opal complained.

'Why is everybody trying to swindle us or eat us?'

'Clever Mayfly is kind of nice,' Tiger-Eye said. 'At least Pebble seems to think so. And there's nothing wrong with Ulrich.'

'That was several islands ago. That chamberlain, Little Stickleback and now...'

'I see him. He is crossing to that building.'

A ship-fish formed the logo above the name of the company.

Shipbreeders Inc.
Sails are for dummies
we breed a fish for every task

'Now what do we do?' Tiger-Eye asked. 'Follow him inside?'

'Let me do the talking. I can sound like a spoiled rich brat who wants a yacht for her birthday. No secretary would dare to stop me.'

'Your clothes look kind of torn and dirty.'

'That doesn't matter. It's a fashion statement. The tone of voice is all that counts.'

There was a secretary inside, very beautiful with hair like spun glass and a satin gown. She slept with her head on the counter and was snoring rather insistently.

'DON'T WAKE ME', the sign said. 'MR. SPLENDID DRIZZLE WON'T SEE YOU ANYWAY.'

Opal was a merchant's daughter. She had met magnates like that and they often had the same kind of secretaries.

They sidled past and went into the corridor. Three doors down, they heard voices.

A door stood ajar and Opal peered through the opening.

Mr. Splendid Drizzle sat behind a gleaming desk made of silver.

No, not silver. It must be a single giant scale from a ship-fish.

'It sounds interesting,' he was saying to the customs officer.

'But how could I make a profit? Get her eggs and breed our own dragon ships?'

'It is a male dragon. No eggs. We wouldn't have the right incantation anyway. We would just get a dragon when it hatched, not a ship.

Aries would never sell us their spell. No, we don't need an egg. That's the beautiful part. Dragons are like lizards, only more so. If you cut a leg off a lizard he grows a new one. Dragons do one better. From the leg grows a whole new dragon. And it would be a ship too, because the spell would still hold. It is the same dragon after all.'

'Now you're talking.' His smile reached from ear to ear.

'Now you're talking.'

'We could easily cut him in a hundred pieces and he would still survive!'

'Where did you put him?'

'That is the funniest part. I knew your son had taken your yacht to the West Island so I put him in your very own berth in The Golden Harbor.'

'And nobody else knows about the dragon-ship?'

'I came straight to you.'

'You did well.' He opened a drawer, reached inside and drew out a loaded crossbow.

'This may look small, my dear Thunder, but the tips are covered with venom.'

'But I, I came straight to you'

'Somebody is going to get extremely rich with this dragon and it won't be you. I never take partners as you know.' He gestured with his crossbow. 'Now you go stand in the corner. Hands on your neck while I call a guard.'

They ran down the corridor, slipping past the still sleeping secretary.

'Great,' Tiger-Eye said. 'We just exchanged a vulture for a tiger.'

Outside a hundred mournful horns sounded.

'An alarm?' Opal said. 'Already?'

'No, it is coming from everywhere. Drizzle is important, but not that important.'

A minute later they understood it was even worse than an alarm.

It was rush hour and all factories and offices were closing at the same time. There were instant lineups at every elevator, each with at least one hundred tired workers and vicious secretaries wearing blood-red high-heeled shoes.

'Is there any other way down to the harbor?' Opal asked a housewife with a howling baby in a sling and a toddler tugging at each hand.

'Only the stairs. But who would ever use the stairs? They...'

Opal didn't wait for the rest. She had already seen them, winding stairs that looked like a giant's corkscrew.

Two boys lounged in the entrance of the stairs.

'You can't go in there,' the biggest said. He was at least a head taller than Tiger-Eye, his muscles bulging in his arms. 'The stairs are our turf.

Only Yellows are allowed.' He pointed to the yellow butterfly tattoo on his cheek. 'And I guess you don't have one, mate.'

'Well,' Tiger-Eye said. 'No problem. We'll just take the next stairs.'

He sounded quite reasonable, though Opal knew he must be fuming inside. But she agreed with him, they didn't have the time for a scuffle.

'The next stairs belong to the Blues.'

'Boy,' Tiger-Eye said. 'Your luck just ran out.' He looked down.

'Hello, Ulrich.'

'Who's that dwarf?' the gang member laughed. 'Your little brother?'

'No,' Ulrich said. 'You were quite right the first time. I am a dwarf. From Cancer.'

'A dwarf....' The boy took a better look this time and blanched. Dwarfs were known as the best street fighters of all MiYu. They never started a fight, but they always won. Ulrich looked up at the boy. 'Is there a problem?' he asked. 'One that could perhaps be solved by rolling you down about one hundred and thirty steps?'

'No, no! No problem.' He jumped back. 'Please pass!'

'I decided to follow you two,' Ulrich said while they ran down the stairs. 'Nobody looks down in a crowd and dwarfs can fit through doors that were only meant for cats.'

'Glad you came,' Opal said.

'Uh, why exactly are we running down these stairs?'

'The customs officer just sold our dragon to a shipbreeder.
He wants to cut him into a hundred pieces.'

'Can't allow that,' Ulrich said. 'He isn't a friend exactly but he is our dragon.'

They arrived too late. The pier was crowded with armed guards.
A chain bound the dragon to a mooring post and his sails drooped in dejection.

'Why doesn't he just break the chain?' Tiger-Eye said. 'It looks quite flimsy to me. The links are no thicker than my fingers.'

'The chain is black,' Opal said. 'A pitch-black stone.'

'Hematite!'

Hematite was the stone that absorbed all spells, turned magic gold back into lead. No dragon, being a magic animal, could ever break a hematite chain. Just touching it made him as helpless as a stranded whale.

'Let's walk a bit closer,' Ulrich said. 'You said that the magnate chained our dragon but he doesn't know us. He doesn't know we are part of the crew. And Modest Thunder certainly won't tell him now.'

He strolled up to the barricade that the guards had erected.

'Hey,' he said, 'what is going on here?' He puffed up his chest.

'I am Irascible Cloud Break, the steel magnate who built the Iron Tower of Dahlgren.' He pointed. 'My yacht is lying behind you people. It's the ship with the golden vulture on the mast.'

'So sorry sir.' One of the guards saluted. 'We had to impound this ship. That's the reason for the chain. His owner moored without paying the fees on a private berth.'

'Hmph!' Ulrich said. 'I hope this doesn't last too long' He gave the guards each a rather large pearl.

'No time at all, sir! The ship is secured. We'll have to stay to guard the ship, but you can just walk past to your own boat.'
'My own yacht,' Ulrich corrected him. 'Good. I'll go tell my captain we can leave after all.'

They met the others on the quay, where they stood waiting for the ferry. Lady Barracuda was balancing three water casks on her head, while the others lugged sacks of meal and dried fruit. Even Clever Mayfly's hares were carrying links of sausages.
'Look!' Ulrich called. 'I bought myself a brand-new crowbar that's big enough to force the gate of a giant!' The crowbar was twice the dwarf's size but he carried it as if it was no heavier than a reed.

'Hematite,' Grandmother sucked her teeth and clacked her tongue.
'That is a problem. I know a lot of spells but so much hematite would absorb them in a second. How they ever collected enough hematite to forge a chain I can't guess.'
'I've got an idea,' Clever Mayfly said. 'Maybe it's stupid and I'm no

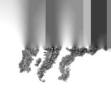

magician. But hematite eats magic, isn't that right? Well, I have met some quite ravenous beasts but there wasn't a single one that could keep on eating forever. It always had to stop before his stomach burst.'

'You want to overfeed the chain? Until it stopped working or broke?

The only problem is, see, I'm rather good at magic after some three centuries. Won't find a better witch in the whole of Leo. But if I unleashed all my spells, all my powers, it wouldn't be enough to fill a single link. And that chain must have hundreds of links.'

'You don't know enough spells,' Pebble said. 'So why don't we buy some more? You once told me that each spell is bound to an amulet.

No stone, no spell. So why don't we buy some more amulets?' She turned to Grubby Chipmunk. 'You are the greediest. Tell, us, what do we have left?'

'We still have quite a few pearls and rubies too. I also took some emeralds along when we fled Aries. I guess we are rather wealthy, at least for destitute vagabonds.'

'We need a magic shop,' Opal said. 'But it's after hours and all the shops are closed.' 'Oh no, not the magic shops,' Grandmother said. 'At least not

the kind of magic shops we need. They're only open after dark when the last ray of sunset fades.'

They took the lift up to the bridge and Ulrich walked straight to the stairs.

The boys still hung around and by the time they saw Ulrich it was too late to run away.

Ulrich pushed the tip of his crowbar against the chin of the gang leader. 'This is just a friendly visit, like,' he growled. 'Now you tell us where to find some real heavy black magic. And I mean black. The stuff even demons shudder to use.'

'There is Little Johnny Sunshine. He's such a mean one he'd sell his grandmother for a handful of pebbles.'

'I would like to see him try with this grandmother!' Ulrich stepped forward. 'Now you show us the way, pronto. If you believe that Little Johnny Sunshine is a bad-ass skunk, you should think again. Compared to us he is a pussycat with a pink bow around his tail.'

Every city (and probably every bridge) had parts where prudent citizens didn't like to walk after dark. Or even in broad daylight.

Having a witch and a dwarf in front prevented most of the usual troubles. The hares also tried to look extra fierce and snapped their teeth at every shadow.

'Here it is,' the gang leader said. They stood in front of a heavy-timbered door, reinforced by strips of black steel. He looked pleadingly at Grandmother Rithka. 'Can I go now? Please?'

'Is there a code to get inside? You know, a password – such as a specific number of knocks?'

'Don't bother,' Grubby Chipmunk said and shook his sack of pearls. 'Customers!'

The door opened instantly.

'Good,' the fat merchant said. 'You look as dangerous as my informants claimed. Now I just got a fine shipment of weyrd-stones: amulets to call the lightning from the sky and the demons from the very depths of the earth. I also trade in amulets of scorching...'

Grubby Chipmunk shook his head. 'Don't bother to enumerate them. We want to buy them all.'

'Say again? All of them? What do you want to try? Blow the whole bridge sky-high?'

'Something even worse.'

'You are right. I don't have to know. Come in and show me how you want to pay.'

'They left two guards,' Grandmother Rithka whispered.

'And I can't even put a sleeping spell on them.'

'Leave it to me,' Ulrich said. 'I've met them before.'

He strolled up to the guards.

'Hello,' he said, 'Do you remember me?'

'Certainly, sir,' one of them said. 'You are the famous steel magnate who built the Iron Tower of Dahlgren.'

'Now I want to show you two things.'

'A sledgehammer sir?'

'And these.'

'Ah. Two big emeralds. More than both of us earn in ten years.'

He saluted, his mate saluted and they quietly walked away, throwing their helmets in the water.

'I thought you'd hit them on the head,' Lady Barracuda said as they stood next to the ship. 'With your hammer.' She sounded a bit disappointed.

'It may sound strange for a dwarf but I don't like to use violence.

Not against such wimps. It isn't sporting.'

'First we try three thunder demon amulets,' Grandmother Rithka said.

'Step back. These amulets are potent enough to level a stone watchtower.'

She spoke the spell to activate them. The amulets lit up with an eerie green glow, sizzled like wet firecrackers and went out.

Opal kneeled next to them. They had lost all their magic and had turned into clear mountain crystal. Worthless.

'Nice,' grandmother said, 'Really nice. The chain didn't even glow.

All right, all right. This time we use seven thunder amulets and a jinn-caller. And why not the claw of dystrodont?'

'What's a dystrodont?' Opal asked.

'You don't want to know. Add a hand of glory, the shadow of a moonlight-walker. Here we go.'

There was a low rumble and the whole pier changed into glass.

The water around the ship froze and two flying bats turned into soap bubbles.

Ulrich felt the chain. 'No change. It didn't even get warm.'

'Bother. Whole armies have been turned into stone with less.

What have we left, Grubby Chipmunk?'

'No,' Ulrich said, 'Stop it before we bring the whole bridge down on our heads. We have been stupid, so stupid.'

'Hey,' Clever Mayfly protested. 'Speak for yourself!'

'No, I am the only one who isn't. We are using all that magic against the chain and it just drinks it up. But think! The chain isn't even as strong as iron, not even as tough as copper. It is carved from stone and stone breaks easily.' He lifted his hammer. 'Especially if one uses this very un-magical sledgehammer.'

They poled the dragon-ship past the entrance of the Golden Harbor. The dragon awoke from his trance and opened his sails. It was midnight when they reached the open sea.

'Better paddle your legs,' Grandmother urged the dragon.

'The shipbreeder will soon come looking for his escaped ship. And we have this.'

The links of the broken hematite chain rattled through her fingers.

'It's worth a few fortunes and could stop a whole army of wizards.'

The sail swooped past and the jagged tip hooked the chain, snatched it away. It plunged into the waves and instantly sank.

'Stop an army of wizards, yes,' the dragon said, 'or bind a dragon. Never again.'

Chapter 13

The Planet Ship of Jupiter

THE PLANET SHIP OF JUPITER

Three weeks went by while they put as big a distance as possible between them and Pisces. Twice they outran a squadron of armed fish-ships. Splendid Drizzle wasn't ready to give up yet.

It was a hot, clammy night and everybody slept on the deck.

Or at least tried to: Opal leaned on the rail and gazed at the stars. Her eyes felt gritty with fatigue, but she was still wide awake.

Something was moving in the distance, at the limits of her vision.

It was huge, as big as a cloud. There was no moon and it was hard to see anything with only the stars to light your way. She blinked but it didn't help. The form remained so indistinct she could have just imagined it. But no, it blotted out the stars for quite a stretch at the horizon. Look, another star winked out.

'Opal?' the voice of her grandmother was calling. 'Opal?'

'Yes?' She walked to Rithka's hammock however the eyes of her grandmother remained closed.

She is talking in her sleep. How cute.

Rithka giggled in her sleep. 'If he only knew! It is so easy.

He only has to say the spell backward.'

Opal jumped forward, clapping her hand over Rithka's mouth.

'I wasn't sleeping,' the dragon said. 'Dragons never sleep. Even if they sail with their eyes closed.'

He started to recite the spell backwards.

Rithka struggled upright. 'What is happening?' She looked at the head of the reciting dragon. 'What is he doing?'

'Breaking his spell,' Opal said.

'How? How did he know?'

'You told him. You talked in your sleep.'

The dragon spoke the final word of the spell, an inverted gurgle and started to change. It went very fast. The hold filled up with scaly flesh, the rudder changed into a tail. The mast shook and dumped the others from their hummocks onto the deck.

'Look out!' Grandmother yelled as one of the sails swept down and turned into a ribbed wing. Opal ducked just in time. The sea lapped against her ankles. She stood between the spines on the dragon's back.

'No more harbors,' the dragon said. 'I'll hunt giant squids and snatch the masts from unsuspecting fishing boats. I'll become the terror of the sea!' He looked down at his cowering passengers. 'Now what should I do with

you? You betrayed me. I could have been free weeks ago.'
He glared at Rithka. 'How long did you know the counter spell?'
'Ever since Capricorn,' she admitted. 'But you are free now.
We saved you.'
'Dragons are wise and merciful. I won't dive right away. Only after I have
brought you close enough to be saved.'
'You'll drop us off at an island?' Grubby Chipmunk asked hopefully.
'I'm not that merciful. No, there is a planet ship sailing there. Jupiter I
guess.' The dragon laughed. 'They hate islanders, you know.
They don't even believe the islands exist. Or if they do that all islands are
inhabited by monsters and devils. So you'd better not tell where you come
from.'

The planet ship seemed to materialize from the dark. The sails started to
glow with the rippling hues of northern lights. Next, Opal saw the lamps
and the carved hull. The ship was gigantic, as big as a mountain.
The masts reached all the way to the top of the sky and they grew from the
ship. Living trees with more sails than Opal could count. On the bowsprit
a mighty ball rotated, like MiYu on the tip of Ysidore's nose.
'This is close enough,' the dragon said. 'I hope you can swim?'
He dove.

Opal struggled up through the dark water, kicking her legs, arms clawing.
The dragon had sucked them under in his wake, like corks in a whirlpool.
There was no light, no air, and the water was freezing cold. Her lungs were
close to bursting when she had a terrible thought: perhaps I'm swimming
the wrong way. Down instead of up.
A cold hand closed on her wrist and she almost shrieked. A cold hand
underwater must be Lady Barracuda. Mermaids don't need to breathe.
She felt herself rising and finally her head broke the surface.
Air! The most precious thing in the world.
Tiger-Eye took her arm and pulled her to the ruby. Ysidore's magic made
the jewel so light it floated. All the others held on to their improvised
lifebuoy.
'They are coming,' Grandmother Rithka said. 'I see them lowering a life
boat.' She waved. 'Hey, hey! Here we are!' She turned to the others.
'Not a word about the islands. We are castaways from the ship of Mars.
Mars cruises so far from their ship that they've probably never met. We
were fishing and a sperm whale smashed our boat. Everybody knows how

foul-tempered these brutes are. Remember.'

Opal saw flaring torches and heard the splash of oars.

Strong arms pulled her from the water.

'Why, what a strange bunch you are!' a gruff voice exclaimed.

'We are from Mars,' Ulrich said. 'The ship of Mars.' And that was the last thing Opal heard before darkness closed in.

Opal awoke in a soft bed, beneath a warm blanket. Sunlight slanted in from a porthole.

'You took your own sweet time waking up,' Grandmother said. 'Sleepyhead, it is almost noon.'

She rose. 'Get dressed. The captain wants to see us.

And remember, we're from Mars.'

'What are you holding in your hand? You were knitting?'

Opal started to laugh.

Her grandmother looked down. 'All the women on the ship are knitting,' she murmured. 'We don't want to attract attention.'

'All women have to knit here?' Opal was aghast. Knitting was about the most un-cool thing she could imagine.

'No, only the older ones.' She tossed her knitting on the bed.

'Let's go outside. The captain wants to speak to us.'

The others were already gathered on the bridge and in daylight the ship seemed even bigger. A meadow sloped down from the bridge to the deck. There were even llamas grazing. You could almost forget you were sailing. Opal craned her neck. The mainmast went on and on, disappearing into the clouds and left a wake of streamers.

So high, she thought. At night they must trail against the underside of the moon.

At the village school the teacher had only mentioned the planet ships once. There was one planet ship for every planet and they had been created at the same time as the islands. They were irrelevant, he'd said. Those monstrous big ships moved so far outside the trade routes that no merchant had ever encountered them.

'Not a word about the islands,' Grandmother cautioned.

A small group was struggling up the slope. Four bearers carried a sedan chair with waving banners. A swarm of parrots hovered above the chair.

'Great, great!' they screeched, 'Thrice great is the Grand Admiral of Jupiter. He steers the mightiest ship of them all!'

'He does not appear to be a modest man,' Grandmother said.

'We'll have to watch our words. Dip all our words in honey and keep on smiling.' The bearers stopped and the curtains of the sedan chair opened.

'So you are our new shipmates,' the Grand Admiral said. 'Well, I have to say I have seldom seen a sorrier lot.'

Keep on smiling, Opal thought, and dip all your words in honey.

She gritted her teeth.

'We are from Mars. A sperm whale overturned our sloop.'

'Mars? Ah, one of the minor ships. You are in luck. Being saved and ending up on the most glorious ship that plies the waterways!' He inspected them as a farmer would inspect a newly acquired flock. 'I see a boy herding hares. Good, hare-herds are always welcome.' He pointed a pudgy finger at Grandmother Rithka. 'You, old woman, can you knit and sew?

I want a new patchwork quilt for my seventh bed. A team of two hundred old women is already busy stitching.'

'Of course I can stitch and sew,' Grandmother said. 'As you said, I'm an old woman.' Her words were soft, dipped in honey. But so is the hiss of an adder, just before he strikes.

'The others are clearly unskilled.' He turned to a man with a ledger.

'Overseer Blount, find them some jobs. Nothing complicated.

They are from a primitive ship.'

'I'll find them a place, sir!'

'Dismissed!' barked the Grand Admiral and he closed the curtains.

Opal got a job in the bowsprit, mending nets with three other unmarried girls. Their names, as they told Opal in the first minute, were Suyla-of-the-East deck, Stir-from-the-third-mast and Adharre-of-bilgesight.

'You have such nice clothes,' Suyla said wistfully and she fingered Opal's torn skirt.

'Nice? Everything is more rag than silk.'

'So what? At least they are colorful and shiny. Your brothers must be rich. We are only wearing grey linen.'

Suyla was right. Compared to the other girls Opal was wearing the dress of a queen.

'You're from Mars. They say. Mars is ever so small.

Only twenty sails. Is that true?'

Dip your words in honey. 'Your ship is much bigger. I bet you have a thousand sails!'

'Only six hundred and thirty-four.'

Opal sat for a full hour mending nets. It was an extremely boring chore and it left her fingertips bleeding.

'You'll get calluses after a week,' Stir consoled her. 'Then it won't hurt so much.'

'Have you ever seen an island?' Opal said.

'I've heard about them. They don't exist and nobody wants to go there. There are devils and all kinds of monsters living there. They don't even have sails!'

So Grandmother was right. The ship never moored at the islands. Opal figured they'd find a way to get off. Steal a sloop?

'On Mars I was a fisher-woman. We always went fishing in a sloop.'

'Your Mars sounds like a strange and peculiar place!' Stir shook her head in amazement. 'No woman ever goes fishing here. It is a man's job. A woman isn't even allowed to touch a ship. It would sink inside a week. They would have to burn the boat.'

So scratch that plan. The fishermen would watch any woman getting close to a boat with eagle eyes.

Opal was bone-tired when she returned to the leaky lean-to they had been assigned. The others were already lying in their hammocks, mostly too tired to lift a finger. They told each other of their days and all agreed it wouldn't be easy to get off the ship.

'They set me forging a new anchor,' Ulrich said. 'This ship has close to three hundred anchors and they are always getting snagged in coral reefs. What I meant to say, I have all the tools there to build our own boat. Saws, chisels, you name it.'

'You can't run around cutting trees,' Lady Barracuda said. 'Wood is quite precious here. They know every single tree and they even name them.'

She was in a foul mood. They had correctly identified her as a lady-in-waiting and set her to making flower arrangements and embroidering tea-cozies.

'Hey,' Pebble said. 'We're missing someone. Where is Smald? Not that I'm really missing him.'

Lady Barracuda pulled the curtain aside. 'There are some people coming with torches.' She narrowed her eyes. 'And halberds.'

Smald was running in front, almost dancing with glee.

'I told them where you are really from! Riffraff and pirates from the islands – barely human.'

The Grand Admiral stepped from the sedan chair. 'Shining Emerald told us everything. That he's the son of the captain of Mars and that you kidnapped him.'

'They did! Even keelhauling is too merciful for them.'

'Of course I didn't believe a word.'

'What? No, no!' Smald waved his hands. 'You're making a mistake!
I'm from Mars! I'm really from Mars!'

'How many sails does your ship hoist? Enumerate the twelve kinds of precious hardwood the master-carpenters used to make the oar.
You should know, being the son of a captain.'

'Uh.'

'You're as bad as the others. Island-scum and not fit to walk the fine meadows of our deck.' He turned to the soldiers. 'Lower a boat in the morning and give them a cask of water. They are exiled.
Let them row to one of their cursed islands.'

'Eh, sir?' Opal said. 'Lord Grand Admiral, are there any islands nearby?'

'Not that I know of.'

CHAPTER 14

THE WHITE CLIFFS OF THE MOON AND BEYOND

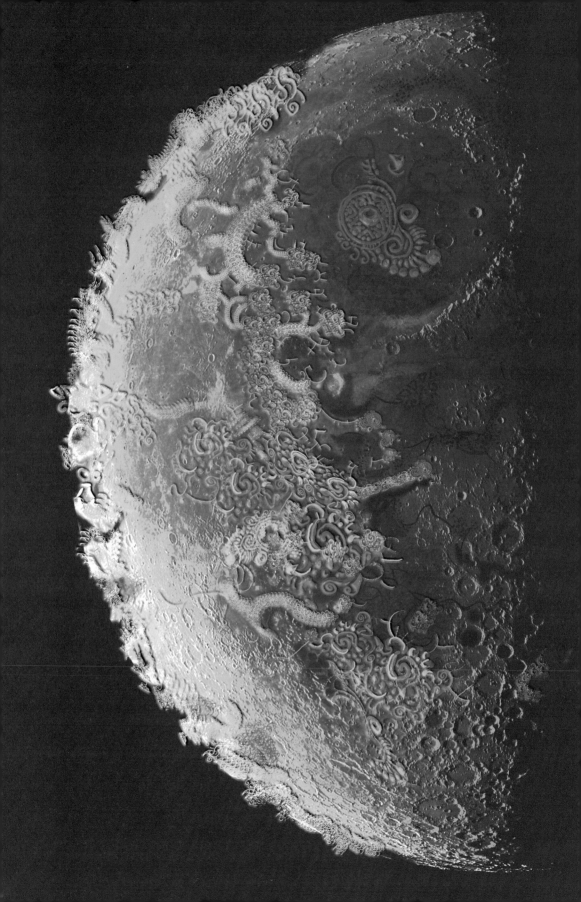

THE WHITE CLIFFS OF THE MOON AND BEYOND

1.

The planet ship was a hazy silhouette on the horizon. No longer real and quite unreachable. Grubby Chipmunk inspected the wallowing rowboat.
'I wouldn't call this a leaky bathtub. That would be bad-mouthing a leaky bathtub.'
Smald sat on the point of the bow, as far away as possible from the rest. Opal would have gladly fed him to the fishes if they hadn't needed him to end their exile.
'I could try calling a water horse to transport us,' Lady Barracuda said.
'But the boat is too unstable. Any little wave and we go down.'
'Any idea where we are?' Grandmother asked.
'I took a bearing last night,' Grubby Chipmunk said. 'Shot the stars as we sailors say. We are quite far to the south. About as far as you can get from the islands without hitting the pole.'
'So there are no islands nearby?'
'Not that I know about.' He tapped his book. 'Or my handbook.'
'Gliph Abar got us into this,' Tiger-Eye said. 'He'll have to give us some advice.'
He looked at the sky though that was the last place where one would think Gliph Abar would reside. He wasn't a seagull after all. 'Great Gliph, please tell Opal how to get to an island.'
Opal rolled the stones.
'Number 3. Let's see.

ASK YOUR SECOND COUSIN

That's a big help! Lustrous Jet must be a thousand miles from here.
Anyway she hates sailing. Even the sight of a goldfish bowl makes her nauseous.' She bit her lips. The book always gave good advice. If you didn't get it, that was your own problem. Gliph Abar was a god for clever people.
A memory popped up. Cousin Jet was nine years older than Opal and as fussy as a grandmother. 'You could have asked me!' she had scolded.
'Look at it, there is water all over the rug!'
Little Opal had clenched her fists. 'Then I'll ask now! Can I have a drop of water? I'm thirsty!'

'I understand,' she said. 'Thank you, Gliph.' She turned to her grandmother. 'Do you have anything left of Ysidore's ball?'

'A few drops at most. We drank it all.'

'A drop is all we need. We'll ask it to show us where we have to go.'

'You can't look inside a drop of water. It's much too small.'

'If I turn my telescope around I can,' Grubby Chipmunk said. 'I'll look through the big lens. It becomes a kind of loupe then, magnifying small things like a water drop.'

'I see a little cloud,' Grubby Chipmunk said. He closed his telescope. 'That is all. I haven't the slightest idea what it means.'

'Is it perhaps that cloud?' Opal pointed behind them. The whole sky was a deep, empty blue. The only cloud hung just above the horizon, no more than a little white puff.

'That is it! Clouds often form above islands, around the mountaintops. But it remains strange. There shouldn't be any island this far from the Great Ring.'

2.

Enormous white cliffs rose from the sea. They were at least three miles high and completely un-climbable. They rowed on and after a few hours the cliffs began dropping lower and lower. A wide bay opened up.

The blue water flashed with silver fish and Opal saw a flock of flamingos flying over.

She frowned. There was something about flamingoes. You never saw them making a nest. Ah, I remember. It was in that book of tall tales Pebble liked her to read aloud. You never see a flamingo chick because they nest on the moon. Opal chuckled. Such rubbish. Everybody knew the moon was much too far out of reach. It would take even the fastest, most tireless bird years to get there.

'All those funny little islands,' Lady Barracuda said. 'They all look like circles. Even the ones underwater.'

'They remind me of something,' Grubby Chipmunk said. 'When I look through my telescope...' He nodded. 'Yes, the moon. They look just like the craters on the moon.'

And now Opal recalled that the book had never said that flamingos nested on the Moon. No, they nested on the Island of the Moon.

'I know where we are. The Island of the Moon. Just as every planet has a ship, the moon has his own island.' The 'changeable island of the Moon' the book had said and Pebble has asked what 'changeable' meant.

Opal was still looking for the answer.

A beautiful city surrounded the whole bay, all white marble and palm trees. Everything was a sparkling silver-white. Indeed, like moonlight.

Beyond stretched the meadows with tall rippling grass like the fur of a snow fox. Snow-white stags with glass antlers were grazing; in the distance shone the tops of the cliffs. 'We could have landed at a worse place,' Grandmother said. Opal wasn't so sure. What did 'changeable' mean when you were talking about an island?

Lady Barracuda looked down in the water. 'It is almost like my own city. There are houses down there, gardens filled with seaweed and sea anemones.'

'Maybe their city sank?' Opal said. 'Like the one on Scorpio?'

'No, there are people living there. You can see lights burning behind the windows. And all those pipes you see poking above the surface?

I bet they're snorkels so they can breathe down there.'

They didn't even try to moor their ship. They threw the water cask and the ruby wheel on the quay and jumped. The boat shuddered, gave a tired gurgle and sank.

'Talk about cutting it fine,' Ulrich said.

They walked down the pier and reached a wide promenade.

People strolled the tree-lined promenade, smiling in a dreamy way.

'Eh, hello?' Grubby Chipmunk said and stepped up to a man who was walking his white Afghan hound. 'We just arrived. Could you...'

He had to jump back. Otherwise the man would have walked right through them.

'I guess he can't see you,' Grandmother said. 'That dreamy smile.
I think they are all sleepwalking.'

'The island of the moon,' Pebble said. 'Moonlight is for sleeping.
Or to sit sighing at your window, thinking sad, romantic thoughts.'

'I never think romantic thoughts when the moon shines,' Clever Mayfly said. He sounded a little bit worried. 'I'm usually so tired after chasing hares all day that I fall asleep right away.'

'Boys don't have to sigh. It's more something for girls.'

It was an eerie experience, like living in a town of ghosts. You could walk into a restaurant when you got hungry. But sitting at a table and waving to a waiter was useless. Just go into the kitchen and load your plate with everything you liked. The food wasn't ghostly at all, but always rather colorless – whitefish, whipped cream, coleslaw and pale asparagus.

No red meat or greens at all.

'Isn't this stealing?' Opal worried.

'They are sleeping,' Grandmother said. 'They don't even know they are cooking and anyhow, money earned in your sleep, is never there when you wake.'

3.

A week passed and Opal grew heartily sick of all that pale, delicate stuff. She also learned to hate sweetly warbling nightingales.

They searched the city, looking for a ship, a sloop, a bathtub, even a couple of empty beer barrels - anything that would float. Maybe there was a spell on the city or on the sea surrounding the island: no matter what vessel they constructed, it sank like a brick.

One morning, about the tenth day, Opal looked from her window and there was the sea, lapping at the steps of the entrance.

She shook Tiger-Eye.

'Get up! The island is sinking!'

They looked out over the city. Most of it was underwater and she realized it had been going on for days. The sea had crept closer and closer. A part of the city had already been submerged when they arrived and all streets looked the same, filled with that pearly glow and the hush of deep slumber. They just hadn't noticed.

'The changeable island of the moon,' she said and Opal felt suddenly cold with fear. 'The island is waning, just like the moon. Getting smaller and smaller and soon there will be nothing left.'

'We can climb to the tops of cliffs. They are miles high. No flood could reach that high.'

'You don't really get it, eh? Come, tell me, how big is the new moon?'

'There isn't any moon left. That is what... oh.'

'Yes, the cliffs would just disappear. Nothing left but sea.'

After that morning the island shrank frighteningly fast. It took only days for the rest of the city to submerge.

They were standing on the hill, just outside the city. The flood was creeping up through the very last street. It didn't seem in a hurry.

Every glassy wave was just a few centimeters higher than the last.

Ulrich jumped up. 'We are such fools! We can just barricade ourselves inside a house and wait for the moon island to grow big again.

There is air inside and the snorkel would let us breathe.'

They ran down the hill, splashed through the water.

The next wave rose to Opal's knees.

Ulrich ran to the door of the last house and tugged at the handle.

'Let us in! Please let us in!'

'We don't want to drown!' Pebble cried.

'Sealed,' Ulrich said. 'Completely watertight.' He stepped back. 'I'll use my hammer.'

Lady Barracuda caught his wrist. 'No, it wouldn't help. The house would be like a ship with a hole. The only result would be drowning the people inside.'

So they ended up at the top of the cliff after all. From the island only a sliver was left, a sickle moon that was rapidly shrinking.

They weren't the only victims. Thousands of rats and chattering cockroaches shared the sinking ridge.

'You are the one with an A for Ritual and Sacrifice, Opal,' her grandmother said. 'I don't know a single spell against sinking islands. Better ask a god.'

The sea retreated but only to take a running leap. With the next wave the water crossed the last meadow, touching the sea on the other side.

'Dinja!' Opal screamed and at the same time she knew it wouldn't work.

If you are any good at prayer you know when you have a connection, when a goddess is listening. Dinja wasn't.

I bet she is kissing with Gliph Abar, Opal thought and she knew with a

terrible clarity that was exactly what was happening. So scratch Gliph Abar too.

'I don't know any other gods!' she wailed and then she remembered the rat in the magic stone shop. Even a very small god is better than none.

'Arre? Arre Umphard?:

'I thought you'd never ask.' She noticed that the rats weren't drowning at all, they were swimming together, hooking forelegs and tails in an enormous float. Arre Umphard, the god of servants, rats and cockroaches was sitting on a throne made of cheese wheels and sausage links.

'Hello fellows. Do you want a lift?' He made a gesture with a glowing sausage and the float grew, curved up and changed into a galleon made of living rats and cockroaches. A cloud of moon moths rose and changed into billowing sails.

'My rats remember your cookies with fondness,' Arre Umphard confided. 'Even if Dinja seldom ate them, they always did.' He looked well fed, no longer the hungry little skeleton Opal had seen in the temple on Cancer.

'I take it back,' Grandmother Rithka said. 'Ritual and sacrifice have their uses.'

4.

If you think that riding a tidal wave made of water horses is fast, you should try a magic ship made of rats. The wings of the moon moths made their own storm. It is said that the flapping of a single butterfly wing in Japan can cause a tornado in Kansas. Now imagine ten thousand of those wings flapping to fill a sail...
The ship bounced like a skipping stone, touching every hundredth wave. It went so fast it outran its own shadow.

'I see the mangroves!' Opal cried. 'We are almost home!'
It was a beautiful clear day and Opal recognized the coast.
There was the jumble of basalt pillars where she had sounded the gong to lure Dardamesh. The cavern must lie somewhere to the right.
The rat ship passed a bit too close to one of the mangrove trees.
An angry chattering arose and a swarm of dragonets swooped down.
They were no bigger than swallows but already fierce as tigers.
'Just sit still,' Tiger-Eye advised. 'They never attack anything that doesn't move.'
'Go away!' Smald cried. He flung a stick of driftwood at a circling animal.
'Don't annoy it!' Opal cried. 'That's no bird, that's...'
It was already too late. The little dragon took a deep breath and yellow flames washed over Smald. When the smoke cleared a statue sat in the stern. It was made of gray limestone, the cheapest stone of them all.

When you arrive home after a tremendous journey, after visiting all the islands of MiYu you don't have to feel let down. There are still some very nice things to do - such as knocking on the door of the high priest, with a little god sitting on your shoulders.
'We've come to return your son,' Opal said. 'We changed him back but he threw a stick at a little dragon and now he's stone again. Slate this time. It will be very easy to turn him back. Very cheap too.'
'That,' the high priest said, eyeballing Arre Umphard, 'is that a god?'
And Opal realized something quite important. The high priest had never seen a god before. She almost pitied him. Gods were everywhere, so many they were almost impossible to miss.
'Excuse me. Shining Emerald?' Opal insisted.
'Just put him somewhere in the backyard. I'll leave him standing for a few

years. Give him time to think.'

- or walking to Tiger-Eye's house, rolling a ruby as big as wagon wheel...

His parents were heavy. It took both of them to hoist the statues onto the giant ruby.

The magic discharged, a blood red thunderbolt that sucked all the color out of the ruby. Leaving it clear as glass. Two people stood swaying on the stone.

'Get behind me!' Tiger-Eye's father cried. 'The dragon has found us!'

The woman didn't duck away. She threw herself against him, trying to shield him from the magic flame.

Both fell down, rolled through the grass.

The man looked around, completely bewildered. 'Where's the dragon? Where are we?'

'Home?' the woman asked. 'Are we home?'

'Well, yes.' Tiger-Eye said.

'And who are... Tiger-Eye?' There are some talents all mothers have – such as the ability to recognize their own children, even after many years.

'The dragon got you, changing you to ruby.' He pushed Opal forward.

'This is my girlfriend Opal. She helped save you. Gathering all this ruby.'

'This here, it was a ruby?' his father said. 'This crystal wheel? You were as rich as a magnate and you threw it all away to save us?'

'O, we are still quite wealthy.' Tiger-Eye opened his money bag.

There was the sheen of pearls, the glitter of rubies and emeralds. Even a couple of moonstones he had picked up at the last island. 'Plenty more where they come from. But I think Opal and I'll wait until the next vacation before we leave again.'

WHO IS WHO ON MIYU?

CLEVER MAYFLY

SMALD

ULRICH SLEDGEHAMMER

LADY BARRACUDA

GRUBBY CHIPMUNK

TIGER-EYE

PEBBLE

HIGH PRIEST

OPAL

MOST DILIGENT MUSKRAT

INTREPID PEONY

RITHKA

OPAL is the daughter of an extremely wealthy merchant. She doesn't like being a stuck-up rich-brat, but what can she do? All the people she knows are in the your-own-flying-whale set. She is fourteen and her parents are already looking for a husband. That is the way it goes with rich people on strange and faraway islands. She has refused all candidates until now. She doesn't need wimps who collect pale blue seashells.

TIGER-EYE is a boy from a hopeless poor family. So poor he has to wear a shirt made of itchy sea grass and sandals with driftwood soles. He is an egg-snatcher, a rather risky job as dragons seldom like their eggs snatched. There aren't any old egg-snatchers.

SHINING EMERALD or **SMALD** for short is the son of the high priest. A nasty little boy but strangely enough everybody wants to be his friend. Maybe it has something to do with the magic amulet he is wearing?

GRANDMOTHER RITHKA is a witch and Opal's favorite grandmother. Witches are so important they don't have to use a gem-name but can choose one that doesn't mean anything at all. If you call her a wise-woman she'll throw you from her mountaintop. Witches are not doddering healing-herb-ladies!

PEBBLE is Opal's younger sister and she is a lot more rebellious than Opal. Her real name is Tourmaline but she has no use for such a precious name.

GRUBBY CHIPMUNK is a pearl smuggler from LIBRA and lives on his ship the "See if I Care". His grandmother was an cannibal and he isn't exactly trustworthy.

LADY BARRACUDA is a mermaid from GEMINI. She is rather bossy and afraid of nothing, but sometimes that is exactly what you need.

ULRICH SLEDGEHAMMER is a dwarf-smith from CANCER. In his free time he carves pretty little statues from rubies or other worthless stones.

INTREPID PEONY is an officer of the Drowned City on SCORPIO. He has the tenacity of a pit bull and never gives up while pursuing criminals like Opal and Tiger-Eye.

MOST DILIGENT MUSKRAT is an customs official on LIBRA. He doesn't like out-islanders and writes all their misdemeanors down in his little notice book.

The **HIGH PRIEST** of LEO talks to All Gods But Gliph Abar. He is the wealthiest man of his isle but still can't spare the tiniest emerald to save his petrified son.

CLEVER MAYFLY is a zebra-hare herder from ARIES and he quite likes Pebble. He is always ready with a brand-new completely crazy scheme and sometimes it even works.

SOME GODS
OF MIYU

DARDAMESH

DINJA

GLIPH
ABAR

YSIDORE

HASDAMIN

ARRE
UMPHARD

AERDELICK
THE SOWER

GLIPH ABAR is the god with a thousand faces. He created the islands from starlight and the sea breeze. He loves adventure and disguise. Had he donned the face of the old woman who pointed you in exactly the wrong direction? Was he the pirate captain who served the other pirates rum with a sleeping draught and untied you?

DINJA is the goddess-with-the-bow and married to GLIPH ABAR. Dinja has a tender place in her heart for Opal because she cried when Grandmother Rithka told her how Dinja ate the very last grape and took her final sip of water while imprisoned by her father in a doorless tower.

YSIDORE is the mighty walrus which balances the whole world of MiYu on the tip of his nose. In his magic dewdrop you can see any place and time. You can call him by licking an ocean-blue gemstone. The Ysidore stone would be the best but any blue stone will do.
Sometimes you have to wait a few dreams before he visits you. You're not the only one who wants to look into his magic dewdrop.

AERDELICK THE SOWER is the local god of SAGITTARIUS and of all that grows green and flowers. He is the 308th son of GLIPH ABAR and DINJA and a bit of a bore. While the other sons hunted bears or went surfing on tidal waves he carefully collected seeds.

HASDAMIN THE ONE-EYED SEA SERPENT is a sea god, with, like name implies, only a single eye. His eye is made of emerald and he wouldn't like to lose it.

DARDAMESH THE MOTHER OF ALL DRAGONS is exactly what the name suggests – the most ancient and powerful of all dragons. Everyone who tries to steal her eggs is turned into emerald with her roaring flame.

ARRE UMPHARD is the god of the poorest servants. He often sleeps in front of the fireplace, in the middle of a heap of purring cats. Usually only slaves, orphans or kitchen boys can see Arre Umphard.

ANIMALS
OF MIYU

GHOST OWL

FLYING WHALES

RAMMSTEIN BUTTERFLY

HUNTING SPIDER

FLYING FISH

WATER HORSES

DRAGON SHIP

SHIP-FISH

SHARK-MOUSE

ZEBRA HARE

STONE MOLE

RAMMSTEIN BUTTERFLIES are steam powered insects with stained-glass wings. They are made by the dwarf smiths of CANCER, who fashion many other mechanical animals. Frog alarm clocks for instance, or windup wasps.

FLYING WHALES are the passenger planes of MiYu. They breed in the Great Crater Lake of Leo.

SHARK-MICE hail from SCORPIO and they are surely the most ravenous animals of the whole archipelago. They are only the size of your hand but they won't hesitate to attack a full-grown dragon. Shark-mice hate water.

GHOST-OWLS build their nests on SCORPIO and they are rather nasty birds. They fly into your dreams and steal your most precious memories.

WATER HORSES or sea unicorns gallop along with the tidal waves or perhaps even cause them. They obey the emperor of the undersea city next to GEMINI.

GIANT HUNTING SPIDERS weave their webs on the islands of AQUARIUS. Their nets are miles wide and they catch great white sharks and sperm whales. A fisherman's boat is also quite all right.

STONE-MOLES live on CANCER and they dig straight through marble and granite. They have crystal teeth and diamond claws.

The **FLYING FISHES** of GEMINI have translucent batwings and quite sharp teeth. Mermaids keep them as pets and they are the hunting dogs of DINJA.

The **SHIP-FISHES** of VIRGO are the size of blue whales and they grow a deck, holds and quite luxurious cabins on their backs. Cannons and harpoons are optional.

The **DRAGON-SHIPS** of ARIES are really sea dragons. The wizards of Aries put them under a spell to turn them into living ships.

The **ZEBRA-HARES** of ARIES are rather fierce little fellows and properly trained, like to hunt coyotes and bears. They are prized for their fur which is used to knot rather plain gray carpets.

MiYu Magic Stones, Dragon Eggs and Magic.

Dragons live on the islands. A world without dragons is an unbearably dull world. Only these dragons are different. MiYu dragons never eat a knight or even the most juicy maiden. They prefer a nice block of soapstone or a bank of crunchy pebbles. They blow their white hot flame across a rock and slurp the bubbling lava.
The hardest pieces crystallize into dragon eggs. All those lovely smooth MiYu stones are in fact dragon eggs! Dragons spawn them like frogs, thousands at the time.
Only one in a million ever hatches. The dragons are very jealous of their eggs. They know the location of every single one.
Egg-snatchers collect the dragon eggs and if you are a witch you can use them for all kinds of nifty spells. To make your herbs grow, to lure whole schools of fat fish in your net, to raise a storm when the fisherman, who dumped you for your best friend, sets sail…

Collecting those magic eggs is an extremely dangerous job and only the poorest of the poor try it. Dragons are a bad tempered lot, always grumbling about the quality of the granite. When they meet a trembling wretch with a bag of their precious jewel-eggs, they take a deep breath and belch a white hot flame right into his face.
The poor man promptly changes into a statue. The more powerful the dragon, the more precious the stone.
It is possible to revive the victim, but it's hard. You have to cover him with his own weight in jewels to turn him back into flesh and blood. The gems promptly lose all their magic and turn into worthless rock-crystal.
If you change into ruby you're out of luck. Your family and your friends will have to spend ten or twenty years to gather so many precious stones. And if you aren't worth the hassle, well, you'll end up an oversized garden gnome with a bird nest in your open mouth.
The most precious gem on the islands is the emerald. Diamonds are worthless. They have whole beaches made from abrasive diamond grit and nasty pointed crystals. People avoid those places.

ARIES

The island of Aries lies sparkling in the deep blue sea. From head to tail it is made of emerald. (A cool stone to help the islanders keep their calm). Because as you know the islanders of Aries are fiery, spontaneous and open hearted. They like action and have quite inquisitive natures. Intrepid explorers in short, with lots of guts. They know no fear and take big risks. They are also very selfish and quite greedy. There is no way they are going to let treasure hunters or pirates take even a single stone.

To keep those people and other treasure seekers away from their island they write in the Handbook for the Able Sailor that there is no emerald at all to be found on Aries. Not even a pebble.

RED JASPER is the famous firestone. The islanders charge it with magical powers by treating it in a red-hot fire. With the right spell, an amulet of Red Jasper will make you almost fireproof. Ask any fireman. Good chance he is wearing a lining of Red Jasper under his shirt.

SODALITE is a deep blue stone which allows you to find water. Very handy on an island almost entirely made of gemstone. Never go out into the desert without a sodalite amulet.

MALACHITE is the stone from the gods. Put on a crown made of malachite and everyone will believe you are a powerful god, or at least a hero.

Or they might be rolling on the floor with laughter.

On the island of Taurus you will only find scorching salt deserts. It doesn't matter, the islanders only need one sip of water a week. In the sands the desert roses bloom. They are harvested with pickaxes and traded for the most precious of gemstones because the islanders love beautiful things. Security and safety are quite important to them. They always keep enough cash stashed away in case something unexpected happens on Taurus.

The beautiful thing about their love for security and safety is that they are very caring and friendly. Once your friend, but only then, you can always count on them. Loyal until eternity. They live for the people they love.

ROSE QUARTZ is colored like the tastiest sea anemones. Take three stones, put them in your net, use the right spell and the fish will come running from miles around. A true fisherman's stone.

HAWK'S EYE every desert rose harvester takes one of these when he goes out in the field. A harvester has to have an eye like a hawk to find the rose in the sand because they are exactly the same color. If you look closely you will see the measuring stripes deep inside the stone. These will tell you the exact distance till the nearest rose. If you want to become a serious harvester, have your contact lenses made out of this stone.

HELIOTROPE is a much-loved stone on this scorching hot island. Put it under your pillow and you dream about swaying palms and swimming pools.

GEMINI is the island of the immortal emperor Sung-Arad who rules the City of Coral on the bottom of the sea. His subjects are mermaids, were seals and great white sharks. Everyone born on Gemini has the ocean in her blood.

The islanders of Gemini are quick, resourceful, intelligent and elusive. They are easily bored and because of that are constantly on the look out for new adventures. They simply adore changes and many islanders have multiple faces, you never know what you can expect.

CARNELIAN is called on Gemini the "meet me in your dream stone." Tap your stone seven times against the stone of your friend and you will meet each other the next night in a dream. Be sure to agree upon a clear meeting point. The statue of the walrus with the broken tusk for instance. Friends who can't see each other for a while often use the carnelian for their dates.

TSUNAMITE (Blue Howlite) is the stone that calls water horses, the sea-unicorns that gallop along with a tidal wave. If you hold the stone up high and pronounce the right spell, you can stop even the biggest tidal wave. Any girl that likes horses should have a Tsunamite to ride a water horse on top of the waves.

PERTIFIED CORAL comes in handy when walking the ocean floor. The smell alone will chase sharks away and makes sea snakes gag. As a powder it will help very well against the sting of the deadly striped mule snail.

CANCER

On the twin islands of Cancer you will find the dwarf smiths. It is a rugged country, with lots of working volcanoes. Its inhabitants are tough guys and gals who bang their hammers all day. They love to drive around on huge steam choppers, listen to heavy metal and dress in leather. They act really tough but in fact they are quite sensitive types. They protect themselves especially against stone-moles and make sure that visitors are not eaten by these wretched animals.

In short, they are quite friendly and can fix about anything that rattles.

AVENTURINE is a stone for connoisseurs. Dwarfs use them as a pendulum to find tasty mushrooms like truffles or buried gold coins. Dwarfs don't care about money but they like to sprinkle gold dust on their fried mushrooms.

TIGER'S EYE is the name of the renowned stone of smiths. In its heart you will see the glow of molten gold and bronze. This stone will make you ludicrously brave: you even have the courage to look a dragon straight in the eye and stick out your tongue. Warning note: it will only work for a little while, after that the dragon's flames will scorch you. It also helps to cure flattened thumbs.

STONE-MOLE TOOTH (Crystal Point) is precisely what it says it is. Stone-moles dig their way through even the thickest walls with their diamond claws. Their teeth are made of crystal and are darned hard. If you use a tooth to scratch a cross on your wall the stone-moles will leave you alone. Unless they are very hungry of course. By the way, banging a hammer on an anvil as hard as you can also helps. Sometimes.

LEO

Leo is the island of dragons that eat stones and the island where they lay their eggs. Here you will find extremely wealthy merchants, sly witches and especially egg-snatchers, who will try to steal the shining, gemstone-eggs from under the dragons. These egg-snatchers are exceptionally brave and will do anything to get rich. If they succeed they enjoy it to the limit and like to share it with family and friends. Islanders of Leo want to be admired. Their houses look like fairytale castles. And at their doors they will even offer hospitality to a beggar who comes knocking. Though that isn't quite as generous as it sounds, for any beggar can be the god Gliph Abar in disguise.

CRYSTAL is the stone that gives power to all the other stones. Every piece of magical jewelry starts out as quartz. As soon as they fill up with magic they start to change color and finally turn into any stone you want. If the magic is spent, they will be colorless again. Quartz is best to be looked at as a magic battery. It will hold the spell of your choice. It works best if you know the magic of a gemstone through and through.

COUNTING STONE (Brecciated Jasper). This stone is here to teach toddlers to count. Count all the red dots and you will have a different outcome every time. If it does not work for you, the stone is empty and needs to be recharged with magic.

YSIDORE (Chinese Amazonite) is named after the divine walrus Ysidore. He twirls the magical world of MiYu like a blue ball on his nose. He carries a big dew drop in which he can see your future. If you balance the stone on the tip of your nose, he will promptly visit you in your dreams. But if you've ever kicked a walrus or screamed a curse to a seagull when he peed on your head, it probably won't work.

VIRGO

The people here are very particular and mysterious. If they trust you they are friendly. But even then are very serious and cling to their beliefs.
In for a joke? Sorry, then you are not welcome. It is terrible but they do not understand even the concept of humor. According to them life's all about making plans for the future and working hard to achieve their goals. But fair is fair: they are architectural wizards. They build the most exquisite things and take great pride in the three enormous floating bridges, connecting the isles of Virgo.

SODALITE ROUGH works as well as any divining rod to track hidden wells. The rough stone works even better than the smooth one. Plumbers often use it to locate a hidden leakage. You can also use it to find the only open ice-cream shop late at night.

ELF STONE (Fluorite). Without a friendly ghost to chase away ghost-owls and mice no house is complete. An elf-stone helps you to attract the better kind of house spirits. Put up six stones in front of an open window to attract a house ghost. As soon as he is in take them down. More than one house ghost in the same house is a recipe for trouble.

YELLOW CRACK CRYSTAL. The cracks inside this stone are actually a labyrinth made by highly trained magicians. An excellent place to store memories. Yellow represents sunlight. So usually you store your summer memories in this stone. To put the memories back in your head all you have to do is peer deep inside the stone and follow the lines.

LIBRA

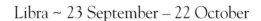

This is the island of nit-pickers and cheapskates. The island of people so precise, it's scary. Everyone, and I mean everyone, carries a copy of the code of law on a silver chain on his belt. You'll find them thumbing through their law book constantly.

Balance is the keyword on Libra. They go out of their way to let everything run smoothly, without any hiccups. But strangely enough it's the Librans who rant and rave to make something go their way.

They are highly praised for their choice in clothes, for the way they tend to their houses and also for their beautiful parks. But sometimes the thought of beauty carries them away and that makes them look a little silly.

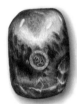

PURPLE PEARL STONE (Amethyst). The purple pearl is by far the most precious deep sea pearl found at Libra. Pearl forgers often use this stone to carve fake pearls. Still, it does hold magical powers. It will almost always help you win when playing marbles.

ROSE QUARTZ ROUGH. For success in love or high grades in school. But only if you can find a way to put it, unnoticed, in a jar of salt, under the table of your loved one or your teacher. There's no chance of a kiss or good grades when you're caught.

UNAKITE is also known as the sea serpent stone. Look at its colors and you will understand why: it looks exactly like sea serpent scales. It heals the bite of the most poisonous sea serpent. It even works when a were wolf has bitten you. Unakite should definitely be in every first-aid kit.

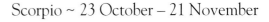

SCORPIO

Scorpio is kind of scary. Most of the dangerous animals dwell on this island, like shark-mice, ghost-owls and karate lobsters.
The islanders live an intense but very serious life, filled with secrets.
The are distrustful of palm readers, rain makers and snake oil peddlers. They know real magic when they see it and accept no substitutes
Any con artist setting foot on the island is chased away by their shark-mice, and that is also a very good remedy against tourists.
This way the islanders of Scorpio can enjoy their beaches in the summer all by themselves.

GARNET The emperor's soldiers used this beautiful gemstone to play dice. But too often it led to fights, bloody noses and chopped-off fingers. To halt this, the emperor decreed that all stones would be cut in two. With one flat side they can't roll, he thought. But clever soldiers glued the halves together with cobweb. And now there's no predicting how they will roll which makes it even more exciting.

POINTING-STONE (Chiastolite). A prudent traveller always carries one. Every pointing-stone shows the shape of a cross and one arm is always longer than the other, even if only a little bit. Suppose you arrived on a cross-road with no signposts? In the distance you hear the barking of bloodhounds. (No, I don't have to know what you did to earn their attention). Throw your stone. The longest arm points to safety. Or you can use the stone for something more important. Four boys asked you to go with them to the prom. Write their names with blue chalk on your class-room table and throw your stone. The stone points to the boy who'll be the most fun.

PHANTOM AGATE It's spots resemble those on the wings of a ghost owl. These birds will fly into your head at night and take your memories. They can be tamed but it is very hard. Sometimes they come in handy though. For example if you want to make your teacher forget about tomorrow's test.

SAGITTARIUS

Sagittarius ~ 22 November – 21 December

Sagittarius is the juiciest island of all. It's the home of Aerdelick the Sower who lives in a dome of bottle-green glass. If Sagittarius is your star sign you often have a great love for plants. It sometimes even seems as if you have roots instead of feet. Many islanders consider themselves eternal students in constant search of knowledge but also for new friends, good times and late night entertainments. Outer islanders who are depressed travel to Sagittarius to bask in the sunshine and listen to the healing rustle of leaves.

TREE AGATE. It's like green roots are growing straight through this stone. Make a circle of tree agates around a tree and its roots will grow through granite. It may take a while though. Note of caution: never ever throw away a used tree agate where poison ivy grows.

SNOWFLAKE OBSIDIAN. On Sagittarius summer is there to stay. But that didn't happen overnight. Aerdelick the Sower captured King Winter with all its swirling snow and locked him in this black stone. It didn't quite work out as planned because you can still see snowflakes shimmering through. Please do not try to crack the stone. Before you know it, your fingers will be frozen solid.

PETRIFIED WOOD. The very first trees that grew on Sagittarius have grown so old, their bark has turned to stone. Use this stone to scratch your wish on a birch and Aerdelick will hear you. If your wish is about scorched parched grass or withered plants it will surely be granted.

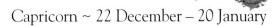

CAPRICORN

Capricorn is paradise for mountain lovers. Thousands and thousands of mountain goats jump from rock to rock. At the heart of Capricorn lays The Secret Garden from which it is said, no one has ever returned.

Islanders believe that once you get there, fabulous riches and infinite power will be yours. These super-wizards and half-gods use these powers responsibly, though. Never wasting a single coin, a second of time or a single spark of magical energy. Islanders who have not yet found the hidden road to the Garden spend a lifetime trying to find it.

ONYX. Even a splinter of this stone is often sharp enough to slice off a piece of moonbeam. It is definitely a nighttime stone. It comes from the depths of volcanoes and can warn you in case of eruptions. When an eruption is eminent it will turn hot and sometimes even starts to sizzle.

BLUE CRACK CRYSTAL. The cracks inside this stone are actually a labyrinth made by highly trained magicians. An excellent place to store memories. The color of the cracks tells you what kind of memories. Blue stands for highlights in your life and exhilarating parties. To put the memories back in your head simply peer deep into the crystal and follow the lines.

IBEX'S EYE improves your eyesight. You can run along a ledge only half an inch wide or jump from peak to peak like a mountain goat. It makes you the king of your local climbing frame.

Aquarius is where the giant spiders trail their webs far in the ocean. They catch whales and great white sharks and sometimes a fisherman's boat. To lure the sailors into their webs they sing the latest top hits. At nighttime Aquarius's cliffs seem to glow. These glowing stones are much appreciated on all the magical islands of MiYu for they are brimming with wisdom and magic.

Living in the magic glow Aquarians are often very wise though a bit peculiar. Their behavior is rather unpredictable. Rules are for the stupid, those people unenlightened enough to need rules. They walk their life's path singing and always continue to look for truth. Don't anger them for they will just walk away, flare up at you or attack like lightning. Sometimes they just act like hunting spiders.

COBWEB AGATE (Crazy Lace Agate). The spiders of Aquarius take great pride in their webs. They use these stones as an example for their weaving patterns. Try using the same patterns on your bridal veil and half the town will want to marry you.

RHODONITE. Important!!!! This stone will only do its magic once! There is a message carved in the stone with tiny black letters. This message is only meant for you and is very important. It can tell you how to get unbelievably rich, very happy or it can even save your life. Use a magnifying glass and hope it's in a language you know.

BLACK TOURMALINE. Aquarian spiders rub their jaws with it before they start singing. This also works with humans. Rub it on your lips three times and sing like a lark. It is said that Shakira carries a black tourmaline in her purse.

PISCES

Pisces is inhabited by dreamy, sensitive but extremely impractical people. They don't have any affinity with worldly affairs or goods like computers, cell phones or shopping malls. On Pisces even egg-snatchers, pearl smuggles and pirates find a deep inner peace. The islanders help them by rocking them gently in oversized hammocks while reading their thoughts and suggesting less stressful careers. Some pirates have even been known to return their booty to the rightful owners!

Hardly any thieves are found on Pisces. But hardly any doesn't mean none.

OCEAN JASPIS. is buzzing with wisdom and truly ancient secrets. It is the favorite stone of the Piscans because it allows them to read the thought of others. Even of their partners which sometimes gives problems.

PURPLE CROCODILE STONE (Amethyst Rough). Pisces's crocodiles will grow up to 15 feet and swallow their prey without chewing. Their stomachs are filled with sharp stones that grind everything to a pulp. When the stones lose their sharp edges they spit them out and they are constantly searching for new, rough-edged stones. If a crocodile is chasing you, throw your stone as far away as you possibly can. He will go after it immediately.

BRONZITE. A coat of amour fashioned out of this stone will make you invulnerable to crocodiles. It looks so beautiful with all its floating specks of gold that no crocodile will dare to scratch it. It will also help you in love and business. When you wearing a coat of armor made of bronzite everyone will look at you as if they have never seen you before.

345

THE STONES OF THE GODS

There are stones that do not belong on any island. Because of that, they are the most powerful. The islanders refer to them as The Stones Of The Gods. But they should be called Gliph-stones.

Gliph Abar is the god who threw them around on all isles, with a big grin on his ever changing face. Each one is extremely precious but at the same time can get you in a heap of trouble.

PYRITE or fools gold is definitely the most powerful and at the same time the most dangerous one. The lies you tell while wearing pyrite will sound so true that everyone will believe everything you say. But there's a catch. It only works when you wear it in plain sight. And then of course everyone will make you out to be a liar. And they will quickly use a diaper to gag you.

HEMATITE shields you from all magic. You are totally safe from curses and spells. But luck is also a kind of magic. If you wear hematite earrings, you will never win the lotto.

GEODE. This is in fact a stone-mole's egg. First the crystal teeth start to grow and later on its diamond claws. Only one in sixty-seven eggs actually hatches. Look carefully to see if the diamond claws have started to grow in your geode.

DESERT ROSE. This stone secretly absorbs all water. Bury it in a forest and the trees will turn to stone. But planted in a desert it will eventually grow into a beautiful palace.

DARDAMESH' STONE

Every now and then, egg-snatchers find an egg that glows in the dark. You recognize it by the single drop that has melted in the stone. It is a fertilized dragon's egg. Only one in a thousand eggs hatch and this is one of them! If you think you have one you can buy a magical MiYu Torch Light. The Torch Light makes it easier to identify fertilized dragon eggs. Go to www.miyumagicstones.com to find the store near you.

Dragon eggs take some time to hatch. If it doesn't crack in your lifetime, your great-grandchildren will surely be happy to have a dragon for their own.

THE CREATORS OF THE BOOK

Afterword

This book is written by a real storyteller: Tais Teng

Also most of the illustrations and the cover are made by Tais.

MiYu Magic Stones B.V. and Tais Teng mention explicitly that this whole book is from cover to cover the product of the brains of the writer. There is no similarity what so ever with reality. Also the power of the stones, the characters, the gods and goddesses and animals in the book are all figments of the writers imagination. There is no pretension to believe that the magic written about in this book can happen in reality. It is a real fantasy book.

EXPERIENCES...

These empty pages can be filled with your own experiences with the magic stones. Write down here what the stones mean or have done for you.

Do you want to learn more on MiYu?
Visit www.miyumagicstones.com!

Magical greetings,

Gliph Aba

High Wizard of MiYu

Hem

Desert Rose

Ibex's Eye

Onyx

Yellow Cra

Blue Crack Crystal

Malachite

Hawk's eye

Red Jasper

Heliotrope

Tree Agate

Rose Quartz

Snowflake Obsidian

Tsunamite (Blue Howlite)

Petrified Wood

Aventurine

Geode

Stone-mole T (Crystal P

Pyrite

Carnelian

Phantom Agat

magic
stones

magic happens!